CANVAS C...

BY

AMÉLIE PIMONT

Copyright

Acknowledgements

R. Michael Wisner
Stephen King
Taylor Meskimen
Jack Standen
Kelvin Pimont
Rikard Rodin
Martine Dufour
Margot Pimont
John Pimont
Lindsay Pimont
Françoise Dalsace
Jean-Pierre Dufour
Bernard Pimont
Kelly May
Frédérique Mollet
Marine Ramelli
Serge Ramelli
Nathanaëlle Hottois Haines
Hélène André

To Love

Contents

Book III

Book IV

Forty-five ∞ Ethiopia
Forty-six ∞ Humanities
Forty-seven ∞ India
Forty-eight ∞ London
Forty-nine ∞ Hope
Fifty ∞ Art
Fifty-one ∞ Fana
Fifty-two ∞ Exhibition
Fifty-three ∞ Vals
Fifty-four ∞ Eternity

BOOK I

One ∞ Tyrakti

It was the middle of the afternoon, late August. The sun shone on Sarah's face. Her green eyes sparkled as she stared off at the village.

The land was vast; there were trees as far as the eye could see. Mountains and jungle surrounded the village; the grass was a vibrant green; nature and wildlife everywhere. The air was thick with humidity. As the wind moved through the trees, they danced. Dogs and cats roamed around aimlessly. People of all sorts worked in the village; some carried buckets, others wood, vegetables, and fruit. There was an old water mill built of timber and bricks that chugged loudly; the sound of the water was appeasing. The village was alive with singing birds and the villagers working in the fields. Life was peaceful and calm.

Sarah wore overalls covered in dirt and sweated as she pulled potatoes from the ground. Her beagle, Toffee, sat next to her watching while she worked. Cheryl, Sarah's younger sister, an innocent girl of 12, walked out of a hut made of mud and straw. Inside, a pot cooked over the fire. There was a bed made of wood and a mattress made of hay, no electronics in view.

Cheryl brought water from the well and handed it to Sarah who drank and touched her sister's head.

"Thank you."

They looked at each other with love; they were connected. Cheryl went back to the hut while Sarah continued to pull potatoes from the ground.

Moments later, the earth trembled. It gradually intensified. Sarah was alert but did not panic as this had happened before. As the trembling got more intense, Sarah looked towards the hut, worried for her sister. Toffee appeared frightened and ran to find shelter.

As the shaking grew more violent, the villagers looked for safety. The fissures in the ground developed large enough to swallow the whole of the dwellings. The huts broke in half as the watermill was engulfed into the earth. Now, stricken with fear, the villagers ran as holes appeared all around them. Trees uprooted and disappeared from view. Cracks spread across the ground as gas released from deep below the surface, taking lives with it.

Sarah got thrown into the air by one of the explosions; she was shaken. As her vision cleared, she saw her home in pieces through the smoke. The outbreaks continued, she rushed to find her sister struggling to stay on her feet.

"Cheryl, Cheryl, where are you?" she yelled.

A violent eruption threw Sarah into the air, once again. She pulled herself up to standing and screamed in desperation.

"Cheryl!! Toffee!!"

Her voice got lost in the clamor of the earth being ripped to dust. The air filled with smoke, her surroundings blurred into strange shapes except for the villagers running chaotically in all directions. A tall man came into Sarah's focus.

"Jeremy? Ha... have you seen her?? I can't see anything. I can't find her! Cheryl?!!"

Jeremy paused and met eyes with Sarah.

"I'm sorry," he mouthed and ran off.

Sarah was frozen in disbelief; she could barely breathe. The explosions intensified. Suddenly, a deafening sound erupted from the sky.

Two ∞ Kawaki

The villagers looked up as a spaceship appeared out of the smoke. Sarah couldn't believe what she saw, a spacecraft the entire village's size descended from the sky. Sarah fell to the ground while villagers scattered.

The spaceship glowed bright white. Blue lights flickered from what appeared to be windows. Solar sails protruded ominously from both sides. A long flexible limb hung from the bottom of the craft. Large black letters read GL 400 proudly on the starboard side.

The trembling of the ground lessened, but the explosions continued. Thick smoke lingered in the air as the spaceship drew close to where the village once stood. The flexible limb folded into itself like an accordion. The ship came to a halt. An automatic ramp lowered to the ground as the door of the spaceship opened. Smoke and dust prevented the villagers from seeing anything. Several people dressed in white uniforms came running down the ramp and rushed to aid the victims.

A fine-looking gentleman named Kawaki stood dressed in a white and gold uniform at the bottom of the ramp, flanked by twenty of his crew members. Sarah watched the villagers move further away from the spaceship and collected themselves in a group. She stood up and walked to the front of the pack, positioning herself with aplomb.

"My name is Kawaki. I am the Captain's deputy of GL 400. We saw the devastation from afar and came to help you. We must hurry - your planet is about to explode!"

Dumbstruck, Sarah and the group stared at Kawaki.

"We must hurry, get onto the ship, we only have a few minutes before everything explodes!" Kawaki stressed.

Sarah saw no other option.

"Get in, get in, let's go, let's go!" Sarah yelled.

While the villagers tried to decide whether to trust Kawaki, a massive explosion erupted behind them. No more deliberation was needed; it was clear the planet was about to crumble. The remaining survivors ran towards the spaceship. Kawaki's men helped them move quickly up the ramp. Sarah stayed back to make sure everyone got on board. She searched the crowd for Cheryl and Toffee, but they were nowhere to be found. Sarah jumped off the ramp and ran back to the hut.

"Cheryl! Cheryl! Cheryl!"

She couldn't find her. Sarah looked back at the spaceship.

"We have to leave now. Everyone is on board!" a uniformed man cried out.

Sarah rushed towards the ship and ran up the ramp. She stared out at the destroyed village, hoping

Cheryl and Toffee would appear. The doors closed, leaving Sarah dejected.

Sarah rested her forehead on a porthole and fixed her eyes on the scorched ground as it moved further and further away. Her sister was gone. Sarah was sad and mad at the same time. Heartbroken that she lost her only family and angry that she couldn't save her. Sarah devoted her life to caring for Cheryl after their parents died. She cried discreetly as she looked down at what was left of her home. She watched as her planet finally submitted to its exploding core. The villagers behind her reacted to the deafening noise. All was lost.

Amid the chaos and crying, Sarah's survival instincts took control. Sarah found her resolve. Her entire demeanor evolved from sad to stern and then determined.

Three ∞ GL 400

The GL400 moved swiftly through the darkness. The remains of Sarah's planet, Tyrakti, had become a tiny red and blue dot. On the ship, there was confusion. The villagers sat depleted on the floor. Mothers mourned the loss of their children and husbands. The men were angry and confused. Many villagers were wounded. The spaceship slowed down, bringing a bit of stability.

Sarah looked around the big room, astonished by what she saw. There were blue lights on the walls. There were light blue holograms with something that looked like a map coming out from the ceiling. Automatic shelves protruded from the seamless white walls offering much-needed water to the distraught villagers.

Kawaki arrived with a few of his crew members. Kawaki's deputy named Halay was standing next to him. Halay was a very tall, buff man with deep, dark hair and even darker skin. Next to Halay was Loyt, a rather skinny, nervous-looking man. On the other side of Kawaki stood an ashen woman wearing a gold uniform. She had platinum blonde hair, blue eyes, and a pronounced facial structure. She seemed cold, fearsome, but firm. Her name was Sirak.

"Listen up!" Halay shouted.

Everyone turned towards Kawaki and his men. A light blue hologram appeared in the form of a microphone in front of Kawaki.

"My name is Kawaki. I am the second in command to Captain Sirak," he pointed to Captain Sirak, "My crew members will show you to your quarters to rest. The wounded will be taken to the infirmary. Most of you are in a state of shock. My men will come by and see each one of you to help you with anything you need. Once you are all well-rested, we will eat."

The villagers' nodded, got up and followed Kawaki's men. Sarah followed Loyt, who was taking a group to one of the quarters. The spaceship was impeccable; the walls were brilliantly white. Bright blue lights adorned the walls. Closed doors lined every corridor. The only noticeable feature was a small black pad with a gentle blue glow next to each door's right side. Sarah was intrigued by what she saw. She had never seen anything so advanced before.

A crew member came out, of one of the doors. As the door swung open, Sarah saw a laboratory with several men dressed entirely in white. In the corner, a man was held in restraints and being injected with a syringe. The crew member caught Sarah looking inside the laboratory and immediately shut the door. He looked at her and smiled. Sarah was slightly confused by what she saw but convinced herself, she must have imagined it. Sarah continued to follow Loyt and the others down the hall. Loyt stopped in front of a door and opened it.

"...And these are your quarters."

Loyt opened the door to reveal an 800 square foot room. Six white bunk beds, three on each side, a white table in the middle of the room with white stools tucked underneath, and a door on each wall. They entered. Everyone looked around, amazed.

"These are your beds, here you have closets," Loyt explained, pointing to the doors, "and these are the showers."

Sarah looked around and entered the bathroom, larger than she expected. She saw four showerheads hung high on the wall and lots of little buttons below.

"What is this?" asked Sarah, pointing to the buttons.

Loyt pressed a button, and water shot out one of the showerheads. A little light blue hologram appeared and displayed the temperature. Then he pressed a red button and the blue button next to it. The hologram read a lower temperature.

"This changes the water temperature, warmer or colder, have you never seen this before?" Loyt asked.

"No, we have never seen anything like this before," Sarah replied in amazement.

"Oh, then I'll also show you how Sonance works."

"Sonance?"

"There are screens in each bunk where you can watch movies, see outside the ship, and our destination."

"What's a movie?"

Loyt was taken aback. He realized that they never saw electronics before. He went towards the bottom right bed and pointed to a thin black pad on the wall that resembled the ones in the hall.

"When you press on this button, Sonance will activate. You can choose a movie to watch. A movie is a story you can watch in three dimensions. If you press on this button, you can see outside the ship, and when you press on this button, you can see our itinerary, speed, and destination."

Loyt paused to see if he was making sense. He pressed the button to start a movie. A holographic screen appeared, and the picture began immediately. Everyone was amazed.

"I will let you get some rest and get your bearings. Dinner will be served soon."

Loyt left the room.

Sarah looked at the other villagers and realized they were all women. She recognized Jennifer, a beautiful blonde with long hair.

"This is very different from what we know. I wonder where we are going?" Sarah said.

Jennifer's eyes welled up with tears.

"I want to go back home," she said.

"Me too, but we have to be strong. Our home, Tyrakti, exploded. We have nowhere else to go for now. I think we should rest a bit."

Jennifer nodded, then laid on one of the beds, quietly crying into the pillow.

Sarah claimed a bed and sat down, feeling the exhaustion take over. She thought about Cheryl. She wondered what Cheryl would have thought about all this and quickly fell asleep.

A few hours later, Sarah woke up to find she was alone in the room. She got out of bed and went to open the door, but it was locked. She banged on the door until a crew member opened it.

"Hi Sarah, you were fast asleep, so we let you rest. Your friends are eating in the dining room. Should I take you there?" he said in a friendly tone of voice.

"But... why was the door locked?" Sarah enquired.

"It must have been a mistake. The doors are always left open. Maybe one of your friends pressed a button when they left."

"Oh, okay," said Sarah, reassured.

The crew member led Sarah through several corridors before they arrived at the dining room. There were holograms everywhere, blue lights on the walls, and big white tables. She was filled with joy to see all her companions sitting happily with plates full of food. Sarah sat next to Jennifer, who looked brighter.

"Did you get some sleep?" Sarah asked.

"Yes, I did, and then I went to the infirmary, I feel much better now."

"Good. Jennifer, I am sure we will find a nice new home," Sarah smiled.

Sarah reached out to the food in the table's center and dished vegetables and meat onto her plate. They seemed different from what she was used to eating; it tasted good, though. She looked at the villagers sitting around, eating almost in silence. She looked at Jeremy, who saw her and waved; she gave a courtesy smile.

At the end of the meal, Sarah went to see Kawaki.

"Hi, my name is Sarah. I wanted to thank you for your help. We are all starting to feel a bit better."

"You are welcome. It's my pleasure to help people in need. I think tomorrow, after more rest, they will start to feel much better. There are quite a few people still in the infirmary. We will proceed with check-ups in the next few days to be sure that everyone is healthy. We want to be sure that there aren't any contagious diseases aboard the ship."

"Oh, of course," Sarah confirmed.

"We also need to think about provisions, we are not used to having this many people on board and will have to stop at a nearby planet to get some food. Our system allows us to recycle water, but we don't have enough food for more than a few days. There is a planet called Kambukta that we have landed on in the past. We can collect everything we need there, but

Kambukta is a bit dangerous. We will have to station there for a few days."

"What does *recycle water* mean?"

"Recycled water is a system where the water we use gets cleaned so that we can use the same water again."

"Oh, yes. We had a system like that on Tyrakti as well. When you say that the planet is dangerous, what do you mean?"

"It's a planet with a lot of wilderness and enormous animals, that can be quite ferocious. It's the closest planet that we can get food from that we know of - we don't really have any other choice."

"Okay. And where will you take us to afterwards? Are you from a nearby planet?"

"We are not from a very close planet. Our planet is called Tikai. It's about one month of travel. It's a very nice planet with lots of wilderness, a bit like Tyrakti. I'm sure your people will like it there."

"Okay. I will tell the others. They've been asking me questions... What were you doing so close to our planet?"

"We are on a mission to look for a rare plant that can help remove bacteria from other plants to prevent them from dying. We saw the explosions when we were coming back from a planet not too far from yours. I hope your people start to feel better and more well-rested. I spoke to a lady who is devastated because she lost her child during the explosion. It must be challenging for all of you. If you need anything, please let me know."

"Thank you."

Sarah went back to her room and explained the situation to the other women.

The next morning, as Sarah left her room, she saw the villagers lining up in the corridor. She spotted a girl named Leila, standing in line.

"What is all this?" asked Sarah.

"Oh, hi Sarah, we were asked to do a check-up to be sure we are healthy," Leila replied.

"Oh yes, Kawaki told me about it."

Sarah looked at the long line extending down the corridor. She continued walking until she saw Captain Sirak.

"Excuse me, Captain, I'm looking for Kawaki. Do you know where I can find him?" Sarah asked.

"Yes, if you go straight down this hall to the right, his office is the third door on the left."

"Thank you."

"Is there something I can help you with, or do you need to see Kawaki?"

"Laura, one of my people, told me something about combat training and a schedule, I wanted to see what that was about?"

"The schedule is for my crew and everyone aboard my ship. As for the training, it's to enhance the immune system after everything you have been through. Your people will be stronger and healthier once they are trained."

"Okay. Do you know how long it will take us to get to Kambukta? Kawaki told me we had to stop there to get supplies."

"Yes, we should get there in about a week."

"Thank you."

As she went back to her room, she saw that the corridor's line was now even longer. The people leaving the infirmary seemed better. There was a crew member in front of the door, directing the people as they entered.

Now in her room, Sarah was alone. A few minutes later, a crew member knocked on her door and entered before she could open it.

"Everyone needs to go to the infirmary to get checked up; I can take you there."

"Of course."

Sarah followed him out of the room and joined the back of the line. Kawaki saw her.

"Sarah, I need your help with something. Go find Loyt. He's in the dining room. Tell him to come to my office right away."

"Yes, of course. I'll go after I'm done at the infirmary."

"No, please go immediately. You don't need to go to the infirmary."

"Oh, okay. I was told that..."

"That's fine," Kawaki interjected.

Sarah was confused by his cold reply but headed off to retrieve Loyt.

Sarah walked into a mostly empty dining hall. Crew members cleaned tables while Loyt sat alone, stuffing his face with gobs of food.

"Loyt?"

Loyt looked up from his food, surprised to see Sarah.

"Kawaki needs you to go to his office."

"Sarah, it's good to see you again. How's your day going on the ship?"

"Uh, it's fine-"

"You know we have the best food on this ship. Don't you just love the food?"

"Kawaki said it's really important."

"More important than *this*?"

"This?"

"Yes, *us*, us getting to know each other."

"I'm just the messenger."

"Well then, I guess you've done your job."

They stared at each other awkwardly. Sarah turned to leave as Loyt took one last bite.

On her way back to her room, Sarah noticed there was no longer a line outside the infirmary. Sarah laid on her bed and pressed the small black pad by her side to start Sonance. The holographic screen appeared, showing outside the spaceship. She paused and stared at the emptiness of space. She thought about Cheryl while watching the stars. She thought about Tyrakti and the life she once knew and slowly drifted into sleep.

She suddenly awakened at five in the morning by someone yelling loudly outside her room. Her roommates stirred one by one. She got up in a rush, opened the door, and saw two people from the village, fighting. One man, Luke, was bleeding; his nose looked broken.

"Hey! What are you doing?!" yelled Sarah.

"I am going to kill you! You knew we were together!" yelled the opponent, David, as he threw another punch.

Sarah tried to intervene but got hit in the face and fell to the floor. Kawaki walked in.

"What is happening here?!" he shouted.

The two men continued wrestling on the floor. Luke beat David severely in the face. Kawaki separated them himself and ordered two crew members to come and remove them.

"We'll take them to the infirmary right now," said a crew member.

Sarah stood up, "I'm sorry, those two have been fighting over the same woman for years."

"There can be no such thing here," said Kawaki.

"Yes, of course. I will talk to them."

Kawaki left, looking worried.

Sarah went back to her room and took a shower, finding the hologram system very amusing. She repeatedly pressed the button to change the temperature, amazed by the hologram that appeared each time. She waved her hands back and forth through the hologram; she couldn't believe her eyes. Out of the shower, Sarah headed to bed. Back to sleep, exhausted.

A few hours later, she found herself alone once more in the room, wondering where everyone was. She got dressed and went to the dining room. As she walked through the corridors of the spaceship, she heard people cheering, and followed the clamoring to a big open space.

The room was filled with people interacting with all different shapes and sizes of holograms. They appeared to be playing games and enjoying themselves. Some had headphones on and were dancing with holographic humans; others played cricket on a virtual field, and people battled in holographic spaceships. Other human-looking holograms served as a fighting game where people practiced punching and kicking. The whole space looked like a high-tech arcade. Sarah watched as her friends played these unusual and unbelievable games.

Suddenly, a loud beeping sound resonated in the entire ship. A 10-foot tall hologram of a red-headed lady with freckles appeared in the middle of the arcade.

"My name is Gem. I am the ship's directory. You can ask me anything. All passengers must report to the dining room for dinner immediately."

As giant Gem disappeared, the gamers were left awestruck. The room began to empty as people went towards the dining room, she followed the crowd.

Kawaki stood behind a bright blue holographic microphone, welcoming everyone into the dining room. The crew members gestured to everyone to take a seat. Sarah took a seat at a table in the center of the room, and Kawaki began.

"Hello everyone, I hope you are all feeling better after enjoying our games! I wanted to gather you all here to go over a few things that will make our time together run smoothly."

The audience looked at him in silence.

"We are installing a few rules that everyone must abide by. The first rule is that there shall be no intimacy between men and women. The incident this morning has proven that this can result in altercations - which must be avoided.

The second rule is that we will be instating a schedule. We are not used to having so many aboard the GL400, and we must stay organized. You will be split into different groups. You will be allocated tasks to pass the time until we arrive at our destination.

Lastly, as some of you may have already heard, we will be doing daily combat training. Kambukta is a dangerous planet, and everyone needs to be in excellent shape by the time we arrive. My crew members will show you your schedules and help you with any questions you might have. Thank you very much."

As Kawaki finished his speech, the microphone disappeared, and he left the room.

Whispers filled the room; Sarah sat silently, deep in thought. As dinner was served, crew members passed instructions and schedules to each person. Sarah looked at the paper and read.

Group - E

Day shift muster: 8 am.

Schedule:
8 am - 12 pm - Clean and maintain the engine room
12 pm - 1 pm - Lunch
1 pm - 6 pm - Combat training (KONAKI room)
6 pm - 8 pm - Dinner and recreation (game room will be open at this time)

Curfew is 8 pm - no one is to leave their room.

Buddy system - no one is ever to be alone. Everyone will be assigned a person that they have to be with at all times. They are mutually responsible for each other.

Assigned Buddy - Sarah, Jennifer.

The dining room began to clear out.

Sarah found her *buddy* Jennifer, and they walked in silence until they were back in their room.

"What do you think about this scheduling thing?" Sarah asked, trying to get Jennifer to open up.

"Yeah, I think this schedule is great. They are doing everything they can to ensure that we survive here until we arrive on their planet. Loyt told me that their planet is filled with trees, beautiful rivers, and mountains. He said it's always sunny. I can't wait to get there."

"Yeah, Kawaki also told me that there are ten times more people on board since they rescued us."

"Thank God they did."

Silence again. Jennifer crawled into her bed. Sarah laid down, her mind racing. She pressed the button to start Sonance hoping the view of space would help her fall asleep, and it did.

Four ∞ Combat Training

The next morning when the women left their room, Sarah noticed a line up in front of the infirmary.

"Have they not seen everybody yet?" she asked Jennifer.

"I dunno, I heard some people saying they felt dizzy or had some kind of cold. I hope they all heal quickly. We have to be careful with diseases being in such a confined area."

"I suppose so... I wonder how they got sick..." Sarah swallowed her words into a whisper.

They arrived in the dining room.

This time, the villagers were segregated into groups. Men, women, and children sat separately. Halay and Loyt checked in with each group to maintain order. The tables now had holograms in front of them with a letter on each, A, B, C, etc. Sarah and Jennifer found their group, E; next to it read: Sarah.

There were four other women at their table, two much older and two in their 40's. Jennifer and Sarah were the youngest, being only 30. The women all knew each other but were not intimate friends. One of the much older women, Sophie, stared at Sarah with her round, sagging face.

"If you think you're gonna tell me what to do, you're insane, I am not taking any orders from someone like you," Sophie scoffed.

"Sophie," Sarah smiled, "Don't get me started. We are no longer on Tyrakti, where you make your own rules. We have to follow the rules of the ship."

"Pffftt... Fuck you, Sarah, I'm not taking orders from a murderer," Sophie gritted her teeth.

Loyt appeared out of nowhere.

"What's going on?" he asked.

Sarah looked at Sophie, then perked up.

"Everything is fine."

Sophie steamed.

"Everything's *not* fine. I want to change groups - I am not going to take orders from *her!*"

Sophie stood up to leave.

Loyt stared at Sophie, unphased by the outburst.

"Sirak herself formed the groups, she will not allow changes. I don't want to hear about this again," said Loyt as he glanced a knowing smile at the two women and left.

The tension between Sophie and Sarah was palpable.

Group E headed to their first shift in the engine room. Led by Sarah, the six women learned how to maintain and clean the ship's engines. The work was grueling, but the time passed.

On their way to lunch, Sophie took another stab at Sarah.

"It's your fault he died," she hissed. "I'll never forgive you for it!"

"You don't know what you're talking about," Sarah retorted.

Sophie turned to Sarah, now inches from her face.

"Don't you fucking dare!"

Sarah walked away, but Sophie grabbed her by the arm. Sarah yanked her arm from Sophie's grasp, looked her straight in the eye, and walked away.

Group E continued through the corridor, encountering Jeremy.

"Hi Jeremy, how's it going with your team?"

Jeremy was pleased to see Sarah.

"It's great, we're learning about electronics, it's actually super interesting. I guess we got lucky," Jeremy smiled.

"A lot of other teams are doing boring stuff, like maintenance."

"We manage the engine room," Sarah said dryly, "Not very exciting... but it's fine."

"Hey, I haven't seen Luke in a few days, have you seen him?"

"No, I haven't seen him since the fight. He must be on the night schedule?"

"Oh, of course, that makes sense. Gotta go. See you later."

After lunch, they gathered for muster. About half of the villagers were present; those on the night schedule and the children were nowhere to be seen. Following muster, everyone was handed protective uniforms for combat training. Sarah put on the silver suit. There was a tiny layer of air or gas between her body and the fabric. A light blue hologram surrounded the entire outfit, which seemed to be a small electric field. Sarah moved around in her suit, feeling it out. Her body felt light, she could move easily and fast. She liked the feeling, although the protective layer's pressure and the strange *aura* made her head throb gently.

The training began. Kawaki's crew members organized the villagers into their groups and explained how the training would work. A crew member was assigned to each group and would act as a teacher. The villagers would learn Konaki, a mix of Kung Fu and Krav Maga, developed over many years by the highest trained fighters on Kawaki's planet. It was a hazardous sport, dangerous, but the protective suits would keep them from getting hurt.

Sophie and Sarah were paired up to practice fights against one another. Sophie was still mad. She hit Sarah fiercely, but Sarah's suit absorbed the rage-filled attack. Kawaki sat at one end of the room, watching the novices as they learned how to fight.

The training continued on all afternoon. When the class came to an end, Sarah was exhausted. She ate dinner in silence, fatigued by the day; then returned to her room with Jennifer. It wasn't until after her shower that she realized their other roommates weren't there. She thought they must be on the night shift.

The next two days went by swiftly. Everyone was adhering to the tight schedule. There was little time for anything but work and Konaki training. Sarah noticed a change in the villagers; they seemed quieter, not like they were when they first arrived on the ship.

"I am so exhausted, but I feel like I am starting to get stronger," Jennifer said as Sarah stared blankly at her hologram movie.

"In training today, I reached 9 points, I am getting much better! How many points are you at?"

"I am at 11 points. I am not sure I fully understand the point system yet, though. I thought that my last fight today would have given me 1 point, but I only got half a point. Loyt said he'd explain it more tomorrow. If we each have to be at 50 points by the time we get to Kambukta, we still have a long way to go," Sarah looked at Jennifer with concern in her eyes.

"Yes, but we are getting better every day. Sophie was nicer today, it's the first time she hasn't said anything nasty."

"Yeah, she's just sad is all, she misses her son. I still can't believe she thinks it's my fault," said Sarah.

"It's because of the rumor..." Jennifer paused.

"Yeah, whatever," Sarah turned back to the movie.

Jennifer awkwardly said, "I am going to take a shower."

Sarah laid still on her bed, pensive. Jennifer closed the door to the bathroom, and Sarah waited a few minutes before getting up. She left the room and walked through the corridors. She saw a child.

"Hi Lucas, how are you?" she asked the boy.

Lucas, an 8-year-old with blond hair and tons of freckles, barely looked at her and didn't reply; he continued to walk past her without so much as a glance. Sarah stood there, surprised.

"Lucas, it's me, Sarah."

He paused, turned around, and looked at her with lifeless eyes for a second before continuing. Sarah was confused by Lucas' behavior. They knew each other well. He used to play with Toffee and help on the farm.

Suddenly Sarah realized that it was past 8pm and she should be in her room.

She hesitated for a second but decided to follow Lucas instead, and did so discreetly. As she turned a corner, she noticed that the lights on the walls, which were usually blue, were red. Lucas stopped in front of a door. Sarah watched from a distance as he used his thumbprint to gain access to a locked room. She had never been in this part of the ship before. As Lucas entered the room, Sarah heard the sound of a man screaming in pain. The big metal door slid closed before she had time to see what was inside. Sarah stood by the door, bewildered.

Her thoughts halted by the sound of Kawaki and Sirak's voices approaching down the corridor. She quickly and silently went back towards her room to avoid being seen. While creeping through the halls, she heard two crew members talking.

"Is everything ready?" said a man.

"Yes, I am going to report to Kawaki now," the other replied.

"Good," said the first crew member.

Sarah stood still, hoping they would not come in her direction. She heard them coming closer, dashed down a corridor to her left, and found a doorway to hide in. Her heart pounded quickly. To her relief, they turned in the opposite direction, where she just came from. Sarah stayed hidden until their voices could no longer be heard. Once she was sure the hallway was clear, she hurried back to her room.

"Where were you? I was getting worried!" Jennifer asked, "I was about to call Loyt. You know we are not allowed to leave our room after 8pm, right?"

"I was just going for a walk, and then I saw Lucas. He didn't recognize me. So... I followed him," Sarah said, breathless from running back to her room, "I heard Kawaki and Sirak talking and crew members behaving weirdly. I think something is happening."

"What are you talking about? I am sure Lucas didn't see it was you," Jennifer replied, "And Sarah, of course, people are talking, they are working. You're making a big deal out of nothing. Don't leave the room after 8pm and don't forget - we have to be together at all times. I don't want to get into trouble."

"Yeah," said Sarah, slightly defeated that Jennifer wasn't understanding, "I guess you're right. Sorry."

Jennifer fell asleep quickly. Sarah laid in bed, thinking of Cheryl, she grew sad. Sarah never showed her sadness in front of anyone; she didn't want people to see her weakness.

The next morning, the routine started again. Everyone went for breakfast, then to daily tasks, and finally to combat training. Everyone's Konaki was improving. Towards the end of the combat training, Sarah fell, her head started pounding instantly. Sirak saw Sarah fall from across the room and signaled to Kawaki to go and check on her. Kawaki and Loyt now stood over Sarah.

"I will take you to the infirmary," said Loyt.

"No, I will," said Kawaki.

Kawaki helped Sarah to her feet. She took off the protective silver uniform, and they started walking towards the infirmary. Kawaki looked to see if anyone was within earshot. No one was.

"I am not taking you to the infirmary," he said quietly.

"Oh, why?" Sarah asked.

"It's too complicated to explain... but... stay away from the infirmary," he said in a punctuated way, "Never show any weaknesses. We will go back to combat training, and you will pretend that you are fine now. Okay?"

"Okay," replied Sarah, slightly confused.

She believed Kawaki had her best interest in mind. She could see that he was trying to protect her. Sarah didn't say anything else. Once they returned to the Konaki room, Sarah went back to her group and continued training with Jennifer.

Sarah and her team were having dinner, along with the other groups. Kawaki entered, the crew members of the ship all stood to attention. Kawaki went to the center of the room, the hologram microphone appeared.

"Hello everyone," he said as the room grew silent, "I hope you are all enjoying learning the art of Konaki. I know some of you are tired. This is normal. As your skill and strength improve, it will become easier. I don't come with good news, however. The supplies are getting low. We will need to tighten the daily rations until we get to Kambukta. The trip to Kambukta is a bit longer than we had planned, but we should arrive there in a couple of days. We must continue to train and become stronger and stronger until our final destination."

The room descended into worried whispers and harmed the morale of everyone on board.

After dinner, Jennifer and Sarah went to the game room. Jennifer wanted to practice her Konaki with a hologram for a bit. Sarah sat, on a floating hologram couch, watching everyone play games. They looked hypnotized as they played. She was waiting for Jennifer, who was fighting a female hologram. The punches moved Jennifer's body as if she was fighting a real human. Jennifer set the level of intensity to the hologram fighting game, starting with easy blows. Jennifer fought well. She artfully dodged several flying kicks and punches. Her opponent, made only of blue light, hit her with a fierce kick in the face; she fell to the ground.

"Game over," said the virtual female fighter.

Sarah looked at her, saw that she was hurt, and signaled her to get up quickly. Jennifer did.

"Let's go back to our room now," said Sarah, "I think it's enough for one day."

"Yes," Jennifer replied, defeated.

They arrived in their room, Jennifer went to take a shower, and Sarah laid on her bed. She pressed on the thin black pad.

"Gem?" called Sarah.

A woman appeared, projected into the middle of the room.

"Yes, what can I do for you?" asked Gem.

"How long have you been on the GL 400 for?"

"I have been on the GL 400 for 311 years."

"You know the plant Kawaki was hoping to find near Tyrakti? When was the plant last found?"

"I don't understand your question. Please rephrase the question."

"Kawaki told me about a rare plant they are looking for that removes the bacteria from other plants. Has this plant ever been found?"

Sarah waited for a reply.

"I don't understand your question. Please rephrase the question."

"That's all right, thank you, Gem."

"You are welcome. Goodbye."

The hologram disappeared. Jennifer came out of the shower.

"Who were you talking to? I heard someone speaking."

"Oh, that was the Gem hologram help thing. I was just asking random questions to see how it... or... she works."

"Oh, that's cool. Can I ask her to tell me a story?"

"Probably, you can try, but wear the hologram headphone things, so I don't hear everything, please."

Sarah smiled.

"Maybe tomorrow, I'm too tired. I'm going to sleep, good night."

Jennifer got into her bed.

"Good night, sleep well," Sarah replied.

Jennifer waved her hand above her head, to make the area around her bed turn pitch black.

Sarah activated Sonance to see outside the spaceship. This had become her favorite part of the day, looking for new stars and planets in the distance, new colors, and shapes as the ship moved through the darkness. She watched for a while until she was certain that Jennifer had fallen asleep. She coughed loudly to see if Jennifer woke up, but she didn't. Sarah was silent as she got out of bed but intentionally left the outside view of the ship playing on her Sonance system.

She opened the door and checked the corridor. No one was there. She exited the room and carefully shut the door behind her. Sarah made her way through the labyrinth of long corridors, retracing her steps when she followed Lucas. She found the door where she last saw him. Sarah hid in a dark corner, hoping someone would exit. She waited there for a couple of hours and didn't see or hear a thing. Deflated, she went back towards her room when she felt a finger poke her three times. This startled her. She jumped and turned around to see a little girl from her village named Maya.

"Oh, Maya, you scared me. What are you doing here?"

Maya looked at her coldly.

"You are not supposed to be here," Maya replied in a monotonous voice.

Sarah didn't recognize Maya. She was very distant, cold, and spoke with authority.

"You are not supposed to be here," repeated Maya looking at Sarah fiercely.

Sarah found herself frightened by this 9-year-old child. She started walking backward. Maya stood there, staring at her blankly. Sarah turned and ran towards her room, checking over her shoulder as she went. Maya, completely lifeless, and pale continued to stare.

Sarah arrived in her room, shaking, with sweat dripping from her brow. Jennifer did not stir. Sarah jumped into her bed, pulled the blanket over her shoulders, and thought about Maya. Sarah had known Maya since she was born. She was always a sweet and cheerful girl. Could this possibly have been the same Maya?

Maya walked calmly down a long corridor with red lights on the walls. She arrived in front of a door and put her thumb up, a hologram appeared, and the door opened. She entered Captain Sirak's office. It was an enormous room. There was an operating table to the right of the door where two children were mutilating a man. The children peacefully used scalpels on the man, tormenting him. They removed matchbox-sized pieces of flesh from his body and placed them in glass containers without making a sound.

The man's eyes were open wide. He blinked almost mechanically every five seconds. The drugs in his system had made resistance or sound impossible. Blue light radiated around the head of both children. A large white desk sat in the center of the room with a giant screen behind, showing the stars. To the left were white shelves filled with little glass containers, adorned with stickers showing unrecognizable symbols.

Sirak sat at her desk. She signaled with her hand for Maya to approach. Maya went towards Sirak and whispered something in her ear. Sirak nodded and Maya left.

The next morning, Sarah woke up to Jennifer, gently patting her on the back; Sarah jumped.

"Sarah, wake up, we are going to be late," said Jennifer.

"Oh shit, sorry, I had a hard time falling asleep last night," replied Sarah.

They went to the dining room and had breakfast; Sarah was looking around, didn't feel very comfortable, and barely ate. Her team went to the engine room. Some of her teammates were cleaning while others worked on an engine. Sarah could not focus on her work, completely distracted by what happened with Maya the night before.

On their way to lunch, Sarah kept looking behind her to see if anyone was there. Jennifer noticed that Sarah was restless.

"Are you okay? You've been weird all morning," Jennifer asked.

"Yes, I'm fine. I just had a nightmare. Didn't sleep well is all."

They got to the dining room and saw all the other groups seated at their tables. Kawaki observed from the sidelines as everyone ate. It was quiet. The mood was heavy. Captain Sirak arrived and went to the center of the dining room. Kawaki followed her. The microphone hologram appeared, and Sirak stood behind it. All eyes were on Sirak. Sarah's heart started to pound.

"There has been defiance. This cannot go unpenalized," announced Sirak, coldly.

People started to whisper. No one knew what she was talking about.

"Silence!" yelled Sirak.

She continued calmly, "As I said, this cannot go unpenalized, you," she pointed to Sarah, smiling coldly, "Come to the center."

Sarah got up and went towards the middle of the room. Jennifer looked at Sarah, worried.

"You will be punished for your impertinence. You will fight the hologram," Sirak demanded.

A large, strong man appeared; he had a spear and looked like a Viking. Sarah nodded and turned to leave the room. Sirak called after her.

"Where do you think you are going?"

"To get a fight suit, Captain."

Sirak started to laugh, "No. There will be no suit."

Sarah realized that she would probably be killed in the next few minutes. Her face went pale. Without warning, the hologram struck her forcefully in the stomach, and she fell to the ground. She got up, shaken, but dodged another punch.

"After this, I am sending her to the pit," whispered Sirak to Kawaki.

"Captain, I believe she might have the correct DNA," Kawaki replied, "I saw different tests from this batch, and some of them were pretty close to the one we want."

The hologram kicked Sarah in the back. Sarah fell to the ground once more, significantly wounded and struggling to catch her breath.

"Why didn't anyone tell me?" said Sirak furiously, "Stop!"

The fighter instantly stopped.

"Enough, now all of you go to combat training."

The groups began to exit the dining hall. Sarah was hurt and shaking.

"Help her up, may this be a lesson," Sirak scolded Kawaki.

"Yes, Captain."

Sirak turned to Jennifer, "And you. You better keep an eye on her next time, or you will get a beating too."

"Yes... yes... Ca... Cap... Captain," Jennifer complied.

Sirak walked off, and Kawaki went to aid Sarah, helping her stand up.

"What have you done?" whispered Kawaki.

"I'm sorry... I went out of my room last night."

"You must be very careful. Next time I won't be able to help you."

"Why are you so nice to me?"

"We can't talk here, Sarah. Go to combat training. I'll see you later."

"Okay."

Sarah caught up with Jennifer, who was waiting by the exit. Jennifer was angry.

"I'm sorry," Sarah said, still in pain and short of breath.

They arrived in the fight room. Sarah's group was close to achieving the 50 point target. To help them get there, Loyt came by and showed the team a few additional fighting techniques.

The Gem hologram suddenly appeared, accompanied by a loud beeping alarm.

"Tomorrow, we will arrive at Kambukta. You must all be fully ready in the dining room for muster at 6am. We will be stationed on Kambukta for two days. Kambukta is a wild and dangerous planet. Follow the rules precisely. Go to your dorms straight after dinner and get a lot of rest."

Gem disappeared almost instantly.

Everyone took off their training suits. Sarah struggled to pull hers off, her side throbbed making her think she might have broken a rib.

At dinner, she hardly ate, and on the walk back to the room, her body pulsated in pain as Jennifer gave her the silent treatment. In the room, Jennifer jumped down Sarah's throat.

"So, *what* did you do?!"

"I went for a walk last night and saw Maya. She saw me and scared the shit out of me, she must have told Sirak."

"Why would you go out of the room?" Jennifer was confused.

"I just wanted to go for a walk," Sarah replied, "I'm tired of staying in this room all the time. I'm homesick and don't feel great."

"Maybe you should go to the infirmary tonight?"

"No," Sarah paused, "Jennifer, we have known each other our whole lives, right?"

Jennifer nodded.

"You can trust me, right?"

Jennifer felt nervous, "Yes, of course, what is it?"

"Just trust me, don't ever go to the infirmary, okay?" Sarah had a genuine concern in her voice.

"I've only been once. The day we arrived, but I've been having headaches, I was planning on going to the infirmary tomorrow morning before muster," said Jennifer.

"Just don't go, please. Keep your headaches, okay? And don't tell anyone that you have headaches, okay?" Sarah stressed.

"You are scaring me; what is going on?"

"Something is going on. I don't know what. But I am sure of it. You have to trust me."

"Fine, fine, fine, I won't go to the infirmary."

Sarah finally relaxed and smiled at Jennifer; she was happy that her friend trusted her.

"Thank you. I'm going to go to bed. Good night."

"You're not going to leave the room tonight, right?" asked Jennifer.

"No, I won't," Sarah replied cheekily.

They giggled gently.

Five ∞ Kambukta

At 6am sharp, Sarah sat in the packed dining room. Kawaki stood at the microphone.

"You all have 15 minutes for a quick breakfast, we will have a roll call, and then prepare to land on Kambukta. Be very careful out there, never be apart from your assigned group. Just remember your training, and everything will be fine."

Kawaki was more official than usual and left immediately after his speech. The room was tense. They had no idea what this planet was like. Once everyone had eaten, and the roll call was complete, they headed to the staging room to prepare.

The staging room was massive; it was entirely white and neatly organized. Armor and weapons sat on recessed shelving inside the walls. There were zip-up suits, black for the crew, and white for the villagers. The suits were marked with sizes. The men and women were taken to separate sides of the room to change. Crew members helped everyone get ready.

Landing on Kambukta was an uneventful affair. Once stationary, the ship doors opened, and the ramp went down. Following Kawaki's orders, the groups exited the ship, accompanied by their respective GL400 chaperones. Kawaki was designated to Sarah's team.

Sarah made her way down the ramp and hopped off, stepping onto the new planet for the first time. She stopped and stared at this new world, taking it all in. There was a jungle with the tallest trees she had ever seen. Giant birds flew over her head. The air was very humid and very heavy; it was difficult to breathe. Sarah looked up at the sky and saw two suns. Light droplets of water fell on her face. She closed her eyes. Kawaki's voice interrupted Sarah's moment.

"Come on, let's go. We shouldn't stay in one place too long, there are dangerous animals here."

The groups scattered in different directions, led by their respective guides. Each group had been assigned tasks that would take them to separate parts of this new planet. Kawaki's men had been here several times to gather supplies in the past. They knew exactly where to go. Sarah's group followed Kawaki, they headed right.

Jennifer felt uncomfortable and tucked herself behind Sarah as they walked.

"We must stay close together," said Kawaki.

The team nodded. They walked for a few hours; the jungle was dense and hard to traverse. Their path was often obstructed by thick branches and impassable bushes that needed clearing before they could continue. To the North, there was a volcano in the distance. Giant birds continued to fly above their heads and swoop down close to the group.

"Get down!" yelled Kawaki.

Everyone dropped to the ground as a giant bird lingered just a few feet from their heads. Sarah glanced at the bird and noticed its sharp teeth before the bird flew away.

"Okay, let's go," Kawaki commanded.

They got to their destination, a small, broken-down farm. The group activated their hologram bags. The bags floated in the air, and each person simply held the side as they filled it with vegetables. The weight of the bag couldn't be felt. They packed the bags with potatoes, carrots, tomatoes, and onions. Once all the bags were filled, the group began walking back to the ship.

Suddenly, they heard the sound of trees breaking down and a loud thud.

"Get down, now!" screamed Kawaki.

Everyone dropped to the ground immediately. A dinosaur-like animal walked, not too far from where they hid, trees broke under its weight as it moved through the jungle. The creature roamed on the path that Sarah and her group needed to follow to get back to the ship. They stayed hidden for a while, watching and waiting for the dinosaur to leave.

"Shit, we need to find another way back," Kawaki thought for a moment, "We are going to have to walk an extra two hours. Okay, be very alert, and don't make any noise."

The group nodded in agreement. There were varying degrees of fear amongst them. They walked for an hour down the new path when Kawaki stopped dead in his tracks. They saw a 15-foot black panther in front of them; the panther stared with terrifying protruding teeth. The group was petrified. The panther slowly walked towards them, eyeing his new prey. Jennifer couldn't hold back and screamed.

Sarah noticed something rustling behind the panther. A muscular man with a naked torso appeared and stood behind the animal, pointing his fist towards it. The man had something in his hand; Sarah couldn't see what it was. With a sudden flick, a burst of energy was emitted from the object, hit the panther, sending it flying in the air. The panther landed 30 feet away, stumbled to its feet, looked at the man, and disappeared into the overgrowth.

"Come this way, it's safer in my territory," said the man.

Kawaki couldn't believe what he just saw. Sarah was amazed and relieved that the panther was gone.

The group followed the man, they came to an area surrounded by a metal fence and entered. As they passed through the gates, they felt a change; it was as if there was some magnetic field.

"We are safe here; the animals can't go past the gate," the man explained.

He continued on, walking towards a 20-foot-high, metal shack, the team followed him. Inside, electronics crowded the long room. On either side of the walls, there were screens and electronics on wooden shelves. Cables went in every direction from one side of the shack to the other. A wooden bed sat in front of a closed-door at the far end of the room.

The man looked around the room and pulled out a bag. Kawaki interrupted him.

"Who are you?" asked Kawaki.

"I crashed on this planet 13 years ago and have been here since."

Kawaki looked confused.

"My name is Eli."

Eli looked at everyone; he noticed Sarah, his eyes fixated on her; he was struck by her beauty. They locked eyes and she smiled at him.

"But, how have you survived by yourself all these years?" said Kawaki.

"I'm a botanist from planet Saké. I was on a mission when my spaceship crashed. I used our technology to create this electromagnetic field to keep the animals away. It's so nice to see other people, I can finally leave this planet and come with you; where are you from?"

"We are from planet Tikai."

"Oh," Eli paused, "I don't think I ever heard of your planet. Where did you land?"

"We are a few miles to the South."

"I know every path very well, I can show you the best way there."

He went through the door at the end of the room, Kawaki and Sarah followed him. Eli remained silent as he gathered belongings. He went outside and retrieved small bags filled with seeds. Eli occasionally glanced at Kawaki and Sarah as they watched him fill a bag with electronic equipment, more plants, and herbs. Eli went about preparing to leave as if he were alone, Sarah and Kawaki watched in fascination. He closed his bag and looked at them with a smile, ready to go.

"I'm ready."

As they exited the shack, Kawaki noticed the weapon Eli used to save them.

"That's a very powerful instrument you have there, what is it?"

"I created it with some of the elements from my planet that I had with me. It emits concentrated electromagnetic gamma rays. I can control the intensity, I've never had to use it at full power."

"Wow," Kawaki was flabbergasted by the seemingly rudimentary device, "What is it called?"

"It doesn't have an official name, but I call it *Gloria* after my older sister, who used to protect me as a child," Eli said, smiling.

They walked out of the shack and left the gated area; Eli led the way.

"It's best to go along the river, there are usually less wild animals, it's because it's closer to the volcano."

Kawaki and Sarah walked right behind Eli, followed by the group. Sarah and Eli glanced at each other discreetly, as they moved along. They walked for about an hour. A few birds flew above them; one bird dived down towards them.

"Get down!" yelled Eli.

They slumped to the ground, the bird got closer. Eli held *Gloria* in the air, the bird stopped, as if it recognized the device and then flew back into the sky.

"The animals sense it," said Eli.

The group continued to walk for a while. They got to a river, walking in a single row. Eli was first, followed by Kawaki, Sarah, Jennifer, and the rest behind them. Jennifer stopped for a second and leaned towards the river; Eli turned around when he heard a change in pace; Jennifer was about to touch the water.

"Don't!" he yelled.

Jennifer was startled and withdrew her hand a second before piranhas, the size of small sharks, jumped out of the water. They snapped their mouths loudly.

"Oh my god!" Sarah shrieked.

"Don't touch the water," Eli reiterated sharply.

In a state of shock, Jennifer replied, "Okay."

Kawaki looked at Jennifer and frowned. They continued along the river for a few hours, a woman in the back of the group, Shelly, about 50-years-old, slowed down.

"I'm tired," said Shelly.

Kawaki looked at Eli.

"Maybe we should stop and rest for a bit?" asked Kawaki.

"Okay, but not too long as we still have a few hours to walk, and we don't want to be outside at night; it gets too dangerous," Eli said, concerned.

Sarah saw that Kawaki took Eli's advice. They walked a few feet away from the river and found a spot to rest. Everyone sat down except for Sarah, she stood with Jennifer.

"I'm so thankful for Eli," said Jennifer.

"I can't believe he survived here for 13 years, alone," said Sarah.

Sarah looked at Eli, who was studying a plant. She was extremely attracted to him and intrigued by who he was and walked towards him.

"What are you doing?"

"I'm a botanist, I study plants, it's been a passion for me since I was a child. They are magical to me - some can heal, others you can eat, and others are poison. It's fascinating," Eli replied, excited to be having a conversation.

He went towards a flower and picked it, smelling the perfume. Sarah was a few feet away from him and reached for a beautiful pink rose.

"Don't touch it, it's poisonous, you'll have a rash for days!"

"Oh... Thanks," Sarah blushed with embarrassment.

She sat next to Eli while he continued to study the flower.

"So, how did you survive all these years here? Did you come alone?"

"There were three of us, but I am the only one who survived the crash. At first, it was challenging; I used the ship as shelter until I ran out of supplies and realized I wouldn't be rescued. I struggled to acclimate to this planet... but... bit by bit, I figured it out. It was definitely not easy," Eli paused and smiled, "But... I am still alive."

They looked at each other intently, he stared at her as if he was looking at the most beautiful flower in the universe. Sarah felt his stare and was a bit intimidated, but liked it. She felt there had been an instant connection the second they laid eyes on each other.

Eli went on, "I almost got killed several times, but there was one time when I really thought it would be the end."

Sarah listened to him attentively.

"A bird came straight at me, stabbed me with his beak in the shoulder, grabbed me with his talons, and lifted me in the air. More birds came and tried to grab me, pulling me in different directions as if they were fighting over me. It was terrifying! In the melee, I was dropped and luckily fell into a thick bush that softened the fall. I made my way back to the spaceship and then created this-"

Eli pulled *Gloria* from his pocket and waved it at Sarah.

"I never go anywhere without her."

Sarah looked at his body. A scar stretched across his chest and over his shoulder.

"I'm glad you didn't die," said Sarah timidly.

They locked eyes again. The moment prolonged. Kawaki interrupted.

"Should we get going?"

"Yes," said Eli, as he stood up.

They all got up, got back in line, and continued to walk. Sarah walked behind Eli, looking comfortably close. Kawaki noticed that they seemed to be infatuated with one another.

"We are almost there," Kawaki said, recognizing where they were, "Probably another 45 minutes, and we will arrive at the ship."

They were all relieved when they finally arrived at the ship, but Kawaki held Sarah back from the group.

"Do not show your attraction to Eli, you will get in trouble. Remember the rules of the ship, okay?"

"I know... I know... Thank you," said Sarah quietly.

"I will tell Eli as well, separately."

"Okay. Thank you, Kawaki."

Sarah joined the group and continued to the entrance of the ship. Kawaki made his way to Eli and pulled him aside, gesturing to the group to keep going.

"I don't have much time to explain things to you, but you will be questioned by the Captain; of that, I'm sure. There are a few rules on the ship; one of them prohibits intimate relationships between men and women. So, be careful what you say or do, okay?" Kawaki gave Eli a friendly smile, "Also, don't say anything about your weapon. You should hide it."

"Okay, thank you for the warning," Eli responded.

Eli did not ask any questions. He paused for a moment and then followed Kawaki into the ship.

Kawaki instructed them to put their foraging bags in the middle of the staging room where there was a circle-shaped area on the floor. They placed their bags and stepped back. The bags lowered into the spaceship, and the platform returned empty.

"It's dinner time, everyone go to the dining room," said Kawaki, "Eli, I am taking you to Captain Sirak. She will want to see you."

The group left, walking off two by two. Kawaki escorted Eli to Sirak's office. At her door, Kawaki put his thumb in front of a pad, a hologram appeared, and the door opened. Eli stayed in the hallway. Sirak sat at her desk. She heard the door open and looked up.

"Yes?" she barked.

"Captain, we found someone on Kambukta. He crashed there years ago, I assumed you would want to talk to him right away," said Kawaki.

"Yes."

Kawaki turned around, opened the door, and signaled for Eli to enter. Eli complied, leaving his bag in the hallway. Kawaki nodded to Sirak and left the office. When the door shut, Kawaki took Eli's belongings and left.

Sirak stared at Eli for a full minute. She was disgusted by his dirtiness, his naked torso, and unshaven face.

"So, you have been on Kambukta for several years?" she said.

"Yes, Captain, my ship crashed there a few years ago when I was on a mission to find rare plants, I am a botanist."

"Where are you from?" Sirak inquired.

"I am from planet Saké, 48 planets West, Captain."

"I see. We are going to Tikai, it's about a month's travel, we are going 22 planets South," Sirak paused, "While you are on my ship, there are a few rules you will need to abide by."

"Of course, Captain."

"No intimate relationships with others are allowed. You will be assigned to a team for work and recreation. Kawaki will give you the details on that; we have combat training every day. We run a buddy system onboard for all non-crew members, you will be assigned to someone you must stay with at all times."

Sirak barely looked at him.

"Yes, Captain."

"You can go."

"Thank you, Captain."

Six ∞ Eli

Eli saw his belongings were no longer in the hall and got worried.

"I will take you to your quarters," Kawaki said, appearing out of nowhere, "I have assigned you to the day shift," Kawaki smiled and lowered his voice, "I put your belongings under the bed in your room, keep them hidden."

"Okay, thank you," said Eli, relieved.

"You are part of Team G. They manage the stocking and cleaning of the laboratory."

"Okay."

Kawaki escorted Eli to his quarters, a crew member was standing guard outside the room.

"You can leave now, I have his new buddy," Kawaki said to the crew member who left right away. Kawaki and Eli entered. A 300-pound young man stood in the middle of the room; he had a kind and goofy look to him.

"Hi Alex, this is Eli, you two will be teamed up for now," Kawaki turned to Eli, "Sean, his previous buddy, was put on the night shift."

"Yes, Sir," said Alex.

Kawaki looked at Eli, "Here are some new clothes, you can take a shower, and then go have dinner. If you have any questions, you can ask Alex."

"Thank you," said Eli.

Eli took a nice long shower; he knew how the buttons worked; he had seen this system many times before. He washed up, shaved, and looked spick and span.

Alex and Eli went to the dining room. Eli looked around as they walked through various corridors.

"Every day we have breakfast and then muster at 8am," Alex explained, "Then we get everything to stock up the laboratory and clean it. After that, we have lunch, then there is combat training. 6pm is dinner time, and then it's our off time; we can go to the game room or to our rooms. You'll see, the game room is amazing! Oh, and never forget, we always have to stay together, and we cannot leave our rooms after 8pm."

"Sounds good, Alex," said Eli.

In the dining room, Eli looked for Sarah. He saw her and gave her a discreet smile. Sarah looked at him quickly and hid her happiness. Although in different groups, at separate tables, Sarah and Eli sat so they could face each other from afar.

Alex introduced everyone on the team to Eli. Alex was clearly starving and began eating quickly.

"Where are you from?" said Eli, picking through his food.

"We are all from planet Tyrakti," replied Alex with a mouth full of food, "There was an explosion on our planet. Luckily, this ship saw it and saved us all."

"Oh, so you are all from Tyrakti, then?"

"Yes, we were living in a farmland village; we didn't have e-lec-tronics on our planet. This is all, very cool to me," said Alex, excited, "I wish we were part of the e-lec-tronics team, I love that stuff. Were there e-lec-tronics on your planet?"

"Yes, there were electronics," Eli replied, as he smiled.

They resumed their eating, Alex continued to chew while he talked.

"So you can teach me stuff then?"

"Yes, maybe," said Eli.

"Cool! Oh, let's go to the game room, I'll show you the coolest game. I've been playing it every day."

"Sure," said Eli, amused by Alex.

They got to the game room, Alex showed Eli the game. Alex was surrounded by a holographic representation of a battle craft. The aim of the game was to destroy all the other spaceships. Alex laughed elatedly throughout. Eli knew this game; he played it a lot when he was a young child.

"Isn't it amazing? I'm at level 17!" said Alex.

"Yes, it's great," replied Eli.

Eli didn't want to spoil Alex's fun by letting him know that he had played it before. Eli stood next to Alex while he played.

"Let's play one together, I'll show you all the best moves," said Alex.

"Sure."

They started a new game, Eli pretended to learn from scratch; hiding the fact that he already knew *all* the moves. He saw that Alex was really excited about the game. Alex proudly showed Eli his latest trick. Alex had become a complete geek since being onboard the GL400. Eli and Alex continued with their game when the Gem siren went off, Gem appearing in the center of the room.

"All passengers must return to their rooms at this time."

Eli and Alex went to their room, and into their beds. Alex showed Eli the Sonance system, he was thrilled to show it off. He switched from film to film and then the exterior view and the itinerary. The itinerary interested Eli the most; Alex was about to switch back to a movie when Eli interrupted him.

"Wait, go back to the itinerary, let me see."

"Sure, look, you press on this button," said Alex, delighted that Eli was showing interest.

"Thank you, I love maps, I'll just watch this from my bed, okay?" said Eli.

"Yeah, I'm going to watch this show I've been watching since we arrived on the ship; it's about this spaceship that attacks all these other spaceships, it's so cool," said Alex.

Eli studied every detail of the map and itinerary; he knew where they were. While Alex watched his film, he farted, didn't apologize, and laughed childishly. Eli found Alex likable despite his manners or lack thereof; he was a good kid.

Sarah and Jennifer were in their room, Jennifer looked at Sarah.

"You really like him, don't you?"

"Yes," replied Sarah, looking coy.

Jennifer looked at Sarah, expecting her to talk more.

"I feel like we have such a strong connection, and I'm pretty sure he feels the same. I keep catching him looking at me. If we were on Tikai, I am sure we would be together. I wish the rules were different."

"In all these years, I have never seen you interested in any man; I am really happy for you," Jennifer chirped.

"Yes," said Sarah dreamingly.

She then turned to Sarah with genuine concern, "But, be careful while we are on the ship, okay?"

"Yeah, I will, don't worry," said Sarah calmly.

The girls got in their beds. Jennifer listened to a story using the hologram headphones. Sarah looked at the stars and smiled; she daydreamed about Eli.

Alex continued to watch his show until he fell asleep, he snored loudly, Eli looked at him hopelessly.

Eli left the room, carrying *Gloria* with him. He sneaked through the corridors, illuminated by blue lights, acquainting himself with the ship. He found himself in an area with red lights on the walls. He turned down another hallway as he heard men approaching. Eli saw a stretcher with a body on it from a distance; he listened in on their conversation.

"Sirak said to put this one in the pit, he doesn't have the right DNA," said a man.

"Yes, but we first need to bring it to the laboratory; she said to keep the lungs," said the other man.

Eli wasn't surprised by the conversation; he waited for them to pass and followed them to see where they were taking the body. He was now in the same area where Sarah confronted Maya days before. The men took the body into the laboratory, and Eli stood in front of the metal door, waiting.

An hour later, the two crew members came out with the same body on a stretcher. The door swung open, and Eli saw three children holding operating utensils. The children had holograms around their heads. Eli followed the crew members, being very careful to not make a sound. They went down three corridors with pink lights and arrived in front of a large black door. One crew member put up his thumb to the keypad, the heavy door opened, and a black ramp appeared in front of them. They pushed the body off the stretcher, and it slid down into a dark hole. Thump. The crew members, unphased, turned around and went back the way they came from, now with an empty stretcher. Eli waited for them to pass, then quietly found his way back to his room.

The next morning Eli and Alex sat down for breakfast in the same spot as they did the day before.

Eli saw Sarah across the room. She looked up, and they looked at each other intensely. No one seemed to notice. As the groups made their way out of the dining room, Eli approached Sarah and whispered in her ear.

"I need to see you tonight after 8."

"Where should we meet?" Sarah whispered back, "We can meet-"

Sarah cut herself off when she spotted Loyt on the other side of the corridor. She turned toward her group to cover.

"Let's go to the engine room now, we have a lot of work to do this morning."

Sarah gave Eli a quick look, and he nodded his head in agreement; they would meet at the engine room. He joined his group, and they headed to the laboratory. This was not the same laboratory Eli saw last night; there were shelves in the walls with all sorts of needles and different sized flasks. The group began their task of cleaning the space. A 10-year-old boy named Steve came into the laboratory and retrieved a vial; Alex knew Steve.

"Hi Steve, it's been a while; how are you?" Alex asked.

Steve was silent. Alex didn't notice Steve's strange behavior.

"I taught him how to play ball, he's a good kid," Alex told Eli.

"Yes, I'm sure," replied Eli.

They continued to clean and organize the laboratory, then went to lunch.

Sarah and her team stood together in one area of the combat training room. Her team was getting better and better at fighting. Jennifer nudged Sarah with her elbow.

"He's looking at you," Jennifer muttered.

"I know."

Sarah looked over at Sophie; she looked depleted of emotions.

"Are you all right, Sophie?" Sarah asked.

"Yes, everything is going well, I am getting much better at this; I have lost 10 pounds since we arrived," replied Sophie in a certain calmness.

Sarah barely recognized Sophie without her feisty attitude. Sarah was called to practice with Jennifer.

They moved through a choreographed fight, Jennifer took a hit and fell to the floor. She struggled to catch her breath. Sarah rushed to Jennifer and helped her to her feet, trying to keep anyone from seeing she was hurt. Sarah looked at Jennifer, indicating for her to be careful, but it was too late. Halay, the tall, dark-haired deputy of Kawaki, saw this and went towards them.

"Is everything fine, Jennifer?"

"Oh yes, I tripped is all," replied Jennifer quickly.

"Oh, okay, if you need to go to the infirmary, just let me know."

"Of course, thank you," said Jennifer.

Halay went back to help another team.

Alex and Eli practiced fighting together; Alex had a hard time.

"I am not really good at this as you can see," he said sheepishly.

"I can help you, you should use your weight to your advantage instead of trying to avoid the blows," said Eli.

Sam, a jockish looking team member, teased Alex.

"There's no hope for you, Alex. You've had the lowest score ever since we started. You should think about losing weight instead of learning how to fight."

Alex looked at Sam but didn't reply; he was used to being teased by his team. Don, the team leader, intervened.

"That's enough, Sam."

Don had a kind face, and his long white beard made him seem wise. He turned to Alex.

"Continue practicing, you'll be all right."

The bullying made Eli even more fond of Alex. Eli was determined to help Alex become a better fighter. They continued with their training until dinner.

After dinner, Alex and Eli went to the game room. Instead of playing the spacecraft game, Eli suggested the hologram fighter. Alex was unsure, but Eli convinced him the game would help. After many attempts, Alex managed to use his weight against the hologram and finally scored a win. Pleased with himself, he continued the simulated fighting.

On the other side of the game room, Sarah and Jennifer learned how to cook with a hologram chef. Jennifer was fully engaged with the chef, while Sarah sat on a floating couch watching Eli help Alex. His kindness made him even more attractive.

The siren sound went on, and Gem appeared once more.

"Attention, all passengers. It's time to go to your rooms," ordered Gem.

Sarah jumped off the couch, grabbed Jennifer, and headed out. Sarah looked back to see if Eli was looking. He was, they both nodded to each other from afar.

Eli and Alex got to their room; Alex laid down and turned on his spaceship show while Eli went to the washroom. In the shower, he closed his eyes and thought about Sarah; he would see her soon. He was excited and nervous all at the same time. He wondered if this would be considered their first date. He opened his eyes and smiled.

Sarah and Jennifer talked in their room.

"But, it's dangerous, Sarah, if you get caught, we'll both be in trouble."

"I won't get caught. I've thought it through, Jennifer. I wouldn't do this if it wasn't important, and Eli is smart, he'll make sure we're careful."

"Fine... but you better not get us in trouble. Sirak scares me."

"I promise."

"Okay. Fine. Go and don't come back too late."

Sarah kissed Jennifer on the cheek.

Seven ∞ Sarah and Eli

Sarah crept through the corridors; she was cautious. Sarah made it to the engine room. It was quiet, without a sound to be heard. She hid behind one of the big engines, one her team repaired two days earlier. She sat on the floor and waited nervously, with her eyes fixed on the entrance. Sarah wondered how long it would take for Eli to arrive. She heard light footsteps approaching. She stayed hidden; it might be someone else. Eli entered, and Sarah's face lit up. They saw each other, and both smiled big. Eli moved towards Sarah and sat next to her on the floor.

"Hi," he said.

"Hi," she replied.

They looked at each other without saying a word. Minutes passed. There was happiness in this silence as they finally had a moment to study each other, up close and uninterrupted. There was a definite connection between the two. They smiled and spoke to each other with their eyes before finally breaking the silence.

"So, here we are," Sarah said.

"Yes..." Eli paused, "There are so many things I need to tell you, but most importantly, you must know that this ship is very... *very* dangerous. I've heard of these people and this ship. Their home planet lacks genetic diversity. They travel the universe, planet to planet, and *save* people, but really, they are kidnapping people for their DNA. You must never go to the infirmary or show any weakness, okay?" Eli said with evident concern in his voice.

"I knew something weird was going on. What does genetic diversity mean?"

"It's a bit complicated to explain, but basically, they test and use the cells from other people to enhance their people."

Sarah was embarrassed by her naiveté, "And... what are cells?"

"Well, essentially, it is everything that your body is made of."

"Oh, Kawaki warned me not to go to the infirmary."

"Never go to the infirmary! They drug people and then hypnotize them with those holograms. I haven't fully figured out why, but Kawaki has also helped me a few times. It's almost like he isn't on their side."

"Huh..." Sarah pondered what Eli just revealed.

"Sirak is the daughter of a very powerful and noble family on Tikai; nothing will stop her. You must stay away from her at all costs. Do you understand?"

"Yes."

"Also, be very careful when you walk in the corridors at night, yesterday I saw a man get thrown down some kind of a shaft. I am not sure where it goes, but I will find out."

"Okay," Sarah nodded.

"Oh, and I figured out that the corridors with green and blue lights on the walls are the ship's safe parts. If you end up in a red or pink lit corridor, get out of there, okay?"

"Yeah, I was following Lucas, a child from Tyrakti, the other night, and I ended up in a red-lit corridor."

"Don't ever go there without me, okay?" Eli said sternly.

"Yes," Sarah replied, enjoying the fact that he evidently cared about her.

She understood the tone in which Eli was speaking to her. He was trying to protect her. The two talked for hours, telling each other where they were from and what they had done. Time flew. They got along effortlessly.

"Cheryl was my baby sister, she was such a happy and kind person," Sarah began to sob, "When our parents died, I took care of her. Despite how tough it was, she was always making the best out of things; she would help me at the farm... I miss her so much."

Eli felt Sarah's immense sadness and took her in his arms. They looked at each other for a minute, silence lingered in the air once more. Eli leaned in towards her and kissed her softly. Sarah's heart started pounding with excitement. The kiss was languorous and passionate. They both felt as if they were floating on a cloud, blissfully transported from the reality around them.

They continued to speak and kiss for another hour, feeling entirely in love in an instant.

"We have to go back to our rooms. I would much rather stay here all night with you, but we need to be careful," Eli said regretfully.

"I don't want to go, but I know you're right," said Sarah.

"I *will* see you every night, okay?"

"Yes," Sarah smiled at the thought.

They got up and went towards the exit, pausing at the door; Eli turned around and kissed Sarah passionately one last time.

They walked through the corridors together quietly. Eli took Sarah to the entrance of her room. They stood there peacefully, looking at each other for a moment before Sarah entered. Eli then went to his quarters, entered silently, and saw Alex, who was fast asleep.

Sarah and Eli laid on their beds, watching the star-filled abyss outside the ship on Sonance. They drifted into sleep, thinking only of one another.

The next morning Sarah woke up in an excellent mood. She woke Jennifer up excitedly. Sarah stood in front of Jennifer with a big smile on her face.

"He is... he is... there are no words, I just like being near him, we understand each other," Sarah stopped and mused for a second, "He kissed me!"

Jennifer, eyes half-open, smiled at her friend.

"Awwww. That's amazing, I am so happy for you."

Jennifer rubbed the sleep from her eyes and popped out of bed. She quickly showered and emerged from the bathroom, fully dressed. Sarah sat on the bed, still smiling from ear to ear.

"Be careful to not look too happy," said Jennifer with genuine concern.

"Of course, you're right," said Sarah, unable to thwart her wide grin, "Jennifer, there are other things I need to tell you."

"What?" Jennifer was immediately nervous.

"Eli told me that he's heard of this ship before. He said the Captain and crew are evil people. They kidnap people from other planets and use parts of their bodies to help their people. We have to be careful, okay?"

Jennifer didn't say anything for a minute, trying to understand.

"What do you mean?!"

"I know... it sounds crazy. I still don't understand it. I just know that we need to look out for each other."

Sarah tried to calm her friend.

"Right, okay, but... I don't understand what they do with other people's bodies?" said Jennifer, still confused.

"It's complicated, you have to trust me."

"I trust you."

The day on the ship went by quickly.

Sarah and Eli met again in the engine room. They spent the evening talking and kissing, they continued getting to know each other. A few hours went by, and then Eli walked Sarah to her room. As they quietly navigated their way around the ship, they ended up face to face with Kawaki. They stared at him in shock, not sure what to expect. He looked at them seriously.

"Follow me, don't make any noise."

Sarah and Eli followed Kawaki to a red-lit corridor they hadn't been to before. They stopped in front of a door, Kawaki put his thumb up to the black pad, and the door opened. Sarah and Eli looked at each other; they were not sure if they were in trouble.

"You don't need to worry, you can trust me," said Kawaki, noticing their reticence.

Eli and Sarah nodded at each other and entered the room.

"This is my office; no one will find you here," said Kawaki.

The office was relatively large; the entire wall behind Kawaki's desk was a fake window showing space outside. There was a blank hologram screen covering the whole right wall. On the other wall, there were shelves filled with little glass containers adorned with unfamiliar symbols.

"Who are you really, Kawaki?" Eli asked.

"I could ask you the same thing?" replied Kawaki.

They looked at each other for a moment, then Kawaki started.

"I was hired by a wealthy family from Tikai to bring down Sirak's family. My patrons - The Lukoses - believe they have found a solution for the lack of genetic diversity on Tikai. The Siraks and the

Lukoseses both wish to rule my planet; they have been fighting over Tikai for decades.

Sirak's family has been enslaving and torturing people from all over the galaxy for hundreds of years. I am part of a rebel group; we are very organized and have a lot at our disposal. My mission is to kill Sirak," Kawaki paused and looked at Sarah and Eli for a reaction, "I think we can help each other. The people of Tyrakti are at risk here, and if we kill Sirak, we can free them."

"I knew it! I wondered why you were helping us," Eli said, excitedly, "I've heard of your planet and Sirak's family before. Our Humanity Commission has sent out several missions to kill her family to no avail. So... how can we kill Sirak?"

Sarah took in all the new information, realizing she was in the middle of some interplanetary war.

"Sirak usually has an exact schedule, but in the last week, she has been in her office most of the time where she is protected by a hologram defense system. If we want to kill her, it will have to be somewhere else on board. She seems certain that someone from Tyrakti has the DNA she's been searching for. She has been warier lately. I will have to find out more about what is going on; she doesn't tell me everything. Eli, with *Gloria*, we might be able to kill her," Kawaki looked at Eli for some agreement.

"Okay. But, if we are going to do this, we will only have one chance," said Eli.

"Let's meet in a week. I'll try and get more information and find out when Sirak will be outside her office. We should arrive on Tikai in four weeks. We must kill her before we land. There is nothing I can do to save anyone once we land on her side of the planet."

Sarah and Eli nodded and said, in sync, "Okay."

"I haven't seen anybody from the night shift since we arrived. Are they okay?" asked Sarah.

"The teams in the other shift are actually the people with similar or close DNA to the one Sirak's family is looking for."

"Oh my god," said Sarah, shocked, "Eli said he saw someone being thrown down some kind of shaft-"

"Listen," Kawaki interrupted, "Be careful when you leave your rooms, and be very careful of the children - they are hypnotized and under Sirak's control."

"Holy shit. I was so confused that Maya and Lucas didn't recognize me. They were acting so strangely. We have to help them!" said Sarah.

"We will come up with a plan, Sarah. In the meantime, keep your eyes open," Kawaki said, slowly.

Kawaki walked towards the door.

"I will make sure no one is outside so you can leave. There are usually children in the corridor to your right; it's not very far from the pit," said Kawaki.

"What's the pit?" Eli asked.

"It's a long shaft where Sirak puts unwanted bodies."

"That must be what I saw," Eli whispered to Sarah.

Kawaki opened the door and heard a noise. He saw Maya standing not too far from his office door.

"Hi, Maya," he said loudly.

"Sirak wants to see you," said Maya in a monotonous voice.

"Of course," Kawaki replied.

Kawaki followed Maya, who accompanied him to Sirak's office. Eli and Sarah stayed where they were for a few minutes until they no longer heard footsteps. Eli had *Gloria* ready in one hand and held Sarah's hand in the other. They left Kawaki's office. No one was there; they went to the left, being very careful to not make any noise. Eli escorted Sarah to her room before returning to his, to process everything he just learned.

Eight ∞ Plan

Jennifer woke up when Sarah came back into the room. Sarah told Jennifer what happened with Kawaki. Jennifer finally realized the extent of what was happening on the ship.

"What can I do to help?" asked Jennifer.

"I think it's safer if you aren't involved, Jennifer, at least for now," Sarah replied.

"But I want to help," Jennifer pleaded.

"I will speak to Eli and Kawaki to see if there is something you can do. But for now, just stay away from the infirmary and don't show *any* weakness, okay?"

"Okay."

"I need to get some sleep."

Sarah collapsed onto her bed.

They woke up a few hours later. Sarah was tired, she started to feel the lack of sleep. They went to the dining room for breakfast. Sarah kept looking for Eli. He finally appeared and sat down at his table; Eli and Sarah glanced at each other.

Sirak and Kawaki arrived; Sirak took up her position in the middle of the room with Kawaki by her side. The microphone hologram appeared.

"Today, you will do your combat training without protective suits. Everyone should have reached 50 points by now," said Sirak sharply.

The hologram microphone disappeared, and she left without another word.

Alex stared at Eli; he was freaking out. They went to the laboratory while Sarah and her team went to the engine room. The other teams got up and went to different parts of the ship to complete their tasks. Alex and Eli talked in the corridor as they walked towards the laboratory.

"I am gonna get my ass kicked," said Alex.

"No, you'll be fine. You'll continue to train as we have been doing, and you'll get better and better," said Eli trying to comfort him.

"Yes, but what about Sam? He hates me."

"I doubt Don will make you guys fight together right away."

"I hope you are right," Alex seemed to relax at the idea.

Sarah's team was busy working in the engine room when Sirak and Loyt arrived. They didn't say a word and simply watched the team work.

"Can I help you, Captain?" said Sarah.

"No," Sirak replied, "Continue, we are simply doing an inspection."

Sarah's heart was beating quickly. She didn't know what to expect from Sirak; she was impossible to read.

Sirak whispered to Loyt as he took notes. After a few minutes, they left. Sirak and Loyt went to the laboratory and inspected Eli's team while they worked.

"Hi, Captain, can I help you with anything?" asked Don.

"This is just a routine inspection, be sure there is always a full stock of supplies in the laboratory," said Sirak.

"Yes, Captain, I have noticed that the storeroom stock is lowering quickly. I didn't realize that there were that many sick people."

"There are many sick people in the night shift," said Sirak, coldly.

"Oh, of course, Captain," Don replied.

"You ask too many questions," Sirak smiled.

"Sorry, Captain," Don was embarrassed and continued with his duties.

Loyt scribbled down some notes and left with Sirak.

The teams finished their morning duties and went to lunch. Sirak, Kawaki, Halay, and Loyt stood at the dining room's right side, looking at everyone while they ate in silence. Tension could be felt. Jennifer looked at Sarah.

"I don't think I'll make it."

"You'll be fine, Jennifer, I promise. Just make the same moves you have been doing with the suit on," Sarah encouraged.

The teams walked to the fight room in silence. Sirak, Kawaki, Loyt, and Halay were standing at one end of the training room, observing the different groups. The fights began. Each fighter was hesitant.

Don assigned Eli to fight Alex. Eli was careful to not hurt him; Alex was grateful. Nearby, Sarah fought Sophie. Sophie hit Sarah in the face; she fell to the floor but stood up instantly. Sarah realized Sophie had been keeping her anger to herself and used these fights to get back at her. Sarah was hurt but didn't care and didn't show it. Then Alex fought with Don, Don also went easy on him. Alex was proud of the fact that he was managing to fight without the suit's protection.

Sirak whispered something to Loyt; Loyt went towards Don's team.

"I want to see Alex fight Sam," said Loyt.

"But Sam is at a much higher level than Alex," Don replied.

"Do it."

Don had no choice and called Sam over. Alex was terrified. The fight began. Sam kicked Alex in the leg and got pushed back slightly. Sirak grinned as she watched. Alex remembered what Eli told him; *to use his weight and strength to absorb the blows.* Sam hit Alex again, this time in the chest. Alex had a hard time breathing but continued to hold his ground; he tried to hit Sam, but Sam ducked from the blow. With all his strength, Sam punched Alex in the chest, he fell to the floor. This time, he couldn't get back up. Alex stayed on the ground. Eli ran over to help him get up.

"I'll take him to the infirmary," Loyt told Don.

"Yes," Don replied, "Eli, follow Loyt to the infirmary."

"Of course," said Eli.

Sarah was nervous as she watched Eli leave with Alex. She was snapped out of it when her name was called for the next fight. The room resumed with training.

Loyt escorted Eli and Alex to the infirmary and left them waiting outside. The crew member standing by the door instructed Alex to enter alone.

"You can wait here," he said sharply to Eli.

Alex entered while Eli and the crew member stood outside, waiting together, not a single word exchanged. Alex came out an hour later and seemed much better.

"How are you feeling?" said Eli, very concerned.

"I can barely feel a thing," replied Alex.

"Okay, should we go and have dinner and then go to the game room?"

"Let's get dinner, and after I'd rather go to our room, I don't feel like anymore fighting today," Alex replied.

"Sure."

They went to the dining room together. Sarah and her team were sitting at their table. Eli looked at Sarah, he saw that she had a slight bruise on her right cheek. Sophie looked at Sarah with hatred, Eli put two and two together. Jennifer couldn't sit still between Sophie and Sarah; she felt extremely uncomfortable.

"Let's go back to our room," Sarah said to Jennifer.

"Okie dokie," Jennifer was happy to leave.

Alex and Eli walked through the corridors without saying a word and arrived at their room

"What a shitty day," moaned Alex.

"I thought you did pretty well!" said Eli, genuinely impressed by his improvement.

"Yeah, well, not good enough. I'm tired of being here," said Alex.

"We should arrive in a few weeks. Not long now," Eli said, reassuringly, "I'm going to take a shower."

Alex laid on his bed and started watching his show. In the shower, Eli was angry at how Alex was treated. He grew concerned about what was done to Alex while he was in the infirmary. Eli got out of the shower and laid on his bed, looking at the itinerary. Half an hour later, Alex snored loudly. Eli got ready to leave his room, excited to have his daily alone time with Sarah.

Eli walked through the corridors carefully and got to the engine room, this time before Sarah. He sat in their usual spot and waited. He waited longer than expected and got worried. He heard a noise, looked towards the door, and saw Sarah enter. He was ecstatic to see her. They hugged and kissed each other passionately. He kissed her bruised cheek softly.

"It doesn't hurt," she said.

She touched his face gently.

"You have beautiful green eyes," Sarah cooed.

They sat and held each other close. They talked about the future they wanted together. They talked about owning a farm, what it would look like, how many children they would raise, and how happy they would be. Eli looked at Sarah intensely, they kissed. He put his hand on her breasts.

"I have never done it before," whispered Sarah.

"We'll go slow, it's just you and me, okay?" Eli said sweetly.

She smiled, her face blushed pink. Eli started to caress her gently, barely touching her with the tips of his fingers. She made soft noises. He slowly kissed her forehead, each cheek, her nose, eyes, and finally her lips. Eli slipped her top off and kissed her neck. Sarah was overcome with new emotions. He lightly kissed her right breast and then her left. Eli touched and kissed Sarah very sensually. He kissed her stomach, slowly going lower and lower until Sarah was in full ecstasy. Her body shook uncontrollably. He kissed her lips three times, slowly. They stared at each other; it was clear they were completely in love. They were both sweating and breathing heavily. Sarah touched Eli's chest, feeling his warm skin, wondering if she was doing it correctly. The movements were slow. He took off her pants entirely and then removed his. Eli moved his body on top of hers. He lovingly kissed her whole body and ran his fingers through her hair. Sarah felt his penis hard against her body. Scared, she reached for his hands. Eli paused, interlocked his fingers with hers, and tightened his grip. He slowly guided her right hand onto his erection. He brushed his hand across her wetness between her legs before slowly sliding a single finger into her. Sarah's skin tingled from head to toe as if an electrical current had erupted from her core. Her body was tense and relaxed at the same time. Sarah nervously stroked him up and down, still unsure of what to do. They kissed passionately. Sarah rocked her hips back and forth against him as it started to feel more natural. Eli moved down to kiss her erect nipples; he used his tongue to tease her uncontrollably. As he returned to kiss her face, Sarah felt him slowly glide into her. Her eyes widened, her breath was taken away. It didn't hurt as much as she had expected. Sarah was experiencing sensations and emotions she didn't know were even possible. She grabbed at Eli's back, pulling his body tight against hers. Eli was gentle with her, as he started thrusting back and forth. Sarah relaxed, and her body began to shake. They locked eyes, Sarah held Eli's face with both hands and moaned loudly. As the world around them seemed to pause, they climaxed together, their bodies entwined like the roots of a tree.

Eli laid next to her, caressing her breasts and stomach. Sarah smiled timidly. They made love over and over and then fell asleep from exhaustion. Time passed, Eli woke up startled, realizing they had been asleep for too long.

"Sarah, wake up, wake up," Eli gently moved her.

Sarah woke up in a dreamlike state, smiling.

"We have to hurry back to our rooms."

"Oh, no. No, no, no, no, no," said Sarah.

They got up, threw their clothes on, and headed for the door to leave. Sarah touched Eli's arm and looked at him before kissing him intensely one last time.

They walked through a red-lit corridor when they heard a noise. They stopped abruptly, four crew members and two children pushed a stretcher at the end of the hall. Sarah recognized the man on the stretcher.

"It's Luke, he is from Tyrakti. He got into a fight a while ago. I haven't seen him since. We have to stop them."

"They are too many," Eli paused, thinking, "Fine, let's follow and see if we can stop them."

Through the ship, they wandered until they reached a pink-lit corridor. Eli made sure that Sarah was always behind him. They hid behind a corner. Eli poked his head around and saw three more men in front of the pit. He turned to Sarah and shook his head, no. The crew members laughed and talked loudly while opening the door to the shaft. Sarah and Eli retreated, making sure to not make a sound. Once Eli was convinced they were in a safe place, he turned to Sarah.

"I am sorry it was too risky. We have to think about our plan."

"Yeah, I know. You are right. It's just hard not doing anything, you know?" said Sarah.

"I know," Eli replied.

Eli took Sarah back to her room, where Jennifer was already awake.

"I was worried. You are going to give me a heart attack," said Jennifer.

"Sorry, we fell asleep," Sarah smiled wide, "And... we um... we made love."

"I was scared something happened to you."

Sarah's mood changed as she saw how affected Jennifer was.

"I'm sorry, Jennifer."

"Don't let that happen again."

Eli entered his room; Alex was still in bed, tossing around. Eli jumped into bed, pretending like he spent the night there, just as Alex woke up.

"It's time to get up, man," Alex yawned.

Eli faked a yawn and got up.

A week went by with the same routine, work in the morning, combat training in the afternoon, and nightly escapades to the engine room for Sarah and Eli. They lived in a bubble together, meeting up, talking, and making love every night.

Nine ∞ Optimism

One night, when Eli and Sarah headed back from the engine room, they overheard crew members talking in a red-lit corridor. They watched as the two crew members pushed a stretcher and stopped in front of a door. Sarah and Eli hid in the hall nearby; they could hear everything.

"She has the perfect DNA," said a crew member.

"Halay said once we drop her off, we need to go and warn Sirak. Can you imagine we might have found the solution after all this searching?" said another crew member.

A crew member put his thumb up to the keypad, a hologram appeared, and the door opened. Sarah peaked around the corner and saw the person on the stretcher. The two men entered the room, and the door closed behind them.

"Oh my god, that was Cheryl. I am sure that it was Cheryl!" whispered Sarah, her eyes welling with tears.

"I thought Cheryl died during the explosion on Tyrakti?" said Eli.

"Me too, I don't know, but I am sure that was her; we have to help her, she's my sister!" said Sarah anxiously.

"Of course."

"How is it possible? They must have gotten her when they landed, I don't know, maybe it wasn't her, but I am pretty sure it was," Sarah said, confused at what she saw.

"Okay... okay... it's okay," said Eli.

"We have to try. I have to know if it's her."

"Okay, let's get help from Kawaki. We have to go to his office."

Sarah felt reassured that they were doing something about it. She thought about Cheryl, her baby sister.

"We must be quiet, remember what Kawaki said, there are often children near his office. Maybe I should go by myself?" said Eli.

"No, I want to come with you," Sarah replied.

"Okay, fine, let's go."

They headed towards Kawaki's office. As they moved through the corridors, they heard voices and stopped. The voices were going further and further away from them. They arrived at the corner of another hall where Kawaki's office was. Eli glanced to see if anyone was there, he saw a child. He touched Sarah behind him to make her stop walking. It was the little boy Lucas. He strolled down the hall, looking at the walls. Eli and Sarah stayed hidden. Eli kept checking until the coast was clear.

"Stay here, I will knock on Kawaki's door and come right back."

Sarah stayed where she was. Eli went into the corridor and gently knocked on Kawaki's door and hurried back to the corner and hid next to Sarah. He poked his head around the corner in case Kawaki opened his office. The door opened, Kawaki looked to the left and then to the right and saw Eli. He signaled for him to come. Sarah and Eli entered Kawaki's office.

"It's too dangerous, you should only come here with me," said Kawaki.

"They have my sister!" shouted Sarah, completely stressed out.

"We need your help," said Eli.

"I didn't know you had a sister on the ship?" said Kawaki.

"I thought she had been killed in the explosion, but I'm pretty sure it was her. They took her into a locked room," said Sarah, exasperated.

"When was this?" asked Kawaki.

"Just a few minutes ago," Eli replied.

"We heard them talk about her having perfect DNA," said Sarah.

"Shit, I hope they haven't found someone with fully matching DNA. Sirak told me she was going through everyone's tests yesterday. We better hurry," Kawaki was concerned that their plan might be foiled.

Kawaki opened the door and checked to make sure no one was there and then signaled them to follow. The trio headed towards the room where Sarah thought she saw Cheryl. Now close by, they heard crew members speaking not too far away. Kawaki signaled them to stop.

"Stay here, I'll go and look at what's going on and come back," whispered Kawaki, "Be sure to stay hidden, okay?"

"Yes," they whispered back.

Kawaki walked to the door and put his thumb up, a hologram appeared, and the door opened. Kawaki saw a girl on an operating table; she was fully drugged. Four crew members watched the girl.

"Who is this?" Kawaki asked.

"We think she might have the correct DNA, Sir," said a crew member.

"Sirak is coming to see her," said another crew member.

Kawaki nodded. He looked at the tag wrapped around the girl's ankle. It read: *Cheryl, Tyrakti Planet*.

The door suddenly opened, Sirak entered.

"Good, you are here," said Sirak, looking at Kawaki, "This might be the one."

"Great news, Captain," said Kawaki, trying to seem enthusiastic.

Sirak had a notepad in her hand and looked at one of the crew members.

"Where are her results?" she asked.

The crew member handed the paperwork to her.

"Here, Captain."

She looked at the results and compared them to her notepad for a minute. She didn't seem pleased.

"Shit! They are off by one," she said.

"Damn it," said Kawaki, smiling inside.

"This might do," Sirak said while she looked at the crew members, "I want you to redo *all* the tests."

"Yes, Captain."

"Come and get me when you are done. Kawaki, you come with me, we have a few things to go over."

"Yes, Captain," replied Kawaki.

Sirak and Kawaki left and went to Sirak's office. Sarah and Eli were still hidden behind the wall where Kawaki left them. Eli saw Sirak and Kawaki walk away from them down the corridor; he turned to Sarah and whispered.

"Kawaki and Sirak just left."

"What should we do?"

"I think we should wait here. Kawaki will come back; we can't get in there without him."

Kawaki came back forty-five minutes later.

"We have to hurry, Sirak wants to start doing tests on Cheryl. If we don't get her out tonight, Sirak will take her to a more secure lab, and we will never get to her."

"So it is Cheryl! Oh my god!" said Sarah in shock.

"Shhh, yes, that's what her name tag said... We only have one chance, I've been thinking about how we can do this."

Eli and Sarah listened to Kawaki attentively.

"There are four crew members in there. Eli, you will have to use *Gloria* to neutralize them. Sarah, you will take your sister, and then we will go to a secret office that only I have access to, okay?"

They looked at him and nodded in agreement.

"What are we going to do with the bodies?" Eli asked.

"We'll put them in the pit. Once we get Cheryl to safety, we can make it look like they disappeared," explained Kawaki.

"It's risky, but a good idea," replied Eli.

Kawaki put his thumb up to open the door, Sarah and Eli were hidden behind him. Eli had *Gloria* ready in his right hand. The door opened, and Kawaki entered. At first, the crew members only saw Kawaki and continued with their work. A second later, they saw Eli and Sarah. Kawaki hit one of the men on the head while Eli, with a single beam from *Gloria*, killed the others. Sarah ran to Cheryl, undid the straps on her arms and legs, and picked up her limp body.

"Hit this one with *Gloria* as well. We want to make sure he doesn't wake up while we are gone," said Kawaki to Eli.

Eli fired a beam at the man Kawaki hit on the head.

"Let me carry her, it will be easier," Eli said to Sarah.

Kawaki went towards the door and opened it. He looked both ways down the hall to see if anyone was there and signaled to Sarah and Eli that it was safe. Cheryl seemed lifeless and unconscious. They traveled through the ship, from the red-lit corridor where Cheryl was being held to the green-lit hall where Sarah's dorm was.

"We are here," Kawaki said.

He stood in front of a wall. Sarah and Eli looked at each other confused. Kawaki raised his hand towards the wall as a black hologram keypad appeared instead of the usual light blue one. His thumb was scanned, and a door appeared inside the wall. They entered the room, and Eli placed Cheryl on a long black floating hologram couch. Sarah tended to her sister, trying to wake her up.

"What is this place?" asked Eli.

"It's my secret office," replied Kawaki.

Eli looked around and saw that everything was black; the holograms on the walls were black, the couch, the chairs, and the desk as well.

"Sarah, you stay here with your sister, and Eli and I will get rid of the bodies, okay?" said Kawaki.

"Yes, of course," Sarah replied.

Eli and Sarah looked at each other, *I love you*, they whispered at the same time.

Kawaki went towards the exit and turned to Sarah.

"I'm the only one who has access to this room. No one even knows it exists. You're both safe here."

"Okay," replied Sarah.

Eli stayed behind Kawaki as they moved through the ship. They turned a corner and heard voices; they hid for a minute to let the crew members pass. They continued on their way and arrived in front of the room where Cheryl had been kept. The four men were still on the floor lifeless.

"Let's get them on a stretcher and take them to the pit. Hopefully, we won't meet anyone on the way there. There is usually someone in front guarding. We'll see," said Kawaki.

"Okay."

Kawaki and Eli stacked the four bodies onto a stretcher and left the laboratory. They wheeled the stretcher through red and pink-lit corridors before arriving near the pit. Kawaki went ahead to check if there was a guard, but luckily no one was there. Kawaki signaled Eli to bring the bodies and opened the door. As it opened, a ramp for the stretcher extended out. There was a foul odor of death. Kawaki and Eli slid the bodies onto the ramp, they heard a loud thump as the bodies fell to the pit's bottom. Kawaki closed the door, and they went back the way they came.

The ship was busy with crew members everywhere. Kawaki and Eli had to hide every time they heard voices nearby. Artfully dodging people as they moved through the ship, they finally arrived back at the laboratory. They entered and put the stretcher back where it was, ensuring no evidence of what had occurred.

"Come on, let's go," said Kawaki.

Eli followed Kawaki, once again being careful not to be seen until they arrived at Kawaki's secret office. Cheryl was awake, Sarah was next to her. When Sarah saw them appear, she went to Eli and hugged him.

"I'm so happy you are okay," Sarah held him tightly.

"We got lucky. There was no one at the pit," said Eli smiling confidently.

They walked towards Cheryl, who was still under the drugs' effect, but she was awake and smiled.

"What did they do to her?" Eli asked.

"She has been locked up and drugged since she arrived on the ship," replied Sarah, "She doesn't remember much, she has told me scraps of things, but it all seems quite blurry to her."

"I can make a concoction with plants for her. It will help force the drugs out of her system."

"Thank you, Eli."

Eli turned to Kawaki.

"So, what's the plan?" asked Eli.

"When Sirak finds out that Cheryl disappeared, she'll be furious; she *will* investigate. Things are going to get crazy. We have to be even more prudent now."

"Right, but how are we going to kill her? Did you get more information?"

"She is in her office most of the time. The only time I see her come out is when she comes to the fights," Kawaki explained, "She is planning a full day of combat training with everyone next week. I don't know what day yet. There's a trophy for the winner; she wants to make this quite an event. She'll be out of her office for that full day, I'm sure. We could plan for it that day?"

"I guess it's a possibility, but it would be easier if she wasn't surrounded by so many people when we do it."

"We don't have any other options; I'll keep digging and see what I can find out."

"What are we going to do about my sister?" Sarah asked.

"She will have to stay here, for now, it's the only safe place on the ship, I'll bring her food every day," said Kawaki, trying to reassure Sarah.

"I want to stay with her, though."

"It's too risky for now. We'll find a way for you to see her regularly but not before things calm down. Tomorrow is going to be a crazy day; we must be careful," said Kawaki.

"Okay, but I want to see her tomorrow. Can I come at 9pm?"

"Okay, we'll meet here tomorrow. I might have more info on Sirak's schedule. I'll work out how I can give you both access so you can come here without me."

Sarah sat next to her sister, who was sleeping. She wrote a note and left it next to her. Kawaki exited first, ensuring no one was outside before sending Eli and Sarah back to their rooms.

It was 6am the next morning. Kawaki was sleeping in his room, his quarters were enormous, a large desk sat at one end of the room with a floating hologram armchair. Sirak came banging on his door in a fury. Kawaki jumped from his slumber.

"Coming!" said Kawaki loudly, adjusting his pajamas.

"Hurry up!" squawked Sirak.

Kawaki opened the door, and Sirak came charging in.

"What's happening, Captain?"

"The girl! She disappeared! The crew members disappeared as well. How did this happen?!" Sirak screamed.

"I have no idea, I didn't see them after I left your office, Captain."

"Find her! I want you to scour the entire ship! I want her found *now*!"

"Of course, Captain, right away!" said Kawaki compliantly.

Sirak left, slamming the door behind her. Kawaki got dressed and rushed out; he went to fetch Loyt and Halay.

"We need to search the ship; the girl must be somewhere. Ask the children if they saw anything last night and send them directly to me if they have," Kawaki ordered.

"Yes, Sir!" they said simultaneously and ran.

The groups were in the dining room for breakfast. Eli and Sarah looked at each other from time to time. Sirak entered, she was agitated. Kawaki stood next to her. The microphone hologram appeared.

"There has been a breach. If anyone has seen or heard anything, you better come forward and tell me now!" Sirak said sternly.

Everyone stared at her, confused; they didn't know what she was talking about. The room went silent.

"No one?!" Sirak barked.

She pointed out to six random people from different tables. Crew members grabbed them and took them out of the room. Everyone was quiet, and now, terrified, Sirak stormed out; Sarah and her group could still hear Sirak.

"Take them to my office now!"

The crew members brought the six people plucked from the audience out to Sirak's office and made them stand against the back wall. Sirak paced back and forth in front of them.

"Call the children," she ordered.

Sirak grabbed the first person's jaw and slammed him against the wall.

"Are you going to speak?" Sirak was practically foaming at the mouth.

"I... I don't know what you are asking, Captain, I haven't seen anything," said the first man.

Sirak looked calmly at the man with a smile.

"Fine, you want to play this game with me, we'll see who wins."

The man was terrified, "I don't know anything, I swear! I don't know anything!"

Two children came in, instantly recognized by those lined up against the wall.

"Lucas... Maya!" said a woman.

The children did not respond. An older woman in line saw Lucas.

"Hi, honey," she said.

She went to hug him, but he didn't even slightly move.

"Lucas, it's me, Mama... What's wrong?"

He didn't budge. The woman started crying. The children had holograms around their heads and a little hologram bag floating around their waists. Lucas and Maya very calmly took out needles and glass vials. Maya took the arm of the first man in line against the wall, another crew member held him, and Maya injected the needle into his arm. The man shook tremendously and collapsed to the floor; his body was still. The other villagers saw this and started screaming in fear.

"Stop! Stop! We don't know anything!" said Lucas's mother.

Sirak looked at the five remaining villagers lined up.

"Still nothing? Fine!" taunted Sirak.

The villagers screamed and shouted for help, "We don't know anything, please! Please!"

Sirak signaled the children to continue. While crew members held the villagers against the wall, Maya and Lucas injected each with the same substance. They shook and fell to the floor one after the other. Lucas was in front of his mother, she cried, looking at her child with love.

"Lucas... it's me. It's Mama... please, don't... I love you."

Emotionless, Lucas took his mother's arm and injected her. She started to shake terribly and collapsed to the floor. He didn't pay her any more attention than he gave the others he injected.

"Throw them in the pit," said Sirak.

The crew members lifted the bodies from the floor and left.

Loyt and Halay went to Kawaki's office.

"Sir, no one has seen anything, and the children haven't heard anything. I'm sorry," said Loyt.

"Fine, have the crew members continue searching the ship for clues," Kawaki ordered.

"Yes, Sir," said Loyt and Halay as they left.

Sarah was with her team in the engine room; Sophie was talking to one of the ladies in her group.

"I wonder what happened?"

"I have no idea, but they must have done something," replied a woman in the group.

The rest of the group quietly got on with their work. Crew members came through the engine room every hour to check on them.

Eli was in the laboratory with his team when crew members came through searching everywhere for Cheryl.

It was lunchtime, the teams went to the dining room. When Sarah arrived, Eli was already seated with his team eating; they eyed each other.

"The villagers Sirak took this morning are not back with their teams," whispered Sarah to Jennifer.

"I know, I looked for Matthew but didn't see him," replied Jennifer.

Sirak entered the dining room. The hologram microphone appeared in front of her; she was cold, but smiled.

"Tomorrow is fight day, you better be ready. May the best one win!" said Sirak and left immediately.

Everyone looked at each other, not understanding.

"What does she mean, fight day? We have been fighting every day," asked Jennifer.

"I'll tell you later, I overheard something," whispered Sarah.

"Okay."

Everyone finished eating in silence before heading off to their last combat training session before the newly announced *Fight Day*.

The training began, once again, without the protective suits. Everyone fought with their team members, the tension was high, but no one got badly hurt. Kawaki observed the fights and approached Eli.

"Don't come tonight, it's too dangerous."

Eli nodded.

The training continued, a few people fell to the floor but got up right away. It was time for dinner. Kawaki walked towards Sarah's team when the training had finished.

"Sarah, how are the fights coming along?" he asked.

"Good, Sir, my team is getting better every day," she replied.

He looked at her seriously and, under his breath, said, "Don't come tonight."

She nodded.

"Yes, we have been practicing in the game room almost every evening."

"Good," said Kawaki as he left.

Sarah thought about Cheryl and hoped she was okay. Sarah looked towards Eli, who was staring at her shaking his head, indicating *no*; Sarah nodded, discreetly.

After dinner, Jennifer and Sarah went to the game room and practiced with a hologram fighter. Sarah trained on the medium level. They practiced for an hour and a half and then decided to go to their room.

"I have so much to tell you... Cheryl... is alive!" said Sarah.

"What do you mean?!"

"Yeah, she was captured and drugged when we arrived on the ship. Eli, Kawaki, and I saved her last night."

"Oh my god! Where is she now?"

"She is in a safe spot with Kawaki. You have no idea how insane the people on this ship are. They kill people... It's... it's unbelievable."

"Oh my god. Oh my god. How are we going to get out of here?"

"We should land in a couple of weeks. In the meantime, all we can do is be cautious and not draw any attention."

"Okay... I've been trying to keep a low profile."

"Ugh, I really want to see Eli, but he said not tonight; with everything that happened yesterday, the crew members are watching the whole ship 24/7."

"You should do what he said," asserted Jennifer.

"But I really want to see him."

"Don't do anything crazy! You *just* said we have to be cautious!"

"You are right, and it's not like he'd be there... I thought I was going to see Cheryl. I'll get some rest, I haven't been sleeping much. I'm stuck in this room, and I can't do anything..."

Sarah took a shower, she thought of Eli and Cheryl. She still couldn't believe her sister was alive. In bed, Jennifer watched a movie, while Sarah watched the stars.

Ten ∞ Fight day

"Hurry up, I want to get to the dining room first so I can see Eli," Sarah said to Jennifer, who was taking too long to get ready.

They sat down for breakfast in an almost empty room. Bit by bit, people from the other teams arrived and sat at their tables. Sarah kept turning around to see if Eli was there. Sophie sat down next to Sarah.

"What do you keep looking at?" asked Sophie.

"Oh, I... I'm wondering what we are going to do today," Sarah replied.

"Fight day, that's what the Captain said!"

Jennifer looked at Sarah with piercing eyes, indicating for her to be careful. A few seconds later, Jennifer saw Eli arrive and nudged Sarah under the table. Eli sat at his table and looked at Sarah adoringly. Sarah smiled; she missed him.

Sirak, Kawaki, Loyt, Halay, and other crew members entered the dining room. People were still eating. Sirak went to the center of the room, the microphone hologram appeared; she was very calm.

"Today is fight day. Fights will go on all day until there is one winner. You are to report to the Konaki room in ten minutes. No suits permitted, of course."

Sirak smiled and left, her crew members following behind her.

The teams hurried to finish breakfast. A heavy tension filled the room.

The fight room began filling up with the teams. Sirak and Kawaki sat on hologram floating armchairs in one corner of the room while Loyt and Halay stood next to them. Crew members organized the villagers into lines; one crew member stood at the end of each line. Halay saw that everyone was ready and went to the center of the Konaki room. A microphone hologram appeared.

"Each fight will last 60 seconds. There are no rules. The first one to the ground loses. May the fights begin!"

Halay's voice echoed around the room. He stood next to Sirak once more, who smiled rabidly. Sirak watched as the fights began; she enjoyed the spectacle. When fighters were wounded, crew members took them away to the infirmary. As the day went by, more and more wounded villagers left and didn't return. Each winner went on to fight the next one in their line. It was starting to look like a blood bath.

A fight between two men began, the first man hit the other on the head, the man fell to the floor with a cracking sound. He died on the spot. The crew members cheered the winner, and Sirak let out a cackle.

Tension built with the people of Tyrakti; they no longer were safe and knew it.

A tall square looking man by the name of Oliver had won the last twenty fights. Now, it was Sarah's turn. Eli could tell that Sarah was terrified but still courageous; she would do everything she could. The match began, they fought for about thirty seconds; it was violent. Oliver punched Sarah in the stomach; she could no longer breathe. She fell to the floor but got up quickly. Oliver, then with all his weight, kicked Sarah on the side of her stomach. She fell and didn't get up. Eli looked at her; he was distraught. He knew that Sarah was a good fighter but hoped that she would stay down. Sarah got up despite barely being able to breathe, Oliver saw and smiled. He punched her in the face with all his strength. She fell back down and stayed there; the fight was over. The crew members cheered. Sarah got up and joined the line of those that had already fought; she was not wounded enough to go to the infirmary. The matches continued.

Six hours later and Oliver was still winning. Now, it was Alex's turn. Alex looked like he was about to cry; Eli tried to encourage him. The fight began, Alex got hit in the face and fell to the floor with a big thump. He stayed on the floor, unconscious; crew members picked him up and took him to the infirmary.

Finally, it was Eli's turn. Oliver punched Eli in the jaw; his jaw barely moved. Eli kicked Oliver in the stomach, Oliver got pushed back a few feet. Everyone looked at Eli, realizing that he was a good fighter. Oliver tried to punch Eli in the stomach; Eli avoided the blow and instead kicked Oliver's hand; Oliver hit himself in the face. Oliver fumed and tried to kick Eli in the face, but Eli dodged, flipped into the air, and kicked Oliver in the head. Oliver fell to the ground with a big thud; Eli won. The people of Tyrakti cheered; they didn't like Oliver. The fighting continued, Eli beat every man and woman, but he was gentle with the women. Sarah watched Eli, falling even deeper in love with him.

A few hours passed, no one had lunch, everyone was starving, and there was no water for anyone. The fights came to an end; there were three people left. Eli fought all three of them and won; he was relieved. Sirak stood up quietly and made an announcement.

"Now, you must fight Halay, this fight will last until one of you win."

Eli was tired at this point; he had been fighting for hours. Sarah looked at Halay and was concerned for Eli. Halay was much bigger than Eli and was a highly trained fighter. The last and final fight began. Halay smiled at Eli; he wasn't afraid at all. Halay hit Eli in the face, Eli felt it and pulled back. He kicked Halay in the stomach, Halay laughed. They fought each other for several minutes, hitting each other and avoiding each other's blows. Eli started to get weak. Halay kicked Eli in the head, and he fell to the floor but got up right away, breathless. Sarah looked at Eli, worried. Halay swung a punch at Eli's face, Eli ducked and landed a powerful blow to Halay's stomach. Halay flew back and hit the floor, unable to breathe or move.

The room descended into silence; no one knew what to expect from Sirak; she stood up confidently and declared.

"So, you are the winner. You have won the right to be part of my personal crew."

Sirak smiled at Eli. Eli looked directly at Sirak, he was surprised and nodded gracefully. Kawaki stood up and went to the center of the room, the microphone hologram appeared.

"All of you are to clean yourselves up and report to the dining room. Those whose buddies are in the infirmary will be accompanied by a crew member. You will be assigned to a new buddy at dinner time."

Everyone dispersed; some were followed by crew members, others with their buddies. Sarah and Jennifer went back to their room. Eli addressed Kawaki before exiting.

"Where should I go?" he asked.

"You are part of the crew now; you can go to your room by yourself. Take a shower, and Loyt will assign you to your new tasks after dinner."

Sarah and Jennifer were in their room; they were both exhausted.

"I can't believe Eli is such a good fighter, he never told me," Sarah said.

"Some of us got pretty lucky. I was afraid to get hit by Oliver," Jennifer replied, obviously not hearing what Sarah said.

"I wonder what Eli will be doing now that he is part of the crew?"

"I bet he'll tell you everything. It's probably going to make it easier for you guys to see each other."

"Yeah... Maybe..."

They both showered and got ready for dinner.

At dinner, people were already eating. Sarah and Jennifer sat at their table. Eli arrived and sat in his usual spot; he looked at Sarah and nodded. She nodded back - they would see each other tonight. Sarah smiled to herself at the thought.

Loyt went to see Eli.

"You should go and sit over there now with the other crew members," Loyt gestured with his hand.

Eli didn't like this as it was further away from Sarah, but he managed to find a seat that still faced her. He sat down and met the crew members. Some of them he had already met, others he was meeting for the first time.

Sirak arrived in the dining room and went to the center of the room, the microphone hologram appeared.

"There will be no more off-time from now on. After dinner, everyone goes straight to their rooms, understood?"

Everyone was silent.

"Understood?!" yelled Sirak.

"Yes, Captain!" everyone said in unison.

Sarah was in her room, pacing back and forth. She wanted to go and see Eli.

"I don't think it's a good idea for you to see Eli tonight," said Jennifer.

"I have to see him, and we agreed to meet."

"Yes, but he's a new crew member, he will probably have new things to learn."

"I don't know, he'll tell me tonight. I'll go at 8pm like I usually do, I am sure he'll be there."

"Fine. In the meantime, can you stop pacing? You're driving me crazy."

"Yes, sorry, I'm just nervous."

"Relax, take a little nap, or watch a movie."

"Good idea, I'll watch a movie... or the stars."

Sarah laid on her bed and thought for a moment.

"I also have to go see Cheryl. What if she didn't get food or if she's afraid?"

Jennifer took off her hologram headphones.

"What?" she said, realizing she missed something.

"Never mind," Sarah replied.

Jennifer continued to watch her movie. Sarah looked at the time on Sonance, it said 7:56 pm. She got up, went to the bathroom, and came out a few minutes later. She was excited.

"I'm leaving."

"Be very careful, okay?" Jennifer said.

"Yes, I will," Sarah replied.

Sarah left the room; she was even more careful than she usually was. Before turning down each corridor, she peeked her head quickly to see if anyone was there. She walked through three halls but stopped when she heard voices coming towards her. She immediately retreated to where she came from and waited. The voices continued but moved further away. Sarah peeked down the corridor again, didn't see anyone, and continued on her way. She arrived at the engine room and went to the spot where they always met. Eli had not arrived yet. She sat and waited for him impatiently.

Eli was with Sirak, in her office. For the first time, she was intrigued by him.

"So, where did you learn to fight like that?" Sirak inquired.

"Growing up, I had basic training on my planet. Then I trained a lot on Kambukta to survive amongst the animals," Eli replied.

"It's very impressive."

"Thank you."

"I want you to work hand in hand with Loyt. Some crew members and a girl went missing recently; they need to be found."

"Oh, how do people go missing on a ship?"

"That's what I said... I might possibly have a spy on my team. I want you to work with Loyt and report any suspicious activity to me, understood?"

"Yes, Captain."

"You can go, you will start your new duties in the morning."

Eli nodded and left Sirak's office. He hurried through the corridors, still paying attention to not being seen or making too much noise. Sarah had been waiting for over an hour; she was anxious and hoped that Eli was okay.

Eli finally got to the engine room, looked inside, and saw Sarah sitting in their spot.

"I am so sorry, I was with Sirak, and I couldn't leave," he said, apologetically.

Sarah was relieved to see him.

"It's fine, you are here now."

He sat next to her, and they kissed passionately.

"It might make all this easier for us. Sirak wants me to report anything that I notice; she told me that crew members and a girl went missing... This means she trusts me. We could use this to our advantage," Eli paused to kiss Sarah's face, "I'll probably know more about what she does and where she goes. I might even end up being alone with her, and then... I could kill her."

"I am worried about you... with all these changes..."

"I'll be fine... and I can defend myself, you know?" said Eli, trying to cheer her up.

"Yes, I know, but still..."

He looked at her, picked up her chin, and kissed her. They got lost in the moment and made love passionately. They talked as they got dressed.

"Two days without seeing you was too long," said Eli.

"Yeah, I couldn't take it. I wanted to come here last night just in case, but Jennifer told me to listen to you."

"Don't scare me. If we decide not to meet, don't do anything differently, okay? It's really dangerous!"

"Yes, I know, I promise."

"Kawaki told me he saw your sister; she is doing much better. I gave him some herbs she is taking twice a day. By the time we land, she will be completely fine."

"Thank you, I miss her so much," said Sarah, grateful for his help.

"In a few weeks, we'll live together, we'll take care of your sister, we'll have a beautiful life, Sarah."

"I know. I can't wait. I dream of it every day."

They kissed, cuddled, and enjoyed a moment of silence as they stared at each other.

"What do you think happens after we die?" asked Sarah.

"I'm not sure; as long as I get to be with you," replied Eli.

"Yes, as long as we are together."

"Everything is going to be fine, you know?"

"Yes, I know."

"We have to go back to our rooms, I don't know if Loyt is going to be looking for me," said Eli.

"Already?" asked Sarah.

"We might see each other less for the next few days until I know what I am doing."

"But, we are still meeting in Kawaki's secret office tomorrow at 9pm, right?"

"Yes, I'll meet you outside your room at five to nine, we'll go together. It's been crazy on the ship since Cheryl disappeared... I wouldn't be able to live with myself if something happened to you."

They got up, and before they left the engine room, they kissed once more.

Eli dropped off Sarah and went to his room. When he entered, Alex was not back from the infirmary. He looked at his bed and wondered where he was; he was worried about him and missed having him there. Eli laid in bed and fell asleep.

Eleven ∞ Rebellion

Sarah and Jennifer woke up at the same time and got ready.

"So how did it go?" asked Jennifer.

"I thought it might be easier now that he works for Sirak, but after last night we realized that it will be trickier than we thought. Anyhow, we'll arrive on Tikai pretty soon, and Eli has a plan," replied Sarah.

"Oh, what's the plan?"

"I'll tell you everything later, we have to go; otherwise, we'll be late."

"Okay."

When Sarah and Jennifer arrived in the dining room, Eli was already there, sitting next to Loyt in his new uniform. Sarah noticed that Sirak and Kawaki were not present. After breakfast, everyone left for their morning duties. As Sarah exited the dining room, she turned to look for Eli. Her eyes settled on him, speaking with Loyt; she knew Eli noticed her.

Sarah's team followed her to the engine room. Jennifer saw that Sarah was not at ease and less talkative than usual.

Meanwhile, Eli and Loyt walked around the ship for hours searching for any clue as to Cheryl's disappearance. As they walked through the hallway, Eli saw Sirak enter a laboratory. This was the first time Eli saw her outside of her office or the dining room. He made a mental note of the time; it was precisely 11:31 am.

They continued through the corridors and walked right in front of Kawaki's secret office. Loyt did not see it as it was disguised as a wall. They arrived to the corner of a red-lit corridor.

"Should we go left? We haven't been there yet," asked Eli.

Eli knew that the left side went to the pit, where only crew members were allowed.

"No, I already checked there yesterday," replied Loyt, sharply.

Eli realized that Loyt didn't fully trust him, and he would have to be more careful.

They continued going through different rooms all morning but didn't find anything unusual.

"Let's go to lunch," said Loyt.

"Okay."

Later at combat training; everyone's morale was much lower. The villagers no longer felt safe, but, instead, felt like they were prisoners. Most team members had been assigned new buddies, as many of the wounded had still not returned from the infirmary.

The combat training for the day began, many were still tired from yesterday's fights. Eli and Loyt stood in the corner of the fight room watching the exhausted fighters poorly perform.

Sirak entered and sat next to them; she observed the team members fight without saying a word to Eli or Loyt.

A 60-year-old man with white hair from one of the teams walked towards Sirak.

"Excuse me, Captain?" said the old man.

"Yes," replied Sirak, coldly.

"My buddy hasn't returned from the infirmary, and I wondered when he was going to come back?"

Sirak stood up slowly and, in a swift movement, cut his throat with a knife. The man fell to the floor and bled to death. A woman from one of the teams saw this and screamed. Everyone turned around to see what was going on. No one said a thing; they stood there in total shock.

Sirak turned to Loyt, "Get rid of this."

Eli went to help Loyt, but Loyt motioned with his hand.

"Stay here, I can handle this myself."

Everyone stared statically as Loyt removed the body; Eli was furious but kept his emotions for no one to see.

"Continue the fights, now!" yelled Sirak.

Everyone, wholly terrified by her, continued to fight. Some of the team members were softly crying. Hours later, combat training finally came to an end.

They all walked to the dining room like zombies. No one whispered a word. They took a seat and silently started to eat. Sarah looked at Eli, who nodded at her discreetly before Jennifer and Sarah went back to their room in a hurry.

"Oh my god, I can't believe it, I can't believe she slit his throat, just like that! She's insane! It's worse than I thought, we have to do something, she is going to kill us all one by one!" yelled Jennifer, in a panic.

"Stop. Stop. I know, but don't yell... Eli and Kawaki are working on a plan," said Sarah, hushing her.

"What's the plan? I want to help."

Sarah explained the plan finishing with, "There is nothing to do but be attentive; it's too dangerous for us to get more involved."

"Okay. I am going to take a shower, I'm exhausted," replied Jennifer dejected.

Jennifer stayed in the bathroom for a very long time. When she finally came out, Sarah was ready to go.

"I am leaving to meet Eli in a few minutes."

"Okay, I'm going straight to sleep, it's been a long day. Be careful, okay?"

"Yes, I will. Everything is going to be fine, I promise."

"I hope you are right."

Sarah poked her head out of the door and saw Eli waiting at the corner. They quickly made their way to Kawaki's secret office. Eli put his thumb up, the black hologram keypad appeared, and the door opened.

"You have access?" asked Sarah.

"You will as well, Kawaki set it up for me today," replied Eli.

Sarah saw Cheryl inside and smiled.

"You already look so much better," said Sarah.

"Kawaki has been really good to me; he brings me food every day, and yesterday he brought me some herbs that have been helping a lot. I am really starting to feel like myself again," replied Cheryl.

Kawaki walked into the room.

"Good to see you all here," said Kawaki.

"Thank you so much for tending to my sister, I have been so worried."

"She is looking better every day," replied Kawaki.

"Yes."

"Okay, let's talk about the plan," Kawaki turned to Eli.

The girls listened in.

"Loyt and I have been assigned to search the ship for Cheryl and the missing crew members. We haven't found anything that could give us away. When we walked in front of your secret office this morning, I was afraid Loyt would notice, but—."

"There is an electromagnetic screen in front of the office; you can only see the door if you have access to it or if I am about to open it," replied Kawaki.

Eli and Sarah knew it was a secret office but hadn't realized to what extent.

Eli continued, "I am not sure they fully trust me yet, but last night, Sirak did tell me she thinks there is a spy on the team."

"Of course they don't trust you, they have no idea who you are, and they know that you are a good fighter. No one has ever beat Halay, so you should be very careful; we never know what to expect from Sirak. This could all be a game to her."

"I'll be cautious. We need to get Sirak alone. We need to stop her before she kills more people," said Eli.

"Yes, I know. The problem with Sirak is that we never know what's going on in her head. One day she's nice, and the next day she's demented. I've seen a lot of crazy things on Tikai. She's a sociopath. I saw her kill an 8-year-old slave with her bare hands because he left her door open."

"This has gone on for too long," replied Eli.

"The next chance you have, Eli, take it!"

"I will."

Sarah was worried about what she heard, she held Cheryl's hand. She knew Eli was brave, but this was a significant risk.

"Sarah, I need your prints to give you access to this office. For emergencies only, do you understand?" said Kawaki.

"Yes, of course."

Sarah got up and went to a black hologram pad; she put her right-hand flat on it, there was a beeping sound and then a continuous beep.

"You can remove your hand now," said Kawaki, "I need to go; Sirak said she wanted to see me before 11pm."

"Okay. Do you know where they took the wounded villagers?" asked Eli.

"No, I asked, but Sirak just said they had been taken care of, not sure if they are still alive or somewhere locked up on the ship," said Kawaki, "I'll check on Cheryl a few times a day."

"Thank you very much," said Sarah.

"Let's meet here next Tuesday at 9pm with a real plan to stop Sirak unless Eli gets the chance before."

"Okay," replied Eli.

Kawaki left.

Eli and Sarah stayed with Cheryl until she fell asleep. They sat on the floor, talking, kissing, and cuddling. They couldn't wait to live together and begin their new life on Tikai. Sarah kissed Cheryl on her cheek before Eli took her back to her room.

When Eli got to his room, Alex was still absent. He wanted to help him, but he had no idea where he was. He decided he would look into it more the next day.

Another week went by with the same routine for everyone. Work in the morning, combat training in the afternoon, and regular meetings for Sarah and Eli in the engine room. Eli spent most of his time with Loyt, making it challenging to discover where the wounded villagers were being kept.

Finally, they reached Tuesday evening.

Sarah and Jennifer were in their room when Sarah noticed her friend was already in bed and appeared to be quite sick.

"I'll ask Eli for a remedy; we need to keep you out of the infirmary," said Sarah, concerned.

"Okay," replied Jennifer weakly as she dozed off.

Sarah was patiently waiting for Eli; minutes later, she heard two taps on the door and knew it was him.

They got to the secret office, and when Sarah entered, she saw Cheryl and hugged her. Cheryl looked like she was fully healed. They waited for Kawaki.

"Jennifer is sick, can you give me something to help her? I am afraid they'll bring her to the infirmary; she's been coughing quite a bit tonight," said Sarah.

"I have just the thing, but I need time to prepare it. I will bring it to your room tonight," replied Eli.

"Thank you."

"You need to wake her up every two hours during the night and have her take it; she will be healed in the morning."

"Okay, thank you."

Kawaki entered, and announced his findings.

"I figured out where Sirak put the wounded villagers. They are in the abandoned infirmary near the pit."

"Oh, that's why Loyt never wants us to go there. Can we get them out?" asked Eli.

"Six crew members, as well as Halay, are watching them at all times. Not sure how to get them out without being seen."

"We need to find a way. Oh, I also figured something out about Sirak's schedule," said Eli, excitedly, "She leaves her office at exactly 11:30 am every Tuesday to go to the laboratory."

"That means we could be in the corridor between her office and the laboratory next Tuesday, and we could kill her. Good work, Eli!" said Kawaki, "That's the plan we've been waiting for, one more week of this nightmare. We should be arriving in eight days, so we can't fuck it up next Tuesday. This will be our only chance."

"Yes," said Eli.

"Once we kill Sirak, it will be easy for me to get the crew under my control. I am the second in command, and they'll have to follow my orders. We'll land on the Southside of Tikai where The Lukoses rule. If we haven't figured out a way to save the wounded villagers soon, we'll help them once we kill Sirak," said Kawaki.

"Okay," replied Eli.

"I can't wait to arrive on Tikai," said Sarah, smiling at her sister, "We'll have a home again."

Cheryl smiled. They all stayed there for a while, enjoying a moment together, until Kawaki got up and left.

"Good night," said Kawaki.

"Good night," they replied.

Sarah and Cheryl looked at each other lovingly; Eli could tell Sarah needed time alone with her sister. He left to make the herbal remedy for Jennifer. Sarah and Cheryl spent hours catching up. They enjoyed their time together and, for a moment, forgot where they were.

Eli returned to the secret office and took Sarah back to her room, and gave her the remedy for Jennifer.

Sarah entered her room; Jennifer was coughing so intensely that she woke herself up.

"Eli prepared a remedy for you," said Sarah.

"Oh, thank you," replied Jennifer.

Sarah touched Jennifer's forehead; she was on fire. Sarah pulled out a little bag with the remedy in it and poured it into a cup. Jennifer drank it, the bitterness of the liquid was evident in her expression; Sarah nursed Jennifer and tucked her in.

"I'll wake you up in two hours to give you some more, okay?"

"Okay," said Jennifer, thankfully.

She fell asleep instantly while Sarah laid on her bed; she was not tired at all. She thought about the events of the day and about the life they would have on Tikai. She looked at the stars as she daydreamed.

Two hours later, she woke Jennifer up. Jennifer had a hard time opening her eyes; Sarah gave her some more of the liquid which she drank and went straight back to sleep. Sarah was tired; she put a reminder on the pad to wake her up in two hours.

Sarah was fully asleep when her alarm went off, she got up and gave some more of the herbal medicine to Jennifer. Jennifer already looked a lot better and no longer had a fever, they both went back to sleep immediately.

The next morning when Sarah woke up, Jennifer was still asleep. Sarah gently touched Jennifer's arm; she opened her eyes and smiled; the color had returned to her cheeks. Sarah gave her some more of the remedy before she went into the shower.

Fifteen minutes later, they were ready to leave.

"Thank you so much, I feel completely healed," said Jennifer.

"He has a gift with herbs. He helped Cheryl, too; she is back to normal already," replied Sarah.

Jennifer smiled, and they walked to the dining room.

Eli and Loyt were sitting next to each other, having breakfast. Sarah saw Eli as she sat at her table; she looked at everyone, having breakfast in silence. Halay entered and walked straight to Loyt.

"Sirak wants to see you in her office right away," barked Halay.

He didn't even look at Eli. This made him feel uncomfortable; it was the first time he saw Halay since their fight. Loyt got up and went to see Sirak followed by Halay. The teams left to do their morning duties.

Loyt was in front of Sirak's office, he put his thumb up, the hologram appeared, the door opened, and he entered.

"Yes, Captain," said Loyt.

"I want you to get me the call book of all the arrivals from Tyrakti and all the tests from the laboratory," commanded Sirak.

"Yes, Captain," replied Loyt.

"Don't ask anyone to do it for you, do it yourself," she said.

"Yes, Captain."

He left her office immediately.

Loyt went to a locked door a few corridors away, got a thick log, and then went to the laboratory where Cheryl disappeared. He looked through a few shelves and finally found a record with lots of tests and names next to them. Loyt brought everything to Sirak's office.

"Good. Continue your walkabouts with Eli," ordered Sirak.

"Yes, Captain."

Loyt headed to the dining room looking for Eli but didn't see him. He went to the fight room; Eli wasn't there either. He then asked a few crew members if they had encountered Eli.

"I saw him near Sirak's office half an hour ago," said a crew member.

"Thank you," replied Loyt.

He continued to search for Eli and found him near the old laboratory where all the wounded villagers were.

"What are you doing? I've been looking for you everywhere," said Loyt, annoyed.

"I was looking for you, I went to Sirak's office, but I didn't see you, so I continued searching the ship for the missing crew members," replied Eli.

"Fine. We don't need to look there, Halay has been searching on this side of the ship."

"Okay."

Loyt and Eli continued going from room to room searching but didn't find anything suspicious.

"Let's go to lunch," said Loyt.

They arrived in the dining room, everyone was seated and ate, once again in silence. Loyt and Eli sat next to each other and didn't talk while the crew members next to them laughed and joked.

Sarah looked around; the tension amongst the villagers was getting worse. Lunch was over, and all the teams got up and walked to the Konaki room. Eli stood, but Loyt grabbed his arm.

"Sirak asked us to search the laboratory once again; she thinks we might have missed something. After that, Sirak wants us to look in the rooms on the other side of the ship."

"Okay," replied Eli.

Loyt and Eli were now the only two left in the dining room; Loyt was still eating. Halay joined them and sat next to Loyt without acknowledging Eli's existence. A crew member brought Halay a plate of chicken and placed it in front of him. Halay took his knife and stabbed a chicken wing viciously. He directed his stare at Eli. They locked eyes for a few seconds; until Halay finally looked away and started to eat like a beast.

Loyt and Eli left and went to the laboratory. They turned everything upside down, looking for any clue they could have missed.

Meanwhile, Sirak was in her office, comparing the two logs and smiled wickedly.

Loyt and Eli didn't find anything in the laboratory, gave up, and went to the other side of the ship. This was Halay's section, and Loyt had never let Eli enter this area before. Loyt was beginning to trust Eli.

They got to the dorms, which were dirty. There were bloodstains on the sheets, and tattered clothes were strewn about the floor.

"Who lives here?" asked Eli.

"No one, these are just old rooms."

Eli put it together; this was where the villagers were kept before getting mutilated. They proceeded to look through this area for a couple of hours and didn't find anything.

"It doesn't make any sense, how can people simply disappear?" said Loyt, annoyed.

"I don't understand either," replied Eli.

"Sirak is going to be very disappointed."

"Yes."

"It's already time for dinner, let's go. I'll report to Sirak after we eat."

They arrived in the dining room. Eli looked at Sarah's table and saw Jennifer and Sarah's team, but Sarah was missing. This worried him, but he had to wait to talk to Jennifer. Eli was seated, his plate was full of food, but he didn't eat.

"Aren't you hungry?" asked Loyt as he gobbled down his meal.

"Oh, yes, of course, I am," said Eli and started to eat.

He kept looking towards Sarah's table to see if she had arrived. Dinner came to an end, and everyone got up in pairs and left for their rooms—still no sign of Sarah. He watched Jennifer, who was accompanied by Sophie and her buddy.

"I'm going to see Sirak. I'll see you later," said Loyt.

"Sure," replied Eli, half absent.

Eli stood up and followed Jennifer and the other two. He pretended to walk past them, waiting in the corridor for Sophie and her buddy to leave, and then went to Jennifer's room and tapped three times. Jennifer opened the door.

"Can I come in?" whispered Eli frantically.

"Yes," replied Jennifer as she quickly ushered him in.

"Where is Sarah?"

"I don't know, a crew member came to take her during the combat training."

"When exactly? Was it at the beginning of training or towards the end?"

"Towards the beginning," replied Jennifer anxiously.

"Okay, I need to go."

Eli left abruptly and went to Kawaki's office and knocked on the door, Kawaki opened.

"What are you doing here? We shouldn't be seen together," whispered Kawaki.

"Sarah is missing, a crew member came to take her while they were training, do you know where they took her?" Eli was desperate.

"No, I haven't heard anything," replied Kawaki perturbed.

"Fuck! Where could they have taken her?"

"There are many possible places, the laboratory, or the test rooms in the ship's backside. But you don't have access to those parts of the ship."

"We need to act quickly," led Eli.

"You search near the laboratory and the pit, and I will go to the test rooms in the ship's backside," replied Kawaki.

"Okay, and we bring her to your secret office?"

"Yes, we'll meet there."

Eli left Kawaki's office and went towards the laboratory to search for any sign of Sarah, but the halls were empty. He walked around listening intently, but silence prevailed. Hours went by, and he still hadn't seen or heard anything that might have led him to Sarah's whereabouts. He decided to go to the secret office to check if Kawaki had had better luck. He entered and was disappointed to find only Cheryl, who was asleep. He left and continued his search for Sarah.

Eli nervously paced back and forth in a hall near one of the laboratories when he heard a door opening. He went to the corner of the corridor and took a look. He saw two children and two crew members coming out of a laboratory with someone on a stretcher. He recognized Sarah!

He took *Gloria* out of his pocket, ready to use. He silently got closer to them and hit one of the crew members on the head; the man fell to the floor with a smack. Eli then shot a beam towards the second crew member and the two children, who instantly fell to the floor. He ejected a beam to the first adult he hit on the head, making sure to kill him. He took Sarah in his arms and quickly rushed her to the secret office.

Cheryl was horrified when she saw Eli arrive with her sister. He placed Sarah next to Cheryl on the couch. Sarah opened her eyes, saw Eli, and smiled weakly.

"What happened?" asked Cheryl in a panic.

"She was drugged," replied Eli.

Eli took the flask with the remedy he prepared for Cheryl and gave some to Sarah. She drank slowly, closed her eyes, and then fell asleep.

"Listen to me, Cheryl, you need to give this to your sister every hour?" said Eli.

"Okay," replied Cheryl.

"I have to go. If anyone comes looking for me, and I'm not in my room, they'll be onto me. Kawaki will come later this evening," said Eli in haste, "Take care of her, I'll come back as soon as possible."

He left the secret office and went straight to his room.

Kawaki and Loyt walked through the corridor together when they saw the two children and two crew members dead on the floor.

"What the hell happened here? Get this cleaned up right away," ordered Kawaki.

"Yes, Sir, I'll get some help," replied Loyt.

Loyt ran to Eli's room, opened the door abruptly, and saw Eli lying on his bed watching a movie. He appeared very relaxed, Loyt was surprised to find him there.

"What's going on, Loyt?" asked Eli, calmly.

"There's been an attack."

"An attack?!"

"Hurry, we have to warn Sirak right away," said Loyt, agitated.

"Of course," replied Eli, jumping out of bed, following Loyt.

They went through the corridor where the bodies were just a minute ago, the bodies were gone, and two crew members were cleaning the floor. When Loyt and

Eli arrived in front of Sirak's office, Loyt put his thumb up, and the door opened.

Kawaki stood next to Sirak.

"What happened?!" yelled Sirak at the top of her lungs.

"I don't know, Captain, Kawaki and I were walking through..." attempted Loyt before Sirak interrupted him.

"I know! What the hell is going on, on *this* ship?!" yelled Sirak.

"I don't know, Captain," replied Loyt.

"And you!" Sirak pointed towards Eli, "Where were you!?"

"I was in my room, Captain," answered Eli.

"I went to get him, and he was watching a movie, Captain."

Sirak stared at Eli. Eli looked straight at her, not lowering his eyes.

"Fine! Go... Find out who did this!" ordered Sirak slamming her hand on her desk as she looked at Kawaki, "Go with them!"

"Yes, Captain," said Kawaki, and they all turned to leave.

They returned to the scene of the crime.

"Where did you put the bodies?" asked Kawaki.

"We put everyone and the stretcher in the laboratory, Sir," said a crew member.

Eli, Loyt, and Kawaki walked to the laboratory and entered. They saw two crew members on the floor next to two children, Steve and Lucas. Kawaki bent down to take their pulse; they were all dead. Kawaki and Loyt looked at the bodies and the stretcher to see if they saw anything unusual.

"I don't understand what could have happened? There is nothing that even shows a fight. Oh wait, except for this one, he has a mark on his head; it looks like he was hit by something. But how could all these people be dead just like that? They haven't been stabbed or anything, it's bizarre," stressed Loyt.

"Bring them to the other lab for tests," ordered Kawaki.

"Yes, Sir," replied Loyt.

The crew members and Loyt put the bodies on a stretcher and took them away.

"Eli, come with me, I want to see if we find anything else," said Kawaki.

Loyt and the crew members went to the left while Kawaki and Eli went to the right. Once Kawaki and Eli made it to the end of the hall, Kawaki checked to see that no one was there before whispering-

"What happened?"

"I saw the crew members with the children taking Sarah from the laboratory somewhere else, and I killed them on the spot. I didn't know what else to do. I brought her to the secret office, she is completely drugged. What do they want with her?"

"I don't know, Sirak hasn't told me anything, she must be up to something," replied Kawaki.

"I told Cheryl to make sure Sarah takes the herbs I prepared every hour, she should be better in the morning."

"I don't know what Sirak will do now that more people have been attacked," Kawaki got worried.

"I want to check up on Sarah," said Eli.

"No, don't go there, you might be followed, don't take any more risks. I'll go check up on her tomorrow when things calm down," replied Kawaki.

Eli said nothing but knew Kawaki was right.

"We need to go to Sirak's office now, I don't want her getting suspicious."

When they arrived in front of her office, crew members were standing outside waiting. Kawaki put his thumb up, the hologram appeared, and the door opened. They entered and found Loyt already inside. Sirak looked up from her desk and said calmly-

"So?"

"We didn't see anything unusual, Captain," replied Kawaki.

Sirak was very calm. Too calm. She didn't say anything for a while and then exploded.

"What the fuck is going on here?!? I want you to find out what is happening!! Someone is trying to sabotage me, and when I find out who it is, I will squash him like a worm! Now get out!! Loyt, you stay here," yelled Sirak.

Kawaki and Eli left. Eli went to his room, and Kawaki went back to his office.

Sirak stood in front of her desk, facing Loyt. She harnessed her fury.

"I want you to let Eli do his searches alone from now on. Make him believe he has our trust and follow him. He is up to something. Be nice to him, let him believe things are better. If he is the one fucking with me, I will cut him up into pieces and add him to my art collection!" said Sirak, laughing maniacally.

The next morning, Jennifer, barely awake, was startled by the sound of Sophie and her buddy moving in. They had been reassigned since Sarah disappeared.

While Eli did his regular rounds on the ship, he went to the engine room to look for Jennifer, who was there working. He wanted her to know that Sarah was safe. He found her, scrubbing a coil and looking extremely tense. He walked by her and nodded. Jennifer smiled; she understood.

A couple of days went by, with everyone doing their usual tasks. Eli had been searching the ship on his own and was missing Sarah terribly being separated for this long. Loyt, on the other hand, was following Sirak's plan and watching Eli closely.

Kawaki went to check on Cheryl and Sarah in the secret office.

"How are you feeling, Sarah?" asked Kawaki.

"Much better, thank you. Cheryl has been taking good care of me. How is Eli? When can I see him?" replied Sarah.

"He's fine, it's too dangerous at the moment. We have to be more careful; Sirak is on the lookout for anything suspicious. There are more children and crew members on the lookout in the halls," said Kawaki.

"But we are still going to follow the plan, right?" asked Sarah.

"Yes, it's our only chance."

Eli felt bold enough to go to the old laboratory to look for the wounded villagers, hoping he would not run into Halay. He walked by a big metal door and noticed it was left slightly open. He quickly checked to see if anyone was behind him and then proceeded to peek inside. His breath stopped short when he saw three guards, four feet away from the door. Eli continued to investigate carefully and saw the room was filled with the injured villagers crammed together on the floor. There was a foul smell coming from inside, and blood was spattered in various places in the room. He scanned through the cracked door and found Alex sleeping or possibly even dead. Eli spotted three crew members on the other side of the room. Halay was in the center of the room, laughing with a crew member standing next to him.

Meanwhile, Loyt stood in the corridor behind Eli, watching everything. Loyt left quickly and went to Sirak's office.

Eli turned to leave, bothered by what he just witnessed.

"What is it?" said Sirak as she saw Loyt enter her office.

"I was following Eli and saw him by the old laboratory, he was looking through the door," replied Loyt.

"I knew he was up to something."

"Yes, Captain."

"Continue following him, he'll take us to the girl," ordered Sirak.

"Yes, Captain."

"Did we get the results yet on what happened to the crew members?" asked Sirak.

"Yes, we've never seen anything like this before; the cells deteriorated from the inside," replied Loyt.

"Get me the report."

"Yes, Captain," said Loyt and left.

A couple of days went by, the crew members were stressed out and tougher with the villagers than usual. The people on the ship didn't understand what was going on. They continued their daily routine with tasks in the morning and combat training in the afternoon. Conversation amongst teams had entirely disappeared, and the mood was dolorous.

It was midnight; Eli was lying wide awake in his room, unable to sleep. He decided he couldn't take it anymore and needed to see Sarah. He left his room without making a sound, careful to ensure no one was there. He went through a few corridors, continually making sure he was not being followed, and finally arrived in front of the secret office. He put his thumb up, the hologram appeared, and the door opened. He entered, and Sarah ran into his arms and kissed him passionately.

"I've missed you so much," said Sarah.

"Me too, I couldn't wait any longer," replied Eli.

They hugged and kissed again. Cheryl was sleeping. They sat against the wall and once again pretended to be in their new home somewhere on Tikai.

"Kawaki has been coming a lot, he's been really good to us," said Sarah.

"Yes, he's been protecting me as much as he can," replied Eli.

"In two days is the big day. Are we all going to meet here and then go with Kawaki?" asked Sarah.

"No, Kawaki and I will go. I don't want you to come; it's too dangerous," replied Eli.

"But I can help, I want to help, I've been losing my mind here. I want to help, please?" asked Sarah.

"I really don't think you should come," replied Eli.

"I want to, we've been in this together since the beginning, let me help."

He looked at her lovingly, raising her chin and kissing her. He found her irresistible and smiled. He couldn't say no.

"Promise."

"I promise."

"This will soon all be over, and we will live our lives where we want and how we want."

"Yes, I know, I can't wait, I dream of our life together every day. It's the only thing helping me keep it together."

"Everything will be fine, I promise," said Eli and then kissed her passionately, one last time, "I have to go."

"Are you coming back tomorrow?" asked Sarah.

"I don't think so, Kawaki would be mad if he knew I came tonight."

"I love you," she said.

"I love you too," he responded and then left the room.

Sarah laid next to her sister, watching her sleep peacefully, she looked at the stars and finally fell asleep.

The next morning everyone was having breakfast. Jennifer looked upset; she missed Sarah. Sophie had been promoted to team leader and was taking advantage of it.

Loyt sat next to Eli and Halay. Halay was saying a joke, Eli didn't laugh.

"You don't like my joke?" asked Halay aggressively.

"Leave him alone," responded Loyt, defending Eli.

"Whatever, he's boring," retorted Halay.

Eli didn't say much; he was stressed out.

They finished breakfast.

"Why don't you do the rounds with all the teams?" Loyt said to Eli.

"Sure," replied Eli.

"I'll go help Halay with the wounded."

"Oh, what are you going to do with the wounded?"

"We need to give them more medication."

"Are you sure you don't need help?"

"No, we're fine, thanks."

Eli got up and started making the usual rounds, he really wanted to see Sarah, but he couldn't see her now; it was too risky. He walked through a corridor when he saw Maya.

"Hello," said Eli.

Maya didn't respond; Eli continued past her and went to see all the teams.

Loyt was in front of Sirak's office, put his thumb up, the hologram appeared, and the door opened.

"What?" asked Sirak as she saw Loyt enter.

"Last night, I was following Eli. He was walking near the women's rooms. I continued following him, and suddenly he disappeared."

"People don't disappear on the ship, go through all the women's rooms," commanded Sirak.

"Yes, Captain."

Loyt left her office. He went through the corridors, and as he got closer to the rooms, he encountered Kawaki.

"Hi, Sir, can I help you with something?" asked Loyt.

"No, I'm fine, I am just getting something to eat; I missed breakfast."

"Of course, Sir."

Kawaki continued on his way, got to the dining room, and sat at a table. A crew member brought him some food. Kawaki was stressed out and ate slowly while thinking. He finished his late breakfast and went through the ship, looking for Eli. He found Eli with one of the teams in the inventory room and signaled for him to come. Eli followed Kawaki, who went out into the corridor.

"For tomorrow, we both meet in the corridor near the laboratory at 11:25 am. I will be coming from my office, okay?" whispered Kawaki.

"Yes," replied Eli.

"Sirak has been asking questions about you, so be very careful, okay?"

"I will."

They heard the sound of light footsteps, and both turned around at once. A boy named Danny, who Eli had never seen before, stood in front of them staring.

"What do you want, Danny?" asked Kawaki.

"Sirak wants to see you," said Danny in a monotonous voice.

"Thank you," replied Kawaki and turned to Eli.

"Continue going through all the workspaces, okay? If you see anything, let me know," ordered Kawaki.

"Yes, Sir."

Eli's heart raced rapidly. He felt more and more stressed out, he had all the weight on his shoulders. If he failed tomorrow, everyone would get killed, and he couldn't even start to think about what would happen to Sarah. Sarah, the love of his life. He toughened up and continued to the next area on the ship. The day rapidly came to an end.

Eli laid on his bed, looking at the stars. He thought about his planet, friends, and family he hadn't seen in such a long time. They must all believe him dead. He dreamed about taking Sarah to see his family. They would love her. He thought about living on a farm with Sarah and their children running around playing with the animals. He smiled. He knew that he would succeed tomorrow, he had no choice.

Eli woke up the next morning, feeling confident. He went to the dining room, and as he walked by Jennifer, nodded at her; she saw this and smiled slightly. He sat next to Loyt and Halay, they were both eating.

"Hi," said Eli.

"Hi," replied Loyt.

Halay looked up but didn't say anything.

"Some of the wounded villagers are feeling better; they'll be coming back in the teams tomorrow," said Loyt.

"That's great to hear," replied Eli.

"Sirak is thinking about letting people go back to the game room."

"That's going to help, their morale is very low," replied Eli.

"Yes, that's what I told her."

"So what are we going to do today? I've looked everywhere and didn't find anything. Should I continue the search?" asked Eli.

"I have some business to attend to this morning; you can just do rounds with the teams, see if everything is going well, I'll see you at lunch, and then we'll get new orders from Sirak."

"Okay," answered Eli.

The teams went to do their tasks, and Halay and Loyt left together. Eli started his rounds by going to the engine room. When he arrived, he saw Sophie throwing hot water at Jennifer.

"Hey! What are you doing?" yelled Eli.

"I'm just playing with her," replied Sophie laughing.

"Don't fool around, get back to work!" ordered Eli.

He continued his rounds. While he was on his way to the inventory room, he saw a crew member walking with Alex.

"Alex, are you okay?" asked Eli, extremely happy to see him.

Alex barely looked up, he looked very weak, but he was alive.

"Fine," replied Alex quietly.

"Where are you taking him?" asked Eli to the crew member.

"I'm taking him to his room."

"I'll take him from here."

"But Halay told me to bring him to his room."

"Let's go together, let me help."

Eli took Alex on one side while the crew member held him on the other side. They got to their room and entered. The crew member and Eli helped Alex onto the bed before the crew member left. Eli looked at Alex's eyes and saw that he was very drugged. He gave him some herbs he had hidden under his bed. Alex managed to swallow.

"You'll feel better soon," said Eli looking at him as a brother.

Alex looked at Eli and did his best to smile. He fell asleep thirty seconds later, snoring loudly. Eli smiled. He was happy to see his friend again, even though he was in a terrible state. It was 11am; Eli left his room and was ready. He went through the corridors towards the secret office. He entered and saw Sarah standing in front of the door, waiting for him; he kissed her.

"I've been waiting for you," said Sarah impatiently.

"I promised I'd come, but I don't want you to come with me; I'll be back right after, but you must stay here," said Eli.

"No! I want to help! Please, please, please," begged Sarah.

"It's dangerous!"

"I know, but how can I just sit here? I can't do that, I have to help, please?" implored Sarah.

"I don't know."

She looked at him with puppy eyes.

"Kawaki is going to kill me."

"Please?"

"Fine... but we have to be careful, it has been crazy the last few days," replied Eli giving in.

"I'll be careful," replied Sarah, "You'll see, I'll help you, I might even save your life."

He looked at Cheryl, who smiled at them.

"Hi Cheryl, you look much better," said Eli.

"Yes, I feel like I'm back to normal; thank you so much for the herbs; they really helped," said Cheryl smiling.

"Of course."

"So you are both going to leave and come back soon?" asked Cheryl.

"Yes, don't worry," said Eli.

"Okay," replied Cheryl.

He looked at Sarah lovingly and kissed her passionately. Sarah felt like she was floating in the air from his kiss.

They left the secret office discreetly; no one was in the corridor. Sarah stood behind Eli; they went through a few halls and didn't see or hear anyone. They were getting very close to the laboratory. It was 11:27 am. They stood at the corner of a corridor. Eli looked down both sides. He didn't see anyone. They walked into the last hallway before they would get to the laboratory. Eli poked his head to the right and got hit in the face abruptly by Halay; he fell to the ground instantly, but quickly got up. Loyt and two crew members came from the left and grabbed onto Eli. They hit him and locked his arms from behind. Eli couldn't move. Two other crew members held Sarah, who was kicking as hard as she could. Halay grabbed Sarah from behind and locked her arms. Sarah and Eli were facing each other. Sirak arrived, pacing slowly.

"I knew you were a traitor. Loyt has been following you for days; I knew you would take me to her, you bastard," said Sirak softly, looking at Eli.

Sarah struggled to get away from Halay but couldn't move.

"It's so sad. Two people in love, you're going to make me cry. Do you know that she's pregnant?" said Sirak looking at Eli.

Sarah and Eli looked at each other surprised by what they heard.

"Let her go! Take me, but let her go!" yelled Eli.

"Let her go... let her go..." said Sirak laughing mockingly.

Halay took out a knife and placed it in front of Sarah's throat. Sarah looked around, saw a pink light to her right, felt the knife to her throat, and looked at Sirak's smile; she then stared at Eli, and tears came falling down her cheeks. Their hopes and dreams of finally being together on a farm as a family vanished in a second.

"No!!!" yelled Eli.

Halay looked at Sirak, who nodded.

"I love you," whispered Sarah, looking intensely at Eli.

She started to imagine going to a world where they were together, just the two of them. Eli looked at Sarah with teary eyes.

"I love you for eternity," replied Eli.

Halay moved, about to slit Sarah's throat.

"I will see you again," whispered Eli.

Sarah looked at Eli, crying profoundly, and managed a nod before Halay slit her throat. She fell to the floor. Eli screamed.

"Extract the embryo, I need her DNA," ordered Sirak calmly.

Loyt stabbed Eli several times, he fell to the floor, barely moving. Kawaki arrived and was shocked by what he saw, Sarah dead on the floor, and Eli hardly moving.

"Kawaki, help the men. We found our traitor," ordered Sirak.

Kawaki and another crew member lifted Eli's body.

"Take him to the pit, I want him to rot," ordered Sirak.

"Yes, Sir," replied Kawaki.

"Loyt and Halay, take the girl to Laboratory D," ordered Sirak.

"Yes, Captain," replied Loyt and Halay.

Kawaki was doing everything he could to not show his emotions; he was devastated. They arrived at the pit with Eli's body.

"I'll finish, go help Loyt and Halay," ordered Kawaki.

"Yes, Sir," replied the crew member.

Kawaki was next to Eli; Eli barely moved.

"I am sorry, I am so sorry," said Kawaki, whispering.

"In my pocket, take *Gloria* and kill her," whispered Eli.

Kawaki looked in Eli's pocket and found *Gloria*, which he hid. Eli closed his eyes; he could barely breathe.

"I am so sorry."

"I'm floating," whispered Eli.

Another crew member arrived at the pit and saw Kawaki with Eli.

"Do you need help, Sir?" asked the crew member.

Kawaki realized that this could look awkward.

"Yes, I need help with the ramp," replied Kawaki.

"Of course, Sir."

He pressed a button, and an automatic ramp appeared. Kawaki slid Eli into the pit with a thud.

Eli could smell the foul odor of death. There was no space; he felt cramped. It was completely dark. He couldn't see anything. Eli started to float; he was bodiless. He went up through the pit, into the ship, and into space.

Sarah's body was on an operating table in a laboratory on the backside of the ship. The laboratory was more significant than the others; floating hologram machines were on each side of the operating table. Two doctors, wearing a white coat, were opening up Sarah's body. There was a floating hologram, in an egg-shaped bassinet, half-open on one of the doctors' sides.

Loyt and Halay were outside the door guarding it when Kawaki arrived. Kawaki put his thumb up, a hologram appeared, and the door opened. Kawaki entered and saw the doctors extracting the embryo from Sarah's body. One of the doctors took out the fetus and placed it in the bassinet. A pink hologram screen came out from both sides of the bassinet covering the top. The doctor took the bassinet and put it in a metal cube in a floating hologram freezer.

"Good job," said Kawaki.

"Yes, Sir," replied a doctor.

Sarah, bodiless, floated above her body and followed Kawaki. Kawaki left; Halay and Loyt were still standing in front of the laboratory.

"Get back to your usual duties," ordered Kawaki.

"Yes, Sir," they said in unison.

Kawaki walked to his office when he saw Sirak in the corridor on her way to the laboratory.

"Is it done?" asked Sirak.

"Yes, Captain," replied Kawaki.

"Good, we'll finally have some peace around here," she said as she walked by him.

Kawaki turned around, facing Sirak, who had her back to him.

"Captain?" said Kawaki.

Sirak turned around.

"Yes?" said Sirak.

Kawaki pulled out *Gloria* and pointed it at Sirak. He pressed a button, a beam shot out, hitting her. Her eyes widened before she fell to the floor. Kawaki went towards Sirak and touched her pulse. It was no longer pounding.

Sarah, bodiless, floated through the ship, above the spaceship, and into space.

A few crew members arrived.

"Two of you go put her body in the pit, now!" ordered Kawaki.

The crew members were confused but followed his orders.

"And the rest of you, follow me, we are going to arrest Halay and Loyt!" ordered Kawaki.

Kawaki, followed by the men, walked through the halls leading to the rooms. Kawaki saw Loyt and Halay in front of the infirmary, laughing.

"Arrest them!" ordered Kawaki.

The men blocked Halay and Loyt and hand-cuffed them.

"What are you doing?!" asked Halay.

"We didn't do anything!" yelled Loyt.

"Lock them up in the back prison. No one is to talk to them!" ordered Kawaki to the crew members.

"Yes, Captain!" the men replied.

"Captain?! What are you talking about?!" yelled Halay.

Halay and Loyt were taken to a cell with pristine white walls and black metal bars on the ship's backside. The crew members left without saying a word.

"There has been a mistake!!" shouted Halay.

A big metal black door closed behind them.

"I want you to arrest all of Sirak's private men and take them to the prison. Don't forget all the doctors and children, but put the children in a different cell," ordered Kawaki to several crew members.

"Yes, Sir!"

Gem, the directory hologram appeared everywhere in the ship with a beeping sound.

"Everyone is to report to the dining room right away!"

Twelve ∞ Tikai

Kawaki was in the secret office with Cheryl, she was crying.

"I am so sorry, I did everything I could. They saved us all, they saved you," said Kawaki, gently.

Cheryl continued to cry.

"Come with me, we don't have to hide anymore," said Kawaki.

Kawaki held Cheryl, helping her walk.

They entered the dining room, everyone was sitting at their tables. Jennifer saw Cheryl and ran to her, taking her in her arms and then sat at her table. Kawaki went to the center of the room, the microphone hologram appeared.

"Sirak is dead. I am the new Captain of the ship. There will be no more fights. There will be no more suppression. There will be no more violence. We will land on Tikai tomorrow, where you will have a new home. There will be an abundance of food in the dining room until we arrive. You are all free to do whatever you want until our arrival. The crew members will help you with anything that you need. The crew members will bring the wounded people of Tyrakti back to their rooms. I apologize on behalf of my planet for any harm that was caused to you. God bless you all."

The people of Tyrakti applauded; Kawaki nodded. He went to sit next to Cheryl and Jennifer.

"There is more I must show you," said Kawaki.

Jennifer and Cheryl followed Kawaki. All the previously locked doors on the spaceship were now opened. They went through several corridors to the backside of the ship. Crew members were carrying wounded men to their rooms. Kawaki entered the laboratory where Sarah's embryo had been extracted.

"Sarah was pregnant," said Kawaki.

Cheryl and Jennifer gasped in surprise.

"This technology will permit for Sarah's baby to be born," said Kawaki.

Cheryl started to cry, Jennifer took her in her arms.

"Sarah would have been happy to know that you will take care of her child," said Kawaki.

Kawaki looked at Jennifer and Cheryl.

"You should both get some rest, you have been through a lot in the last few weeks," said Kawaki.

"Yes," replied Jennifer.

Kawaki walked them back to their room.

"Get some rest, and let me know if you need anything."

"Thank you," replied Cheryl, still sobbing.

Jennifer and Cheryl entered the room.

"I need to take a shower," said Cheryl.

"Yes, let me show you how this works," said Jennifer looking at her lovingly.

Jennifer showed Cheryl how the shower worked and left her alone. Jennifer laid on her bed, she started to cry as she watched the stars while thinking of Sarah.

Cheryl came out of the shower. She laid down next to Jennifer, and they fell asleep.

Cheryl woke up a couple of hours later, Jennifer was already awake.

"I'm hungry," said Cheryl.

"Let's get some dinner," replied Jennifer.

They went to the dining room; as they walked through the halls, they heard a lot of noise, people were talking, others running and laughing. The ship was very much alive again.

Kawaki arrived in the dining room, there was lots of food on all the tables. There was music, some people were dancing, others were laughing and eating. Cheryl looked around, amazed by the amount of joy; she looked at Jennifer and smiled. Alex entered the dining room, he stood alone, looking at the tables.

"You can sit with us if you want?" Jennifer said to Alex.

"Yes, thank you," replied Alex shyly.

The festivities went on into the night.

The next morning, Jennifer, Cheryl, Kawaki, and all the others were in the game room looking outside the ship as it prepared to land. They saw a planet that was very green with lots of trees, mountains, and rivers. The sun was shining.

BOOK II

Thirteen ∞ Thebes, Ancient Egypt

Eli, a buff looking slave, walked through the desert, shirtless. His feet and hands were chained, as well as the other slaves walking in front and behind him. Adler, the slave driver, was at the head of the line.

"Hurry up, keep the pace," yelled Adler.

The slaves, chained up to one another, walked faster despite how tired they were. The only thing in view was a vast desert. The slaves walked for hours without stopping for water when Eli saw a city from a distance; he paused to observe the town but was pulled by the other slaves that continued to walk.

The city got bigger and bigger as they approached it. As they entered the city, Eli looked up and saw massive sculptures of Pharaohs and tall, ornate pillars. He had never seen anything this impressive before. While he walked past them, he looked up towards the columns; they seemed to touch the sky.

Every time the slaves slowed down, Adler tugged on the chain that tied them together.

They walked through a small alley beside the pillars. A vast passageway brought them to a considerable interior plaza surrounded by more pillars and breathtaking architecture.

Farmers, priests, doctors, engineers, and artists rushed through, stood, and talked to one another. Adler took the slaves past the square and went through a few little alleys until they arrived to a spectacular garden with fountains and palm trees. Columns surrounded the garden making it very private. The ground was paved with old carved terracotta stones.

Fourteen ∞ Princess Sarah

Princess Sarah, a tall, slim brunette with silky skin, laid across a wooden carved bench in the garden surrounded by slaves. She gently pet her Saluki dog, who sat right next to her. Two slaves held parasols above the princess while other slaves stood by with platters of fresh fruit.

She saw Adler walk by with chained up slaves. She looked at the workers and fixated on Eli; she saw his green eyes.

"Adler," said Sarah.

"Yes, Princess," he bowed.

"Bring me that one," she said, pointing towards Eli.

"He is not a eunuch, Princess," said Adler.

"Just bring him to me, don't tell my father," ordered Sarah.

Adler obeyed, knowing Princess Sarah's character. He undid the chains that attached Eli to the other slaves and brought him to Sarah. Eli stared at Sarah in awe; he had never seen such a beautiful woman in his life.

"Unchain him," ordered Sarah.

"Of course, Princess," replied Adler.

Adler unchained Eli completely.

"Where should I put him, Princess?"

"Leave him here, tell Kosey to come and see me," ordered Sarah.

"Yes, Princess," replied Adler.

Adler went into the palace.

Sarah scrutinized Eli as if she had just bought a piece of art. Eli had a lot of charisma, and she liked this. She examined him for a few minutes and felt incredibly drawn to him for no apparent reason. Eli stood in front of Sarah, who studied him, he appeared uncomfortable.

"Turn around," ordered Sarah.

Eli turned around. She continued to look at him and finally stood up, wearing a beautiful white dress. She walked behind him, still analyzing him. She touched his shoulders with the tip of her fingers and then touched his back. She went around him and stopped to face him. He saw her perfect face, her impeccable make-up, and her jewelry. He could breathe her perfume; it smelled like jasmine. She touched his face.

"You have beautiful green eyes," whispered Sarah.

Eli smiled timidly. He stared at her, not knowing what to think or do.

A skinny 11-year-old boy with a kind looking face came running out.

"Yes, Princess?" said Kosey.

"Prepare my room, take the slave to my chambers, make sure he is bathed and give him some new clothes," ordered Sarah.

"Yes, Princess," replied Kosey.

Eli followed Kosey. As Eli walked away, he turned around to look at the princess; she saw this and liked it.

Eli and Kosey went into the palace. The entrance was grandiose; there were pillars on each side with an opening to an incredibly large living room with light coming through from the sky. There were beautiful tall sculptures made out of gold and smaller sculptures made out of glass in every corner of the room. There was a colorful stone fountain in the middle, decorated with gold carvings on the outer part. There were steps made out of marble embellished with lapis lazuli to the pillars' right and left. Kosey went to the right; Eli followed him, but paused to look at the palace's beauty; he had never seen anything this grand before. He looked around in awe as he followed in Kosey's footsteps.

Kosey led him up the stairs, through a beautifully decorated corridor leading into a majestic room. A large bed sat in the middle of the room with two decorated pillars at the back. There was a rich burgundy couch with gold details and a vanity to the right wall with a statue made out of obsidian. Gold jewelry and precious stones visible on the furniture.

"Come," said Kosey, kindly.

Eli followed him, not saying a word. Kosey walked in front of the vanity table and into a huge bathroom. The bathtub was the size of a small room and was made out of marble, embellished with precious stones.

There were small couches on each side of the tub. There was a big sculpture of Princess Sarah made out of gold to the right. Slaves poured water into the bathtub, and one of the slaves added oil.

"While you wash up, I will get you some new clothes," said Kosey.

Eli didn't really know what to think and simply stood there.

"Go inside the bath," said Kosey, making a sign with his hand.

Eli was shy. He looked at the slaves who filled water into the bathtub, wondering if they would stay there. Kosey noticed and told the slaves to leave by waving them away.

"Now you go in, I'll be back with some clothes," said Kosey as he looked at Eli.

Eli nodded. He slowly took off his dirty linen kilt and went into the tub. It smelled divine. His feet were black and darkened the water as he entered. He washed up and started playing with the water like a child. Kosey came back with some new clothes and saw Eli playing, and smiled at him. Kosey made a sound with his throat to make his presence known; Eli stopped playing with the water immediately but knew that Kosey saw him and smiled timidly.

"What's your name?" asked Kosey.

"My name is Eli."

Eli spoke rather eloquently despite being a slave.

"I'm Kosey, where are you from?"

"I was born in Aswan. My mother was a slave there, I stayed in the same camp as her."

"I have been a slave here since I was four years old, Princess Sarah has been good to me," said Kosey.

"Do you know what she wants from me?"

"No, it's the first time she has asked for a slave to be brought to her chamber," replied Kosey.

Sarah was in a beautiful private living room relaxing on a dark green couch, slaves bathed her feet. Her dog, Akil, sat next to her.

"Call for Lapis," ordered Sarah.

One of the slaves left to get Lapis. Lapis had been a slave for Sarah since the age of five, they knew each other well. A minute later, Lapis arrived; she was of medium size and had a pretty face.

"Hi, Princess, are you ready for your massage?" asked Lapis.

"Yes, I want the lavender and rose oils today," replied Sarah.

"Right away."

Lapis left while the slaves finished bathing Sarah's feet, dried them off, and then took their leave. Lapis came back with the oils, Sarah was on her stomach. Lapis took out the rose oil, put it on her back, and started massaging her. Sarah was relaxing.

"I heard you picked a slave?" asked Lapis.

"Yes, something is different about him," replied Sarah.

"But he is not a eunuch Princess, what will your father say?" dared Lapis.

"My father never refuses me anything, I am sure I will figure something out. If he disagrees, I will refuse to meet any more prince's," said Sarah smiling.

"I am sure he will agree, especially now with the ceremony coming up in a month," said Lapis.

"I know... I dread this ceremony each year. There has never been a prince that even cared about who I am; they simply want the money and power," said Sarah, annoyed at the thought of another ceremony.

"Yes," replied Lapis sympathetically.

"Make my skin look like silk Lapis," said Sarah.

"Yes, Princess."

Lapis was the only person Sarah spoke to, but she was still her slave and knew this although she genuinely loved Sarah.

Kosey left Eli in Sarah's room to wait for Princess Sarah. Eli looked around but didn't dare touch anything. He was uncomfortable and wondered what was to become of him.

Fifteen ∞ Jabari

Jabari, Sarah's father, entered the private living room where Sarah was being massaged. He was tall and charming. Sarah's dog, Akil, got up as he came in. Lapis stopped rubbing Sarah and stood upon his arrival. Jabari signaled with his hand for Lapis to leave, who did so immediately, before he sat next to his daughter.

"You remind me so much of your mother, so beautiful, so perfect, if only she could see you, she would be so proud," said Jabari.

Sarah's mother died when she was very young. Sarah was an only child. Jabari had given Sarah everything she ever wanted; however, she had grown to be rather lonely. When she was a girl, she studied regularly, gained a lot of knowledge, grew up to be athletic and beautiful but bored and spoiled.

"In one month, is the big day," said Jabari.

Sarah nodded; she didn't care much. Each year her father gathered the wealthiest men and princes from the nearby cities for her to choose a husband; she always found faults in the men he presented her with.

Sarah smiled at her father.

"I don't need a husband, I'm fine here with you."

"This year it will be different, there is a man by the name of Ammon. He is very wealthy, comes from a reputable family, and rumors say that he is also *very* handsome."

Sarah lightened up when her father told her he was handsome; she wondered what this Ammon is like.

"We'll see," replied Sarah.

"Yes," said Jabari, losing hope, as he got up to leave, "I will see you later."

"Yes."

A minute later, Lapis came back.

"Should I continue?"

"Yes."

Lapis continued to massage Sarah.

"My father told me about a man named Ammon. Apparently, he is *very* handsome," said Sarah, giggling.

"Oh, a handsome prince?" said Lapis, smiling.

"He is not a prince, but he is very wealthy. My father thinks I might like him."

"That would be a first."

"Yes, we will see," said Sarah.

Lapis continued to massage Sarah until she fell asleep. Lapis put a silk sheet on Sarah's body so that she wouldn't get cold.

Sarah woke up a few hours later, completely relaxed. Her dog Akil was next to her, wiggling his tail as she stirred. She was in an excellent mood and hummed a tune.

Lapis arrived.

"Did you have a nice nap?" asked Lapis.

"Yes, I had a beautiful dream, I was somewhere else, it looked like another planet, the slave was there with me. I want to see him, is he in my room?" asked Sarah.

"Yes," replied Lapis.

Lapis accompanied Sarah to her room, followed by Sarah's dog, Akil.

Kosey stood in front of Sarah's room, on guard.

"Stay," said Sarah to Akil.

When Sarah entered her room, she saw Eli asleep on her bed. Lapis was stressed out and went to wake him up, but Sarah interrupted her.

"No, let him sleep, you can leave," ordered Sarah.

"Are you sure you want to stay here alone with him?"

"Yes, don't worry, I will be fine; Kosey and Akil are outside if I need anything."

Lapis nodded and left.

Sarah sat on the bed next to Eli, who was still asleep, and watched him. She gently touched his hair; he opened his eyes, saw the Princess, and abruptly sat on the bed.

"I am sorry, I... I fell asleep," stammered Eli.

Sarah smiled; she was amused by his reaction.

"What's your name?" asked Sarah.

"Eli... my name is Eli."

"Where are you from?"

"I was born in Aswan, Princess."

"Hm..."

"Um... what would you like me to do, Princess?" asked Eli.

"Just relax, Eli. Do you have a wife?"

"No, Princess."

"Did you have one?"

"No, Princess, not really."

"What do you mean by not really? Did you have a wife or not?" demanded Sarah.

"I was with someone a long time ago," replied Eli.

"Where is she now?"

"She died, Princess."

"Oh, I see," replied Sarah.

Sarah and Eli looked at each other for a moment. He was waiting for the Princess to tell him what she wanted. Sarah undid the top of her dress, making it very clear. Eli stared at her beauty; she smiled. She took his hand and put it on her right breast; he was very timid, not because he had never slept with anyone before but because she was a Princess. He went towards Sarah and kissed her. She smiled at him. He gently caressed her and leaned in towards her. They started making love passionately. Sarah was amazed at how much she enjoyed his presence, touch, and ease of connection. It all seemed natural to her as if they had already known each other.

Kosey was outside in front of the door when Lapis arrived.

"Did she ask for anything?" asked Lapis.

"No," replied Kosey.

"What are they doing?"

Kosey got embarrassed.

"I think they are um... you know um... I don't know," replied Kosey.

Lapis giggled.

"Let me know if she calls for me," said Lapis as she left.

Sarah and Eli talked for a few hours and then made love again and again. Sarah called for Kosey by jingling on a gold bell; he arrived.

"Yes, Princess," said Kosey.

"Bring me some food."

Kosey left and came back with two servants with various trays of food. The servants put the platters on the table and left the room right away. Kosey stood in front of Sarah, waiting in case she needed anything else.

"You can leave," said Sarah.

"Yes, Princess."

Sarah looked at Eli, who stared at the food.

"Eat."

Eli was starving, Sarah could tell. He ate and smiled timidly.

"I don't want to see you bed anyone else," ordered Sarah.

"Um... of course, Princess," replied Eli.

"Call me Sarah."

"Yes."

They spent the night together, whispering, eating, and making love.

Sixteen ∞ Game day

The next morning Sarah woke up in a better mood than usual. She turned to Eli, but he was gone. She called for Lapis by tolling the bell and Lapis arrived.

"Where is he?" asked Sarah.

"I saw him with Kosey, Princess," replied Lapis.

"Oh... Fetch him," commanded Sarah.

"Should I dress you first, Princess?"

"No, fetch him."

"Yes, Princess," said Lapis and left immediately.

Lapis came back with Eli a few minutes later.

"I didn't tell you to leave Eli; where did you go?" asked Sarah, annoyed.

"I got you these beautiful flowers from the garden, Princess."

"Oh, thank you," replied Sarah, slightly embarrassed, "I want you to stay with me unless I tell you otherwise."

"Okay, Princess."

"Call me Sarah."

"Yes."

Eli handed her beautiful purple and rose-colored flowers; Sarah smelled them, the scent was divine.

"Lapis, bring me a vase?" said Sarah.

"Yes," replied Lapis and left quickly.

"Sit," said Sarah to Eli.

Eli sat; he looked straight ahead, towards the door. Sarah saw that he was not looking at her and made a sound to get his attention. She wanted him to look at her; he saw that she was very capricious but found it cute.

Lapis came back with the vase and put the flowers in it next to the bed.

"Dress me now," ordered Sarah.

Lapis dressed Sarah while Eli sat on the bed; Sarah teased Eli to be sure that he was observing her.

"I thought we might play some games today. Lapis, tell Kosey, Eboni, and Nenet to join us for the day. We'll play hide and seek," said Sarah, smiling.

Lapis was surprised as Sarah usually liked to play Senet or Mancala.

"Yes, Princess, of course," replied Lapis.

She finished to dress Sarah and then left. Sarah turned to Eli.

"I want you to find me all day."

"Of course, Sarah," replied Eli as he smiled at her.

It was the first time Eli called Sarah by her name; she liked it but realized that no one but her parents had ever called her like that.

She pretended to be an animal, moved towards Eli, and then backed away from him; she was playful. He finally grabbed her, and they started kissing passionately.

Half an hour later, Sarah and Eli left the room. Lapis, Eboni, Kosey, and Nenet were waiting for them in the playroom. Eli followed Sarah into the grandiose room and saw games he had never seen before. The playroom was gorgeous; the back wall was made out of marble with designs in it. There were precious stones on the statues on each side of the marble wall, and beautiful green and burgundy couches that circled a wooden carved table with games on it. Nenet was gorgeous, very slim, and charming. Eboni was a bit bigger and looked sweet.

"Let's play hide and seek," said Sarah.

"*You* are it," Sarah said to Eli as she touched him.

Everyone went to hide, Eli started counting; he was to find everyone. He finished counting and started to look around. He found Lapis, Kosey, and then Eboni. He was searching for Sarah but instead found Nenet. As he opened a door and looked behind it, Nenet got frightened and jumped. They laughed. Sarah saw this from her hiding spot behind a dark statue and didn't like it and stood up.

"Nenet, get some food for us," ordered Sarah.

"Yes, Princess," said Nenet and left immediately.

Eli understood that Sarah was jealous, and he had to be careful when he interacted with other women. He liked the attention but, at the same time, realized that he was in a delicate situation. They played board games for the rest of the day. They ate, laughed, and enjoyed themselves. Sarah was no longer annoyed with Nenet seeing that Eli was only paying attention to herself.

"Lapis, come with me to my room," said Sarah.

Kosey, Eli, and Nenet were sitting on the couches.

"Eli, Kosey will bring you to my room a bit later; the rest of you can leave," said Sarah.

"Yes," said Eli.

She smiled at him flirtatiously as she left, followed by Lapis.

"He is different, I think I might like him, a new distraction," said Sarah.

"Yes, Princess, he seems nice," said Lapis.

"What do you mean by *he seems nice*? Did someone say something?" asked Sarah.

"No, not at all, I mean that he seems good for you," said Lapis quietly.

"Oh... yes... he is good for me," said Sarah reassured.

Lapis looked at Sarah and smiled.

"I want you to dress me in a beautiful gown and do my make-up. I want to be perfect for him," said Sarah.

"Yes, Princess," replied Lapis.

Lapis put make-up on Sarah at her vanity table; there was a knock on the door.

"Who is it?" asked Sarah.

"It's your father," said Jabari.

"Oh, come in."

"Lapis, leave us."

"Yes, Your Highness," replied Lapis to Jabari.

She left, closing the door behind her. Jabari sat next to Sarah in front of the vanity table.

"I heard a rumor, Sarah," said Jabari.

"Yes?"

"You are bedding one of the slaves?! This must be a falsity?"

"No, it's true, I like him, he amuses me," said Sarah coldly.

"But you cannot, what will your future husband say?" said Jabari.

"I don't care."

"You must stop this at once!" said Jabari, raising his tone.

"I will not! I prefer to not get married at all!"

"Sarah, please, why is it so hard to find you a husband?"

"I will find a husband in due course, but I am having fun with the slave, please, let me have him?"

"I can't refuse anything to you, can I?"

"Please?" implored Sarah.

"Fine, have fun with your slave, but when you meet Ammon, you will spend time with him, yes?"

"Yes, father, I will be good to him," said Sarah, smiling.

She hugged her father; he shook his head, not knowing what to do with his daughter anymore. He left her room; Lapis was standing outside and then entered.

"What did he say?" said Lapis.

"I can keep him, as long as I show some interest in Ammon, I can keep Eli, I told you he would say yes," said Sarah smiling.

"Yes," replied Lapis.

Lapis finished Sarah's make-up and took out a beautiful red gown. She put it on Sarah, who looked astoundingly gorgeous. Sarah admired herself in the mirror.

"Thank you, Lapis," said Sarah.

"You look stunning, Princess."

"Call for Eli now."

"Yes, Princess," said Lapis as she left.

Sarah laid on the bed, waiting for Eli.

He knocked on the door.

"Come in," said Sarah.

Eli opened the door and entered; he looked at Sarah and found her riveting. He closed the door and stood there for a minute, staring at her beauty.

"What have I done to deserve this?" asked Eli.

Sarah giggled.

"Make love to me," said Sarah.

He got closer to her and laid next to her; he started caressing her hair and then kissed her passionately. He was surprised by how quickly he fell in love with her despite her impractical character. They made love as if they had been together for years, knowing each other's bodies perfectly. They spent the evening talking and making love again and again.

Three weeks went by. Sarah was very much enjoying the time she was spending with Eli; she was completely in love with him. She didn't expect this and started to think that this would become a problem for her.

It was tricky for Eli because he was unconditionally in love with her. Still, she had the duties and nature of a princess.

He softened her character, she became kinder and gentler to her slaves while Sarah taught him how to read. They made a good team.

They spent lots of time speaking to each other; Eli told Sarah that an old man in one of the slave camps taught him to speak correctly. Sarah was amazed by Eli's stories, where he traveled, where he had been a slave, and how he almost died strangled by a snake. He had a tough life and, despite that, had remained cheerful and kind.

Eli knew that the big day was coming quickly and didn't know what to do if Sarah was to choose Ammon as a husband. He didn't dare ask her. Sarah had spent so much time with Eli that she didn't think about Ammon at all; she knew that the day was coming and she would have to choose, but she was with Eli now; she knew she couldn't marry him but was living on a day to day basis.

Jabari frowned upon her relationship with Eli. He usually didn't care much about her whims, but this time he saw that Sarah was very attached. Jabari wanted what was best for his daughter. Being with a slave was far from anything he could imagine being desirable. He hoped she would like Ammon, and Eli would be a distraction from the past.

Seventeen ∞ Overthrown

Two days later, at 5am, Sarah woke to screams and loud banging's. She was afraid; she looked to see if Eli was next to her, and he was. Relief washed over her. Their room door was thrown open, and they saw a group of men fighting Sarah's slaves in the hallway. The palace was being overthrown.

Jabari's army marched in, while screams came from all sides. Sarah ran to the window, men fought her father's army in the yard. People were getting killed in every direction. Sarah yelled for her father, but he didn't come. She was utterly panicked and looked to Eli, who reassured her.

Five men managed to enter the room; they threatened Sarah and Eli. Her dog Akil barked ferociously. A man smacked the dog, and it went flying to the room's corner. The men closed in on Sarah. The slaves rushed in, tackling three of the men. Eli fought one while another grabbed Sarah by her hair and hit her across the face. Eli was enraged and threw the man he was fighting across the room, knocking him unconscious. He turned to the man hitting Sarah. He threw a punch, but the man caught his fist and threw Eli to the floor. Eli struggled as the man kicked him ferociously in the ribs. Eli was near death when he took a small knife on the floor and stabbed the man in the calf. The man fell to the floor, and Eli stabbed him in the stomach. He ran to Sarah, who was shaking in the corner of the room.

"Let me take you to a safe place," said Eli, still holding the knife in his hand in case they got attacked.

Sarah followed Eli out of the room. They continued to hear fighting and screaming in and outside the palace. Eli went to a wall to the right, outside of Sarah's room. He pulled on a stone, revealing a secret passageway.

"Kosey showed me this entrance to the oil room," said Eli, looking back to make sure no one was following them.

Sarah barely nodded. They entered a hall made of bricks; it was a thin corridor. They end up in a small, square room made out of masonry stones. The room was cold. It looked like a small apothecary. Bottles and jars of different oils were kept there to stay protected from the heat.

Sarah was still shaking; Eli took her in his arms and leaned her against the brick wall.

"I need to go to see what's happening. I'll be right back," said Eli still in pain.

"No, don't leave me alone," said Sarah, slightly sobbing.

"I am just going to look from the end of the corridor."

"No, don't leave me, please-"

"Don't worry, I'll be right back."

He took the knife out of his pocket while standing next to a pink jar; Sarah looked at him for a moment and then became completely hysterical.

"Don't go!! We'll get killed! I don't want you to go!! Don't go!! Please, I beg you!!"

Eli saw the fear in her eyes and sat next to her.

"It's okay."

He took her in his arms once more, holding her tight until she fell asleep. Eli gently removed his body and laid her down. He left the secret oil room, back down the hall, slightly opened the door, and glanced around the corner. Dead bodies covered the floor. He saw men from Jabari's army. Eli was about to return when he heard Jabari call out for his daughter.

"Sarah, Sarah, where are you?!" yelled Jabari.

Eli walked out of the doorway.

"The princess is here, Your Majesty," said Eli.

"Where?!" demanded Jabari.

"In the oil room."

Jabari pushed past Eli and entered the secret corridor. He saw Sarah on the floor. She woke up and saw her father and started crying. Jabari took her in his arms and carried her back to her room; Eli and the slaves followed behind him.

Jabari's men won the battle, but many were wounded.

Eli stood in the corner of Sarah's room, unsure of what to do. Sarah's dog, Akil, went to Sarah's bed, limping. Slaves tended to Sarah's wound across her face, while Jabari held her hand.

"I thought I lost you, what would I do without you?" said Jabari.

"I am fine, father, I am fine, I just need to rest."

Jabari looked at Eli in the corner and scowled. Eli left the room; Sarah saw this but didn't say anything.

"Remove the dead bodies!" ordered Jabari to the slaves.

A few hours later, the palace started to look a little cleaner. Jabari had placed guards around the palace, as well as in front of his daughter's room.

He went back to Sarah's room; she was in bed. He sat next to her and took out a dagger.

"Sarah, I want you to have this with you at all times," said Jabari.

Sarah looked at this beautiful dirk made out of gold with sapphires on the hilt.

"It's beautiful."

"I would feel better if you took fighting lessons with Kamar."

"I don't want to."

"Please... think about it."

"Yes, Father."

"I will let you get some rest."

He kissed Sarah on the forehead and left.

At the the end of the day; Eli waited in front of the princess's door; the guards wouldn't let him in. Lapis left the room, and Sarah saw Eli in the hall.

"Come in," she called to him.

The guards stepped aside and let Eli in. He entered her room and looked at her with loving eyes.

"I am so sorry," he said as he sat next to her.

Akil was next to her on the bed. Eli leaned in and hugged her before kissing her passionately.

"Thank you... Eli, you saved my life. I love you, you know?"

"I love you... I cannot live without you."

"My promise to you is that we will spend our life together. I want to bear your children," whispered Sarah.

Eli's eyes welled with tears as he kissed her face.

They made passionate love and then Sarah fell asleep; Eli watched her for hours. He imagined what his new life would be; a child is a thought he never had. He was destined to a life of slavery. Here, he was entirely and utterly in love with a princess who wanted a life with him.

The next morning they woke up wrapped in each other's arms. Sarah's wounds had stopped aching. She looked at Eli and felt complete.

"Let's go for a walk in the gardens today?"

"Yes, my love."

Lapis came in and dressed Sarah. Eli was on the bed staring at Sarah with stars in his eyes. They had breakfast together in her room.

Sarah was at peace, she was calm and knew how lucky she was to be alive. While they had breakfast, she looked at Eli, smiling and admiring him.

The two lovers went to the gardens. They strolled along a pathway of colorful flowers. Eli delicately touched the flowers and plants, as he whispered to them.

"What do you say to these flowers?" asked Sarah.

"I tell them that I see that they are here and wish them well,' replied Eli.

"I have never met anyone that whispers to plants before."

He smiled at her.

The sun shined bright. Slaves covered both of them with parasols. The slaves looked at Eli; they did not consider him to be one of theirs anymore; it created a slight discomfort.

Sarah and Eli sat on a bench near a beautiful fountain.

"Eli, I will speak to my father tomorrow. I want to cancel the event. With all that has happened, I am sure my father will understand."

"Yes, that would be good."

They sat for a while, laughing and talking to each other like children.

An hour later, they went back to the palace and headed to Sarah's room to bathe. They played in the bathtub together, throwing water at each other. They whispered about their future life together—their children. Eli was ecstatic. Sarah saw how happy he was and smiled. They got into bed, made love, and fell asleep. Despite the day's events, life could not have been better for both of them.

The next morning Jabari knocked on Sarah's door; Sarah sat on her bed alone and he walked in.

"Sarah, my darling, you look well."

"Yes, father, I feel much better, but I want you to cancel tomorrow's event."

"Yes, I already have, but what about Ammon?" asked Jabari.

"I don't want to see him."

"He has already arrived, when he heard of the attack, he came right away. He is staying in the guest's palace."

"Ammon is here?" asked Sarah, surprised.

"Yes, I told him you needed to rest, you will meet him tomorrow."

"But I don't want to meet him!" Sarah raised her voice.

"Quiet now. You will do your duty as a princess and meet your guest tomorrow. He is a distinct man. He arrived with many men in case we needed support for our army."

"Fine, I will meet him tomorrow, but I will not marry him, I assure you of that."

Jabari looked at his daughter. She sulked deeper into her bed. Jabari saw Sarah's mother in her face. He stroked her cheek.

"Get some rest now," said Jabari and left.

Sarah fell asleep for hours and awoke to Lapis entering the room.

"I don't know what to do. I promised Eli. He is the love of my life. If only he was from a rich family, it would be so much easier."

"I am sorry, Princess," replied Lapis.

"I will never get married and simply be with Eli. My father wants me to be happy, he will understand, right?" asked Sarah.

"I think so, Princess. I don't know. Should we pick your outfit for tomorrow?"

"No, I don't care about what I wear for tomorrow. Will you call Eli, please?"

"Yes, right away, Princess."

"Thank you, Lapis, you are a good friend to me, you know?"

"Yes, you are as well," Lapis smiled and left the room.

Sarah laid back on her bed, dreaming of Eli. Moments later, he arrived.

"Where were you?" asked Sarah.

Eli was quiet.

"I was helping Kosey with the tables for the event tomorrow."

"Come here, my love."

"I know I promised you I would cancel the event, but Ammon showed up when he heard of the attack. My father wants me to welcome him. I can't do otherwise. I am so sorry, but it will be fine, you will see."

"I understand."

She could sense that Eli was scared to lose her; he was a simple slave, and Ammon was a wealthy man. Eli didn't say anything, but Sarah saw his worry.

"It will be fine, I am sure of it, my father would never *force* me to get married to him."

"Yes... I hope so."

Sarah looked at him, lifted his chin up, and kissed him. They looked at each other and made love; once again, they were one.

Eighteen ∞ Ammon

The next morning when Sarah woke up, Eli was gone. She didn't like it. Sarah called for Lapis, who arrived in an instant.

"Should I dress you? Everyone is setting up for the event, Princess."

"Where is Eli?" asked Sarah.

"He is helping set everything up, Princess."

"Oh..."

"What dress would you like to wear?"

"I don't care," Sarah sulked.

Lapis dressed Sarah, who looked gorgeous as usual. They left Sarah's room together, Lapis and Akil walking behind.

They arrived in the grand dining room where Sarah's father was sitting next to Ammon, mid-conversation.

Sarah observed Ammon. He was a handsome, tall gentleman. She was surprised by his elegance and found him to be very attractive. As she walked into the dining room, her father stood.

"Sarah, this is Ammon," announced Jabari.

"It's very nice to meet you, Princess," said Ammon smiling profusely.

"It's nice to meet you too," said Sarah, without a smile.

Sarah sat at the table, barely looking at him. Twenty slaves waited on the table. Eli was among the slaves, watching Sarah from afar. Sarah could feel his stare and glanced back at him. He seemed to be hiding his jealousy but not very well.

Near the end of the meal, Ammon signaled to one of his slaves to bring him something. The slave presented Ammon with a beautiful box. Ammon took the case made of gold and laid it before Sarah. She opened it and found a beautiful necklace with hundreds of emeralds and precious stones embedded into it. It was the most beautiful piece of jewelry Sarah had ever seen. She gasped but quickly pretended like she didn't care. Ammon saw this and smiled.

"Please accept this gift from me to thank you for your hospitality."

Jabari didn't let Sarah reply for fear of her response. He cut in-

"Thank you, Ammon, it's a pleasure having you here," said Jabari.

Sarah stared at her father, then Ammon. Her face was cold. Sarah got up to leave, but her father interrupted her departure.

"Will you take Ammon for a stroll in the gardens?" ordered Jabari.

"Yes, father," Sarah replied with disdain.

Ammon got up, excited to spend some time alone with Sarah. She started to walk, Ammon followed.

They walked for a while, Ammon tried to get Sarah to speak, but she remained quiet. He told her of his palace and his extraordinary life. She had no interest in him.

"I am getting tired. Will you take me back?" asked Sarah.

"Of course, after what happened to you, I am sure you must need rest," replied Ammon.

"Yes..."

"My palace is a very safe place."

"I am sure of it."

They arrived at the palace.

"It was a pleasure," said Ammon.

"Likewise," replied Sarah.

Sarah walked quickly back to her room, where Lapis was waiting for her.

"Where is Eli? I need to see him," demanded Sarah.

"I haven't seen him, let me go and look," said Lapis, as she left.

Sarah was alone in her room, eagerly waiting for Eli to arrive, but Lapis came back alone.

"I cannot find him, Princess."

"Thank you, Lapis... You can leave."

"Is everything all right, Princess?"

"Yes, I am fine, I am worried for Eli is all. Good night."

"Good night, Princess."

Lapis walked out.

Sarah wondered where Eli could be when she realized that she *knew*; he was in the oil room.

She took the secret passageway, following the light coming from the window. Eli sat with his back against the wall where they hid when the palace was under attack. He looked sad and lonely. She sat next to him and touched his face; he didn't look at her.

"There is nothing between him and me... There never will be, I told you, you are the love of my life," said Sarah.

"What will we do? I can't marry you. Maybe it's better if you marry him. I saw your face when he gave you the necklace. Don't tell me you didn't like it," replied Eli.

"Yes, it's a pretty necklace, but I want you, I choose us. Our love and connection is more precious than any sapphire," said Sarah.

She looked at him, and his expression slowly changed to a smile. She touched his face and brought his lips to hers. They kissed deeply.

"We will be fine," said Sarah.

"I can't live without you, you know?" said Eli.

"Me neither."

They went back to Sarah's room and got into bed. They laughed together and then made love. Eli felt better. He thought to himself, they would be together forever, their connection is what brought them together and it would last forever. Ammon would soon leave, and this would all be in the past.

The next morning Sarah awoke to her father, Jabari, sitting next to her. She was startled and looked to see if Eli was next to her, but he was gone.

"So my dear, what do you think of Ammon?" asked Jabari.

"Father, he is nice... but I love Eli. I want to spend my life with him."

Jabari exhaled loudly.

"You know you cannot marry him. What will you do?"

"I don't care, he makes me happy, he makes me smile like mother made you."

"Yes, but you won't be able to have children with him. Are you willing to give up children to be with him?" said Jabari firmly.

"I will have children with him, I don't care what people think. He is my one and only love."

Jabari was overcome with frustration, he stood up.

"I can't hear more nonsense like this."

"I love him, it's no nonsense, father."

"Ammon will be staying here for a few days. I expect that you keep him company and remain a worthy princess."

"Yes, father," Sarah gave in.

Jabari left.

Sarah was upset. She called for Lapis, who arrived to dress her as usual. Lapis sensed how unhappy Sarah was, she tried to calm her.

"Do you want to talk about it, Princess?"

"No, no, I need to relax."

"Would you like a massage, Princess?"

"Yes, that would be great, but use the rose oil. Eli prefers the scent."

Lapis smiled, grabbed the rose oil and began to massage Sarah.

"Thank you, Lapis, this is exactly what I need."

"I am happy you are feeling better."

An hour later, Sarah was dressed and went to the dining room with Lapis. Ammon and her father were there talking and having what looked like a good time.

"I thought we could play Senet today," said Jabari.

"That sounds like a great idea," replied Ammon.

"Ah! Here she is!" said Jabari.

Ammon turned around to look at Sarah, followed by Akil.

"You look beautiful this morning, Princess," said Ammon.

"We were thinking about playing Senet, will you join us?" asked Jabari.

"Yes, father."

"Are you hungry?" asked Jabari.

"No, father, I am fine."

The two men got up, and they all went to the playroom. Ammon walked next to Sarah.

"Did you rest well, Princess?" asked Ammon.

"Yes, thank you," replied Sarah.

They sat on the couches around the big game table and started playing Senet. Ammon glanced up at

Sarah; Sarah felt this but avoided looking him in the eyes.

They played games all afternoon. While they played, Ammon moved one of the counters and touched Sarah's hand. She pulled back her hand abruptly. Ammon smiled. Sarah was uncomfortable but thought Ammon was a nice man with a gentle expression. If she were not in love with Eli, she would enjoy Ammon's company. But she chose Eli, and she loved him.

"I am hungry, let's have a feast tonight!" said Jabari.

"Yes, that sounds terrific," replied Ammon.

The evening proceeded, and Ammon found his seat next to Sarah at the table.

"I think we should go sailing tomorrow," said Jabari.

"What a splendid idea!" replied Ammon.

"I guess it would be nice to go sailing," said Sarah, forced into agreeing with their enthusiasm.

She looked to see if Eli was nearby but didn't see him. She wondered where he was.

Dinner began. The slaves brought platters and platters of food.

"Bring the musicians, what is a feast without music?" said Jabari to one of the slaves.

"Yes, Your Highness."

The musicians arrived and began to play. There was a great ambiance in the room; food, music, and wine.

"Will you do me the honor of a dance, Princess?" asked Ammon.

Sarah hesitated for a moment. Her father shot a stern look her way.

"Yes, of course," she replied.

Ammon put out his hand, Sarah was uncomfortable but obliged.

Ammon found Sarah charming, beautiful, and interesting. A moment during the dance, Ammon made Sarah twirl in a circle, and she finally let out a smile. Ammon's heart opened; he had hope for the first time. The dance came to an end and they returned to the dinner table.

"I am getting tired," said Sarah.

"Yes, you must rest, for tomorrow is a big day," said Jabari.

"Good night, Princess," said Ammon.

"Good night," replied Sarah as she left.

Ammon watched her leave with a smile on his face; Jabari was pleased.

"She is perfect," said Ammon.

"Yes, she is like her mother, I would be honored to have you as my son in law, but there is a problem we must manage first," said Jabari.

The two men stayed at the dinner table discussing a plan and had some more wine.

Sarah arrived in her room, she called for Kosey.

"Can you get Eli, please?" said Sarah in a slightly worried voice.

"Yes, Princess. I saw him in the galley working. Is everything fine?" asked Kosey.

"Yes, I just want Ammon to leave."

"He is very nice to us, he gave us each a new kilt."

"Yes, he is charming, but Eli is my love."

"I think Eli is upset."

"Yes, I know, please fetch him."

Kosey fetched Eli. Eli was delighted to see Sarah and kissed her the moment he entered the room. They sat on the bed together.

"We are going sailing tomorrow," said Sarah.

"Yes, I heard... When do you think he will leave?"

"Probably in a few days, I think he knows that I am not interested."

Eli smiled. They laid in bed, whispering. Their hands were intertwined, they kissed each other and made love. Sarah fell asleep in Eli's arms.

The next morning Sarah woke up, and Eli was next to her. Her dog Akil was sleeping at the foot of the bed next to her feet. She turned to her left and saw a vase of beautiful flowers next to her bed. She looked at them and smiled. She turned to Eli, he was still asleep. She touched his hair, his face, and then kissed his cheek. He opened his eyes and smiled. They had breakfast in her room before Lapis arrived to dress Sarah.

Sarah met her father in the living room, they were preparing to go sailing. Jabari ordered which slaves would stay at the palace and which slaves would assist with the sailing. He made sure to leave Eli behind; Sarah saw this and mouthed that she loved him. He looked at Sarah, and it was as if time had stopped; he mouthed back that he loved her.

Sarah, Jabari, and Ammon left with the slaves; amongst the slaves were Lapis and Kosey.

They sailed off into a beautiful day full of sunshine and giant clouds. Sarah leaned on the boat's rail, she looked at the water's reflection, lost in her thoughts. Jabari sat next to her.

"I told you, he is great, no?" asked Jabari.

"Yes, father, but I told you I love Eli," replied Sarah, barely looking up from the water.

Jabari did not respond and Ammon interrupted them.

"It's beautiful, isn't it?" said Ammon.

"Yes," replied Sarah.

"I love sailing, I regularly go sailing in Memphis, I am sure you would like it there, Princess," said Ammon.

"No," said Sarah abruptly.

Jabari and Ammon were very surprised by her instant response; Jabari looked at his daughter.

"I mean, I love it here," said Sarah.

"Yes, I understand," replied Ammon.

They sailed for hours, enjoying the breeze and the sun. Ammon tried to spend as much time as he could with Sarah, but she didn't engage with him.

"That's a beautiful dagger you have there," said Ammon, pointing to it.

"Yes, my father gave it to me; he wants me to be protected at all times," replied Sarah.

"A rare beauty like you needs to be safe at all times," said Ammon.

Sarah smiled politely.

"I have the oldest dagger in Egypt at my palace. It would be an honor for me to give it to you."

"Thank you, but this one is perfect."

Ammon attempted to impress Sarah with his wealth, but she did not budge; Sarah blocked Ammon out and spent her time next to Lapis, daydreaming about Eli.

At sunset, they sailed back to the palace and arrived in time for dinner.

"This was a long day. I will go to my room," Sarah said to her father.

"Don't you want to have dinner first?" asked Jabari.

"No, I am too tired."

"Okay, good night, sweetheart."

"Good night, father, good night, Ammon."

Ammon stood up and kissed Sarah's hand before she could avoid it. Ammon and Jabari sat at the dining table and started to talk.

Sarah entered her room and saw Eli waiting for her on the bed; she was thrilled to see him and ran to kiss him. He knew that she didn't care about Ammon; he could feel it. He didn't seem worried at all anymore.

Sarah sensed this, and it reinforced their relationship. They spent the evening talking, laughing, and making love.

Sarah rang the bell and Kosey entered.

"Can you bring us some dinner, Kosey, please?" asked Sarah.

"Yes, Princess, right away," said Kosey as he left the room.

Dinner was brought a few minutes later, and they enjoyed a meal in bed.

Another day went by. Sarah didn't pay any attention to Ammon as she fell deeper in love with Eli; they were on a cloud of their own.

The next day Jabari and Sarah were in the game room playing senet.

"I don't understand you, he is wonderful," said Jabari.

"Father, I told you I am in love with Eli, I will never be with Ammon."

"But what will you do? You cannot marry Eli."

"Father, I am happy, isn't that all that matters? You have told me your whole life that you wanted me to be happy, well, I am."

"Yes."

Jabari loved his daughter and was happy to hear this, but at the same time, he thought he knew what was best for her.

Jabari and Sarah spent the afternoon playing games and enjoying their father-daughter time. Sarah loved her father, enormously; they had always gotten along, the only disagreement they had ever had was about finding a husband.

"I will go to my room now, father," said Sarah as she stood to leave.

"Have a nice evening, my dear."

Jabari kissed his daughter on the forehead.

Sarah was excited to see Eli. When she got to her room, Eli was there waiting for her. They had another wonderful evening together. The next morning they woke up and laid there staring into each other's eyes enjoying every second of it.

"I have to go to the galley, but I will miss you," said Eli.

"Not as much as I," replied Sarah smiling at him.

Lapis arrived half an hour later. Sarah was sketching a picture of Eli while humming a tune.

"That's beautiful, Princess, I haven't seen you draw since you were a child," said Lapis as she took out a dress.

"Thank you."

"Should I dress you?"

"Yes."

Lapis dressed Sarah. Sarah's mood was infectious; she was full of joy.

"Thank you, Lapis. Should we go for a walk in the gardens together?"

"Yes, Princess, like when we were children."

"Yes, I'll be done very soon, and then we can go, I'll meet you outside."

"Okay, Princess."

Lapis was happy to have time with the Princess, she smiled and left the room. Sarah and Akil laid on her bed while Sarah finished her sketch of Eli. A knock at the door.

Nineteen ∞ Kosey

"Yes?" Sarah called.

Kosey opened the door and entered.

"Hi, Kosey."

"Hi Princess, I need to speak to you about something," replied Kosey timidly.

"Of course, what's the matter?" asked Sarah.

"I saw something, I should have told you yesterday, but I was afraid," said Kosey.

"What is it?" asked Sarah, worried about Kosey's tone.

She had known Kosey for many years and had never seen him this terrified.

"Tell me... What is it?" asked Sarah impatiently.

"I... I saw him... with Nenet."

"You saw *who* with Nenet? What are you talking about?" Sarah got hysterical.

"I saw Eli and Nenet sleeping together when we came back from sailing," said Kosey.

"That's impossible! Are you sure it wasn't someone else?" yelled Sarah.

"I promise, Princess, I saw him, I know it was him," replied Kosey, terrified of the repercussions.

"What?! Get him now!!"

"Yes, Princess," replied Kosey as he ran out of her room to get Eli.

Eli arrived minutes later by himself; he opened the door and was happy to see Sarah as if nothing happened. Sarah started yelling at him the minute he walked in; she was out of her mind like some kind of possessed by a demon.

"How could you!! You are just a slave!! I gave you everything!!" yelled Sarah.

"What are you talking about, Sarah?" replied Eli in shock.

"Don't you dare call me Sarah!!" Sarah cried.

Eli didn't understand why she was so upset; he tried to go towards her, but she pushed him away.

"You are just a slave!!" screamed Sarah.

Eli was perplexed.

"What are you talking about?! I didn't do anything!" replied Eli yelling back at her.

"How dare you lie to me!! Kosey saw you!!" she said, crying and yelling hysterically.

Eli started to walk towards Sarah to calm her down. In an outburst of rage and folly of jealousy, she took her dagger from her waist and threw it at Eli without thinking. The blade went straight into Eli's heart; Eli stopped abruptly and fell to the floor while looking at Sarah in despair. Sarah realized what she had just done and ran to him, crying hysterically.

"I love you for eternity, I will see you next lifetime," whispered Eli in confusion, before his eyes closed.

"I loved you, I don't understand how you could do this to me. I thought we were forever? I am sorry, I am so sorry," whispered Sarah while on top of him.

Akil whined in the corner of the bedroom. Kosey and Lapis came running into the room. They saw the mess, Kosey was shocked, and Lapis didn't know what to do. She got closer to Sarah who was crying and shouting.

"Get away!! Get away!! Don't touch him! Don't touch me!" yelled Sarah from the top of her lungs.

"Let me help," said Lapis gently.

"Go away!!! Get out!!!" yelled Sarah.

Jabari came rushing in.

"Get out!!! All of you get out!!" yelled Sarah.

Lapis walked silently to the vanity table, giving Sarah space.

"Come with me," said Jabari to Kosey, "You stay here," whispered Jabari to Lapis.

Sarah wouldn't let anyone near Eli or herself. Lapis stayed in the corner, watching Sarah as she cried for hours and fell asleep of exhaustion on top of Eli's dead body.

Twenty ∞ Eli and Sarah

A few hours later, Lapis took Sarah and put her on her bed; Sarah was asleep, mumbling, she was lost. Lapis spent the night comforting Sarah while Akil laid beside her. Jabari ordered Kosey and a few other slaves to take Eli's body to a cold room next to Sarah's.

Sarah woke up in the middle of the night and saw Lapis next to her.

"Was it all a bad dream?" murmured Sarah sadly.

Lapis looked at Sarah in despair.

"I am so sorry," replied Lapis.

Sarah looked on the floor and saw that Eli's body was no longer there.

"Where is he? Where is he? Where did they put him?!" yelled Sarah anxiously.

"He is in the cold room next door."

"Take me to him now," Sarah trembled.

Lapis held Sarah and took her to Eli's body, followed by Akil. Sarah entered the cold room and signaled for Lapis to not come with her. Lapis and Sarah's dog stayed outside while Sarah stayed with Eli for hours, crying.

"I am sorry, I am so sorry," she repeated.

Sarah shivered from the cold and fell asleep on the floor. An hour later, Kosey and Lapis took Sarah back to her bed. Sarah was delusional. She kept calling Eli's name throughout the night.

The next morning when Sarah woke up, she was very sick with an intense fever. She cried and screamed for Eli. Jabari came to her, but Sarah turned away from him, burying her head in the bed. He stayed in her room for a while before realizing his daughter wouldn't speak to him.

"She won't talk to anyone," Lapis told Jabari.

Jabari didn't reply; he was distraught and left.

A few days went by, Sarah didn't eat, barely slept, and wouldn't stop crying. Her fever was getting worse; she only got out of bed to see Eli in the cold room. Her father became very worried about her; he got hourly updates from Lapis. He sent for several doctors, but every time they managed to examine Sarah, they all said unanimously that she needed to sleep and eat more. Sarah still didn't let anyone approach her except for Lapis and Akil.

Sarah woke up in the middle of the night. Lapis and Akil were fast asleep; Akil stirred when Sarah got up.

"Shhh," said Sarah to Akil.

Sarah tiptoed out of the room and went to see Eli's body; he was still in the cold room.

"I am so sorry, I love you, I love you for eternity, I had chosen us, remember?" Sarah whispered.

She got up and was going back to her room when she heard Ammon and Jabari whispering to Kosey. She got closer so that she could see them. Sarah heard the conversation and understood that she had been fooled. Ammon and her own father paid Kosey to tell her that Eli had slept with Nenet. Eli hadn't slept with another woman; he would never do that. Sarah felt deeply betrayed, but at least understood what had happened. She stood there in shock and then went back into the cold room. She leaned over Eli's body.

"I am so sorry, I should have known you would never do that, I love you for eternity, you are my one true love, I will see you again."

She went back to her room and sat in front of the mirror at her vanity table. She looked at herself; she was exhausted, dark circles around her eyes. She looked at Lapis, who was sound asleep behind her. Sarah watched Lapis and Akil lovingly. She stared at herself in the mirror; she felt like Eli was there next to her, watching her. She continued to look in the mirror and saw the reflection of Eli beside her, smiling. She knew he was there, bodiless.

"I will see you next lifetime," whispered Sarah.

She walked to her bed and laid down. She pet Akil and kissed him on the head.

"You have been a good dog," whispered Sarah, before closing her eyes.

The next morning Lapis woke up and went to see Sarah. Sarah was no longer breathing; Lapis screamed. Jabari and Kosey ran into the room and saw Sarah's lifeless body. Jabari was devastated, took his dead daughter in his arms, and yelled while Kosey began to cry.

"It's my fault, I am sorry, I am sorry, it's my fault," said Kosey.

Lapis didn't understand what he was talking about and did not pay much attention to him. Everyone was completely overwhelmed by their own grief.

Sarah departed bodiless from her room, floating through the palace, and above, now looking at Thebes from the sky.

BOOK III

Twenty-one ∞ Saint-Dié-des-Vosges, France

It was midday on the 30th of January 1905 in Saint-Dié-des-Vosges in the Great-East of France. The land was expansive, with hills in the surroundings. There were two adjacent farms and no sign of any other habitat. All that could be seen was snow on the leafless trees and the ground. Everything was white. The air was freezing. The wind blew through the trees, making them dance gracefully. The sun shined, giving a beautiful glittering effect across the snow.

Bernard Durand, a tall man with brown hair, paced back and forth in front of a farmhouse wearing a warm jacket and a scarf. He smoked a cigarette with a shaky hand.

A woman inside the farmhouse screamed as she gave birth. Bernard finished his cigarette and went back into the house. The entrance led into the living room where a fire burned in the chimney, warming up the entire house. As Bernard entered, he took off his coat and scarf and hung them on the coat-hanger. He sat near the fire to warm his hands.

A minute later, he stood up and started pacing in front of the fireplace. He heard his wife scream with labor pains. He poured himself a glass of wine from a bottle on the wooden coffee table and drank it in one shot before putting the glass down. He walked towards the front door and started putting on his jacket to smoke another cigarette when he heard a baby cry; he dropped his coat and ran upstairs.

Bernard opened the door and saw his son, Eli, for the first time. His wife, Marguerite, looked ecstatic and exhausted all at once. She cried with joy. Her face was red and sweaty. Eli had brown hair and green eyes; he was a gorgeous little boy with lots of hair. Bernard looked at his son and then his wife.

"He is perfect," said Bernard.

Marguerite looked at Eli and Bernard lovingly and smiled.

Jean-Pierre Manigault was on the farm next door, sitting in front of a big fireplace quietly reading a book. His wife was yelling upstairs in agony, also giving birth. Jean-Pierre patiently read his book while he sipped a cup of chamomile tea. He looked towards the stairs when he heard his wife yell louder and then turned back to his book, reading silently.

An hour later, he heard a baby cry. He put his open book on the side-table next to his chamomile tea and calmly went upstairs. He was timid and somewhat nervous. He opened the door and saw his wife, Françoise, with a tiny girl in her arms. He sat next to Françoise on their bed. He looked at his daughter; she was beautiful, with a natural smile, very dark hair, and stunning eyes.

"She is as beautiful as you," said Jean-Pierre.

Françoise started to cry as she looked at her daughter and then her husband.

"What do you think about Sarah?" asked Françoise.
"I think it's perfect," replied Jean-Pierre.

Twenty-two ∞ Childhood

Seven years went by, the Durand and Manigault families got along exceptionally well. They had been neighboring farmers for decades. The two families were good friends; enjoying everything together. The Durand family had lots of goats and chickens, while the Manigault family had lots of cows and pigs.

Sarah and Eli were now both seven years old. The two families celebrated their children's birthdays in the Manigault house. The parents sang happy birthday to their children, and Sarah blew her candles first.

"What did you wish for?" asked Eli.

"I can't tell you; otherwise, it won't come true," replied Sarah.

Eli blew his candles and made a wish to himself. The two children looked at each other and smiled.

"Go open that door, your gift is behind it," said Jean-Pierre to Sarah as he pointed to a closet.

Sarah stood up, smiled, and wondered what could be behind the door. She opened it to discover a big box on the floor. She looked back at her parents, trying to get a hint when the box moved slightly; she squealed.

"What is it?" asked Sarah.

"Open it! You'll see," replied her parents.

Sarah opened the box and saw a Labrador puppy in it. She took him out and kissed him all over; she was enchanted.

"Thank you, thank you, I promise I will take good care of him," said Sarah.

The parents looked at Sarah lovingly.

"I am going to call you Yuki," said Sarah to her puppy.

The puppy Labrador cuddled itself into Sarah's arms, and Eli pet him on the head.

"He's going to be our best friend," said Eli.

"Yes, our best friend!" replied Sarah.

Sarah and Eli smiled at each other while they played with Yuki.

Bernard and Marguerite stood up.

"Eli, we have to go outside to see your gift," said Bernard.

"Outside?" asked Eli.

"Yes, come," replied Françoise.

Sarah held Yuki in her arms while he two families went behind the Manigault farm next to a tall, beautiful tree. There was a big white drape around a small shack, Eli couldn't discern what it was. The two men took the cover off and revealed a beautiful greenhouse. Eli was in shock; he ran to his parents and hugged them.

"Thank you!" said Eli.

They all entered the greenhouse; it was full of life. Eli looked at all the flowers and plants one after the other. He stood in front of a beautiful pink rose and whispered something to her.

"What did you say?" asked Sarah.

"I told her that she is beautiful," replied Eli.

"Oh," says Sarah, surprised.

He continued to look at the flowers and was enchanted.

"We are going back inside," said the parents as they left.

Eli and Sarah sat on the ground next to each other, Yuki was next to Sarah. Eli looked around as if he was just given a chocolate factory. Sarah looked at him and saw how happy he was; she took his hand in hers. Eli smiled at her and pet Yuki.

Sarah and Eli were best friends; they were inseparable. If you were looking for Sarah, you could be sure that she was somewhere with Eli. Sarah and Eli both had good grades at school. They woke up at 7am and were in front of the farms at 7:30 to go to school together. They stayed in school until 2pm and then went to the farms to help for a few hours before having dinner all together. Each evening after dinner, they listened to Marguerite or Françoise read a story. The children had a beautiful, free childhood. They spent their free time running in the hills, playing hide and seek, and building shacks for Yuki.

That February, Marguerite and Françoise finished cooking dinner for everyone as they did each evening. Françoise went to the front of the farm and tolled an old bell that hung next to the door. The bell was at least 200 years old, rusty, but still in excellent shape.

The children would play in the hills until they heard the bell toll.

"Dinner is ready!" said Eli, smiling.

"I wonder what we are having tonight? I am starving!" replied Sarah.

When the bell was tolled, everyone knew it was time to eat. The men and children walked back up to the house and they had a wonderful dinner together, and afterwards, Marguerite read them a story in the living room.

Saturday afternoon, on the 10th of August, the children were on the top of their usual hill. They sat in the grass surrounded by wildflowers. Yuki ran in circles around them. Eli looked at Sarah timidly.

"Sarah, will you marry me when we are older?" asked Eli.

"Yes, I will," Sarah smiled.

Eli made a ring out of a strand of grass and gave it to Sarah; she put it on. They looked at each other and smiled.

The two children continued to grow up together, spending a lot of time outside during the summer holiday, and helping at the farm daily.

On the 14th of August 1914, Sarah, Eli, and Yuki played hide and seek near the barn. Sarah decided to climb up a tall tree. She hid, waiting for Eli to come, but he didn't. Yuki stood in front of the tree and waited patiently for Sarah. Sarah, tired of waiting for Eli, decided to climb back down. She tripped and grabbed onto a thick branch to avoid falling onto her head. She hung from the tree upside down—Yuki started barking like crazy. Bernard heard Yuki and ran out of the house to find Sarah hanging from the tree, and helped her get down. Eli came running a few seconds later and saw Bernard helping Sarah.

"I am so sorry, I was hiding in the tree, and I tripped," said Sarah.

Bernard hugged his daughter as he got over his fright.

"You must be careful, that's a tall tree," said Bernard.

They all went to the kitchen, and Bernard prepared a hot chocolate for the children.

"You are a good boy Yuki," said Bernard to the dog.

Sarah kneeled down in front of Yuki and kissed him on the nose.

"You saved my life Yuki," said Sarah, hugging him.

They forgot the mishap and had dinner. Sarah discreetly gave Yuki pieces of food under her chair without being seen by her parents; Eli saw her, but of course, didn't say anything.

The next morning Sarah, Eli, and Yuki went to the barn to play. They climbed to the mezzanine in the barn; they were right below the roof. They usually didn't go up there because the ladder was dangerous to climb. Sarah and Eli sat next to each other, and Sarah looked at the boxes.

"I wonder what all these boxes are?" asked Sarah.

"Let's look inside," said Eli.

"But Papa always says we shouldn't come up here," replied Sarah.

"I think it's because we were too young," said Eli.

They opened the first dusty box together and saw a lot of old letters and ancient toys. Sarah felt guilty as she realized they were going through her parents' belongings.

"I think we should go back down," said Sarah.

"Let's just open one more?" asked Eli.

"Fine."

She opened the second box and saw the French flag and a small rectangular box with decorations; she opened the box and pulled out a rusty knife; it looked like an old hunting knife. Her father's initials were engraved into the spine of the blade. Sarah pulled it out and looked at it.

"Put it down!!" yelled Eli.

"What is wrong with you? It's just an old knife, you're the one who said to open another box," said Sarah.

"Just put it away! I am leaving!" yelled Eli.

Yuki heard the children quarrel and started to whine.

"Fine, I am putting it away; why are you acting so weird?" said Sarah.

"I don't like knives, okay?!"

He hurried down the ladder, almost fell, while Sarah put the knife back in the box and closed it. Eli sat on the floor next to Yuki; he was reticent. Sarah came down the ladder and sat next to him.

"I didn't want to upset you," said Sarah.

"I know, I'm sorry, I just... I just... I don't know... I don't like it, that's all," said Eli, quietly.

"Should we go to the hill?" said Sarah.

"Okay," replied Eli.

"Catch me if you can!" said Sarah as she ran off with Yuki.

Twenty-three ∞ World War I

It was the 18th of August, 1914. The two families were in front of the fireplace in the Manigault farm; they listened to a story read by Françoise. The children and Yuki sat on the floor near the fireplace when Yuki started barking.

All of a sudden, loud banging sounded on the front door. Bernard and Jean-Pierre got up, surprised by the noise. They opened the front door and saw sixteen German soldiers standing there with rifles. Bernard and Jean-Pierre were horrified; the mothers screamed and took their children in their arms. General Wagner, the German general in command, stood in front of the soldiers.

"We are at war! We are taking over the house," said General Wagner.

Jean-Pierre started to tremble and fell to the floor.

"Get him up before I decide to shoot him!" said General Wagner firmly.

Bernard quickly helped Jean-Pierre up and took him towards the living room.

"You can sleep in the attic. My men will be staying on the farm. The women can do the washing, the cooking, and the men and children will help at the farm to ensure that my men have enough food," said Wagner.

"Yes," said Bernard, more composed.

"You are lucky I don't just shoot you," said Wagner.

The children were petrified and trembled with fear; the life they knew was about to come to an end. General Wagner saw Yuki and pointed his gun towards the dog.

"No!" said Sarah standing in front of her dog.

General Wagner admired the courage of this little girl.

"He better not be a nuisance; if I hear one peep, I will shoot him!"

"Yes," said Sarah, with tears in her eyes.

The German soldiers entered the house, not respecting the place at all. One of the soldiers knocked down a vase with his bag; Françoise rushed to clean up the broken vase. While she cleaned, a piece of porcelain cut her thumb, Jean-Pierre saw this and went towards her to help her.

"Leave her!" yelled Schmidt, another soldier.

Françoise finished cleaning up the broken vase, blood dripped on the pieces of porcelain, making a mess. The group of soldiers gathered in front of the fireplace.

"Now, go!" said General Wagner, "You!" Pointing towards Bernard, "Show me where the food and wine is."

"Yes," replied Bernard.

Bernard was walking towards the kitchen when Schmidt pushed him from behind, nearly falling down. The Germans laughed at him.

"Quiet now," said Wagner.

The soldiers instantly cut the laughter. They got to the kitchen, and Bernard showed Wagner where the food and drinks were.

"Good. Make sure your family stays out of my men's way, no funny business," said Wagner.

"Yes," replied Bernard.

"You can go now," said Wagner.

He turned and went to the living room to join the others.

The two families went upstairs. As Françoise arrived on the second floor, she opened a closet and quietly took out blankets before continuing to the attic. The attic was an organized mess, an old bed frame, torn up mattresses to the right and a pile of old furniture to the left.

Marguerite started to cry.

"What will we do?" she sobbed.

"We must stay strong and work together," said Jean-Pierre.

"I didn't believe Julien when he said the war was coming," said Françoise.

"None of us believed it. We must do the best we can. If we do as General Wagner says, he probably won't kill us," said Bernard.

"I hope you are right," said Marguerite.

Eli and Sarah were surprisingly strong under the circumstances.

"We should get some sleep," said Marguerite.

They set up the mattresses on the floor.

"Eli and Sarah, you should sleep on the bed," said Françoise.

The children and Yuki went on the bed while the parents laid on separate mattresses on the floor. The parents whispered to each other while the children looked at the stars. Yuki cuddled beside Sarah, and everyone fell asleep.

The next morning the families were awakened by a gunshot. They jumped out of bed; Eli looked outside the window and saw a German soldier shooting into cans and laughing. He was drunk.

The families went downstairs. General Wagner and Schmidt were sitting in the kitchen. Françoise and Marguerite started making coffee.

"Get me some eggs, Sarah," said Françoise.

"I'll go help her," said Eli.

The children left the house. Bernard and Jean-Pierre stood in front of General Wagner, waiting for orders.

"You will continue to manage the farm and provide us with food, but if you do anything suspicious, you will be shot at once," said Wagner.

"Yes," says Bernard.

The two men left and went to work at the farm. Marguerite and Françoise prepared breakfast, while Schmidt looked at Françoise with a flirtatious smile.

The children came back with a basket of eggs and handed it to Françoise.

"You may eat once we leave. A few soldiers will stay here on guard," said Wagner.

"Thank you," replied Françoise.

"The children should help on the farm," ordered Wagner.

"Yes," said Marguerite.

The children left the house with Yuki to meet up with their fathers. There were more soldiers outside.

"Papa, what do you want us to do?" asked Eli.

"Why don't you both go milk the cows?" replied Bernard.

"Okay."

The children went to milk the cows, Yuki followed behind them. The children were working when Eli broke the silence.

"We have to do something," whispered Eli.

"What do you mean?" asked Sarah.

"We have to fight back."

"I don't know how we can do that..."

"The French will come to save us, I am sure."

"Yes."

Weeks went by, the situation got worse and worse. The children and parents were exhausted with their daily farm work on top of caring for the German soldiers.

It was the 19th of October 1914; Schmidt ran out of the house yelling in German.

"What are you doing?!" yelled Schmidt.

Bernard was feeding the pigs, he didn't understand why Schmidt was upset.

"What are you doing?!!" yelled Schmidt.

"I'm feeding the pigs," replied Bernard.

Schmidt motioned to Bernard to follow him, and they went into the barn. Schmidt started beating Bernard with a stick; Eli heard something and walked to the barn just as Schmidt left. He ran to his father on the ground bleeding.

"I will bring you inside; you will be all right, Papa," said Eli worried.

Bernard had a wide bruise across his face; he could hardly get up. Eli helped his father to the house; Marguerite saw her husband limping and rushed towards him. Françoise gasped when she saw Bernard. Marguerite signaled to Françoise to stay in the kitchen in case a soldier came asking for something. Eli and Marguerite took Bernard to the attic and put him on the bed. Marguerite cleaned Bernard's wound.

"Go back to work, if someone sees that we are all missing, things will get much worse," said Marguerite.

Eli ran back outside and caught up with Sarah, who was gathering eggs.

"Schmidt beat my father," said Eli angrily.

"What?! What happened? Is he all right?" replied Sarah.

"Mama is taking care of him, he'll be okay. I think Schmidt is the worst of them all."

"Yes..."

"We need to find a way to get out of here," said Eli.

"But there are soldiers everywhere."

"We will find a way. We have to."

Months went by, the winter was crude, the food supply diminished quickly. The two families worked more and more caring for new soldiers that arrived daily. The two farms were crammed with men. The children hid cheese and meat in a spot in the attic, and the families ate it at night when the Germans were asleep.

Spring arrived, there were leaves on the trees, and an abundance of vegetables began to sprout out of the ground. The German soldiers had curbed their aggression; things became tolerable.

General Wagner was suddenly called to Germany for an emergency. He left the farm abruptly, leaving Schmidt in charge.

A few months went by. There were rumors that people from the village were dying of malnutrition and disease daily. The tension at the family farms once again became unbearable. Schmidt did everything he could to make things harder for the families. He started their work at five in the morning and pushed them to work until midnight. The families were worn out and sleep-deprived; Jean-Pierre grew incredibly weak.

It was the 2nd of September 1915, late morning, Schmidt called a general meeting on the town square.

He was assigning labor jobs to the villagers. Schmidt had a list with names and called out at random.

"Fabien Danton, Sandrine Dupont, Jeremy Sanglin, Melanie Dufour, Fabienne Casteuil, Caroline Dupuis, Paul François, Victor Leblanc, Louis Charpentier. You will work in a German camp. These soldiers will take you there at once."

A small 11-year-old boy stood shivering; his name was called on the list.

"But, he is only eleven years old, please," pleaded his mother.

A soldier came towards her and grabbed her son out of her arms.

"Please, I am begging you," she said.

Bernard watched from the back of the group; the mother held onto her child with all her strength.

"Sir," Bernard called out.

Schmidt immediately drew his gun and shot Bernard in the abdomen, Bernard fell to the ground with a thump. The people of the village started screaming. The little boy was ripped out of his mother's arms and thrown onto the truck along with the others. Marguerite cried, Eli took her in his arms to prevent her from seeing Bernard's now lifeless body.

"That's enough!" yelled Schmidt.

Two German soldiers yelled at the villagers, threatening to shoot. The crowd quieted down, terrified. Schmidt finished with his orders, naming many more people to leave for the German labor camps. There was mass confusion in the town square as families were ripped apart. Marguerite trembled and cried, Françoise tried to reassure her. Eli went towards his father to see if he was still breathing; as he got close to his father, a German soldier smacked Eli away.

"Don't touch him!" said the soldier.

Eli looked up at the soldier with a hatred he had never felt before. Eli, Marguerite, Françoise, Sarah, and Jean-Pierre got pushed back by several soldiers, preventing them from approaching Bernard.

"Get back to work!" yelled Schmidt.

The villagers started to disperse from the town square. Eli, his mother, and Sarah's family walked back to the farm, directed by Germans; Eli looked back, trying to get one last look at his father.

They returned to the farm. Jean-Pierre and Eli were in the barn getting ready to kill a pig for food. The women worked in the kitchen. Sarah scrubbed the floor in the entrance with Françoise while Marguerite cooked. Marguerite cried while she worked; Schmidt stood in the kitchen doorway observing her.

"Why are you crying?" said Schmidt softly.

She didn't dare reply, but he insisted.

"Why are you crying? Tell me," said Schmidt.

"My husband," replied Marguerite, uncontrollably sobbing.

Schmidt laughed.

"Now, you can be mine," he whispered.

She was horrified by the thought and started shaking uncontrollably as she washed the potatoes. He grabbed her ass and got closer; she didn't say anything and walked further into the kitchen to get vegetables from the walk-in fridge. He followed her. She looked back and saw that he was following her; she was terrified and speechless. Schmidt entered the walk-in fridge, menacingly.

"Help," whispered Marguerite.

Suddenly, a loud siren went off. The Germans started to make noise outside. Schmidt left the walk-in fridge but stopped abruptly-

"You got lucky this time, but I'll be back for you," he smiled.

Marguerite fell to the floor, trembling.

The French Army was attacking a village nearby, and all the German soldiers were called to fight. Only four German soldiers stayed behind; the families were relieved to see soldiers leaving.

The families continued their work and kept to themselves as much as they could. Some of the soldiers never came back, while others returned wounded. Schmidt didn't come back, and Marguerite was grateful. The women took care of the wounded on top of the cooking and cleaning. Sarah helped with the injured soldiers; Sarah had a very delicate hand when it came to sewing the wounds.

Eli and Jean-Pierre were left alone to care for the farm. They were exhausted by the workload. They came home late at night when the others were already sleeping in the attic.

Months went by, and the winter was harsh. There were more and more wounded German soldiers returning from battle. The women were completely overwhelmed by the number of soldiers they needed to care for. Despite the difficult situation, Sarah was learning to be a nurse. She was extremely busy, which prevented her from overthinking about their situation.

The war continued; it felt as if it would never end. Winters were challenging because there was less food and the soldiers tended to stay indoors and get drunk.

One evening, on the 19th of February 1916, General Wagner came back to the farm, holding a cane. He limped into the kitchen and saw Marguerite. To her surprise, she was reassured to see him; she went towards him to help him sit down.

"Thank you," said Wagner.

"I will get you a cup of hot chocolate," said Marguerite.

She went to the stove and prepared a hot chocolate. General Wagner looked older and damaged by the war.

"What a terrible war, all this suffering for land, it's hard to understand," said Wagner, quietly.

Marguerite was surprised by his comment.

"Yes," she said.

"Where is Françoise?" asked Wagner.

"She is helping the wounded soldiers."

"Ah, yes, of course."

Eli walked into the kitchen; he shook from the bitter cold. Marguerite looked down at his hands; they were a muted blue.

"Come here, let me get you something warm," said Marguerite.

Eli saw that General Wagner was sitting there and stopped abruptly.

"It's okay, boy... You should listen to your mother," said Wagner.

"Thank you," replied Eli.

Eli, still shaking from the cold, moved towards his mother.

"Here, I have some hot soup, this will warm you up," said Marguerite.

Eli sat in the kitchen and quietly drank his soup, warming up while Wagner observed. Eli finished his soup and got up.

"Take this to Jean-Pierre," said Marguerite, handing him a bowl of soup.

"Thank you, Mama," said Eli.

He nodded to General Wagner as he left the kitchen. Marguerite continued preparing the food.

"I have a son about his age," said Wagner.

"Yes?" replied Marguerite.

"He is a good boy, he is very good with clocks," said Wagner.

"Yes. Children are incredible. Eli loves working with plants; we gave him a greenhouse a few years ago," said Marguerite.

"It's reassuring for us parents to see our children take an interest in things."

"Yes."

"I will see you tomorrow," said Wagner as he pulled himself up with his cane.

"Yes."

Sarah and Françoise cared for a wounded soldier on the second floor; he screamed in pain. Françoise held the soldier down with another man while Sarah amputated his leg. There was blood everywhere; Sarah had a difficult time keeping her poise. The soldier went unconscious and the screaming stopped. Sarah finished removing the limb, and Françoise helped her stop the bleeding.

Sarah, exhausted, went to the kitchen to sit down in silence for a moment.

"I have hot soup, would you like some?" asked Marguerite.

"No, I am not hungry," replied Sarah.

"Hot chocolate?" said Marguerite.

"Yes," said Sarah with a weak smile.

The next morning at 5am, more wounded soldiers arrived at the house. Sarah and Eli stayed asleep with Yuki next to them.

Françoise got up and quietly left the attic.

Twenty-four ∞ General Wagner

Françoise made her way down the stairs. When she reached the first floor, she stopped in her tracks. Schmidt stood there with six other soldiers.

"Where are the rest of you?" yelled Schmidt.

"They are upstairs," replied Françoise, nervously.

"Go get them!" he yelled.

"Yes, right away," said Françoise.

"My men are hungry!"

Françoise hurried upstairs and woke up the family. Sarah was so tired she could barely stand while Jean-Pierre looked very frail. Eli grabbed Jean-Pierre by the arm and headed to the barn. Marguerite went to the kitchen. Françoise and Sarah took care of the soldiers in the living room.

"Get me some wine," Schmidt barked at Sarah.

"There is none left," replied Sarah.

"What?!" yelled Schmidt.

Schmidt got up furiously and went to the kitchen, followed by another soldier. He stood in the kitchen, looking at Marguerite; she looked up and saw him. The last time they were in the kitchen, he was attempting to have his way with her after murdering her husband. She stopped, petrified by these memories.

He smiled at her.

"I want some wine," said Schmidt.

"I... I am sorry, there is none left," replied Marguerite.

He got closer to her, still smiling.

"Well then, maybe I can have a piece of you," said Schmidt.

He looked towards the other soldier.

"Watch the entrance, no one is to enter," ordered Schmidt.

The soldier went outside the kitchen and guarded the door; Marguerite began to shake.

"Please," said Marguerite.

"Come here."

Marguerite backed away further into the kitchen. She was reliving the nightmare from before. He moved in on her like a fox after a chicken. She moved back; he got closer, then slapped her across the face. She fell to the floor, knocking down pots with her. Schmidt got on top of her and ripped her dress apart. Marguerite screamed and fought back. General Wagner walked in at that moment.

"Get off her!" yelled Wagner.

Schmidt violently hit her and pulled at her clothes; he wouldn't stop. General Wagner took out his gun and shot Schmidt between the shoulder blades. Marguerite dragged herself out from under his limp body, crying. Wagner went towards Marguerite and helped her up, covering her at the same time; she was in a state of shock.

"It's all right... It's finished," said Wagner.

"Thank you," replied Marguerite in a trembling voice.

General Wagner touched Schmidt's pulse, he was no longer breathing, and left the kitchen, furious. He went to the living room where Sarah and Françoise helped with the wounded.

"Help Marguerite upstairs, please," Wagner said to Sarah.

"Yes, Sir," replied Sarah.

Sarah went to the kitchen, Yuki followed behind her. She saw Marguerite shivering in the corner and helped her upstairs and into bed. Marguerite fell asleep immediately.

Sarah returned to the living room to continue helping the injured. Françoise was shakily sewing a soldier's arm. Wagner observed from a seat against the wall.

"Let me do it," Sarah said to Françoise.

Françoise was relieved.

"I will go to the kitchen," said Françoise.

"Yes," replied Sarah.

Wagner noticed that Sarah had become an expert in taking care of the wounded.

Months went by. Under Wagner's control, the German soldiers became more respectful to the French families. Sarah and Françoise continued to care for the wounded soldiers while Marguerite took care of the meals. Jean-Pierre and Eli took care of the animals and the farm. General Wagner allowed the French families to work less and sleep more. When summer arrived, there was an abundance of food once again.

One warm evening, on the 21st of September, 1916, General Wagner and the French families had supper in the kitchen. There was a pleasant breeze that blew through the opened windows. Sarah and Eli looked plum and happy, no longer famished and exhausted. Yuki relaxed under the table. They enjoyed dinner together.

Suddenly a loud noise came from outside–a motorized vehicle driving towards the farm. Soldiers yelled in German. Wagner stood up to go towards the entrance when a higher-ranked German named General Hauler entered with several soldiers behind him. He looked stern. General Wagner saluted General Hauler. Wagner knew of General Hauler's reputation and was instantly frightened for the French families.

"You have been called back to Germany, you will leave in the morning, I will be taking over this section," said Hauler.

"Yes, Sir," saluted Wagner.

The families quickly cleaned up in the kitchen before General Hauler had time to enter. He walked into the kitchen, not saying a word, observing these French farmers.

"What are you waiting for? Get my men some food," said Hauler.

Marguerite, Sarah, and Françoise quickly took out the pork and cooked vegetables. Eli and Jean-Pierre stood in the middle of the kitchen, not moving.

"What are men doing in the kitchen? Get back to work!" yelled Hauler.

Jean-Pierre and Eli hurried out of the kitchen while six of General Hauler's soldiers entered. A soldier stopped Jean-Pierre and Eli.

"Where are you going?!" said the soldier.

"We are going to work at the farm, Sir," replied Eli.

"No bullshit," said the soldier.

"Yes, Sir," said Jean-Pierre.

Eli and Jean-Pierre got to the barn and fed the cows.

"This guy looks worse than Schmidt. There must be something we can do to get rid of him, maybe we can talk to General Wagner?" said Eli.

"I don't know, I don't see much we can do but to hope for the war to be over," said Jean-Pierre.

"I heard that there is a group of resistance," said Eli quietly.

"It's too dangerous," replied Jean-Pierre.

"I want to help," said Eli.

"If something were to happen to you, your mother would not forgive me. We don't know anything about this resistance, we don't even know how to contact them," said Jean-Pierre.

"I could find out," replied Eli.

"We need to get back to work, don't say another word of this, you will get us all killed," said Jean-Pierre.

Eli didn't say anything and continued to feed the cows; he felt helpless.

Eli and Jean-Pierre finished in the barn and went back to the house. As they entered, they heard the soldiers singing, drunk and quietly went upstairs. They opened the attic door to see Françoise, Marguerite, and Sarah, whispering with General Wagner.

"You must be very careful with General Hauler; he has a nasty reputation, he has killed babies in front of their mothers," said Wagner.

Eli and Jean-Pierre were shocked to see Wagner in the attic.

"I will leave tomorrow at dawn; it will get mad here," said Wagner.

"We must leave," said Eli.

"The entire region is surrounded by German soldiers; if you get caught, you will be killed at once," replied Wagner.

"There is nothing we can do then?" asked Eli.

"I fear not," replied Wagner.

General Wagner took a gun out of his jacket and handed it to Jean-Pierre.

"Take this, you will need it," said Wagner.

Jean-Pierre looked at the gun and then at Wagner.

"Thank you," said Jean-Pierre.

"I must leave now, I hope we will see each other again one day."

Wagner got up and walked out, leaving the family alone in the dark.

Twenty-five ∞ General Hauler

The next morning things changed rapidly. The German soldiers were drunk and disrespectful to the three women. The families worked harder than ever. Sarah and Françoise took care of the wounded, Marguerite cooked and cleaned, and the men worked very long hours at the farm.

One evening, in January 1917, twelve wounded men came back from battle. Sarah, Françoise, and Marguerite tended to them. The farm was once again packed with Germans.

General Hauler entered the living room where the women tended to his wounded soldiers.

"I need more room for my men," said Hauler.

Sarah cleaned a wound on one of his men.

"There is no more room," said Sarah without realizing who she was speaking to.

General Hauler took his rifle and stabbed Sarah in the back with his bayonet. She started bleeding. Françoise and Marguerite pleaded to General Hauler.

"Please, we will find room," said Françoise.

Sarah proudly continued to tend to the soldier despite being in terrible pain.

"Put them in the attic, you go to the barn with the animals," said Hauler.

"Yes, Sir," replied Marguerite.

"The next time you disoblige me, it will be death," said Hauler looking at Sarah.

Sarah nodded and General Hauler left.

Eli and Jean-Pierre came into the house a few hours later and went to the attic; Françoise got their belongings and put the gun in her dress pocket.

"We will stay in the barn from now on," said Françoise.

"But it's freezing there," replied Jean-Pierre.

"I know," said Françoise.

Jean-Pierre helped Françoise take their things to the barn. Françoise hid a few wool blankets in a bag and hoped that no one would stop her on her way to the barn. She managed to get to the barn where Sarah, Eli, Marguerite, and Jean-Pierre were waiting. Sarah laid on the floor; wounded. Marguerite cleaned Sarah's wound when Françoise arrived and took over. She took out a needle and thread and looked at the wound. It seemed rather deep but hadn't damaged any organs.

"Don't move," said Françoise.

Sarah was in so much pain; she couldn't think straight anymore. Eli held her hand tightly.

"You will be fine," said Eli.

Françoise started sewing up the cut. Sarah tried to keep quiet for fear of the Germans. Françoise finished and dabbed alcohol on the wound. Sarah laid on her stomach and closed her eyes, trying to escape to a new world. Jean-Pierre and Eli carried her to a haystack and laid her down. They used the blankets Françoise took from the attic and slept tightly together to keep warm. The cows and pigs made noise during the night, waking Eli up, making him think it was the Germans.

The winter was more brutal than ever. Jean-Pierre had a cold; he coughed most of the time. Françoise worried about him when she looked just as frail. Sarah continued to tend to the wounded soldiers with Françoise. Marguerite spent all her time in the kitchen alone, cooking.

One Morning, General Hauler entered the kitchen to get coffee.

"Here you go, Sir," said Marguerite, handing him a mug.

General Hauler slapped Marguerite in the face spilling the coffee on the floor.

"I didn't speak to you!" said Hauler.

Marguerite shook herself back, not saying anything. General Hauler took a cup of coffee himself.

"Were you never told to only speak when you are spoken to?" said Hauler firmly.

Marguerite didn't know if she could reply to him, she nodded.

"Did you hear me?!" yelled Hauler.

"Yes, Sir," said Marguerite.

"These French pigs!" mumbled Hauler as he left the kitchen.

A few very tough months went by. The families had their routines and stayed out of *trouble* to the best of their abilities.

Spring arrived, there was more food, but life wasn't any better for the families. The families continued to struggle but were happy to be in the barn to avoid the Germans during the nights. They had a few moments of peace.

The warm days went by quickly. The farms were flooded with injured Germans, some soldiers stayed in the living room. Sarah was overwhelmed by the amount of work she had, but Françoise helped her; they made a good team.

Twenty-six ∞ Françoise

On the 24th of October 1917, two German soldiers came into the house utterly drunk. Jean-Pierre and Françoise were leaving the kitchen when one of the German soldiers grabbed Françoise, pulling on her dress. Jean-Pierre got between them. Françoise knew how it would end for Jean-Pierre if he intervened. The German soldier was very drunk, and looked decided on molesting her; Françoise looked at Jean-Pierre.

"Go, I will be fine, you should go, I will see you soon," whispered Françoise.

"I can't," replied Jean-Pierre.

"Please, go, I love you," said Françoise.

She was prepared to get raped to keep her husband safe. Jean-Pierre tried to control himself from hitting the soldier, but the other soldier had a gun drawn at him. Jean-Pierre could do nothing but get killed; he went to the barn with tears running down his face, completely emasculated.

Once in the barn, he and the rest of the family heard Françoise scream from the house.

"I can't do this," said Eli.

"You will stay here, or we will all get killed if you go," replied Jean-Pierre.

Françoise came to the barn half an hour later. At the entrance of the barn, she fell to the ground. Jean-Pierre ran to her, picked her up, and laid her in the hay. He laid next to her, holding her tightly. Françoise was numb and bruised while Jean-Pierre had tears in his eyes. They fell asleep, cuddled together.

The next morning when they woke up, Françoise was sick; she had a very high fever and was delusional. Sarah covered her up with all the blankets they had.

"Bring her hot soup," Sarah told Marguerite.

Marguerite went to the kitchen and discreetly came back to the barn with a bowl of soup. Jean-Pierre looked at his wife in despair.

"Workers!" yelled Hauler.

Sarah helped the new soldiers who had just arrived, and Jean-Pierre and Eli went to the farm.

Jean-Pierre was in a rage; he didn't know what to do to help his wife. Throughout the day, Eli and Jean-Pierre took turns to check up on Françoise. She was not doing better; her fever was still very high.

Sarah helped with the wounded German soldiers all day. She discreetly went through all the medical supplies looking for anything that could help her mother but found nothing.

Sarah, Marguerite, Jean-Pierre, and Eli sat in front of Françoise.

"We need to get some aspirin from Madame Dussault, she always has some, she is our last hope, we have to get her fever down," said Jean-Pierre.

"It's very dangerous, but I think it could work," replied Marguerite.

"We will go together, it will be easier," said Eli.

"You both be very careful, okay?" said Marguerite anxiously.

Sarah hugged Eli and Jean-Pierre before they left.

The night excursion was challenging; they went through the village hiding behind hedges, buildings, and trees, making sure they were not seen. They arrived at Madame Dussault's house and quietly knocked on the backdoor. An old lady opened, she had a very kind look to her. When she saw who it was, she let them in quickly.

"What are you doing? It's very dangerous to walk in the streets at night," said Madame Dussault.

"Françoise has a very high fever, I was hoping you had some aspirin?" said Jean-Pierre impatiently.

Madame Dussault looked at Jean-Pierre, who was entirely in despair.

"Come this way," said Madame Dussault.

They followed.

"Help me lift out this plank," said Madame Dussault.

They lifted a plank and saw boxes of aspirin and a handgun.

"Take a pack, and give her 4 tablets as soon as you get back," said Madame Dussault.

Eli saw the gun and looked at Madame Dussault.

"Where did you get the gun?" asked Eli.

"One of my good friends gave it to me, the time will come, the time will come," replied Madame Dussault.

Jean-Pierre put the aspirin in his coat jacket.

"Thank you very much, we are very grateful for your help."

"Of course, be careful on the main street, there are often soldiers on the Westside."

"Thank you," said Eli, wondering how she knew these things.

They left Madame Dussault's house being prudent not to make any noise. They walked through the village again, using small streets. They got very close to the forest when they heard Germans speaking and stopped abruptly. The Germans stayed there talking and laughing, Eli and Jean-Pierre waited for a few minutes. The Germans were not leaving. They decided to get to the forest from behind the street they were hiding in. They were very quiet and went to the end of the road, over a small brick wall and into the forest. They went through the woods being very careful; many soldiers were in the woods, especially at night. They could finally see the farm. They were very close to the farm when they saw General Hauler smoking a cigarette outside. They waited a few minutes; Hauler stayed there and lit up another. They decided to get to the barn from the other side of the farm. They walked through the woods in front of the farm until they got close to the barn. They now needed to walk across the farm to get behind it. There was no one in sight. They quietly passed, finally arriving behind the farm; no one was there. They quickly got to the back door of the barn.

Sarah and Marguerite were startled by their entrance but were profusely crying. Jean-Pierre was perplexed; he got closer to Françoise and saw that she was no longer breathing. Jean-Pierre took his wife into his arms.

"I am so sorry, I am so sorry, I should have, I should have, I am sorry," said Jean-Pierre.

He cried. Sarah tried to comfort her dad by taking him in her arms. He looked at his wife and touched her face.

"You are so beautiful," said Jean-Pierre.

Sarah cried, and Eli took her in his arms. Jean-Pierre laid down next to his cold wife, holding her tightly. He fell asleep in total despair.

A few hours later, Jean-Pierre woke up in the middle of the night. The others heard him and woke up as well. Jean-Pierre's eyes were bright red.

"We have to bury her, Papa," said Sarah.

"Yes, I know," replied Jean-Pierre.

The four of them wrapped Françoise in a blanket and took her behind the barn.

"We will bury her here, next to this beautiful tree she loved so much," said Jean-Pierre.

They started to dig a hole in the ground next to the tree. It was pitch black; they could barely discern where they were digging.

An hour and a half later, they had finally dug a big enough hole. They gently put Françoise in the ground. Jean-Pierre touched his wife's body wrapped in a blanket one last time before placing dirt on her. Françoise was now fully buried.

"Thank you, my love, for the wonderful years you have brought me, I will never forget you, rest in peace," said Jean-Pierre.

"I love you, Mama, rest in peace," said Sarah, crying softly.

"I love you, Françoise, you were like a second mother to me, rest in peace," said Eli.

"Goodbye, my friend, we will never forget you, we love you, you will live in our hearts forever, rest in peace," said Marguerite.

Daylight began to appear. They shivered from the cold and grief. They heard noises coming from the farm; the soldiers were getting up. Sarah, Eli, and Marguerite went inside the barn while Jean-Pierre stood there for a minute, looking where his wife was buried.

"Goodbye, my love, I will see you on the other side."

Twenty-seven ∞ Friend returns

Another day of work began. Sarah helped the wounded soldiers this time alone. Marguerite went to the kitchen and prepared breakfast. Jean-Pierre and Eli worked in the barn with the animals.

Weeks went by, the winter was colder than usual. Jean-Pierre had lost all hope; he got on with life, living it as if he were no longer there. He couldn't bear the thought of his wife being raped and then dying so suddenly. He regretted not intervening that night and wondered if things would have been different. The terrible events had hardened Sarah and Eli's characters. They behaved like adults, even though they were children.

Marguerite was in the kitchen by herself most of the day. Sometimes she got the unpleasant surprise of General Hauler. This morning was one of those mornings. Hauler entered the kitchen silently; he looked drunk.

"So what are you cooking for us today?" said Hauler, smiling calmly.

"Some pork with potatoes," replied Marguerite.

"Pork?! You think I am a pig?!" said Hauler.

"No, Sir, I said we will have pork for lunch," said Marguerite.

He started laughing hysterically. It looked like he completely lost his mind. He tripped and fell to the floor and continued laughing; Marguerite went to help him up.

"Don't touch me!" said Hauler, loudly.

Marguerite distanced herself from him; he started laughing even louder.

"You are scared of me, aren't you?" said Hauler.

"No, Sir," replied Marguerite.

He got up abruptly and held her jaw firmly in his right hand; Marguerite was in pain but didn't say anything.

"You should!" said General Hauler.

He let go of her jaw. Eli entered the kitchen.

"You! I will squash you like a worm!" said Hauler as he slapped Eli in the face.

Hauler walked away, laughing.

The soldiers got ready for battle. Gunshots could be heard in the distance. The house emptied out, aside from the wounded. Sarah was swamped with work.

Marguerite went to the barn to see Jean-Pierre and Eli, they were milking the cows. Yuki was next to Eli.

"Eli, could you help Sarah for a bit? She hasn't stopped for a second since this morning," asked Marguerite.

"Yes, of course," replied Eli, "Yuki, stay here."

They left Jean-Pierre with Yuki; he had become a taciturn man; Eli was worried about him. Marguerite and Eli walked back to the house together.

"Do you think he will be all right on his own?" asked Eli.

"Yes, he'll be fine, Yuki will keep him company," replied Marguerite.

They arrived back at the house to find Sarah in the living room, with blood smeared all over her clothes and bloodstains on her face and hair. Eli looked at her, realizing what she was dealing with throughout the day. He admired her for a moment, observing her courage and poise.

"Tell me what to do," said Eli.

"You can put a bandage on this man," replied Sarah pointing to a soldier on her right.

"Go get some food," said Eli.

"I can't, I need to sew this soldier's leg first," replied Sarah pointing to the left.

"If you don't get some food, you won't be able to help anyone, I'll be fine, get some food," said Eli, insisting.

Sarah looked at Eli, realizing that he was right.

"Okay," said Sarah.

Sarah could barely stand up because she had been sitting for such a long time in the same position; Eli helped her up.

Sarah went to the kitchen and sat down next to Marguerite. Marguerite put a plate of pork and potatoes and a cup of hot tea in front of where she sat. Sarah gazed in the distance for a moment and then burst into tears.

"I miss her so much," said Sarah.

"I know, honey," replied Marguerite as she took her in her arms.

"I can't do this anymore, we have to leave, or we will all die."

"Get some food, it will give you some strength."

Sarah ate, she looked at Marguerite and smiled for the first time in weeks.

"This is so good," said Sarah.

"Thank you," replied Marguerite, smiling at Sarah.

Marguerite could tell that Sarah didn't want her to worry. Sarah finished her meal, toughened up, and went back to the living room to tend to the soldiers. Sarah and Eli worked together; Eli helped Sarah hold the soldiers while she sewed. The sound of bombs went off in the distance.

A few hours later, new wounded soldiers came to the house. General Hauler was one of them. He had been shot in the stomach. He was carried by two soldiers; they rushed him into the living room.

"Hurry up, help him now," screamed a soldier.

Sarah dropped what she was doing and took care of Hauler, who bled profusely. She cleaned the wound and could see that an organ had been hit. She sew him up but knew he wouldn't make it through the night. When she was finished, the two men carried General Hauler in front of the fireplace.

She tended to the other wounded soldiers with Eli's help. A few hours later, all the injured soldiers had been cared for.

It was two in the morning; Eli and Sarah went to the kitchen to get food. They found a warm soup with vegetables and ate it up quickly, hoping that no one would enter the kitchen.

They finally got to the barn, Marguerite and Jean-Pierre were already asleep. Yuki heard them arrive and wagged his tail. They cuddled up next to each other and fell asleep instantly.

The next morning Eli woke up before the others and woke Marguerite up.

"I think we should let them sleep, Mama," said Eli, whispering.

"Yes," replied Marguerite.

They left the barn and went to the house. Marguerite went straight to the kitchen, and Eli went to the living room to help the wounded. He went to see Hauler and found that he was no longer breathing.

"Hauler didn't make it," said Eli.

"Well... Fine..." replied Marguerite, not daring to speak her mind.

Jean-Pierre woke up a few hours later; he felt rested. He started to tend to the animals in the barn.

A few minutes later, Sarah woke up, she looked much better; Yuki was cuddled next to her, keeping her warm. Sarah looked at Yuki and smiled at him while petting him.

"You are so loyal, but you must stay here with Jean-Pierre, I don't want anything to happen to you," said Sarah.

Yuki, as always, obeyed Sarah. Sarah went towards the house, as she walked there, she saw a lot of soldiers wandering about. Some soldiers played card games, others smoked cigarettes pacing in front of the house. She didn't know what to think. She went inside the kitchen and saw Marguerite, who was in a better mood.

"What's happening?" asked Sarah.

"General Hauler died last night, I think they don't have a chief anymore," said Marguerite.

Sarah's tension came down; she was relieved and smiled. She had a hot chocolate with some bread and butter and then went to the living room. Eli was there tending to the soldiers. Sarah observed him for a few moments, thinking how well he was managing. Eli had already removed Hauler's dead body.

A few months went by, many of the remaining soldiers were now fully healed. About thirty soldiers died, and there were twenty soldiers left on the farm. They hadn't gone to battle since General Hauler died. The soldiers had come to appreciate Sarah and felt indebted to her for saving their lives. For the most part, they were kind to the French families.

On the 13th of March 1918, General Wagner returned to the farm. Marguerite saw him from the kitchen window and went to greet him.

"General Wagner, you have come back," said Marguerite joyfully.

"Hello Marguerite, yes, they found out that General Hauler had been killed in battle and sent me to replace him," replied Wagner smiling.

"Yes, Sarah did tend to him, but he didn't make it," said Marguerite.

"Where are the children?" asked Wagner, worried by Marguerite's possible response.

"They are fine; they are probably in the barn helping Jean-Pierre," replied Marguerite.

"Oh, good," said Wagner, relieved.

Marguerite warmed up some coffee and gave a cup to Wagner.

"Thank you," said Wagner.

Twenty-eight ∞ Resistance

General Wagner went outside; all the soldiers lined up in front of him.

"We will go to battle tomorrow," said Wagner.

The soldiers didn't look happy about it but knew they didn't have a choice.

"You may rest for the day, be prepared to leave at six in the morning," said Wagner.

The soldiers dissipated in different directions. Sarah and Eli heard Wagner's voice and ran outside with Yuki.

"Hello," said Wagner.

"You have returned," said Eli.

"Yes," replied Wagner.

"Look at your beautiful dog," said Wagner, petting Yuki.

He remembered his shameful reaction to Yuki the first time he arrived on the farm. Wagner touched Eli's head sympathetically.

"You have grown," said Wagner.

"Yes, I'll soon be a man," replied Eli smiling.

Jean-Pierre came out of the barn and looked towards Wagner; Jean-Pierre looked much older and used by life.

"Should we get some breakfast?" said Wagner.

Jean-Pierre came towards them but didn't say anything.

"What happened to him?" whispered Wagner.

There was a moment of silence.

"My mother died," said Sarah.

"I am very sorry," replied Wagner, feeling the tension.

They all went to the house silently. Marguerite welcomed them with a big breakfast; the kitchen smelled delightful. There was toasted bread with butter and jam, eggs, bacon, and some coffee and hot chocolate. It seemed as if they were not at war for a moment. They all enjoyed a nice meal together. Even Jean-Pierre had the strength to smile, being the first time he smiled since Françoise died.

Later that day, after the family had dinner with Wagner in the kitchen, they walked to the entrance door.

"Where are you going?" asked Wagner.

"We are going to the barn," replied Marguerite.

She realized that Wagner was not aware that they had been sleeping in the barn all this time.

"What? No, you will go back upstairs, General Hauler is no longer here," said Wagner smiling.

The family was relieved to know they would be sleeping in a bed once again.

They got the few belongings they had in the barn and set up in the attic once again. The children slept on one of the floor mattresses while Jean-Pierre was on the other, and Marguerite on the single bed.

Sarah laid in bed, looking at the sky, Yuki was next to her. She felt some kind of peace for the first time since her mother died. She wondered where she was, and if her mother was thinking about her like she was.

They all fell asleep peacefully and got a good night's sleep for the first time in a very long time.

The next morning there was movement and noise in the house. Marguerite and Sarah prepared breakfast while the remaining soldiers got ready to go back to battle for the first time in a while. General Wagner was in the kitchen finishing his coffee.

"All the soldiers are coming with me as we are already short-handed, do you still have the gun I left you?" asked Wagner.

"Yes, we do," replied Marguerite, surprised that they would be on their farm alone for the first time since the beginning of the war.

"Good," said Wagner.

Everyone left, the farm was suddenly much quieter. Marguerite went to the barn to get Jean-Pierre and Eli. The four of them had breakfast in the kitchen on their own. Eli ate quickly.

"Take your time, it's the first time we can enjoy a meal alone here," said Marguerite.

"I have a lot of work at the barn," replied Eli.

"I was thinking of reorganizing the attic today," said Sarah.

"That's a great idea, I think I might cook a nice meal for tonight," said Marguerite.

They finished their breakfast, and all tended to their tasks.

Sarah went to the attic and started moving furniture around while Yuki slept in the corner.

Eli and Jean-Pierre were in the barn; Jean-Pierre milked the cows.

"I am going to the chicken coop, I will clean it out entirely, I will see you in a few hours," said Eli.

"Okay," replied Jean-Pierre.

Eli went out of the barn, and instead of going to the chicken coop, he went to the small barn on the farm next door. He opened the barn door, the squeaky door had not been opened for years, and spider webs were everywhere. He saw his small bicycle, brushed off the spider webs, and sneaked out of the farm.

He biked to the village and didn't hear or see anyone on the way. When he got to the village, he saw some soldiers. He arrived at the town square and remembered the last time he was there. He stared at the ground where his father laid dead a few years before. He snapped out of his thoughts and went to Madame Dussault's house. He got to the back door and put his bike against the brick wall before knocking on the door. Madame Dussault opened and was surprised to see him alone. She looked to see if anyone was there and then let him in.

"What are you doing here?" said Madame Dussault.

"I want to help," replied Eli.

"Help with what?" asked Madame Dussault.

"I know you are up to something, let me help," said Eli.

"You have a lot of courage, but it's too dangerous for you," replied Madame Dussault.

"Let me help, the soldiers would not suspect me as much as someone else," pleaded Eli.

"That is true, let me speak to the others," said Madame Dussault.

"Thank you," said Eli, as his face lit up.

"For the past two months, there have been fewer soldiers in the village, but you must be careful nonetheless, don't take the main roads," said Madame Dussault.

"Okay," replied Eli.

"Come back tomorrow, I will have an answer for you, don't speak of this to anyone," said Madame Dussault.

"I won't," replied Eli.

"Now go, and be careful," said Madame Dussault.

"Yes," replied Eli as he left.

Eli carefully headed back to the farm. He rid his bike through the forest, happy with himself. He arrived at the farm, put his bike behind the barn, and then went to the chicken coop and started cleaning; Jean-Pierre arrived.

"Where were you? I came by earlier and didn't see you," asked Jean-Pierre.

"I just went for a short walk," replied Eli.

"Be careful, I don't think your mother would appreciate it if you wandered around the farm," said Jean-Pierre.

"Yes," replied Eli thinking that she would have a heart attack if she knew what he was really up to.

"I just finished a big batch of Camembert cheese, Marguerite was thinking of making some Camembert bread bowls tonight with some pork," said Jean-Pierre.

"My favorite," replied Eli with a smile.

"Yes, so, how much longer until you are done?" asked Jean-Pierre.

"Probably an hour," replied Eli.

"Okay, I am going to the barn to prepare the pork; come and help me when you are done," said Jean-Pierre.

"Okay."

Jean-Pierre went back to the barn while Eli continued to clean out the chicken coop.

An hour later, once Eli was finished with the coop, he went to the barn. Jean-Pierre was attempting to cut up a pig, blood was everywhere; he struggled to do it alone.

"Let me help you," said Eli.

This reminded Eli of his father. When Sarah and Eli were younger, they used to come and watch their two fathers cut up the pig, and would squeal about all the blood. Eli helped Jean-Pierre cut up the pig, and then they both brought the pork to the kitchen. Marguerite was in the middle of baking bread, she had flour all over her face.

"Put it over here," said Marguerite.

They put the meat on the large counter to her right.

"Thank you," said Marguerite.

"Should I cook the meat, Mama?" asked Eli.

"That would be great; I messed up some of the bread and had to start over," said Marguerite.

"I will see if Sarah needs help," said Jean-Pierre as he left the kitchen.

Eli grilled the pork while Marguerite finished baking the bread.

An hour later, the soldiers returned from battle; Wagner entered the kitchen.

"It smells really good," said Wagner.

"Thank you, I am making Camembert bread bowls with some pork," replied Marguerite.

"It sounds like a feast," said Wagner.

"It will all be ready in a few minutes," said Marguerite smiling.

"Thank you, I have a few wounded soldiers, where is Sarah?" asked Wagner.

Sarah entered the kitchen.

"I am here," said Sarah.

"Oh good," replied Wagner.

"Eli, help me bring the wounded soldiers to the living room," said Sarah.

"Yes," replied Eli.

Eli and Sarah left the kitchen together and picked up the four wounded soldiers from the entrance, and saw new soldiers outside they hadn't seen before.

Sarah started to sew up a deep cut in one soldier's gashed leg while Eli cleaned the arm of another wounded soldier. The two other soldiers waited next to the fire. One was bleeding from his arm while the other one seemed better off. Sarah finished sewing the soldier's leg and then tended to the next soldier. Eli and Sarah worked well as a team; he prepared everything, and she did the sewing. They finished caring for the wounded men while the other soldiers had dinner. The day came to an end and the soldiers, including Wagner, retired for the night.

Marguerite, Eli, Jean-Pierre, and Sarah had dinner in the kitchen by themselves.

"Thank you, Mama," said Eli as he devoured his meal.

Marguerite smiled, she looked at him in a motherly way, satisfied that her son enjoyed the feast she prepared. Jean-Pierre and Marguerite cleaned up the kitchen while Sarah and Eli went to check up on the wounded men.

They finally all went to the attic. Marguerite opened the door and stopped abruptly with excitement. Sarah had set up the entire attic as if it were a real room; there were closets, curtains, and flowers everywhere; it looked charming. Sarah even put family photos on display. There was a book on one of the mattresses; Marguerite turned to Sarah and hugged her.

"Thank you, this is beautiful," said Marguerite.

The four of them got into bed, and Marguerite started to read the book aloud. The children fell asleep quickly. Marguerite stopped reading once everyone was asleep and closed her eyes.

Two months went by, things started to look better, and the family got used to this new routine. A few new German soldiers arrived at the farm regularly, of which most were wounded. Sarah tended to the soldiers with Eli's assistance.

Eli spent his time helping Sarah and helping Jean-Pierre on a part-time basis. This gave him the liberty to leave the farm secretly to go and help Madame Dussault. Eli had been helping Madame Dussault by delivering messages to people that were part of the resistance in nearby villages. He was very proud of himself when he went on his secret errands.

One late afternoon in May, Eli returned from one of his secret errands for Madame Dussault. He went to hide his bike behind the small barn. While he walked back to the main farm, he bumped into Wagner, who was smoking a cigarette outside. Eli was startled; the soldiers usually didn't come back to the farm until night time.

"Be careful, boy," said Wagner.

Eli was not sure how to answer. He didn't say anything; he was frightened.

"I wouldn't want anything to happen to you," said Wagner patting Eli on the head.

"Yes."

"Don't tell your mother, she'd be worried sick," said Wagner.

"I won't."

"This will be our little secret," said Wagner.

"Okay," replied Eli.

"Now, go in."

Eli went inside the house, not knowing what to think.

"Do you need any help, Sarah?" asked Eli as he entered the living room.

"Yes, a few soldiers just came back, apparently there are more coming later," said Sarah.

Eli helped Sarah with the wounded men as usual. Marguerite was in the kitchen humming as she cooked, and Jean-Pierre was in the barn with Yuki working with the cows. The days all looked alike.

In the summer of 1918, the German soldiers were becoming more and more scarce in the village. A lot of soldiers were called to fight elsewhere. To the French, it felt like the war was coming to an end.

On the 11th of October 1918, Sarah walked to the barn, hoping to find Eli, to ask him for help with some wounded men. As she entered, she saw a drunk German soldier standing behind the barn door. She walked towards the exit, but the soldier stood in front of the door. Sarah was frightened. He was right in front of her face and grabbed her jaw. He leaned in and touched her breasts; she screamed. He put his hand in the air to slap her, when Eli arrived from behind, stabbing the soldier in the back with a garden fork. The soldier yelled. Eli dropped the fork to the ground when he realized what he had done. The soldier fell to the ground, bleeding profusely. Eli and Sarah stared at the soldier as he bled out before he convulsed and died. Sarah was trembling, Eli took her behind the barn next to the tree where Françoise was buried.

"Are you okay?" said Eli.

"Yes, I'll be fine, nothing happened," replied Sarah.

They sat there, hiding. Eli held Sarah in his arms. They were not sure if anyone heard them, stayed hidden for ten minutes, but no one came. Eli and Sarah went back into the barn quietly and hid the soldier's dead body under a haystack.

"We have to go back into the house. I came to get you so you could help me, there are lots of wounded soldiers that just arrived," said Sarah.

Eli knew that Sarah had a tough character and didn't permit herself to be weak; otherwise, she wouldn't make it through the war. They went back to the living room and tended to the wounded soldiers as if nothing had happened.

The night came, and Marguerite, once again, read a story to all of them; they all fell asleep except for Eli.

Eli got out of bed and went back to the barn. He buried the soldier they left under the haystack; no one heard or saw him. Two hours later, he made his way back to the attic and went to sleep without waking anyone.

The next morning they woke up and went back to their usual routines. Eli left the farm on his bike in the middle of the day to do one of his secret errands for Madame Dussault. He biked through the forest not far from the road when he heard a car. He stopped abruptly and laid down on the ground waiting for the vehicle to pass, but it stopped—three German soldiers fired at Eli. General Wagner was in the car.

"What are you doing?" said Wagner to the soldiers.

"We saw someone," replied a soldier.

Wagner recognized Eli's bike.

"Stop firing!" said Wagner.

Eli moved slightly; the German soldier farthest from Wagner saw this and started firing again, just missing Eli. Wagner took out his gun and shot the soldier that was firing at Eli. The other two Germans realized that Wagner was betraying them. One of the soldiers fought with him; Wagner managed to shoot him, but the other one got away.

"Traitor!" said the soldier to Wagner as he ran off.

Wagner hopped into the driver's seat and started driving to catch up with Eli, he saw that Wagner was alone and got into the car.

"I told you to be careful!" said Wagner.

"I am sorry, I didn't hear the car until it was too late," replied Eli.

"What will we do now? The other soldier must have gone to warn the others," said Wagner.

"We can hide in the small barn. No one ever goes there," replied Eli.

"That's a good idea, they wouldn't think we would go back to the farm," said Wagner.

Eli was pleased that he found a solution.

"I will tell my mother when night comes, and she'll bring us some food."

"Okay," said Wagner.

They drove the closest they could to the farm and hid the car in a field and then walked to the small barn and hid there until night fell. They were sitting on a stack of old hay.

"So what did you do before the war?" asked Eli.

"I was a bridge engineer," replied Wagner.

"Wow, that must be a fascinating job."

"Yes, it was a lot of work, my wife would bring my son to see the new bridges I was working on."

"So, you have a boy?"

"Yes, he is a good kid, you remind me a lot of him," replied Wagner.

"When did you last see him?"

"At the beginning of the war, he went to his grandparent's house near Dresden with my wife."

"It's been a long time," said Eli.

"Yes, I can't wait for this war to be over," replied Wagner.

"Thank you for saving my life today."

"You're welcome, kid."

"I will see if I can get my mother's attention from the back window, okay?" said Eli.

"Yes, be very careful, I don't know if they saw that it was you; if they did, your mother would have heard of it," said Wagner.

"Okay."

He left the small barn and went to the back kitchen window of the farm. He looked through the window and saw his mother cleaning the kitchen by herself; he quietly tapped on the window, Marguerite jumped and opened the window.

"You frightened me. Where have you been? I have been worried!" said Marguerite.

"So, no one is looking for me then?" asked Eli.

"Yes, I *am* looking for you!" replied Marguerite.

"I know, but I mean, is anyone else looking for me?" asked Eli.

"No, what have you done, Eli?" said Marguerite, very worried all of a sudden.

"It's fine, you are sure no one came looking for me?" reiterated Eli.

"Yes, I am sure!" replied Marguerite.

"Okay, I am coming through the front door then."

Eli, slightly worried, walked slowly towards the house in front of the German soldiers. They spoke to each other in German; they seemed confused. No one noticed Eli. He recognized the soldier that escaped from Wagner, but the man didn't recognize him as he passed by. He walked into the kitchen.

"I was so worried! Where were you?" asked Marguerite.

"Don't talk too loudly, Mama, I don't want anyone to notice I wasn't here," said Eli.

"What happened?" asked Marguerite.

"I have been helping Madame Dussault for the last few months, and today I was on a secret mission for her when some Germans saw me and started shooting at me. Wagner was there and defended me and killed the other Germans, he now has to hide as he is considered a traitor," whispered Eli.

"Oh my god, Eli, are you trying to kill me?!" said Marguerite.

"I am sorry, Mama, I couldn't stand there and do nothing, it's my country, my people and my family," replied Eli.

"It's fine, thank god you are here, safe and sound," said Marguerite, as she did the sign of the cross on herself.

"Yes, but there is more," said Eli.

"What?"

"Wagner is hiding in the small barn on the farm," said Eli.

"Oh my god."

"I need to get him some food and blankets."

"Not now, there are too many people, we will wait a bit, and I will come with you," said Marguerite.

"Okay."

Eli went to see Sarah in the living room and helped her.

"Where were you? I was looking for you earlier," asked Sarah.

"I'll explain it to you later," whispered Eli.

Sarah looked at Eli, wondering what he had got himself into.

Twenty-nine ∞ Prisoner

Wagner sat by himself on a pile of hay. He was cold, hungry, and worried. He wondered if Eli made it to the other farm. Wagner looked around the barn and imagined everything the families must have gone through. Living in a cold barn for years with almost no food, terrified about what might happen to them.

Back in the house, things became quieter and quieter as work wound down. The house was completely silent. Eli signaled to Sarah to follow him in the kitchen. Jean-Pierre and Marguerite were in the kitchen cleaning.

"I need to bring some food and blankets to Wagner; he is in the small barn," whispered Eli.

"What happened? I heard some German soldiers say he was a traitor," said Sarah.

"He saved my life while I was on a secret errand for Madame Dussault," replied Eli.

"I can't believe you didn't tell me," said Sarah.

"Don't make so much noise, no one can know he is here; I didn't want to tell you because I knew you would be worried," replied Eli.

"Fine, I'll get some blankets upstairs, I'll go with you," said Sarah.

"Okay."

"Here, take this, it's a warm soup and some pork," said Marguerite.

"I'll be right back," said Sarah.

She went up to the attic and took a few blankets. On her way down the stairs, she heard some noise coming from one of the rooms. She stopped for a second, no one appeared, and then continued down quietly. Eli was ready to go.

"Papa and Marguerite, I think you should wait for us here so that it doesn't look weird when we come back in case someone wakes up," said Sarah.

"Okay," replied Marguerite.

Eli and Sarah left from the kitchen's back door to go behind the farm. They walked behind Eli's greenhouse and continued until they got to the small barn. They quietly opened the barn door, it made a squeaky sound. Wagner was startled by the noise and hid in one of the stables. Eli and Sarah entered.

"Wagner?" whispered Eli.

Wagner was relieved to hear Eli's voice, his head appeared from the top of one of the stables.

"I was worried something had happened to you," said Wagner.

"No, I am fine, I wasn't recognized, but there are lots of soldiers at the farm, and we didn't want anyone to see us," replied Eli.

"Okay, and did they say anything about me?" asked Wagner.

"I heard two soldiers saying that you were a traitor," replied Sarah.

"Yes," said Wagner.

"Here is some food," said Eli.

"Thank you," said Wagner as he took the warm soup.

"And we brought you blankets, I will put them right here," said Sarah.

She put them on the stack of hay next to where they stood.

"Thank you very much," said Wagner.

"What are you going to do?" asked Eli.

"I don't know," replied Wagner while he ate some soup.

"We will bring you food tomorrow; we will probably know more about what they think," said Eli.

"Thank you very much, you are both really great," said Wagner.

Sarah and Eli left the small barn and went back to the house, taking the same route. They entered the kitchen from the backdoor; Marguerite and Jean-Pierre were waiting for them.

"Is everything fine?" asked Marguerite.

"Yes, he'll be fine for tonight, but we have to find a better solution," replied Eli.

"Let's go upstairs," said Marguerite.

They all went to the attic, not making much noise as they took the stairs. They arrived in the attic and sat down next to each other.

"We need to find a place where we can hide him," said Eli.

"Yes, I know," replied Marguerite.

"Why don't we hide him here? No one ever comes up here," said Sarah.

"That's not a bad idea," replied Eli looking at how to rearrange the attic, "Maybe we could use the furniture to create a small hiding spot behind there; if someone comes, they wouldn't see him."

"You realize that if someone finds him here, we will be in serious trouble?" said Jean-Pierre.

"He saved my life," said Eli.

"And mine," said Marguerite.

"Yes, I know... Fine, but we must be cautious," said Jean-Pierre.

"Yes, as soon as the soldiers go to battle tomorrow, we will reorganize the attic," said Sarah.

Sarah stood up and looked around.

"We could put a mattress in the corner over there, under the roof, and we could surround it all with the furniture," said Sarah.

"Yes, that would work," replied Eli.

"Okay, let's get some sleep," said Marguerite.

"Will you read tonight?" asked Sarah.

"Fine, but only for a bit, it's very late," replied Marguerite, smiling as she took out the book.

Everyone laid in their beds, and Marguerite read the story out loud. The children listened eagerly as they cuddled with Yuki. They fell asleep shortly after. The house was now completely silent, only the wind could be heard.

Early the next morning, the soldiers rushed around getting ready for battle. Six soldiers were too wounded to move. Sarah tended to them with Eli's help. Marguerite was in the kitchen once again cooking for everyone, while Jean-Pierre went to the barn carrying a little box. He left from the backdoor of the barn and walked behind the farm towards the small barn. He opened the back door to the small barn discreetly and saw Wagner sleeping on the hay. Jean-Pierre got closer to Wagner and touched him softly on the shoulder; Wagner jumped in surprise.

"Ahh," said Wagner loudly.

"Shhh! I brought you some food," replied Jean-Pierre.

"Oh, thank you, I am sorry, I didn't hear you come in," said Wagner, shivering.

"You look like you are freezing?"

"It's all right, thank you, so Eli told you what happened?"

"Yes, we have a plan," said Jean-Pierre.

Wagner ate some eggs while he listened to Jean-Pierre.

"We will wait for the soldiers to leave, and we will take you to the attic, there is a place where you can sleep, and no one would see you," said Jean-Pierre.

"But it's too dangerous for your family," replied Wagner.

"We cannot leave you here; you will freeze to death," realized Jean-Pierre.

"Thank you so much for your kindness," said Wagner gratefully.

"We will come back a bit later to get you."

"Thank you."

Jean-Pierre left through the backdoor and went towards the other barn where he milked the cows.

Sarah and Eli took care of the soldiers in the living room. They needed to set up the wounded in a way where they would not see the staircase when Wagner went to the attic.

"We should move the soldiers in front of the fireplace, so they don't get too cold," said Sarah loudly.

"Yes," replied Eli.

Eli put mattresses in front of the fireplace. They took the wounded men one by one and put them closer to the fireplace, away from the staircase's view.

An hour later, Sarah went to the kitchen. Eli's mother was there with Jean-Pierre.

"We are ready, Eli and I will get Wagner. We put the soldiers closer to the fireplace so they don't notice us when we pass with him. I thought that maybe you could bring food to the soldiers while we walk by?" said Sarah.

"Yes, I also thought that Jean-Pierre could help create a diversion, he could be standing near the staircase with some blankets, and we could use an open blanket to hide you when you pass with him?" said Marguerite.

"I don't know, it might be too obvious, no?" asked Sarah.

"I think it could help," replied Marguerite.

"Okay, fine, we are leaving now," said Sarah.

"Okay, we will be on the lookout for you," said Marguerite.

Sarah went to the living room to get Eli, and they left the house.

Jean-Pierre took a pile of blankets from the entrance closet, he was nervous.

"It's going to be fine," said Marguerite.

"Yes, I hope so," replied Jean-Pierre.

Ten minutes later, Eli and Sarah appeared with Wagner. Marguerite and Jean-Pierre saw them through the kitchen window and nodded. They all met at the entrance. Marguerite went towards the wounded soldiers and brought them soup while Jean-Pierre looked like a clown with an open blanket in front of the staircase. Sarah and Eli started to walk behind it with Wagner.

"Okay, so here is some soup," said Marguerite loudly to cover up the possible noise of the three going up the stairs, "It will keep you warm."

"Thank you," said a soldier quietly.

"And Jean-Pierre has some more blankets if you need," said Marguerite even louder.

The three passed behind the blanket. As soon as they did, Jean-Pierre went towards the soldiers and covered one of the men with an additional blanket. Marguerite looked at Jean-Pierre; he was agitated.

"And here you go," said Marguerite, handing each soldier some warm soup.

Sarah, Eli, and Wagner got to the attic. There was furniture surrounding a mattress on the floor in the right corner. It looked cozy. Wagner looked at the children; he was moved by their kindness.

"Thank you very much," said Wagner.

"Of course, you'll be much better here," replied Sarah.

"You can settle in, we will bring you food and check up on you later," said Eli.

"Thank you," replied Wagner.

The children left smiling and went back to the soldiers. Sarah had bandages in her hands.

"I need to change this bandage," said Sarah.

"I will help your father at the farm," replied Eli.

As the weeks went by, fewer and fewer soldiers came back to the farm. The tension of the war drastically decreased. Wagner stayed in the attic and became a part of the family. He listened to the nightly stories read by Marguerite. No one suspected his presence.

The end of the war was announced three days later. The few remaining soldiers left the farm in a hurry. The French family finally had their own home once again.

Sarah and Eli went to the village, they saw it start to revive. People were in the streets once more. They could significantly sense the loss and destruction of the war, but the villagers were happy to walk in their town and talk to their friends once again.

It was the 13th of November, 1918. Three British soldiers arrived at the farm and knocked on the front door; Marguerite greeted them.

"Hello, may I help you?" asked Marguerite.

"Hello madam, we wondered if we could trouble you for some food?" said soldier Campbell.

"Of course, come in! We were just about to have lunch," replied Marguerite, thankful for their help in the war.

The three British soldiers entered the house, Marguerite took them to the kitchen. Sarah, Eli, Jean-Pierre, and Wagner sat in the kitchen. When Wagner saw the British soldiers enter, he was frightened.

"Hello!" said Campbell.

"Hi," replied the French family in unison.

"Please take a seat," said Marguerite.

The soldiers sat. There was a slight silence while everyone looked at each other. Marguerite placed all the food on the big kitchen table, and they began to eat.

"This is delicious, thank you," said Campbell.

"All the produce is from our farm," replied Marguerite proudly.

"What's your name, son?" asked Campbell to Eli.

"My name is Eli."

"How old are you?" asked Campbell.

"I am thirteen!" replied Eli.

"Almost a man!" said Campbell.

Eli smiled confidently. They all ate and enjoyed the meal. Campbell looked at Wagner that hadn't said a word during the whole meal.

"And what's your name?" asked Campbell to Wagner.

"His name is Bernard, this is my husband, he hasn't talked since he has been back from the war," said Marguerite before Wagner had time to respond.

"I am sorry, the repercussions of the war are immense, I am sure in due course he will get better," said Campbell.

Wagner looked at Marguerite, not knowing how to thank her for her wit. The meal came to an end.

"Thank you for this lovely feast, madam, I wish you all the best," said Campbell as they left.

The French family was relieved when the soldiers left the house for Wagner's sake.

"Thank you once again, I don't know how I can pay you back for your help," said Wagner.

"You have helped us in difficult moments," said Marguerite as everyone left the kitchen.

It was the beginning of the evening; Wagner was in the entrance with a little bag, he was getting ready to leave. Sarah, Eli, Jean-Pierre, Marguerite, and Yuki, stood next to him. Marguerite had prepared a bag of food and handed it to Wagner.

"Thank you," said Wagner.

"And here are my husband's papers; for the time you are in France and you will need them to cross the border," said Marguerite.

Wagner took the documents and held Marguerite's hand, thankfully.

"I will never forget your kindness," said Wagner to the family.

He touched Eli on the head.

"And you, be a good boy," said Wagner with a heavy heart.

Eli smiled and hugged Wagner. They said goodbye, and Wagner left.

Thirty ∞ Farm life

The next morning Marguerite, Jean-Pierre, Eli, and Sarah started to fix up both farms; they decided to unite the two into one big farm.

Five years went by, the repercussions of the war could still be felt in the village's commerce and the farm. Times had grown severe for the family. They barely got by; the adults discussed selling a part of the farm.

Eli had gotten back into his greenhouse activities. He spent most of his time with his plants and worked at the farm.

It was the 30th of January 1923; Eli was in his greenhouse working on his flower experiment. He had been working on this experiment for two years. Sarah entered the greenhouse with Yuki.

"Anything new?" asked Sarah.

"Yes, there is a bud coming out, it looks like it might be a green and pink rose," said Eli excitedly.

"Wow, let me see," said Sarah.

They observed the bud of the flower for a while. It looked unlike anything they had seen before. Eli had cut up seeds of his favorite flowers and put them together to grow, attempting to create a hybrid rose.

"You are beautiful," he whispered.

Eli had always talked to his flowers; Sarah was used to this and found it charming.

"I have named this rose *Sarah* after you," said Eli, timidly looking at her.

"You are so cute," replied Sarah.

There was a moment of silence; they were both a bit shy.

Meanwhile, Marguerite received a parcel from Germany. It was addressed to the children; she didn't open it.

At three in the afternoon, Sarah and Eli ran to their hilltop. Sarah ran ahead of Eli while he tried to catch her. When he did catch up to her, she tripped and fell onto the frozen grass. He stumbled and fell on top of her. They stared at each other for a minute; Eli leaned in and kissed Sarah. It was a long passionate kiss. He removed his lips from hers and admired her for a while, looking at each detail on her face.

"You are so beautiful," said Eli.

Sarah giggled.

"You are the love of my life, Sarah."

"And you are mine," replied Sarah timidly.

They kissed again, it was a gentle, warm kiss. Eli outlined Sarah's face with his finger. He then kissed her right eye, then her left eye, then her nose, then her right cheek, then her left cheek, and finally her lips. They spent the rest of the afternoon walking around with Yuki while holding hands and kissing each other.

In the evening, they celebrated Sarah and Eli's birthday in the living room, next to the chimney. They both blew their candles at the same time. Marguerite handed them each a gift. Sarah opened hers first. It was a knitted sweater Marguerite made.

"Thank you very much," said Sarah.

She was very thankful for her gift; she knew how tight things had been lately and didn't expect a present at all. Eli opened his gift; it was a nice pair of knitted gloves.

"Thank you, Mama," said Eli.

They both kissed Marguerite and Jean-Pierre to thank them.

"There is something else," said Marguerite as she got up.

"Something else?" asked Eli, surprised.

"This came by mail this morning, it's addressed to the both of you, it's from Germany," said Marguerite as she handed them each a parcel.

"Wagner! That means he is alive!" said Eli, excitedly.

"Oh my goodness, after all this time!" said Sarah.

There were four letters and parcels, one for each of them and one thick envelope addressed to Marguerite. There was a beautiful music box addressed to Sarah. When she opened the music box, a beautiful gold ballerina danced. It was an antique piece with little rubies on the side of it. Sarah looked at the ballerina in amazement; she had never seen anything quite this beautiful in her whole life. Eli received an elegant old fashioned gold pocket watch with his name engraved on its back. He held the pocket watch in his hand and stared at it, smiling while he thought about Wagner. There was a lovely cashmere scarf for Marguerite and a beautiful pair of warm leather gloves for Jean-Pierre. Marguerite put the scarf on immediately.

"It's so soft!" said Marguerite rubbing her neck into the scarf.

Jean-Pierre tried on his gloves.

"This is perfect for the winter," said Jean-Pierre.

They all opened their letters and read them to themselves. Eli read his letter.

My Dear Eli,

You were like a son to me; you brought me love and hope when I thought all was lost. You are such a good boy; continue to help your mother like you have always done. I have told my son a lot about you, your strength, honesty, and courage. This pocket watch belonged to my father. He was a man of honor, I thought it would be fit for you to have it.

Much Love,
Hans Wagner

Eli was very moved by the letter.

Marguerite opened her envelope and found her husband's documents in it. She started reading her letter. She stopped reading and opened the bigger envelope; the others did not pay attention to her as they were reading their own letter.

"We are saved! We are saved!" shouted Marguerite as she opened a big envelope with a pile of money in it.

Everyone looked up, gasping.

"He wrote, *I have never forgotten your kindness. Please accept this gesture for everything you have done for me. You have brought me back to life; I realized my life goal because of you and your family. At the beginning of the war, I was a broken man. Your family saved me. You made me realize that we are all people regardless of our nationality or different cultures and that war is never a solution. Since I have returned to Germany, I have dedicated my time to helping and teaching people about kindness and helping one another. I have created an association, and I continue in my endeavor each day to make up for the damage I caused during the war. I wish you all the best, and thank you for your friendship. Much love, Hans Wagner,*" Marguerite cried with joy, "He is doing well, and he is with his family."

"Look at the photo of his son," said Eli, showing the picture.

"And this. Wagner did a drawing of the farm," said Sarah, showing everyone.

"We don't have to sell the farm anymore!" said Jean-Pierre.

They stood up and danced and laughed. The family spent a great evening together and then went to sleep.

Eli laid in bed, thinking about Sarah; he wanted to go and see her. He tossed around in his bed, unable to sleep for hours. He finally decided to get out of bed; opened the door, listened for any noise, and went quietly towards Sarah's room. He stood in front of her door, hesitant. He didn't want to knock because he didn't know if it would wake up the others. He stood in front of her door for three minutes, not knowing what to do.

Sarah, from inside, went towards her door and opened it. She saw Eli and smiled; Eli was bewildered but entered her room.

"How did you know?" whispered Eli.

"I just did," whispered Sarah.

"But how?"

"You are my soulmate."

They smiled at each other, and Sarah went into bed while looking at Eli; he followed her. They kissed intensely. Eli caressed Sarah on her breasts and then everywhere. They made love tenderly. They were both still virgins and a bit nervous. As they made love, everything came naturally to them. They became one, physically and spiritually.

The next morning Eli went to the kitchen to see his mother.

"Hi honey, you look happy?" said Marguerite.

"I am, I love Sarah, I always have, but now we are together, I want to marry her," replied Eli.

Marguerite gasped.

"What? I didn't know you were together!" said Marguerite.

"Yes, we are," replied Eli.

"I am so happy! You will get married! Oh my god, this is the best news I have ever heard! Wait here, I'll be right back," said Marguerite.

She left the kitchen and came back five minutes later. Eli was waiting, daydreaming about Sarah and their night together.

"Here, take this, my mother gave it to me," said Marguerite.

She handed him a beautiful old fashioned ring with a red ruby on it; Eli stared at the ring.

"It's beautiful, she will love it, thank you, Mama," said Eli.

"When will you ask her to get married?" asked Marguerite.

"I don't know, don't tell her anything, I want it to be a surprise," said Eli.

"Of course, I won't say anything," replied Marguerite.

Jean-Pierre heard that they were together from Marguerite and was just as delighted.

Sarah and Eli spent months together, working at the farm, and loving each other more each day. They spent their evenings in Sarah's room, whispering, reading, and making love.

Thirty-one ∞ Proposal

It was the 30th of January 1924. Sarah and Eli were in the barn together, milking the cows. Eli stood up, and without saying a word, took Sarah by her hand.

"Where are we going?" asked Sarah.

"You will see, close your eyes," said Eli smiling.

"Close my eyes?"

"Yes, trust me," said Eli.

Sarah closed her eyes; Eli took her to the greenhouse and opened the door. They entered.

"You can open your eyes," said Eli.

She opened her eyes and saw lit candles absolutely everywhere. There were green and pink hybrid roses in all corners of the greenhouse. There were different colored plants, flowers, and roses decorating the greenhouse's walls and ceiling. There were petals on the floor, leading them to a blanket with a basket on it, next to it a bottle of wine. It looked like the greenhouse had been turned into a fairytale. It was breathtaking; Sarah turned to Eli and kissed him.

"You are so romantic," she said.

Eli kissed her lovingly. They sat on the blanket and Eli poured some wine and gave her some bread with butter and cheese. They enjoyed a magical lunch when Eli paused to look at Sarah. He put his hand in the basket and took out a little jewelry box. Sarah looked at him and started to cry of joy. He opened the small box and displayed the beautiful ring from his grandmother.

"Will you marry me?"

"Yes! Yes, a million times yes!"

They kissed passionately. He took the ring out of the box and put it on her finger.

"I will be yours, and you will be mine for eternity," said Eli.

"Yes, for eternity," replied Sarah.

Sarah felt like she was the luckiest woman alive. They made love in the greenhouse on the blanket. It was different this time. It was sensual and very passionate, but they made love knowing they had decided to spend eternity together. As they made love, they felt bodiless, as if they were floating in the air. It was a sensation neither of them had ever felt or experienced before. There were such strong emotions between them that it felt like their hearts were going to burst.

A few hours later, they went to the kitchen together to see Marguerite and Jean-Pierre. Sarah had a huge smile on her face and extended her hand in front of their parents.

"Oh my god! Congratulations!" said Marguerite.

Sarah's father had tears in his eyes. He hugged his daughter and Eli. They spent a wonderful evening together, celebrating their children's birthdays and talking about the upcoming wedding.

"We will decorate the town square with flowers. The whole town will be there. It will be incredible!" said Marguerite.

The new couple was delighted by how excited Marguerite was. It finally gave her something to look forward to instead of spending all her days in the kitchen and Jean-Pierre was amused by Marguerite's excitement.

The next morning when Eli and Sarah arrived in the kitchen, Marguerite had prepared various meals and cakes to taste.

"What is all this?" asked Eli.

"It's for the wedding! Taste them and tell me what you prefer!" said Marguerite as excited as she was the night before.

Sarah and Eli laughed. The house was filled with joy, a joy that no one had felt since before the war.

The next few weeks were dedicated to wedding preparations. The entire town was looking forward to the wedding; people talked about it everywhere they went.

Sarah went to a small boutique with Marguerite to pick out the wedding dress. Antoinette, the boutique owner, was very proud to help Sarah pick out her dress.

"So here you have the old fashioned dresses," said Antoinette.

"Oh, how lovely," said Marguerite.

Sarah looked at the dresses and stopped in front of a beautiful, simple gown. There was a thin lace around the neckline and the sleeves.

"I like this one," said Sarah.

"It's beautiful but are you sure you don't want something more modern? I have other dresses here if you like?" said Antoinette.

"No, this one is perfect, Eli will love it," replied Sarah.

"Okay, I will get it ready right away," said Antoinette.

Sarah tried on the dress, it fit her perfectly; she was dead drop gorgeous. She looked elegant but simple in her way; the dress was made out of thin fabric.

"Thank you," said Sarah as they left.

As the ladies got home, they saw Eli and Jean-Pierre preparing boxes.

"What are you doing?" asked Sarah.

"It's a surprise!" replied Eli grinning.

Sarah blushed; how could there be more surprises, she thought.

"Okay," said Sarah cutely.

She kissed him and went back to the house. Sarah helped Marguerite prepare the food for the wedding, which was now in two days. Sarah was in the kitchen, cutting up meat when all of a sudden, she started gagging.

"Are you all right?" asked Marguerite, a bit worried.

Sarah looked at Marguerite for a moment and then realized that she was pregnant.

"Oh my god, I am pregnant, I missed a period and have been nauseous for a few weeks," replied Sarah.

Marguerite was ecstatic.

"Oh my god! A grandchild! How wonderful!" said Marguerite hugging Sarah.

"What will Eli say? How did this happen so quickly?"

"Don't you worry, honey, everything will be perfect!" said Marguerite.

"Yes, but we didn't plan this."

"I will be here to help you both," said Marguerite.

"I have to go see Eli."

She left the kitchen and went to the barn, but the men had left; she went back to the kitchen.

"He is not there, do you know where they went?" asked Sarah.

"They will return soon enough; Eli is preparing a surprise for you," replied Marguerite.

"Okay," said Sarah pensive.

She wondered if she would be a good mother and if Eli would be okay with the news.

"I will cut the meat; you can mix the bread dough," said Marguerite.

"Yes," replied Sarah quietly.

A few hours later, the bread was in the oven, and the meat was in a big pot simmering with red wine. Sarah had flour in her hair and on her face. Jean-Pierre and Eli walked into the kitchen; Eli had a big smile on his face. Sarah had a serious look on her face.

"What's the matter?" asked Eli as he went towards Sarah to remove the flour on her face.

"We have to talk," said Sarah.

Eli was immediately worried.

"What's happening?" asked Eli.

"Come, let's talk in the dining room," said Sarah leaving the kitchen.

Eli followed her. She stood in front of him, looking at the floor.

"What is going on?" asked Eli.

"I am pregnant," replied Sarah, not knowing what reaction to expect.

"Pregnant!! Oh my god, we are going to have a baby!" said Eli jumping with excitement.

He took Sarah in his arms and squeezed her tightly.

"You are okay with it?" asked Sarah.

"Okay? I am happier than I could ever have imagined! We are going to have a child together! He will have your eyes and lips, oh, and your nose, of course," said Eli.

Sarah giggled.

"It might not be a boy, and he might have your eyes and your lips," said Sarah.

Sarah was relieved by Eli's reaction. She knew that everything would be fine now. They kissed gently, and Eli put his hand on her stomach.

"You can't feel anything yet, I'm probably only a few weeks pregnant," said Sarah giggling by Eli's naivete.

"I know, but in case he can feel something, I want him to know that I am here," replied Eli.

They hugged, Eli kissed Sarah on her head, holding her tightly. Jean-Pierre and Marguerite entered the dining room.

"Congratulations! I am so happy! I will be a grandmother!" said Marguerite.

"Congratulations!" said Jean-Pierre.

"Thank you," replied Eli.

"Thank you, Papa," said Sarah.

They had a wonderful evening together.

Jean-Pierre went to the dining room to read while Marguerite stayed in the kitchen, going over the few last preparations for the wedding.

"You kids go and have fun," said Marguerite.

"Okay, good night, Mama," replied Eli.

"Good night," said Sarah.

They left the kitchen. Marguerite started to sing while she continued to prepare the meal for the wedding. Steam came out of several pots, she smelled the fumes; it was almost ready.

"I will be a grandmother, I will be a grandmother, I will be a grandmother," she hummed to herself.

Sarah and Eli spent a romantic evening together.

"Do you think you got pregnant in the greenhouse?" asked Eli.

"Probably," replied Sarah.

"I bet you we will have a boy," said Eli.

"I think you might be right," said Sarah smiling.

The next morning Sarah helped Marguerite with the last preparations. They were in the kitchen, baking cakes.

"We will make the tarts afterwards," said Marguerite.

"Okay," replied Sarah.

"Can you get the small box of pears I left in front of the barn?" asked Marguerite.

"Yes, of course," replied Sarah.

She went to get the pears when she saw Eli pacing back and forth outside, rehearsing his wedding speech. She admired him from afar. He was so cute. He turned around and saw Sarah looking at him. He went towards her and took her in his arms.

"Are you spying on me?" asked Eli.

"Yes, I am, you are so cute... I love you for eternity," said Sarah.

"I love you for eternity and even more," replied Eli.

"No, I do," said Sarah.

"Let's say we love each other equally?" said Eli.

"Yes," replied Sarah, giggling and kissing him.

"I need to get the pears for the tarts."

"Okay, see you later."

She brought the pears back to Marguerite, and they started baking pies. Marguerite was in the kitchen singing as they made the tarts. She was in heaven. Sarah, on the other hand, wondered how it would be to be a mother. They finished with all the cooking preparations, they were both quite exhausted from the day's activities.

Eli and Jean-Pierre came into the house, having just finished all the farm work for the day.

They all had dinner in the kitchen, excited about the wedding the next day.

Eli and Sarah went up to their room together. Eli was walking up the stairs behind Sarah holding her hand. They looked adorable together. Sarah opened the door and saw Eli's hybrid flowers everywhere in the room. There were petals on the bed; it looked beautiful. She turned to him, hugged him, and kissed him deeply. He took her to the bed and laid her on her back; he started to kiss her, caress her, and they made love.

The next morning the two love birds woke up and stayed in bed for a moment.

"So, it's the big day, you are going to be my wife," said Eli.

"Yes, I will, I will be your wife," replied Sarah smiling.

When they went down to the kitchen, Marguerite was rushing around.

"The meat is ready, the cakes are ready, the tarts are ready, I just need to get the wine from the cellar," said Marguerite.

"Let me help you with the wine, Mama," said Eli.

"No, you get ready, dear, Jean-Pierre will help me with the wine, everything else is under control, and Marc and Philippe are coming to give us a hand," said Marguerite.

"Okay," replied Eli.

"Honey, I will help you with your dress and hair in twenty minutes," said Marguerite to Sarah.

"Thank you," replied Sarah.

"Okay, I'll get dressed," said Eli.

Sarah tapped Eli on the behind as he left the kitchen; he looked at her cheekily.

Jean-Pierre entered the kitchen.

"So everything is ready in the town square," said Jean-Pierre.

"Oh good, can you get the wine out of the cellar? I am going to help Sarah," said Marguerite.

"Of course," replied Jean-Pierre.

He looked at Sarah and kissed her on the cheek.

"You are so beautiful," said her father as he looked at her lovingly.

"Thank you, Papa," said Sarah.

"Once you bring the wine out, you can leave with Eli. We will meet you at the town square," said Marguerite.

"Okay," replied Jean-Pierre.

Marguerite and Sarah went upstairs to Marguerite's room. There was a photo of the six of them on the cupboard. Sarah looked at her mother in the picture.

"She would have been very happy for you, dear," said Marguerite.

"Yes, I am sure," replied Sarah missing her mother on this big day.

Thirty-two ∞ Wedding

Sarah put on the gorgeous gown she chose with Marguerite; she looked beautiful. Marguerite did her hair while Yuki was on the floor next to Sarah. Sarah sat in front of the mirror, looking at herself for a moment and all of a sudden got very sad.

"I hope Eli is fine," said Sarah out of nowhere.

"I am sure he is, why would he not be?" replied Marguerite.

"I don't know," said Sarah turning around to look behind herself.

"Is everything okay, honey?" asked Marguerite, seeing that Sarah was worried.

"Yes, yes, everything is fine, I am sure everything is fine, I want to see Eli is all," said Sarah.

"I am almost finished, just one more minute, voila, all done, you look magnificent," said Marguerite.

"Thank you, it looks great, okay, let's go," said Sarah.

"Oh my, you are in a hurry."

"Yes, I just want to see Eli."

They left the room and went downstairs, followed by Yuki; the men had left as planned.

They walked to the village, Yuki walked with them. Sarah walked hastily.

"Why are you walking so fast? You are going to ruin your dress," said Marguerite.

"I want to see Eli, I told you."

Marguerite stopped in front of Sarah.

"My dear, everything will be fine, this is one of the best days of your life, everything will be perfect," said Marguerite.

Sarah started to cry.

"But what if something happened to Eli?"

"Nothing happened to Eli; he is waiting for you at the square, I promise," said Marguerite holding Sarah's shoulders.

"Okay, okay, I am sure you are right," said Sarah calming down.

They continued to walk hastily and arrived at the town square.

It looked beautiful; there were plants and hybrid roses everywhere, candles and flowers on the tables, chairs set up, and an aisle in the middle with petals on the ground. There was a small band playing to the right. The entire village was there. Everyone cheered when Sarah arrived. She started to smile timidly. She looked for Eli but didn't see him. She looked towards the center of the aisle and finally saw him. She had a sudden huge relief; everything would be fine, she thought to herself, he was safe. She smiled effusively. Eli came towards her and kissed her. The kiss melted her heart. She smiled; she was in heaven. Jean-Pierre saw his daughter and hugged her.

The wedding music started to play. Marguerite walked with Eli, and Jean-Pierre accompanied Sarah. Marguerite and Eli went down the aisle first, and then

Sarah and Jean-Pierre followed. They arrived in front of a plump, friendly priest. Sarah and Eli faced each other. The priest began the wedding ceremony while the village was silent, aside from Marguerite, who sobbed.

"You may say your vows," said the priest to Eli.

Eli looked at Sarah.

"I promise to love you, care for you, understand you, and help you. I promise to love you despite all difficulties we might encounter, I promise to help you attain your goals. I promise to love you and make you happy for eternity," said Eli.

Sarah had tears in her eyes.

"I promise to love you, always be there for you, understand you, and help you. I promise to love you and make you happy for eternity," said Sarah.

"Sarah Marie Manigault, do you take Eli Adrien Durand to be your husband?" said the priest.

"I do," replied Sarah.

"Eli Adrien Durand, do you take Sarah Marie Manigault to be your wife?" asked the priest.

"I do," replied Eli.

"I pronounce thee husband and wife, you may kiss the bride," said the priest.

Eli and Sarah kissed each other. They looked at each other and started laughing with joy. Marguerite and Jean-Pierre hugged the newlywed couple.

"Oh, I am so happy!" said Marguerite, crying.

The band started to play music. Eli took Sarah's hand, and they began to dance. The villagers circled around them. Everyone danced, ate, and enjoyed themselves.

The wedding was a great success, everyone had a wonderful time.

The next day Eli woke up and looked at Sarah, who was still sleeping, for an hour. He found her astoundingly beautiful and calm. She finally opened her eyes and saw him looking at her.

"Are you spying on me?" said Sarah giggling.

"Yes, I am, Madame Durand," replied Eli.

They looked at each other, kissed, and made love. Their life as a married couple began.

They loved each other and understood each other more every day. They worked at the farm and helped their parents like they always had.

On the 21st of February 1925, Sarah was in Marguerite's room giving birth to their child. Marguerite was next to Sarah. A midwife by the name of Hélène had come from the village to help Sarah give birth. Sarah screamed; she had not imagined the pain it would be; she could barely feel her body.

Jean-Pierre sat in an armchair in front of the chimney in the living room while Eli paced back and forth in front of him. Yuki sat on the floor. They could hear screaming from above.

"Is she all right? Do you think she is fine? I wonder if everything is fine," said Eli.

"Everything will be fine, sit down for a minute," replied Jean-Pierre.

"I can't, I can't, do you think she is fine?" asked Eli, completely stressed out.

"Yes, she is fine, it's normal," replied Jean-Pierre.

Eli sat down on a chair next to Jean-Pierre for five seconds and then got up again, pacing back and forth.

An hour later, Sarah gave birth to a little boy. Jean-Pierre and Eli heard a baby wail.

Eli ran up the stairs and barged into the room, followed by Yuki. He looked at Sarah, who was sweating and holding their baby in her arms.

"You were right; it's a boy," said Sarah looking at Eli and their son.

Eli sat next to Sarah and kissed her. He looked at his son for a moment and kissed him on the head.

"I promise to take care of you and help you with everything you need," said Eli to his son.

Jean-Pierre entered the room and looked at the boy and Sarah.

"John Bernard Durand?" said Sarah to Eli.

Eli looked at his wife lovingly.

"Yes, John Bernard Durand is perfect," replied Eli.

"Hi John, we are your parents, we are going to take care of you," said Sarah.

"We are going to take care of him as well," said Marguerite smiling.

Jean-Pierre smiled and admired his family, he felt at peace and thought that his wife would have been so very to see them.

"Can I hold him?" said Marguerite, already completely in love with the boy.

"Yes," said Sarah and handed her John.

Marguerite took John in her arms and looked at this beautiful baby boy in awe. She hummed a calm tune to him as she swung him gently.

One year went by, Sarah was learning how to be a mother and did well. She got along very well with John and did the best she could to understand his needs and wants. He was a very calm and easy baby; he occasionally cried, usually only when hungry. He seemed to want to grow quickly, attempting to crawl everywhere.

Eli loved his son and spent his time playing hide and seek talking to him.

It was John's first birthday, they celebrated all together in the dining room. Marguerite held John up on his feet.

"Look! He took his first step!" said Marguerite excitedly.

John smiled, looking at them all proudly. He took a few more steps and then started to crawl again.

"That's my boy!" said Eli, encouraging him.

Sarah and Eli looked at their son and kissed each other. John crawled towards Yuki and laid next to him;

he loved Yuki. Yuki had taken as his mission to protect John; he always slept next to his crib.

The whole family was doing very well. Eli and Jean-Pierre continued to manage the farm, although Jean-Pierre was starting to get older and tired quickly. Marguerite spent her time taking care of the house and John.

One evening in August 1926, Sarah was reading a story to John in the living room. Eli entered, kissed Sarah and then picked up his son. John grabbed onto Eli's pocket watch and looked at it with lots of interest.

"You like it?" asked Eli.

"Dada," said John, smiling.

He started to speak words and continued to play with Eli's pocket watch.

"Let's have another one?" said Sarah.

Eli looked at his wife lovingly.

"Yes," said Eli, kissing Sarah.

Life on the farm was peaceful, and John had brought them more joy than they could have imagined.

Thirty-three ∞ Yuki

Sarah was in the living room in front of the fireplace, reading a book while Yuki was right in front of the crackling fire. Yuki usually slept in John's bedroom, but he was getting older and had a harder time making it up the stairs.

"You are such a good boy," she said as she sat next to him.

He moved slightly; Sarah knew that Yuki was coming to the end of his life. Yuki was fourteen years old, for a Labrador, that was old.

"Thank you for everything, you have been such a good friend."

Sarah was overwhelmed by sadness; she sensed that Yuki was saying goodbye. Eli came into the room and saw Sarah and Yuki.

"I think I am going to spend the night here with him," said Sarah.

"Do you want me to stay with you?" said Eli, knowing how difficult this must be for Sarah.

"No, that's okay."

Eli pet Yuki and kissed him on the head.

"Good night, honey."

Eli left the room and Sarah got a blanket, put it on the floor next to Yuki and laid next to him.

In the middle of the night, Eli checked on Sarah and Yuki. They were both completely asleep; he placed another blanket on top of Sarah and added a log to the fire.

The next morning when Sarah woke up, Yuki wasn't breathing anymore.

"Goodbye, Yuki, thank you for everything," she cried quietly.

She kissed him on the nose and pet him. His body was cold. Eli entered half an hour later and saw Sarah crying and took her in his arms.

"He was so good to us," said Sarah.

"Yes, he was," replied Eli.

Eli took Yuki's body and wrapped it in a blanket. He went outside with Jean-Pierre, and they dug a hole next to where Sarah's mother was buried. Jean-Pierre struggled as he was reminded of his wife's death.

Marguerite was in the kitchen with John and Sarah when Eli came back in.

"It's time," he said, looking at Sarah.

"I will stay here with John," said Marguerite.

"Thank you," replied Eli.

Sarah was terribly sad; Eli took her in his arms once more as she cried. They walked to the front entrance, Eli picked up Yuki's body.

"Let me see him one more time," said Sarah, removing the blanket from Yuki's face. She kissed him on his head and then covered him back with the blanket.

They went next to the tree; Jean-Pierre stood in front of the hole. Eli placed Yuki in the ground, and they covered him up with dirt. Sarah wept quietly. Eli and Jean-Pierre finished tapping the soil on top of Yuki's body and stood there silently.

"I would like to be alone with him," said Sarah.

"Are you sure you don't want me to stay with you?" asked Eli.

"Yes, I'll be all right."

Eli kissed Sarah on the cheek, and they left her.

"Goodbye Yuki, thank you for all the times we played together, thank you for your help and love, you have been so good to me, I love you," whispered Sarah.

She stood there silently and then made her way back to the kitchen.

"I am sorry, honey," said Marguerite as she hugged Sarah.

"I am going to rest for a bit," said Sarah.

Eli accompanied her; she got into bed, he covered her with a blanket, kissed her, and laid next to her. She fell asleep immediately. Eli watched her sleep; he felt her pain and had a hard time bearing it, he knew how much she loved Yuki. He thought about all the times they played together as children; he thought about the time they dressed up Yuki in a skirt and a necklace. He thought about the time Yuki saved Sarah's life when she almost fell off the tree and he thought about how excited Yuki was to meet John. Yuki's death brought sadness to the farm, but Sarah worked through her pain with the love and help of her family.

John grew quickly, making his family laugh a lot. He had a very logical mind. He loved to play with clocks; he constantly took them apart and put them back together.

It was the 14th of October 1926. Sarah, John, and Marguerite were in the kitchen. John was on the floor, taking apart an old clock Eli gave him while Sarah and Marguerite prepared dinner.

"Dinner will be ready soon, will you ring the bell?" asked Marguerite.

"Yes, of course," replied Sarah.

She went in front of the farm and tolled the old bell. She waited for a minute and saw Jean-Pierre appear but not Eli. She went to the greenhouse, opened the door, and saw Eli surrounded by his roses; she hadn't been in the greenhouse in a while; it looked as beautiful as ever.

"Dinner is ready," said Sarah.

"Thank you," Eli replied.

"This one is beautiful," Sarah pointed to a hybrid rose Eli was examining.

"Thank you, I've been working on it for a while now; hopefully, it will be as beautiful as *Sarah*," said Eli.

Eli stood up in front of his wife, admiring her beauty.

"I am so lucky, you know?" said Eli.

"What do you mean?" replied Sarah.

"You, I have you in my life."

He started kissing Sarah, the kiss turned heated.

"I love you so much," Eli said.

He started to caress her, and they made love in the greenhouse; it was very intense. When he was inside her, she stopped and gazed at him for a moment.

"I love you for eternity," she said.

"I love you for eternity," he replied.

They once again had the feeling of flying bodiless as they made love. They orgasmed and laid on the floor in the greenhouse, completely breathless.

"We probably have to go and have dinner?" said Eli, smiling.

They burst into laughter.

"Yes," replied Sarah.

They got up and walked to the kitchen; Jean-Pierre, John, and Marguerite were having dinner. As they entered, Marguerite looked at them and could tell they had sex; she didn't say anything but smiled.

"Are you hungry?" asked Marguerite.

"Starving," they both said at the same time.

Time flew, and winter arrived. Marguerite spent her evening's knitting sweaters for the family while Sarah had taken over the nightly reading. Eli and Jean-Pierre had taken up chess.

It was February 1927, Sarah started to show. She was pregnant and due to give birth in July. John, who was now two-and-a-half years old, spent most of his time with Eli on the farm. He loved having time with his father and helped him in the small ways he could.

Sometimes he brought a small bucket while Eli milked the cows, and he also fed the pigs.

Eli and John were in the greenhouse together on the 13th of March; Eli watered a rose.

"They can hear you, you know," said Eli.

"What do you mean?" asked John.

"The flowers and roses can hear you, if you tell them you love them, they will tell you they love you back, they won't tell you with words, but they will tell you in their own way by becoming even more beautiful," said Eli.

John was a bit perplexed by this and thought about it for a while.

"You mean if I talk to them, they will hear me?" asked John.

"Yes," replied Eli.

"Okay, I will talk to them," said John.

Summer arrived, the farm looked beautiful with its flowers and vegetables. Eli and his son spent afternoons together in the greenhouse; John enjoyed how much his father loved being with his flowers.

On the 19th of July 1928, John played hide and seek with Marguerite in front of the farm.

"Where are you? I cannot find you," said Marguerite loudly.

John giggled; he was hiding behind a barrel a few feet away.

"Where could John be? I really wonder," said Marguerite loudly.

John giggled again.

"I wonder if he is behind the hay?" Marguerite walked towards the hay.

John let out another chuckle.

"Or near the table?"

John giggled again.

"What do I hear? Could it be that *you* are behind this barrel?" said Marguerite as she walked towards the barrel.

John laughed out loud.

"I found you!" said Marguerite.

"You found me!" replied John.

She hugged him; she loved him so much and enjoyed each moment she could get with him. Sarah came walking out of the house, holding her belly that was now enormous.

"I think it's time," said Sarah, trying to catch her breath.

Marguerite looked at Sarah.

"Eli! Eli!" shouted Marguerite.

Eli came running.

"Take John, Sarah is going to have the baby, tell Jean-Pierre to go to the village and get Hélène," said Marguerite.

"Yes, right away," replied Eli.

He picked up John and went to the chicken coop to get Jean-Pierre. Marguerite helped Sarah to her room. Sarah's contractions were fast.

An hour later, Hélène entered the room and got right to work; Sarah was screaming, in full labor.

"Ahhhh!" yelled Sarah.

"Push, push, push, I can see his head," said Hélène.

Marguerite held Sarah's hand.

Eli, Jean-Pierre, and John were in the living room; Eli was stressed but not as much as the first time.

"Why is Mama yelling?" asked John.

"She is giving birth to your brother, she will be fine, it's all right, don't worry," replied Eli.

"I'm scared," said John.

"It's fine, Mama is doing fine," said Eli trying to reassure his son.

"Let's go for a walk, John," said Jean-Pierre.

"Thank you," said Eli to Jean-Pierre.

Jean-Pierre took John by the hand, and they went outside.

"But I want to see Mama," whined John.

"We will come back after, and you will meet your brother," said Jean-Pierre.

"Okay, okay," replied John looking back towards the house.

Eli paced back and forth in the living room; he thought about Yuki, remembering that he was next to him last time Sarah gave birth.

An hour later, Sarah gave birth to a little girl; Hélène took the baby and handed her to Sarah.

"Oh, you are a girl," said Sarah.

"She is so beautiful," said Marguerite looking at this tiny baby.

Eli heard the baby crying, ran upstairs, and entered the room. He saw Sarah holding a baby in her arms; she smiled as she saw Eli.

"It's a girl," said Sarah.

"A girl? Oh my... she is so beautiful," said Eli as he got closer to them.

He stared at Sarah and then at their daughter. She had lots of dark hair.

"What do you think about Margot?" asked Sarah.

"I love it," replied Eli.

"Margot Françoise Durand," said Sarah.

"Yes," said Eli looking at this precious little girl.

He touched her hand, she grabbed onto one of his fingers, he fell in love with her instantly.

Thirty-four ∞ Margot

"Meet your baby sister," said Sarah, waving at John to get closer to her.

John touched Margot's face gently.

"Very gentle, she is a little baby," said Eli.

"Her name is Margot," said Sarah.

John was curious about his little sister; she looked so small and fragile; he stared at her for a while.

The next day Marguerite went to the toy store at the village to pick out a doll for Margot.

"Congratulations! Hélène told me it was a girl," said the shopkeeper.

"Thank you, yes, we are thrilled," replied Marguerite.

"What would you like?"

"I was thinking of a doll, perhaps."

"The dolls are over there."

"Thank you."

There were a few dolls and some soft toys. Marguerite saw a giraffe that looked very cute. She hesitated between a little doll and a giraffe before deciding to get the giraffe. As she went to pay, she saw a red tractor made out of metal. She picked it up and looked at it.

"Boys love the tractor; you can take it apart and put it back together," said the lady.

"I will buy this for John," said Marguerite.

Marguerite got back to the farm with her gifts.

"John?" said Marguerite.

John came running down the stairs.

"I got you a gift," said Marguerite.

"A gift for me?" replied John.

"Yes," said Marguerite.

He opened the gift.

"A tractor!" said John.

"Yes, you can take it apart and put it back together."

"Thank you, I love it," said John, already playing with it.

Marguerite went upstairs. Eli and Jean-Pierre were sitting next to Sarah and Margot.

"Look what I got for Margot," said Marguerite.

"A giraffe?" Sarah said, surprised.

"Yes, it's really soft, I thought she would prefer it to a doll," said Marguerite.

"Thank you," said Sarah, taking the giraffe.

"Look what your grandmother got you," Sarah said to Margot.

She put the giraffe next to Margot's hand; she grabbed the giraffe with her little fingers. Margot fell asleep next to it.

A year went by, Margot grew quickly. Sarah was in heaven, with a boy and a girl. They were all sure it was going be another boy for some reason. Margot began crawling. She spent a lot of time smiling; she was an incredibly easy baby as well and slept with her giraffe every night.

The men continued to manage the farm. Marguerite and Sarah took care of the house and the children. John grew into a smart little boy. He put together and took apart anything he could put his hands on. He had taken apart every clock in the house; Marguerite found small bolts on the floor every once in a while and wondered how the clocks still worked. The house was filled with joy.

Time flew; the children got older. Margot was now talking. She went everywhere with her giraffe, Gigi. Gigi was her best friend.

It was Christmas Eve, 1930. Jean-Pierre and Eli had put a Christmas tree in the living room. The children were incredibly excited. They had become good friends and spent a lot of time playing together. John was older but had a lot of patience with his sister. Sarah and Marguerite had prepared a lovely dinner and set up a beautiful table in the dining room.

"Christmas dinner is ready!" said Eli.

"Yay!" replied John and rushed to sit down.

Eli helped Margot in her chair and then took the heavy pot from the kitchen and brought it into the dining room. Everyone was seated, ready for the feast.

"When are we going to open the presents?" asked John.

"After dinner, honey," replied Sarah.

"Would you like to do the honors, Mama?" said Eli to Marguerite.

"Yes," replied Marguerite.

They all put their hands together.

"In a world where so many are hungry, may we eat this food with humble hearts. In a world where so many are lonely, may we share this friendship with joyful hearts. Amen," said Marguerite.

"Amen," said everyone.

They had steak with mashed potatoes and a big salad.

"Mama, can I have a sip of wine, please?" asked John.

"You can only dip your lips in it, honey, no more," replied Sarah.

Eli handed his glass of wine to John, who barely dipped his lips in the glass.

"I'm like an adult," said John, smiling.

"Yes, okay, that's enough," said Eli, taking his wine back.

John was always negotiating to have a sip of wine to be like the adults. They had a wonderful dinner together.

"It's time for the Yule log," said Sarah getting up.

The children got very excited; they loved the moment with the Yule log as they wondered who would get the prize that Sarah, or Santa-Claus, they believed, had hidden in the cake. Marguerite helped Sarah take the plates away and came back with the Yule log. Marguerite put a dessert plate in front of each person.

"Gigi wants one too," said Margot smiling.

"She can eat with you, okay?" said Marguerite.

"Okay," replied Margot.

Sarah gave everyone a slice of the log. The adults ate their piece of cake while the children looked into it to find a prize.

"I found it!" said John taking out a tiny action figure.

Margot looked disappointed.

"Honey, continue looking, there might be one in yours as well," said Sarah.

"Oh," replied Margot, brightening up and continuing to search.

She put her hand through her entire cake and found a small plastic teddy bear.

"I have one too!" said Margot, extremely happy.

"You both win!" said Sarah.

"Is it time for the presents?" asked John impatiently.

"Yes, but first wash your hands, honey," replied Sarah.

John raced to the kitchen to wash his hands. Eli took Margot out of her chair and helped her wash her hands. Margot liked to do everything herself, so Eli was merely *helping her*.

Jean-Pierre, Marguerite, Sarah, Eli, and the children all gathered around the Christmas tree in the living room in front of a warm fire. There were gifts under the beautifully decorated tree. Marguerite and the children had made little clay decorations for the tree.

John and Margot each opened presents. John got a few cars that he could take apart and put together while Margot got a pretty doll and some books. They were both very excited. Margot sat on the floor with her new doll while she started to pretend like Gigi was talking to her doll.

"Hi, what's your name?" said Margot in the stead of Gigi.

"My name is Melanie," replied Margot as the doll.

"You can be my friend," continued Margot.

"I will make some chamomile tea; who wants one?" asked Sarah to the adults.

Jean-Pierre, Marguerite, and Eli all wanted one.

"Let me help you," said Eli as he stood up.

Eli and Sarah were in the kitchen together; Sarah warmed up the water on the stove and prepared the teacups; Eli came from behind her and kissed her in the neck.

"Hello, you," said Eli.

Sarah turned around, facing him, and kissed him. They were satisfied with their lives.

"Look how happy they are," said Eli.

"Yes," replied Sarah.

"My gift will always be you, my love."

"And mine, you."

Sarah spooned honey into the chamomile teas.

"I know," said Sarah as Eli looked at the quantity of honey she put in the teas.

"It's good for the body," they said together.

Eli teased Sarah with her honey theory; she believed that honey helped the body stay healthy; they laughed. Sarah and Eli came back to the living room with the tea. Jean-Pierre was watching the children play, half dozing off while Marguerite was playing with John.

"It's time for the story," said Sarah.

She sat in her armchair and took out a book. The children stopped playing and laid down on the floor looking up at their mother, ready for their nightly story. They loved to listen to her read; she made different voices for each character and sometimes acted out scenes. This was their favorite family moment every day. The children fell asleep on the floor, and Jean-Pierre fell asleep in his chair.

"Good night," said Marguerite getting up.

Sarah touched her father on his shoulder to wake him up.

"Ah, yes, yes," said Jean-Pierre, waking up from his doze.

Eli took John in his arms while Sarah took Margot, and they brought the children to their room and put them to bed. Sarah put Gigi next to Margot.

The next morning the children woke up. Margot was whispering to Gigi.

"Then, I went flying to the chicken coop with my magic telescope."

John heard Margot.

"What do you mean you were flying? We can't actually fly, you know," said John.

"I can, I go flying every night."

"You mean you were imagining that you were flying?" said John.

"No, I mean Gigi and I went flying to the chicken coop," replied Margot.

"Okay, fine. I am hungry, should we get some breakfast?" said John.

"Yes," replied Margot as she got out of bed, hugging Gigi.

They ran down the stairs; John ran behind Margot playing their usual game.

"I am going to get you!" said John.

"No!!" replied Margot, running down the stairs.

"I am a wolf, and I am going to get you!" reiterated John.

"Ahhh!" yelled Margot as she ran faster down the stairs.

She got to the bottom.

"I won!" said Margot proudly.

"Yes, you won!" said John pretending like he couldn't go faster than her.

Sarah was in the kitchen preparing breakfast while Eli was having his coffee.

"Hi, Papa, hi, Mama," said the children.

"Good morning! Did you sleep well?" asked Sarah.

"Yes, I am starving," said John.

"Here you go, I made an omelet," said Sarah.

"Good morning," said Eli, kissing his children.

The children sat for breakfast.

"I thought we could make a snowman today," said Eli.

"Yay!!" the children shouted.

They quickly ate, and Eli helped them put on their coats. Sarah was in kisses from Eli and the children before they left the house.

"Have fun!" said Sarah.

"Yes!" they said as they left.

Sarah went back to the kitchen and looked at her family lovingly through the window as she sipped her coffee. Marguerite entered the kitchen.

"Hi honey, where are the children?" asked Marguerite, surprised by the house's silence.

"They went outside to make a snowman," replied Sarah.

"How nice," said Marguerite, making herself a cup of coffee.

"Eli is so happy when he is with them, look," said Sarah, pointing through the window.

"Yes," replied Marguerite, observing them lovingly.

"I was thinking of making a ratatouille with pork for lunch," said Sarah.

"That sounds great, do you want some help?"

"No, it's fine," said Sarah, as she started to take out vegetables to wash.

The children were still outside with Eli making a snowman. Margot went to look for two sticks for the arms; she found a branch.

"Look, Gigi, I found an arm, now we need another one," said Margot to Gigi.

Eli looked at his daughter, talking to her giraffe, loving every moment of it. John and Eli finished making the round body of the snowman.

"Now let's do the upper part," said Eli.

"What are we going to use for the nose?" asked John.

"What do you think?"

"A carrot?" said John.

"Yes!"

Margot came back with two sticks.

"Look, Papa, we found the arms," said Margot.

"Thank you, honey," replied Eli.

"Can I put the carrot on?" asked John.

"Yes," replied Eli, handing John the carrot.

"All done! What's his name?" said John.

"What do you want to call him?" asked Eli.

"I think we should call him *Snowman*," said John.

"Yes, I like *Snowman*," said Margot.

"*Snowman*, it is!"

They started rolling snowballs and tossed them at each other. They finally fell into the snow next to each other exhausted from running around. They laid back and made snow angels; Margot made one for Gigi as well.

"Gigi's is the smallest one," said Margot.

"Yes, she has a smaller body," replied Eli.

"I love Gigi," said Margot.

"Me too," said Eli.

"Me too," said John.

Thirty-five ∞ Jean-Pierre

A few hours later, Jean-Pierre had still not shown up in the kitchen. Sarah went to the living room where Marguerite was knitting.

"Have you seen Papa?" asked Sarah.

"No, I haven't seen him all morning," replied Marguerite.

"I will check in his room," said Sarah, as she started going up the stairs.

She knocked on her father's door, there was no answer.

"Papa?" said Sarah.

No answer. She entered the room and saw her father still sleeping. She pat him on the shoulder and he woke up.

"Are you all right, Papa? It's 11:30."

"Yes, I am tired is all."

"Do you need anything?"

"No, I am fine, thank you, I'll be down in a minute," replied Jean-Pierre as he slowly woke up.

"Okay."

She went back to the kitchen, a bit worried about her father; he had been sleeping more lately.

Five months went by, Marguerite spent more time with her grandchildren while Sarah ran the house, and Eli managed the farm. Jean-Pierre helped Eli, but he tired easily and worked at a much slower pace.

Eli and Jean-Pierre were in the barn; Jean-Pierre milked the cows while Eli cut up the meat. Jean-Pierre was sitting on a stool milking a cow when he fell to the floor; Eli ran to help him.

"Are you all right?" asked Eli.

Jean-Pierre tried to get up but struggled.

"I am fine, don't worry, boy," said Jean-Pierre.

Eli took Jean-Pierre to the house and brought him to the kitchen.

"What happened?" asked Sarah.

"I am just a bit tired," replied Jean-Pierre.

He took a seat, and Sarah gave him a warm cup of soup.

"Drink this," said Sarah.

Jean-Pierre sat there, quiet, and drank the cup of soup.

"I am going back to the farm, will you be okay?" asked Eli.

"I'll take care of him," replied Sarah.

He kissed his wife as he left. There was a silence in the kitchen; Sarah broke the silence.

"Margot has been reading lately; she's really good at reading."

"Good," said Jean-Pierre.

"She wants me to teach her how to write," said Sarah.

"Good," replied Jean-Pierre quietly.

"Do you want to sit in the living room, Papa?" asked Sarah.

"No, I am fine," said Jean-Pierre.

Sarah continued to prepare dinner while her father sat there, not saying a word, simply looking at her.

"You are so beautiful, Françoise," said Jean-Pierre.

With teary eyes, Sarah looked at her father and realized that he was lost in his thoughts, thinking about his wife. Sarah went around the kitchen counter and took her father in her arms.

"It will be all right, Papa," said Sarah, keeping it together.

Jean-Pierre didn't say anything; he continued to look vaguely into the kitchen as he drank his soup quietly. Sarah didn't say anything but simply observed him.

Ten minutes later, Jean-Pierre struggled to get up from his chair, Sarah helped him to his feet.

"Why don't you lie down on the couch in the living room while I finish preparing dinner?" said Sarah.

"Good idea," replied Jean-Pierre.

Sarah took her father to the couch and covered him with a blanket. She went back to the kitchen and finished preparing dinner. Marguerite and the children came back to the house after a long hike.

"Hi, Mama!" the children entered.

"Hi, did you have fun?" asked Sarah.

"Yes, I found a lot of acorns in the forest!" said John.

"Oh good," replied Sarah.

"Yeah, I'm making a collection of them," said John.

"And we saw a deer with babies," said Margot.

"How nice, dinner is going to be ready soon," replied Sarah.

"Okay, children, let's go wash up before dinner," said Marguerite.

Eli came into the house; he was done for the day. He went into the kitchen to see Sarah.

"Hi you," said Eli as he kissed Sarah.

"Hi," said Sarah in a not too joyful voice.

"What's wrong?" asked Eli.

"It's Papa, he's not doing great, he talked to me as if I was my mother, he seems really tired lately, I am starting to get really worried," said Sarah.

"I'm sorry, honey, it's true that he has been sleeping a lot lately, maybe he's simply getting a bit older, do you want me to check up on him?" asked Eli.

"Yes, he's on the couch in the living room," said Sarah.

"Okay," replied Eli.

"Thanks love," said Sarah.

Eli knew that Sarah feared the worst. They had already gone through a lot and couldn't fathom the thought of another death in the family. Eli went to the living room and saw that Jean-Pierre was sleeping; he got closer to him, he could hear Jean-Pierre breathing loudly, it didn't sound great. He went back to the kitchen to see Sarah.

"He is sleeping," said Eli.

"Okay," replied Sarah.

"But I think you should go see him; he has a hard time breathing," said Eli.

"Okay," replied Sarah, leaving the kitchen immediately.

Eli followed her. Sarah saw her father, he was sound asleep; she heard that he had difficulty breathing. She sat on the floor next to him, while Eli stood behind her. She started to cry; she knew her father was on his way out; she had seen too many dying men in her life.

"I'll be fine," said Sarah, as she abruptly stood up.

Eli saw that she was trying to stay tough as always.

"Should we wake him up for dinner?" asked Eli.

"No, we should let him sleep, I'll come and see him after," replied Sarah.

"Okay."

They went back to the kitchen. Sarah was very quiet. The children came running into the kitchen; Sarah hid her emotions and cheered up.

"Dinner time, are you both all cleaned up?" said Sarah, smiling.

"Yes," the children replied.

"Okay, take a seat, I'm coming," said Sarah.

Eli took the children to the dining room, and Marguerite helped Sarah bring in the food.

"Where is grandfather?" asked John.

Sarah got tense.

"He is taking a nap," said Eli.

"He is taking a nap this late?" asked John.

"Because he is tired," said Margot innocently.

"Yes, he is tired," said Eli.

Marguerite looked at Sarah and noticed her silence; she understood that something was wrong. They all had dinner, and then Sarah started to clean up with Eli's help.

"What story are you going to read tonight, Mama?" asked Margot.

"No story tonight, honey," said Sarah.

"Why? We want a story," said Margot.

"Marguerite will read you a story in your room tonight, okay?" said Sarah.

"But we prefer it when you do the story," said John.

"Yes, but tonight your grandmother will read you a story, okay?"

"But why?" asked John.

Sarah started to tear up.

"Because your grandfather is sick, I want to stay with him, now go up in your room," said Sarah.

"Okay, Mama," said John, having never seen his mother like this before.

"Don't be sad, Mama, he told me he will be fine," said Margot.

"What do you mean *he told you he will be fine?*" asked Sarah.

"Yesterday, when grandfather fell, he told me he would be fine, he said he would see grandmother," said Margot.

Sarah started to cry; she couldn't hold back her tears anymore; her children stared at her.

"Yes, honey, you are right, grandfather will be fine," said Sarah, as she tightly hugged her daughter.

"I love you, Mama," said Margot.

"I love you too, honey," replied Sarah, smiling.

"Okay, come on children, I will read you a story," said Marguerite.

John ran into his mother's arms and hugged her tightly.

"I love you, Mama," said John.

"I love you so much, my darling," replied Sarah.

"Good night," the children said together.

"Good night."

As Margot went towards her room, she saw Jean-Pierre in the living room, went to him, and touched his hand to say goodbye.

"She already knew," said Sarah, crying in Eli's arms.

"She is very intuitive," replied Eli.

Sarah sat next to her father in the living room; she could hear his breathing get heavier and heavier. Eli sat in the armchair near Jean-Pierre. Sarah took her father's hand, he moved slightly and opened his eyes to see his daughter.

"It will be fine, my darling, you have made such a beautiful life, and you have an amazing family," whispered Jean-Pierre.

"I don't want you to go," said Sarah.

"You will be fine, Eli and the children will take care of you, and I will see your mother again."

"Yes," whispered Sarah, as she cried.

"I love you, you have given me everything a father could ever ask for."

"I love you too," whispered Sarah.

She held onto his hand tightly. He closed his eyes. His breathing slowed down. Sarah got closer to him, and he then stopped breathing completely. Eli teared up and Sarah cried profusely. Eli took her in his arms while Sarah continued to sob, unable to control her tears. Slowly, Sarah tired and laid down on the floor next to her father. Eli put a blanket on top of her and sat next to her, holding her tightly. She fell asleep on Eli's lap. Eli stayed there and eventually fell asleep as well.

At six in the morning, Eli woke up, Sarah was still sleeping. He touched Jean-Pierre, his head was cold. Sarah woke up, immediately looks towards her father. Maybe this had been a bad dream, she thought, but no, her father was breathless on the couch. Sarah had red eyes. She touched her father's arm and removed her hand immediately when she felt his cold body. She looked at Eli, devastated, he held her tightly. She felt his warmth; and was comforted that Eli was there.

"I need to get some coffee," she said.

He followed her, not saying a word. They got to the kitchen.

"We have to remove his body before the children wake up," said Sarah.

"Yes, I'll handle it," replied Eli.

"Thank you," said Sarah holding back her tears.

Eli went back to the living room and wrapped Jean-Pierre's body in a blanket. He gently took his body to the entrance. Sarah heard him from the kitchen and went to the door.

"Let me see him once more," said Sarah, crying.

Eli removed the blanket from Jean-Pierre's face. His face was lifeless; the soul had departed.

"He is gone... Where do you think he went?" asked Sarah, crying.

"I think he went to see your mother, I'm sure he'll come back to check up on us," said Eli.

"Yes, I think you are right, but there are so many more things I wish I could have told him," said Sarah.

"You can still tell him what you want to tell him, I think he'll hear you," replied Eli.

"Okay."

She looked at her dad and whispered, "Bye, Papa."

"Can you bury him next to my mother and Yuki?"

"Yes, of course," said Eli.

Sarah put the blanket back on her father's face. Eli kissed Sarah on the forehead and left before digging a hole in the ground next to where Françoise and Yuki were buried. He was sweating, although Autumn had arrived, it was chilly. Red leaves covered the ground.

Two hours later, Eli had finished digging a hole big enough for Jean-Pierre's body. He gently rolled Jean-Pierre in the spot and covered him with dirt. He came back into the house, his white t-shirt smeared with soil.

"Did you do it?" asked Sarah.

"Yes, he is right next to your mother," replied Eli.

"At least he is with her now."

"Yes."

The children and Marguerite came into the kitchen. The energy was heavy, and the children could feel it.

"Where is grandfather?" asked John.

Margot sensed and didn't say anything. Sarah crouched down to be eye to eye with her children.

"Grandfather went to see grandmother," said Sarah, trying to keep it together in front of her children.

The children understood immediately and didn't ask any more questions. Marguerite prepared the children for the funeral.

The family went to the back of the house near the tree and the greenhouse. The dirt on the ground was still fresh from Eli's digging. Eli officiated the funeral ceremony.

"We thank you for being a part of this family and for everything you have brought to us. We wish you a nice adventure in your afterlife, we wish you to be reunited with your love, we will see you again," said Eli.

"Thank you for everything, Papa, we all love you," said Sarah, crying.

Everyone started to head back to the house while Margot stayed behind for a minute.

"I am happy you are with grandmother, I love you," whispered Margot.

Jean-Pierre and Margot had a special relationship since she was born; they simply understood each other well. Margot knew he would be fine. She kissed her hand and then put her hand on the dirt where Jean-Pierre was buried. Sarah and Eli saw this. Sarah looked at Eli with loving eyes; Margot came running to catch up to her parents and took their hand. They all went back into the house.

"I am going to sleep a bit," said Sarah to Eli and Marguerite.

"Yes, I will take care of the children," said Marguerite.

Sarah kissed Eli on the lips.

"Should I come up with you?" asked Eli.

"No, I'm fine," replied Sarah.

She wanted to be alone for a moment. The children sat in the kitchen silently.

"Who wants pancakes?" asked Eli.

"Me!!"

Eli prepared pancakes. He did everything he could to bring back some joy to the house. He flipped the pancakes in the air and caught them in the pan. The children laughed.

"Do it again, do it again!" the children cheered.

Eli obliged. They spent a good part of the morning laughing and making pancakes. Marguerite was amazed by her son's strength.

Ten days went by, Sarah slept more than usual and spent most of the time in her bedroom. Eli managed the farm, and Marguerite took care of the children and the house.

Margot entered Sarah's room one afternoon.

"Mama?" said Margot.

"Yes, honey?" replied Sarah.

"Do you want me to read you a story?" asked Margot.

Sarah was amazed at Margot's empathy and how she was trying to help.

"I would love that," said Sarah, looking at her daughter lovingly.

Margot laid next to her mother in bed and started to read a story.

"Once upon a time, there was a beautiful Mama, and she had two incredible children. They lived on a beautiful farm, and they had lots of chickens. Their Papa was the most incredible Papa on the planet. He was kind and worked a lot, and he loved their mother more than anyone else in the world. They also had a very nice grandmother that loved to knit. What always kept the whole family happy was that they loved each other to the moon and back."

Sarah listened to the story and realized that Margot was talking about their family. She looked at the book and saw it was a different story.

"Honey, did you make up that story?" said Sarah proudly.

"Yes, it's our story, I want you to be happy again, we miss you, Mama," said Margot.

Sarah started to cry, not because she was sad but because she was so happy to have such an amazing daughter and family.

"You are right, honey," whispered Sarah to her daughter.

Margot looked at her mother with compassion for a long moment. Sarah looked at her daughter and hugged her tightly.

"Thank you," whispered Sarah.

Margot kissed her mother on the cheek.

"Should we go bake a cake?" said Sarah joyfully.

"Yes!" replied Margot.

Sarah got out of bed for the first time in ten days. Margot took her mother by the hand and directed her downstairs as if Margot was the mother and Sarah the daughter. Marguerite was in the kitchen preparing dinner when she saw Sarah walk in with Margot.

"Hi honey, how are you doing?" asked Marguerite.

"I am doing better, everything will be all right; thank you for taking care of the kids and the house," said Sarah.

Marguerite took Sarah in her arms.

"Yes, everything will be okay, dear," said Marguerite.

Thirty-six ∞ Family

Sarah, Marguerite, and Margot baked a cake and had fun in the kitchen. Eli and John worked in the greenhouse together. Eli watered his plants while John whispered to the roses.

"Do you think Mama is going to be okay?" asked John.

"Yes, Mama is strong, she is sad because she misses her father, but she will be fine, come here," said Eli, welcoming his son in his arms, "It will be all right, I promise."

"I miss her," said John.

"I know, me too," replied Eli.

An hour later, Eli and John went back to the house. On their way to the house, John found an acorn.

"Look, Papa, I found an acorn."

"That's great, honey."

"I'm going to add it to my collection."

They approached the house, and from outside, Eli saw Sarah laughing in the kitchen with Margot and Marguerite. They were throwing flour at each other.

"Look!" said Eli, pointing towards the kitchen window.

"Mama is back!" said John.

"Oh yes, she is," replied Eli, laughing.

They entered the kitchen, Sarah looked at her husband and son. John ran into his mother's arms to hug her. Eli kissed Sarah lovingly. Margot threw a handful of flour at Sarah.

"I will get you!" said Sarah, laughing.

The boys joined in on the flour fight; the kitchen was a disaster with flour everywhere. Eli dumped flour on Sarah's head, got closer to her, stared her in the eyes, and kissed her.

"Ooooh, you're kissing," the children said as they looked, making a grimace.

"Okay, I think it's time for dinner, let's get cleaned up," said Marguerite.

The children followed Marguerite upstairs to clean up. Sarah and Eli were still in the kitchen, kissing romantically.

"God, I love you so much," said Eli, looking at his wife.

"Me too, thank you for being who you are," replied Sarah.

They cleaned up the kitchen and went upstairs to wash up. Eli took his clothes off and went into the shower. Sarah watched him, undress. She undressed and then joined him in the shower.

"Oh?' said Eli in a playful manner.

"May I?" replied Sarah, cheekily.

"Well, yes, you may," said Eli, as he grabbed his wife.

They made love in the shower.

Two years went by, the children grew. The farm was doing well. Margot started to read and was learning how to write well; she wanted to become a writer. She read all her stories to her giraffe. John helped his father on the farm and spent time with him in his greenhouse. He learned all the plants' names and even started to help his father create hybrid roses. He went to school in the village and had a knack for mathematics and science. He dreamed of becoming an inventor when he grew up.

One evening in the winter of 1933, Margot read a story to the family. They sat in the living room, listening to her and staying warm by the fireplace.

"Then, Jack, the little boy went downstairs. He saw his mama baking a cake in the kitchen. He had to exit through the kitchen, or else his mother would hear the front door. He quietly walked through the kitchen without being noticed. It was late at night, and he knew that his mother would disapprove of him going out. He went out of the house, turned around, and saw his mother from a distance. She hadn't noticed anything. He was very silent and quietly walked to his treehouse. He went up the stairs and turned on the light. He waited for his elf friend to come," read Margot.

Margot interrupted her reading.

"Did you hear Gigi? He has an elf friend."

Margot's family found it sweet that she still talked to Gigi as a real friend.

"His elf friend was called Jim, they had become best friends. Jack and Jim spent every evening together, playing chess."

John laid on the floor, listening to his sister when he saw a daddy long leg spider. He was not afraid of insects or spiders and took it in his hand and played with it. Sarah sat in her armchair next to Eli while Marguerite was on the couch, half-asleep. John sneaked behind his mother and put the daddy long leg spider on his mother's scarf. He started giggling.

"What is it?" said Sarah.

"You have a spider on your scarf," replied John, giggling.

Sarah jumped up.

"What? Ahhh, get it off me!" yelled Sarah.

Eli took the daddy long leg spider off of Sarah and put it on the floor; John laughed out loud.

"Did you do this?" asked Sarah, in a playful manner.

"Yes! I did!" replied John, owning up to it and cracking up.

Sarah started to laugh, although still a bit frightened.

"You cheeky boy!" said Sarah, smiling.

John was on the floor, he could not stop laughing. Margot started to laugh, as well and Eli smiled.

"It's not funny!" Sarah protested.

Marguerite woke up.

"What's happening?" said Marguerite.

"Everything is fine," replied Eli.

"Fine for *you*, you mean," said Sarah, smiling at her husband.

"You want to read a bit more, honey?" Sarah asked Margot.

"Okay," replied Margot.

She continued to read until it got late, and they all went to bed.

A few weeks went by, the family enjoyed the winter with Margot's stories, and the warm fires Eli made every night.

It was Christmas Eve, everyone was excited. Marguerite and Sarah were in the kitchen while the children decorated the Christmas tree with Eli in the living room.

"This looks great, let's set-up the table now," said Eli.

They set the table with their father using the nice plates and silverware. Eli lit up tall candles on the table. Sarah came into the dining room with oysters and smoked salmon, while Marguerite brought escargot and mashed potatoes. They sat at the table and put their hands together for the prayer.

"Thank you for this wonderful meal, thank you for this loving family, and we thank you for those we love that are not here with us, Amen," said Sarah.

"Amen."

"Can I have some salmon, please, Papa?" asked John.

"Here, honey, and here are some mashed potatoes," replied Eli.

"Thank you."

"Can I have some escargot," said Margot.

"What's the magic word?" asked Sarah.

"Please, Mama," replied Margot.

"Here you go, honey," said Sarah.

The family enjoyed a great dinner, and Sarah brought in the Yule log. The children were still excited year after year about the Yule log because of the small hidden toys inside it; it never got old. Each year they made a wish when they found their little plastic toy.

"I got a little pink doll!" said Margot, excitedly.

"Margot likes everything that is pink," said John, proudly knowing what his sister liked.

"Yes," said Sarah, touching her daughter's hair.

"Oh! I got a monkey!" said John.

John closed his eyes.

"What are you wishing for?" asked Margot.

"I am not going to tell you; otherwise, it won't come true," replied John.

"Oh yes, that's true," realized Margot.

They had a wonderful Christmas.

Thirty-seven ∞ World War II

Six years went by; it was the month of February in the year of 1940.

John was now a teenager; he was brilliant and invented a watering system for his father's greenhouse. Margot, who was now eleven years old, wrote her own full stories. The farm was doing very well. Sarah and Eli loved each other more each day; their love never ceased to grow. They were proud of their children and the life they had created. Marguerite spent most of her time with the children and knitting sweaters for everyone.

In the village, people talked about nothing else but war. Eli got nervous as tension in the farm and village grew. Marguerite got agitated when she heard anything related to the war. She closed this chapter of her life and couldn't bear the thought of another war. Food was getting scarce for some of the villagers.

Frank Dumas, the general store owner of the village, came to the farm one morning.

"Hi, Frank," said Eli.

"Hi, Eli," replied Frank.

"What brings you here?"

Eli and Frank had known each other for years but had never been close friends.

"I've come to ask... um... for some help, I am having a hard time feeding my family, no one comes to the store anymore," said Frank, embarrassed about his situation.

"Oh, of course," replied Eli.

Eli knew that Frank must be in a very delicate situation; otherwise, he would not have taken the trouble of asking him, a mere acquaintance, for help.

"Please come in," said Eli to Frank.

Frank followed Eli into the house. They sat down in the living room. Frank was a nervous wreck but tried not to show it; Eli saw this and remembered the harder moments they endured and could relate to Frank very easily.

"We will help you, Frank, don't worry, we must help each other in these times," said Eli.

"Thank you very much."

"I will ask Sarah to put together a basket for your family."

Frank was extremely thankful. Eli got up and went to see Sarah in the kitchen; Sarah already knew what Frank had come for.

"I know, they keep coming," said Sarah.

"We have to help him, he has two children and his wife is pregnant," said Eli.

"Yes, of course, I am just worried it will come to a point where we will have to give out rations; otherwise, we will run out of food to give."

"We will do the best we can," said Eli.

"Yes," replied Sarah.

Eli took Sarah in his arms.

"Go back to see him; I will bring the basket," said Sarah.

"Thank you," replied Eli, as he left.

Sarah went to the back and prepared a basket for Frank's family with meat, vegetables, bread, cheese, and butter. Eli brought Frank a warm coffee.

"Drink this. It will keep you warm. Sarah is preparing a basket for you," Eli handed the mug to Frank.

"Thank you, thank you very much, Eli," replied Frank.

"I hear that the German's are retreating; the war might be over sooner than we think," said Eli.

"I hope you are right, but I heard that it was getting worse, my cousin from Strasbourg told me that he was called to fight," said Frank.

"Yes, I heard that the French army was gathering all the men they could, but hopefully it's for precaution," replied Eli.

"We'll see," said Frank, not very hopeful.

Sarah entered the living room with a basket of food.

"Here you go, I hope this will be enough to get you by for a bit," said Sarah, smiling at Frank.

"Thank you, thank you, I will repay you for this," said Frank.

"That's all right," replied Sarah.

Frank stood up and took the basket Sarah handed to him. Eli stood up as well and walked Frank to the door.

"Thank you very much," said Frank.

"You are welcome," replied Sarah.

Sarah and Eli stood at the door and watched him leave. Sarah went back to the kitchen; Eli followed her; she was pensive and worried.

"It will be all right, my love," said Eli.

"As long as we are together, we will be fine," replied Sarah.

"Yes."

"Do you think you will be called to the frontline?"

"I don't know."

"I heard that men were being gathered in Strasbourg."

"I heard the same."

"I can't do this without you, Eli."

"I will always be with you, wherever I am, you are my only home."

"All this is scaring me. I can't live without you."

"You won't, I promise you."

He looked at Sarah intensely and kissed her.

"We are together for eternity, remember?" said Eli, giving his wife a cute smile.

"Yes, I remember, for eternity."

"Everything will be fine."

Sarah was slightly reassured, but Eli could sense that she was still worried.

The children came into the kitchen with Marguerite.

"Mama, Mama, John hid Gigi, and he won't tell me where he put her!" said Margot.

"What is going on?" asked Sarah.

"Margot took my clock and won't tell me where she put it," replied John.

"I don't want you fighting, these are tough times, and we need to help each other, not fight, so I want you both to go figure this out on your own, okay?"

"Yes, sorry, Mama," the children replied.

The children left the kitchen while Marguerite stayed. Sarah looked at her children from the kitchen, she could barely hear what was being said, but she observed them.

"I am sorry, I put your clock under your pillow," said Margot.

"I am also sorry, I put Gigi under the blanket on the couch," replied John.

The two children looked at each other for a few seconds, and then John hugged his sister. They got along most of the time and loved each other dearly. Sarah looked at her children admiringly. They were good kids; she felt fortunate.

A few weeks went by, more and more villagers came to the farm to get food. More and more men were being called to fight.

Sarah's worst nightmare came knocking on the door on the 17th of April 1940. She was in the kitchen cooking when she heard the front door. She went to open the door and saw a French soldier.

"Yes?" said Sarah.

"All men are called to help at the front," said the soldier.

"But I only have my husband, what can I do if no one takes care of the farm?"

"I am sorry, madam, all men from the age of 18 to 65 are called to fight," said the soldier.

Sarah started to cry; Eli arrived from the farm and saw the soldier at the door.

"Are you Eli Durand?" asked the soldier, as he saw Eli approach.

"Yes," replied Eli.

"Here, all men have been called to go to war," said the soldier as he handed him a document.

"Madam," said the soldier, as he nodded and left.

Sarah was in a state of despair and stared at Eli.

"No, no, I can't," said Sarah, crying.

Eli took Sarah in his arms, trying to comfort her. Eli was very frightened himself but did not show this to his wife; he didn't want her to be more worried than she already was.

Marguerite and Margot arrived in the house and saw Sarah crying.

"What is going on?" asked Marguerite.

Sarah didn't respond.

"I have been called to the war," said Eli.

"No!"

"This document says I must leave tomorrow," said Eli.

Marguerite could see that Eli was frightened; she knew her son even when he hid his feelings and took him in her arms.

"It will be all right, son, you are a tough man," said Marguerite.

"Are you leaving us, Papa?" asked Margot.

"I will come back, honey, I am going to help our country fight the bad guys," said Eli.

"But when are you coming back?"

"I don't know."

Sarah was crying; she couldn't stop.

Margot ran out of the house and went to the greenhouse. She opened the door in such a hurry that it startled John, who was arranging some plants.

"Papa is leaving, Papa is leaving!" yelled Margot.

"What are you talking about?"

"Papa has to go to the war," said Margot.

"Oh," replied John.

John got up quietly and walked to the house without saying another word. Margot followed behind him, holding Gigi. She didn't say anything; she knew her brother was distraught.

John entered the house and saw his mother weeping. He looked at his father and hugged him for a while. Eli looked at his son; he had become a young man.

"I will take good care of the greenhouse while you are away, Papa," said John.

"Thank you," replied Eli.

He took his children in his arms.

"Let's have dinner, shall we?" said Marguerite, trying to cheer everyone up.

"Good idea," replied Eli.

"Margot and John, can you come and help me?" asked Marguerite.

"Yes," the children replied as they followed her into the kitchen.

Eli looked at Sarah, who had red eyes; she couldn't stop crying.

"Should we take a little walk?" said Eli.

"Okay," replied Sarah, sniffling.

Eli took her by the hand, and they went outside.

"Look how beautiful our farm is," said Eli.

"Yes, it is," said Sarah, sulking.

"Look at that beautiful tree there, you remember when we climbed to the top?"

"Yes, it was such a great day. We had so much fun."

"And look at that well, you remember when I almost fell in it?"

"Yes, I remember, I was so scared," Sarah laughed.

They continued walking when Eli stopped in front of the greenhouse. Before Eli had time to say anything, Sarah spoke.

"Yes, I remember, that was the most romantic day of my life," Sarah giggled.

"God, I love you so much, we have created such a beautiful life together," said Eli.

"Yes, we have, that's why I don't want you to leave."

"I know, I don't want to leave either, but I will come back, and we will continue our life together. I will see our beautiful children grow, John will go to an amazing engineering school, and Margot will become an amazing writer. You will write to me every day?"

"Of course, I will, we will all write to you every day."

"I promise you; I will come back. Remember, you and me for eternity?"

"Yes, I will always remember, for eternity," Sarah kissed her husband.

"Let's have a nice evening, okay?"

"Okay," said Sarah, holding tightly onto Eli.

They headed back to the house; the children and Marguerite had prepared dinner. Sarah was more cheerful; she wanted to have a great evening with her family before Eli left. The family enjoyed a nice dinner; John made jokes throughout the meal. The evening felt light despite the events.

"I just finished writing my latest story; I wanted to read it to you all tonight," said Margot.

"We would love that," replied Sarah, smiling at her beautiful daughter.

Sarah and Eli were on the couch while Marguerite, John, and Margot sat in armchairs. Gigi, Margot's giraffe, was in a small armchair Eli built for Gigi. Margot started to read.

"It all started when a little boy named Lethabo, from a farm in Greyton, South Africa, had no friends because he was born deaf. His life was hard. His parents left him at a very young age but his neighbor adopted him. His neighbor was an older woman named Leona that was unable to have children herself. Lethabo helped Leona on the farm every day. He became friends with the animals on the farm and gave them each a name. His best friend was a pig which he named Peto. He spent hours talking to Peto, pretending like he was a person. Leona was delighted to have Lethabo on the farm. She lived on her farm alone for years when she saw this little boy walking on the street's side by himself. She offered him something to eat, and he never left."

The family listened to Margot attentively. Margot was proud; this was her first full story.

"It's beautiful, honey," said Sarah.

Margot made a sound with her throat to indicate that she would continue reading.

"Lethabo never queried why Leona had let him stay. They simply got along. Things were simple. It was like it was meant to be. Leona learned sign language so that she could communicate with Lethabo. Lethabo was very grateful to Leona and helped her in any way he could. One day, Peto, the pig, got very sick. Lethabo and Leona didn't know how to heal Peto, so they decided to concoct a remedy with herbs that Leona's grand-mother had left her."

Marguerite started to doze off.

"Your story is great, honey. It's getting late, though; is it okay if you continue tomorrow evening?" asked Sarah.

"Okay, but Papa won't hear it," said Margot.

"You can finish reading it to us, and then we can send it to him to read?"

"Okay," replied Margot.

Everybody got up. Margot took Gigi with her as she went to her room. They kissed each other goodnight and went upstairs to their respective rooms. Sarah tucked the children into bed; Margot stared at her mother.

"You are so beautiful, Mama," said Margot.

"Thank you, honey, you are so beautiful, too," replied Sarah.

She kissed Margot goodnight. She tucked John in as well.

"I know, I know, you are a man now, but I still want to kiss you goodnight, young man," said Sarah before John had time to say anything.

Sarah went to her room, Eli was preparing a bag when she entered; she looked at him and got emotional.

"Let me do it, my love," said Sarah.

"Thank you," replied Eli.

"Everything will be all right."

"Yes," said Eli, as he looked at his wife deeply.

He started kissing her and made love to her as if it was the first time. Kissing and caressing every ounce of her body and taking in every detail to remember her. They made passionate love and fell asleep.

The next morning Sarah woke up unusually early. Eli was still sleeping. She looked at him sleep for a while and then got out of bed and prepared his bag with all the warmest socks, shirts, pants, and sweaters she could put her hands on. She put photos of her and the children in his bag, along with a few books. She went back into bed and started kissing Eli to wake him up. She made love to him in the gentlest way; they were wholly together as one.

"I love you so much, no words exist in this world to describe how much I love you," said Sarah.

"The emotions I have for you describe how much I love you, but there are no words, my heart feels like it doesn't have enough space in it," replied Eli.

The rest of the morning grew sad. They went downstairs, the children and Marguerite were already in the kitchen preparing breakfast. Eli put his bag in the entrance, before they all had breakfast together. It was silent. Eli got up; ready to go. They all stood at the front door.

"I love you so much," he said to Margot.

"I love you, Papa, I will write to you every day, and I will send you all my stories," replied Margot.

Eli hugged his daughter tightly in his arms. His eyes welled up with tears. Eli almost tipped over when John jumped in his arms.

"I am counting on you, you are the man of the house now, you will help Mama?" said Eli.

"Yes, and I will take care of the greenhouse, and when you come back, we will do some new hybrid roses together," said John.

"Yes," replied Eli.

He hugged his son one more time.

"I love you," said Eli.

"I love you too, Papa," replied John.

Eli hugged his mother.

"I love you, Mama," said Eli.

"I love you, darling, I will see you soon," replied Marguerite.

"Yes."

He stood in front of Sarah and took her hand.

"You will be all right?"

"Yes, I will be all right."

"I will come back to you, I love you, I love you for eternity, remember?" said Eli.

"Yes, I remember, I love you for eternity," replied Sarah.

He kissed his wife passionately one last time and left. The family looked at him, leaving. He turned around several times as he walked away until he could no longer see his family or the farm.

Two weeks went by. It was difficult on the farm without Eli. Margot finished reading her book to the family and then sent it to her father.

Thirty-eight ∞ Germans

The German soldiers once again took over the entire village. The nightmare began again; five German soldiers came banging on the front door one cold morning. Sarah opened the door, the soldier pushed her to the floor.

"We need food now!" said a German.

Sarah got up. John heard the noise from the kitchen and came running with Margot behind him.

"Why are you not at war?!" yelled a German soldier pointing to John.

"He is just a boy," said Sarah, interrupting John before he replied.

"How old is he?" asked the German soldier.

"He is 13," lied Sarah.

"Fine. Get us some food, we need a place to stay; my comrades will be arriving soon, we need space for everybody," he said.

"Yes," replied Sarah, terrified.

Marguerite got up from the couch; she looked like she aged twenty years in five minutes.

"John, go tend to the farm, will you?"

"Yes, Mama."

Margot, Marguerite, and Sarah all went to the kitchen, followed by five German soldiers. Sarah took out meat and vegetables and started preparing some food for them.

"Make some coffee Margot, will you?"

"Yes, Mama."

A German soldier looked at Margot.

"How old are you?" said a soldier to Margot.

"She is ten years old," lied Sarah.

"She looks older," replied the soldier.

Sarah didn't say anything and sliced up the meat. The Germans sat at the kitchen table and spoke in German. It sounded like one of the soldiers was making a joke, the four others laughed. Marguerite cut vegetables when she lost her balance and fell to the floor; Sarah rushed to help her up.

"Are you all right, Marguerite?"

"What is wrong with her?" said a soldier.

"She is tired is all," replied Sarah.

The Germans laughed.

"Margot, will you help her upstairs?"

"Yes, Mama."

Sarah continued to cut the vegetables. She put the meat in a big pot with the vegetables. The coffee was ready. Sarah took out cups, poured coffee, and handed them to the German soldiers.

"Here you go," said Sarah.

"I hope this coffee is good," replied a soldier.

Margot came back to the kitchen.

"Can you go and help John, please? If you could bring back some eggs?"

"Yes, Mama."

"So who lives here?" asked a soldier.

"My children and their grandmother," replied Sarah.

"It would be better for you if I didn't find anyone else," said the man, looking at Sarah menacingly.

"There is no one else," said Sarah, afraid of this crazed soldier.

"Good. Twenty comrades will be arriving in an hour; we all need a place to sleep."

"Yes," said Sarah, remembering how the set-up was during World War I.

Margot came back with eggs in a basket.

"Here, Mama."

"Thank you, honey, can you go check up on, grandmother?" whispered Sarah.

"Yes," said Margot, as she left again.

The meat and vegetables finished cooking; Sarah took plates and served the Germans.

"I will go prepare the rooms," said Sarah.

"No funny business!" said a German soldier.

"Yes, of course," replied Sarah, as she left the kitchen.

She went straight away to see Marguerite who was in bed, exhausted. Margot was next to her with a wet cloth in her hands; she patted the damp cloth on Marguerite's forehead.

"It will be okay," said Sarah.

"I am too tired for this," replied Marguerite.

"You will be fine," said Sarah.

Sarah looked at Margot, who seemed worried.

"Stay with Marguerite, I will move our things into the attic before the other soldiers arrive," said Sarah.

"Okay, Mama."

Sarah left in a rush. She gathered all of her children's necessary belongings and brought them to the attic. She entered the attic; it was very dusty. She hadn't been there since the end of World War I. She stopped and looked at the place for a moment. All the terrible memories came rushing back. She started to feel overwhelmed with emotion but immediately got herself together; her look changed to a determined look once again.

She dusted off the furniture, cleaned the attic, and turned the mattress on the bed upside down. She put all her children's belongings on the mattress. She hurried back down and got her things and brought them up. She fixed the place up in the best way possible; it started to look decent. She went downstairs to see Marguerite and Margot. Margot was still next to her, patting her forehead with a humid cloth while Marguerite was half asleep.

"We must bring her upstairs," said Sarah.

"But she is finally falling asleep," replied Margot.

"I know, but we need to get her out of here before the soldiers come; I don't want anything to happen to her, come on help me."

"Okay," said Margot, realizing how dire the circumstances were.

Sarah gathered all of Marguerite's belongings in a bag.

"Let's bring her up first, and then I'll come back to get her stuff," said Sarah.

"Okay."

Sarah gently pat Marguerite on the shoulder.

"Marguerite?"

Marguerite didn't answer.

"Marguerite?" repeated Sarah.

"Hm," said Marguerite, half asleep.

"We need to bring you to the attic," said Sarah.

"I don't want to go anywhere," whispered Marguerite.

"The soldiers are coming soon, we need to move you before they come to your room."

"Oh," said Marguerite, barely moving.

Sarah took Marguerite by the shoulders and started to move her; Margot helped bring her up the stairs. They got to the attic; Marguerite was breathless. Sarah and Margot put her down on the bed and covered her up with blankets, she fell asleep instantly.

"Stay here with grandma, I'm going to get her stuff, I'll be right back."

"Okay," said Margot, feeling the stress in her mother's voice.

Margot started to put her brother's clothes in the closet. She dusted off the bigger mattress on the floor and tidied up a bit.

Sarah came back with Marguerite's clothes and a family picture. She set the family picture near Marguerite on the window sill. Sarah put Marguerite's clothes on a chair at the tail end of the bed. They heard a loud banging coming from downstairs.

"Stay here, it must be the soldiers," said Sarah, panicked.

"Okay," replied Margot.

"Promise me, you will stay here, Margot, okay?"

"Yes, Mama."

Sarah closed the door as she left and went downstairs. She heard soldiers yell louder and louder in German; it sounded like there was a fight at the front door.

As she stepped on the first floor, she saw John being pushed around by two Germans. She ran down to her son and stood in front of him. The Germans were surprised to see a woman and quieted down. A general came in at that moment and saw what was going on.

"That's enough!" said the general.

The soldiers instantly stood up straight and calmed down.

"I am General Weber, I am sorry about my men, they are drunk, it has been a long day," said Weber.

"Yes, he is just a boy," replied Sarah, still frightened as she looked at John.

General Weber motioned to the soldiers to get out of the entranceway.

"Where are my men to eat and sleep?" said Weber.

"I cooked some food, and I have taken out all the blankets and put them in the rooms," replied Sarah.

"Good, take me to the biggest room," said Weber.

"Yes, of course, it's on the second floor."

General Weber signaled for her to show him; Sarah took John by the hand and took him with her. She went to the second floor and showed General Weber to Marguerite's room, the largest.

"Good," said Weber.

Sarah was about to leave with John when Weber stood in front of her.

"One of my soldiers told me there were two children and a grandmother here?"

"Yes."

"Where are you sleeping?"

"We are in the attic," replied Sarah.

"Good, you may leave now," said Weber calmly.

Sarah left with John and went to the attic. She looked at her son; he seemed to be all right.

"Did they hurt you?"

"I am fine, Mama."

He opened the door to the attic and saw Marguerite.

"What's wrong with grandmother?" asked John.

"She fell while she was cooking," replied Sarah.

John went next to his grandmother and didn't say anything while Margot tidied up some more.

"Thank you, honey."

"I found another mattress over there," said Margot.

"Yes, we once had a friend here for a while; it was a long time ago."

"Who was it?" asked John.

"A friend that helped the family," replied Sarah.

"Oh," said John.

"Margot, come here, I am going to cut your hair."

"No, why?" asked Margot.

"We are both going to cut our hair, okay?"

"But I don't want to."

"Stop fussing, come here so I can cut your hair."

"But why?"

"We must look like men for now, okay?"

Margot stood in front of her mother, sulking.

"Thank you, honey, it's better for now with all the Germans here, okay?" said Sarah.

"Okay," replied Margot.

Sarah cut off all of Margot's beautiful hair, she now looked like a boy.

"It will grow out," said Sarah, trying to reassure her daughter.

Sarah took the pair of scissors and cut off her own hair to the best of her abilities, it looked completely crooked.

"John, can you help me?"

John knew that his mother was trying to look the least appealing to the Germans.

"Yes."

"Cut it as short as you can."

"Yes."

He cut off his mother's hair; she looked older with shorter hair.

"Thank you. We should go to sleep now, you should both sleep on the mattress over there," said Sarah.

"But I want to stay with grandmother," replied John.

"Okay," said Sarah, unable to refuse anything to her children in these times.

"I want to sleep with you, Mama," said Margot.

"Okay, come here, honey."

John squeezed next to his grandmother while Margot and Sarah slept together on the mattress on the floor. Everyone was in bed.

"What's going to happen, Mama?" asked Margot.

"I don't know, honey, but it's going to be okay, sleep now," replied Sarah.

"Good night, Mama, I love you," said Margot.

"Good night, my loves, I love you," replied Sarah.

She kissed Margot on the cheek and the children fell asleep quickly. Sarah stayed awake for a while, thinking about Eli; she was wondering where he was and if he was all right.

The next morning John woke up before the others. He touched Marguerite and felt her cold body. He moved her shoulder, but she didn't move. He looked at Marguerite lifeless. He kissed her on her forehead; Sarah woke up and saw John staring at Marguerite.

"What's the matter, honey?"

"Grandmother died in the night," John cried.

Sarah looked at her son and then Marguerite; she took John in her arms. Margot woke up.

"What's happening?"

She looked at Marguerite and understood; Sarah held her sobbing children in her arms.

"Your grandmother went to see your grandfather," said Sarah quietly.

John got up; he looked at his grandmother.

"What are we going to do with her?" asked John.

"We need to bury her near the greenhouse," replied Sarah.

"But how?"

"We will find a way."

They heard noise coming from downstairs; the soldiers were awake. Sarah was unsure of what to do. Last time, she was a child and became a nurse. This time it was different. She had children of her own, and Eli was not here to help her. They went downstairs; General Weber was in the kitchen with a lot of soldiers talking in German.

"Good morning," said Sarah.

Weber looked up but didn't say anything. He looked at John and Margot; then, he stared at Sarah for a moment.

"You cut your hair," said Weber.

"Um, yes," replied Sarah.

"Why did you cut your hair?"

"It's easier to clean," lied Sarah.

Weber didn't reply.

"We need some food, we will leave in half an hour, and we will be back tonight," said Weber.

"Yes," replied Sarah.

"Margot, why don't you get some milk?"

"Yes, Mama," said Margot, as she left.

"John go and feed the animals, will you?"

"Okay, Mama."

He left, Weber watched him go away.

"Your children are polite," said Weber.

Sarah nodded; she didn't know what to say. She started to mix an omelet in a big bowl and added herbs to it. Weber stared at her; she felt him gazing and didn't like it. Margot came back with some milk.

"Thank you."

Sarah added milk to the omelet. Margot stood next to her mother, not knowing what to do. There was tension in the kitchen. Sarah finished cooking the omelet, while Weber continued to stare at Sarah. She felt like he wanted to violate her but was restraining himself from doing so.

"Get me some plates, Margot," said Sarah quietly.

Margot took out plates and put them on the kitchen counter. Sarah took a few big platters of omelets and placed them on the counter.

"Can you get me the bread, please?"

Margot ran to the back and returned with bread, and added it to the kitchen table.

"Thank you, honey."

Margot stood next to her mother. The soldiers took the omelets and bread and went to the dining room.

Weber stayed in the kitchen as he filled a plate with an omelet; he was now only looking at Margot.

"Do you have a boyfriend, little one?" said Weber as he smiled at Margot.

Sarah almost choked hearing this.

"No," said Margot, shyly as she looked at the floor.

"You are beautiful. I am sure you will marry young," said Weber, as he ate noisily.

Sarah was extremely uncomfortable; his intentions were confusing. She wondered if he was a monster or a father himself. He finished eating and went to the dining room.

Everyone stood up, and they all left together. Sarah's heart beat quickly. She couldn't bear these men in her home but didn't have any choice. She looked at Margot.

"Honey, we have to be very careful with these men, okay? Make sure you are never alone with any of them, okay?"

"Okay, Mama," replied Margot.

Margot was old enough to understand everything that was going on. She knew she needed to be strong and help her mother, but she was worried, and her mother could feel it.

"Come with me, let's get your brother, we need to bury Marguerite before the soldiers come back," said Sarah.

"Okay."

Sarah went to the barn, followed by Margot. John was milking the cows when they entered.

"We need to move Marguerite's body," said Sarah, knowing how tough this was on her children.

"Did they leave?" asked John.

"Yes."

"Okay."

He was sad but tried not to show it; he was the man of the house now and felt he needed to act like it.

When there was not a single German in view, they went up to the attic. Marguerite was lifeless on the bed. They wrapped her in a blanket and carried her downstairs; she was very heavy. John was the first to go down the stairs holding on one end while Sarah was at the other end. Margot helped with the doors. They arrived near the greenhouse next to the beautiful tree. John went into the barn to get a shovel, came back, and started digging a hole. He looked serious. Sarah was next to him and tried to take him in her arms. He continued shoveling as if he was unaffected.

"You don't have to hide your emotions with me; talk to me, honey," said Sarah.

John started to cry and let his emotions free; Sarah hugged him close.

"I don't know what to do, I don't know what to do, I am not Papa," whispered John.

"I know, honey, you are perfect just the way you are, you don't need to be like Papa, just be yourself, we will figure this all out," whispered Sarah.

"But I told him I would take care of you, but I don't know how to."

"We will all take care of each other," said Sarah.

John started to compose himself a bit more.

"Yes," said John.

"We are a strong family, we will make it through."

"Okay," said John calming down.

Sarah took the shovel from his hand and started to dig. They took turns. They finally finished digging the shallow grave and gently rolled Marguerite into it before putting dirt onto her wrapped up body.

"We love you, and we wish you to be happy where you decide to go," said Sarah.

"I love you, grandmother," said John.

"I love you," said Margot.

They paused.

"Let's go into the greenhouse," said Sarah.

Her children followed her into the greenhouse; there were lots of roses everywhere; it was a breath of fresh air.

"This is our sacred place, your father and I always used to come here when we were children, we called this the magic house," said Sarah.

"Really?" replied Margot, her eyes lighting up for the first time since the Germans arrived.

"Yes," said Sarah.

"Why is it called the magic house?" asked Margot.

"Because this is where we made both of you," said Sarah.

The children giggled.

Thirty-nine ∞ Front

Eli fought on the frontline. There were wounded and yelling men all around him. It was a complete nightmare. To the right and left, all he saw was pain and blood. Minutes later, a soldier came to replace him. Eli went down the wooden stairs into the trench. He was exhausted and had a wounded leg. He limped to a spot in the ditch and slid down against the mud wall. He looked at his leg; it was completely infected. All he heard were explosions. People rushed past him in all directions. A man slipped next to him and fell onto him; the man got up, didn't say anything, and continued on his way. Eli was in so much pain; he could barely think. His temperature was rising. He opened his jacket and took out letters from his family.

The sounds of the explosions drowned out. He heard the sound of the wind at the farm. He heard the sound of the well and the birds chirping. He heard his children laughing and his wife humming in the kitchen. He reread the words of Sarah's last letter; he finished the latest story from Margot and smiled. He thought about his son and how brave he must be. He thought about Sarah's beauty, how much he loved her. He closed his eyes, imagining his children play. He imagined making love to his wife. He knew he was not going to make it through the night. After a while, he opened his eyes and started writing a letter to Sarah. A soldier stopped in front of Eli.

"Eli, what are you doing? I've been looking everywhere for you; General Moreau said I should make sure to get you to the infirmary," said Gabriel.

"I want to stay here," replied Eli, knowing he had very little time left.

"But your leg-" said Gabriel, looking and understanding the situation.

"I need to write this letter for my wife," said Eli.

"Okay."

"Can you come back and make sure this letter gets to her?"

"Yes, of course."

Sarah and the children made it through the evening; the German soldiers were happy with Sarah's meal and exhausted from their day. They all went to sleep early.

Sarah went to the attic with her children. They slept on the mattress on the floor. Margot and John wanted to sleep with her; she let them, of course.

"Good night, my loves," said Sarah.

"Good night, Mama."

They fell asleep immediately exhausted from all the emotions of the day. She cuddled with her children, each on one side. She fell asleep dreaming of better days to come.

Sarah woke up in the middle of the night; she couldn't sleep. She looked to the side and saw her children. They were both sleeping deeply. She looked out the attic window and thought about Eli. She started to cry but didn't make any noise, careful not to wake her children. She looked at the moon and wondered where Eli could be. She went back to sleep, remembering her childhood with Eli, how much fun they had, and how brave they were.

The next morning Sarah woke up agitated; she felt an intense discomfort. Her children woke up; there was no noise in the house, it seemed as if the soldiers were not up yet.

"Let's go to the kitchen before the soldiers wake up," said Sarah.

"Okay," replied Margot.

"I think you should go to the barn right away," Sarah said to John.

"Okay, Mama."

"I will bring you some breakfast when the Germans leave."

"Okay."

The three of them went downstairs quietly. Sarah and Margot got to the kitchen, and John went straight to the barn. Sarah and Margot started preparing breakfast. Margot made coffee while Sarah warmed up the bread and made eggs for thirteen soldiers.

General Weber entered the kitchen.

"Good morning General," said Sarah.

He didn't reply.

"Omelet again?" said Weber coldly.

"I thought..." replied Sarah.

General Weber interrupted her.

"Don't think, make some porridge," said Weber.

"Okay."

He looked at Sarah and didn't say a word. He looked at Margot and smiled. Margot brought him a plate with an omelet, some bread, cheese, and butter.

"Thank you," said Weber.

As Margot turned around, Weber touched her hair.

"Your hair is very soft," said Weber to Margot.

Sarah was petrified; it's as if someone had just stabbed her in the heart. Margot didn't answer while Sarah started to shake.

"Margot, get me some milk, will you?" asked Sarah.

Margot left the kitchen to get some milk from the barn.

A few German soldiers entered to get some food; Sarah was still shivering but cut some bread. More soldiers came into the kitchen to get food, they went to the dining room to eat, Sarah heard them talk loudly. Margot came back with some milk.

"Thank you, honey," said Sarah.

"Now go and help your brother in the barn, okay?"

"Isn't she going to have something to eat first?" said Weber.

"We were planning to eat afterwards," replied Sarah.

"Sit Margot, have some food," ordered Weber.

Margot looked at her mom, got a plate, and sat at the kitchen table away from Weber. She started to eat silently. Weber observed her obsessively. Sarah saw this and thought of ways to kill him. Weber got up abruptly.

"Off for another day," said Weber, smiling at Margot.

Margot nodded.

"Don't be shy with me," said Weber, as he touched Margot's cheek.

Sarah's heart beat faster and faster. He left the kitchen. Sarah and Margot stood stiff as the soldiers left the house. Sarah was in front of the sink, feeling sick and then threw up.

"Are you okay, Mama?"

"I am fine, don't worry," said Sarah.

The house was silent again; all soldiers had left.

"Go get your brother, honey, we'll have breakfast together," said Sarah.

"Okay, Mama."

She ran out of the kitchen and came back with her brother. The three had breakfast together in the kitchen. Sarah was quiet while the children were more joyful than yesterday. Sarah got up and vomited in the kitchen sink again. John was anxious.

"What's happening, Mama?" asked John once Sarah started breathing again.

"I must have eaten something bad, I'm fine, don't worry," replied Sarah.

Sarah went back to sit at the kitchen table. She seemed absent, lost thinking about Eli. She was worried about him; they hadn't heard from him in weeks.

"I am going to take a walk, get some fresh air," said Sarah.

"Let me come with you," said John, still worried.

"No, I'm fine, honey, eat your breakfast," replied Sarah.

She left the kitchen.

"I wonder what's wrong with Mama," said John.

"She vomited earlier, I think it's because of the German soldier," replied Margot.

"What do you mean?" said John.

"He's been nice to me, and Mama doesn't like it," said Margot.

Sarah walked around the farm. She looked at everything they had created. All the trees they planted as children. She thought about the time Eli almost fell in the well. She walked towards the greenhouse. She stood in front of it and felt Eli's presence. She went inside the greenhouse and looked at all his flowers.

"Where are you, Eli?" whispered Sarah.

She thought she heard him reply and turned around, but he wasn't there. She looked at the hybrid rose he put in the town hall for their wedding.

"I love you," whispered Sarah.

She heard I *love you* back. She turned around again but still didn't see him. She started to cry.

"I miss you," whispered Sarah.

Sarah heard *I miss you too; I will always be with you, remember?* She felt like he was next to her. She sat on the floor where they made love and looked at the different flowers he planted. She was sad but didn't feel completely alone.

She got up and walked back to the house, slowly observing their beautiful farm. She started to smile. She saw her children in the kitchen through the window. They laughed together. She smiled lovingly, before going back to the kitchen.

"How do you feel, Mama?" asked John.

"Much better, honey," said Sarah, kissing him on the cheek.

"I am so lucky to have you both," said Sarah.

Margot giggled.

"I am going back to the barn, I have a lot to do," said John.

"Okay, honey, we will prepare lunch and dinner," replied Sarah.

Margot got up and brought in the plates from the dining room. She did the dishwashing while Sarah started to cook a boeuf bourguignon for dinner. Sarah cut the meat and felt nauseous again. She went towards the sink, thinking she needed to vomit but did not.

"Are you all right, Mama?"

Sarah thought for a moment.

"Of course, I am pregnant. I couldn't bear the smell of meat when I was pregnant with John," said Sarah.

"Oh my god! Papa is going to be so happy!" replied Margot.

"Yes, yes... he will," said Sarah very quietly.

"Do you want me to cut the meat?" asked Margot.

"Yes, but be careful, okay?" replied Sarah.

"Okay."

"I will cut the potatoes and vegetables," said Sarah.

They cooked while they had a bit of fun in the kitchen.

"So you think it's a boy, Mama?"

"I don't know, honey, we will see," said Sarah silently.

Sarah wondered how in the world she managed to get pregnant during the war. She was worried about her baby and missed Eli terribly; she couldn't stop thinking about him. What would he say if he were here? He would make things work like he always did. He would be so happy to know her pregnant; they had wanted a third child for many years. Sarah got pregnant two years after Margot's birth, but she lost the baby. They tried to get pregnant again but had no luck until now. Sarah was happy and sad at the same time.

The day went by quickly. Sarah and Margot spent most of the day in the kitchen while John worked on the farm. The soldiers got back to the farm at 8pm.

"I am starving," said Weber.

"We made a boeuf bourguignon," replied Sarah, as he entered the kitchen.

"Did you help make this?" asked Weber to Margot.

"Yes," replied Margot.

"Well, it must be delicious," said Weber.

The soldiers entered the kitchen and took some food before going to the dining room to eat. Sarah started to wash the pots while Margot gathered the pots and pans around the kitchen.

"Sit down and eat," said Weber to Margot.

"I already had dinner," replied Margot politely.

"I said, sit down and eat!" yelled Weber to Margot.

Sarah and Margot were startled; it was the first time they heard him yell. Sarah boiled inside, but she knew that he would hurt her children if she did anything.

"Yes," said Margot, very frightened by him.

"Don't be scared of me; I am a good man," said Weber.

Margot sat at the table with a plate of boeuf bourguignon. She ate timidly. Weber stared at Margot throughout the meal.

"What do you like doing, Margot?" asked Weber.

"I like reading," replied Margot.

"That's good, that's good," said Weber calmly.

Margot was done eating but did not dare get up.

"You should eat some more, you are too skinny," said Weber.

"Um... but..." replied Margot.

She saw that General Weber was about to explode with anger and changed her mind.

"Yes," said Margot as she got up to get some more.

She came back with more food on her plate and forced herself to eat. Weber stayed seated, observing every bit of her while she ate.

"Good," said Weber, as he got up.

He stood in the middle of the kitchen for a couple of minutes. He looked at Margot, then at Sarah and again at Margot. His behavior was bizarre.

"Good night," said Weber as he left the kitchen.

Ten days went by; the atmosphere got worse and worse. Sarah was worried about her children; General Weber got more toxic.

One morning Sarah received a letter from the frontline. She held the letter in her hand, observing it while her heart accelerated. She hadn't heard from Eli in weeks. John was in the barn while Margot was in the kitchen cleaning up.

"Honey, I am going for a walk; I will be back, okay?" said Sarah to Margot.

"Okay, Mama."

Sarah went into the greenhouse and sat on the floor. She opened the letter; it was from Eli.

My love,

I am not going to make it. I know I promised you I would be back, but I will have to break my promise. I want to thank you for everything you have given me; thank you for all your smiles, thank you for your elegance, thank you for your grace, thank you for all your kisses, thank you for all your caresses, thank you for all the times we made love, thank you for our beautiful children, thank you for your incredible beauty, thank you for our friendship, thank you for always understanding me, thank you for your trust, thank you for your kindness, thank you for your courage, thank you for making everyone around you smile and laugh, thank you for being my rock, thank you for being a fighter, thank you for all your good intentions towards others.

I will always be with you, and I will always love you. You will always be the love of my life. I ask of you one last thing; fight for our children. God knows how much I love them. Make it through the war; I know you can do it. You are the strongest person I have ever met. I will wait for you. I will see you next lifetime. I love you for eternity.

With all my love,
Eli

Sarah cried and cried; she was relieved to read his words but couldn't bear the thought of not seeing him again. She reread his letter several times. She missed him profoundly. She touched her stomach. He would never know she was pregnant. She knew she would not see him again, at least not this time. She looked around and felt like he was there looking at her; she could feel him. She smiled through her tears. She decided at that instant that she would fight. She would get her children and herself through the war.

"I promise you I will get us through this, I love you for eternity, I will see you next lifetime," whispered Sarah.

Sarah was determined. She got up and went to see John at the barn.

"We need to leave here, we can't stay here anymore, it's too dangerous," said Sarah.

"Where are we going to go?" asked John.

"We will figure it out, but we must leave, we must leave today," said Sarah.

"What? What about Papa?"

Sarah started to cry.

"Papa is not going to come back, honey, I am so sorry," said Sarah.

John yelled at the top of his lungs. Sarah took him in her arms and he started to cry.

"We must be strong, honey, we have to find a new home," said Sarah.

John couldn't get his head around the thought that he wouldn't see his father again. Sarah and John walked into the kitchen. Margot was washing the dishes.

"Honey, I have to tell you something; it is something difficult to hear, okay?" said Sarah to Margot.

"What is it?" asked Margot.

"Papa is not going to come back, he... the war, I'm so sorry," said Sarah, completely heartbroken.

Margot cried hysterically. Sarah took Margot in her arms. She held both of her heartbroken children. Sarah transformed from bitter sadness into a determined, strong look, once again. She looked at both her children in the eyes.

"I promised your father we would make it through the war, I will keep my promise to him, okay?" said Sarah.

"Okay," replied both children at the same time.

"We must leave from here today," said Sarah.

"But where are we going?" asked Margot.

"I don't know, maybe America?" replied Sarah.

Eli departed bodiless from the kitchen; he went above the house, above the farm, and above Saint-Dié-des-Vosges into the sky.

BOOK IV

Forty ∞ Los Angeles

It was the middle of a warm afternoon in Los Angeles, California, on the 19th of April 2017. Sarah was in a Spanish style apartment in Los Feliz, a neighborhood of Los Angeles. The apartment was cute, but small with European decor. She woke up next to her dog, Poppy.

"Hi baby," Sarah said to Poppy, as she pet her.

She got out of bed, jet-lagged. She flew in from Cambodia the night before.

She went to the kitchen to make herself a Nespresso coffee. Poppy followed her. She waited thirty seconds for her coffee to finish and went into the backyard she shared with her neighbor to enjoy the day's first light. She drank her coffee while the sun shone on her face. She was content with her last mission. She relaxed for half an hour and got up to go back into her apartment when her neighbor, Victoria, came out. Victoria was gorgeous, tall, and athletic.

"Sarah! You're back?" said Victoria.

"Yeah, I got home last night; how are you?" asked Sarah.

"Doing great, I just sold another house."

"That's fantastic. Congratulations!"

"Thanks, I got to run, but let's meet up later, okay? I want to hear everything about Cambodia."

"Okay, bye."

Sarah went to her living room; there was vintage and modern looking furniture. She went through a pile of photos while she sat on the floor. There were old and new cameras of all kinds on a red shelf. Sarah had been a photographer for 15 years. She traveled the world as a photojournalist for Amnesty International.

Sarah's phone rang; it was Emma, her best friend. She had known Emma for over a decade.

"Hi honey, yes, absolutely, okay, see you tonight," said Sarah.

Sarah spent the day going through her photos. She put some pictures in a stack on the left and other images in a pile to the right. A few hours went by; she had a large stack of photos to the right. She went through them again. Poppy sat next to her; she stopped for a moment to pet her; Sarah and Poppy had a strong bond.

She went through the stack of photos and put twenty pictures in a big envelope. She wrote *Jake* on the envelope and put it on the kitchen counter. She opened the fridge; it was almost empty, a box of mozzarella balls from Trader Joe's and some blueberries. She ate some cheese and the remaining blueberries.

She took a shower. Poppy followed her to the bathroom and sat on the floor mat while Sarah was in the shower. She got out of the shower and dressed for the day.

"You want to go for a walk?" asked Sarah.

Poppy's tail wagged like crazy. The two of them went for a twenty-minute walk in the cute neighborhood of Los Feliz. Red leaves littered the sidewalk. The sun was just right. It was a beautiful day.

They got back home after the walk. Sarah took the envelope of photos, and they got into her old Fiat. They drove to Downtown. Sarah blasted loud music in her car as usual. She loved to drive and getaway. Poppy stood on the center armrest in the vehicle, observing the streets and people. They arrived at the office of Amnesty International, Sarah parked in her usual spot.

Carlos was there. Poppy loved Carlos and greeted him before entering the elevator.

"Hi, Sarah, did you have a good trip?" asked Carlos.

"Hi Carlos, yes, it was all right, happy to be back, all good with the family?" said Sarah.

"Yes, the little one is finally using the potty," replied Carlos, proudly.

"That's great!" said Sarah as she walked through the parking lot to the elevators.

They got to the 5th floor. There was a vast open space with lots of people at desks on phones. Sarah nodded and waved as she walked past. Across the room, she arrived in front of a door and knocked.

"Come in," said Jake.

Sarah opened the door and entered with Poppy. Jake, brown hair, medium-sized, plump, greeted them.

"Hi, Jake," said Sarah.

"Hi Sarah, let me see what you've got," replied Jake.

Sarah sat down, Poppy, on the floor next to her. She opened the envelope and took out the photos. Jake went through them one by one.

"Pretty good, this one is fine," said Jake.

He stopped in front of one of the photos and looked at it a while longer.

"This one is good, I'll send this to the press," said Jake.

"You like it?"

"Yeah, it's all right," replied Jake.

"Does this mean I can get a raise?" asked Sarah.

"No, no, no, we talked about this many times, once you hit the front cover, we can *talk* about a raise," said Jake.

Sarah didn't respond; Jake loved to boss her around.

"Okay, so I'll see you in a couple of weeks?" said Jake.

"Yes," replied Sarah.

"Unless you'll have dinner with me?" said Jake, smiling, trying to charm her.

"No, thank you, you know I can't go on a date with my boss," replied Sarah, uncomfortable.

"I know, I know... It's probably for the better, I am sure we wouldn't get along anyway; you are too serious for me," said Jake.

"Okay, see you later," replied Sarah, as she stood up.

"Bye," said Jake smiling at her in a sleazy manner.

She walked through the office. Jenny, a cute, perky copywriter, was on the phone and waved at her. Sarah and Poppy stood in front of Jenny's booth, waiting for her to finish. Jenny hung up the phone.

"Hey! How are you?" asked Jenny.

"I'm good, I flew in last night, a bit tired, but all is well; how are you?" said Sarah.

"Very good! I got engaged! Ta-dah!" Jenny showed off her engagement ring.

"Oh, wow, that's great. Congratulations!"

"Thank you, I am so excited, I have to jump on a call, but I wanted to show you my ring."

"I am very happy for you."

"Thank you, I'll see you around."

Sarah and Poppy got back to the parking lot.

"Bye, Carlos," shouted Sarah.

"Bye, Sarah, get some rest, huh?"

"Yes, I will, thank you," said Sarah, as she hopped into her car with Poppy.

They drove back to Los Feliz.

"I need to go get some groceries, so I'll drop you off at home and come back, okay?" Sarah said to Poppy.

Sarah arrived in front of her house, went in with Poppy, and gave her a bone.

"Bye Poppy, I am coming right back," said Sarah.

Poppy sat on the couch with her bone in the living room.

Sarah got back into her car and drove to Trader Joe's; she got her groceries and went to pay.

"Wow, you've got a lot of mozzarella," said the salesperson.

"Yes, there's a lot of protein, and I love them," replied Sarah, as she smiled.

"Yes, ma'am."

Sarah left with her groceries and headed back home while blaring her music in the car.

She drove down Franklin Avenue. There was a lot of traffic, as usual, but she finally got home. Poppy came running to see her at the door.

"Hi baby," said Sarah, as she pet her.

She put the groceries away.

"Should we take a nap, Poppy?"

Poppy followed Sarah to the room; Sarah closed the curtains and fell asleep next to Poppy.

They woke up an hour later from the sound of the phone vibrating. Sarah took her phone from the nightstand and read: *Pick you up in an hour*; the text message was from Emma.

Sarah struggled to get out of bed while Poppy jumped off as her usual peppy self. Sarah went to the bathroom to freshen up; she got ready and went to the kitchen. She made herself a cup of coffee. Poppy whined; she recognized Emma's car arriving. A minute later, Emma knocked on Sarah's door.

"Hi, honey, you look great!" said Sarah.

"Thanks, I am so happy to see you!" replied Emma.

Emma was gorgeous; she had red hair, big green eyes, and was very bubbly and lively. They were happy to see each other because Sarah had been away for weeks. Poppy stayed seated but wiggled her tail until Emma noticed her.

"Hi Poppy, I see you, I see you," said Emma, petting her.

"Are you ready to go?" asked Emma.

"Yeah, still trying to wake up, I shouldn't have taken a nap, but I was so tired," said Sarah.

"We'll have dinner, and then we'll go to this art exhibition; you'll feel better, besides I have so much to tell you," said Emma excitedly.

"What exhibition?" asked Sarah.

"It's this great painter; I love his work."

"Great," replied Sarah.

Sarah put on her jacket.

"Be a good girl, Poppy, I am coming back, okay?" said Sarah as she gave her a bone.

"I love that she obeys you so well," replied Emma.

"Yeah, she's great."

They drove off into Emma's Prius.

"So how was your trip?" asked Emma.

"No, you go first, what did you want to tell me?"

"Okay, so I met a guy."

"What? Who is he? Where did you meet him, how old is he, tell me everything!" said Sarah.

"His name is Liam, he's very cool, we met on set, he directed this little TV show I was on, he's 34-years-old, he's smart, he's kind, he's sexy of course, we laugh all the time, I think I'm already in love with him!" said Emma, her face exploding with a smile.

"Oh my god! That's amazing. I can't believe it!"

"Yeah, he really wants to meet you, he thought of coming to the exhibition later if you don't mind?" asked Emma.

"Yes, I would love to meet him. If he is going to steal you away from me, I want to see what he is like!"

"I haven't felt this way in years. It's so unexpected."

"It often happens when you don't expect it at all. You look radiant!"

Emma had been single for a while. Her last boyfriend was a complete loser, and it had been tough for Emma to consider dating again.

"So how about you? How was your trip?" asked Emma.

"Oh, it was good, kind of the usual, it's always so hard for me to see these people living in such poverty, every time it gets to me, you know?"

"Yeah, it must be tough."

"Anyhow, aside from that, it was fine. I took some photos. Jake liked one of them... I think; I asked him for a raise again, and he said no. I don't know what to do. And then he asked me on a date again..."

"I'm sorry. I hope you get a raise soon, you've been there for years," said Emma.

"I know, I've asked him so many times, I don't know what to do anymore."

"I can lend you some money if you need it?"

"Thank you, I'm fine for now, I just need a raise. I have to go to Paris to see my father; he is really not doing good, and going there is expensive."

"Yeah, I get it. Why don't you sell your photos elsewhere?" said Emma, sorry for her friend.

"I don't know; I don't think they are good enough."

"Sarah, your pictures are great, don't say that," said Emma.

"It's fine, don't worry, honey."

"Okay, let me know if you need help, okay?"

"Yes, thank you. Oh, also, Lucas sent me an email saying he wanted us to get back together, so random, two years later," said Sarah.

"That is random, and? Are you considering it?" Emma got worried.

"No, absolutely not, remember how crazy he was? No, I can't date him again."

"Yeah, I remember. I'm sure you'll meet shoe to your foot."

"That's not an expression."

"Yeah, but it's exactly what I mean."

"I know, you're so cute with your funny expressions."

They arrived at Little Next Door, their usual spot in West Hollywood.

"Bonsoir, ladies! How are you tonight?" asked the waiter.

"Good, thank you, how are you?" said Emma.

"Hello," said Sarah.

"Good, thank you for asking, you can sit where you want."

The girls sat at a table outside. The weather was perfect, not too hot, not too cold. Emma and Sarah had their usual glass of 2015 Bourgogne Pinot Noir. They ordered a Cheese and Charcuterie Platter and a Croque Monsieur. They always ordered the same things and shared them. They'd been coming here for years and had tried just about everything on the menu, except for the Escargot; Emma didn't want to try; she thought it was weird and loved snails. They enjoyed their dinner while chatting away.

"So did you book that part for the TV show?" asked Sarah.

"I'm on hold, I went on a callback, it went well, my agent said she'd know by the end of the week," replied Emma.

"That's great."

"This part could change my career. It would get me out of the same parts I'm cast for. I want this one."

"I'm sure you'll get it, maybe don't think about it for a few days."

"Yeah, I think you're right, every time I forget about a part, I got it, it's kind of weird."

"Things work better when there is not too much thought or force in it; that's what I have always seen."

"Yeah, that's what happened with the film I did in Texas, remember? I totally forgot about it, and I booked it."

"See!"

"Should we go? Liam just texted me; he said he'll be there in half an hour."

"Yes, so what exhibition are we going to?"

"Remember that painter I talked to you about, Eli Johnson. He does a mix of contemporary and classic, I've never seen anything like it."

"Oh yeah, I remember."

"I'm surprised you have never seen his paintings, he is extremely popular, people come to see his exhibitions from all over the world."

"Maybe I saw his paintings and didn't know it was him. You know how bad I'm with names."

"If you had seen a painting of his, you'd remember."

Forty-one ∞ Paintings

They got to the art gallery.

"Should we wait for him outside?" asked Emma.

"Whatever you want, honey," replied Sarah.

"Wait, let me text him, see when he's arriving."

Emma texted Liam, he replied right away.

"He's already inside, I can't wait for you to meet him."

Emma took Sarah by the hand and hurried into the exhibition. As they entered, Emma saw Liam; she let go of Sarah's hand and rushed to him. They kissed, completely in love. Emma pulled away and looked towards Sarah.

"Sarah, this is Liam, Liam, this is Sarah," said Emma.

"Nice to meet you."

Sarah was happy for Emma. She noticed how comfortable Emma and Liam looked together; she wouldn't have suspected they had only been dating for a month. It was the first time in years that Sarah's saw her friend this happy in a relationship.

The three of them walked around the gallery and looked at the paintings. The paintings were enchanting, taking them to dream worlds. Sarah got overwhelmed with emotion from the paintings. Many of the portraits featured a woman without a visible face. One of the paintings had a beautiful pink, and blue hybrid rose next to a woman. Sarah stared at it, mesmerized.

They continued to make their way through the exhibition and arrived at a painting of the Karnak Temple in Egypt with a woman's silhouette. Titled: *Thebes, The City Of Love.*

Liam and Emma continued to walk, while Sarah stood in front of the painting. She was bewitched by its beauty. She got closer to it and, without realizing, touched it. Tears rolled down her cheeks. The image seemed so real to her.

Emma and Liam noticed Sarah and walked back to her.

"Are you all right, honey?" asked Emma.

"Yes, it's just very beautiful," replied Sarah.

"Oh, honey," said Emma.

They continued on their tour of the exhibition. Sarah was bewildered by her connection to the paintings. She had never experienced this level of emotion from an artist.

Hours went by before Liam and Emma decided to leave.

"We are going to go, should we drop you off?" asked Emma.

"No, I want to stay a bit longer, you guys go, have fun," replied Sarah.

"Okay, good night."

"Good night, honey."

"It was really nice to meet you!"

"I can finally put a face to all the stories Emma has told me about you," Liam smiled.

"Bye, have a good night, bisous."

Emma and Liam left Sarah standing in the middle of the exhibition. She admired the artwork, feeling whole. All her anxiety disappeared. She noticed another painting of a woman. The painting was of a stunning hilltop landscape, with a beautiful woman's silhouette and wind blowing in her hair. The title read *The Girl With No Face*. Sarah stared at it, transfixed.

A man interrupted her moment, startling her.

"Ma'am, we will be closing our doors in ten minutes; we open again at 10am."

"Oh yes, of course, thank you," said Sarah.

Sarah went back to see the Karnak Temple painting, looked at it one last time and left.

She took an Uber home, lost in her thoughts. She hardly remembered getting home.

When Sarah arrived, she was greeted by Poppy and took her to the backyard.

"Titi, Poppy," said Sarah, encouraging her to do her business.

Victoria saw Sarah in the backyard and called from her balcony.

"I am coming down!" said Victoria.

Sarah was happy to see Victoria despite how tired she was. They had barely seen each other since Sarah returned.

"Sure!" replied Sarah.

They sat outside and chatted.

"So how was your trip?" asked Victoria.

"It was fine, I am just tired, and I'm leaving for Paris to see my dad."

"Oh, but that's nice, is he doing any better?"

"Not at all, I don't know what to do, he's lost, he doesn't even play the piano anymore."

"I'm sorry, I hope you'll cheer him up a bit," said Victoria.

"Yeah. So how are you?"

"I'm doing so good, I sold another house, making money! How about you? Did your boss finally give you that raise?"

"I am so happy for you! No, he's giving me such a hard time."

"I'm telling you, that guy is a macho asshole."

"Yeah, not sure what to do, I'm just hoping he'll give me a raise, I love my job, but it's tough," said Sarah.

"Yeah, being an artist is hard; like I said, if you want to make money, you can work with me?"

"Thanks, I know, I just wish I could do what I love and *make* money, you know?"

"Yeah, just let me know if you need anything?"

"Thanks, honey, I have to go to sleep because tomorrow I have a busy day."

"Okay, sleep well, I'll see you tomorrow!"

"Good night."

Sarah washed up and went to bed. She felt peaceful and fell asleep.

She woke up abruptly at 3:45am. She was entirely awake as if someone had grabbed her by the shoulders and woken her up. She took her phone, and Googled a photo she took in a town in India. It was the most popular photo from her portfolio of work. She found it to be such a strange thing to do in the middle of the night. She felt as though someone was looking at this same photo right at that instant. She didn't understand what she was doing and went back to sleep.

The next morning when Sarah woke up, she thought she dreamt of her late-night Google search. She looked at her phone to discover the search page was still open on the photo she took years ago. She realized it wasn't a dream. She got up, grabbed some coffee, and did a YouTube exercise class in her tiny living room. She stayed busy and forgot what happened in the middle of the night.

Sarah prepared for her trip to Paris. She hurried to finish retouching the photos she took in Cambodia. She worked all day to meet her deadline. She spent the evening watching the film *Love, Actually* with Poppy. She had dinner on her couch. Sarah had been single for three years; she was set in her ways. She had a busy life and traveled often.

The next morning Sarah packed her bags and got ready for her Paris trip. She chatted with her dad on the phone and got excited about seeing him. She loved her father dearly; what bothered her the most about living in Los Angeles was that she didn't see her father as much as she would have liked.

"Hi, honey, how are you?" said Sarah as she picked up the phone.

"I'm great! How are you?" replied Emma.

"I'm good, finally got over my jet-lag."

"And now you are going to Paris, how ironic."

"I know it's crazy, but it was the cheapest flight."

"Yes, so are we still meeting at Home Restaurant for lunch?"

"Yes, I'll see you there, bisous," said Sarah.

"Bisous," replied Emma.

Sarah finished packing. She took the leash on the kitchen counter, Poppy wagged her tail, she knew it was time for a walk. Sarah did not put the leash on Poppy but had it in case she needed it. They walked through the neighborhood, walking down three blocks of quaint California homes before reaching Hillhurst Avenue. The sun shined bright as usual. Sarah and Poppy arrived before Emma. They sat outside near the fountain. Sarah listened to birds chirping.

Emma arrived, and the girls had a lovely lunch together. They talked a lot about Liam. Emma was completely in love with him. Sarah told Emma what happened in the middle of the night, waking up to look at a photo she took years ago in India. How it felt like someone was watching that exact same photo at the same time.

"Do you think you know this person?" asked Emma.

"I have no idea, I could just see someone looking at the photo I took, it was strange, I thought it was a dream."

"I think it's really cool, can you imagine if we could all see what other people were thinking? I'd like to see what Liam is thinking right now!" Emma laughed.

"Yeah, it would be cool. I'm going to have to go soon, or I'll miss my flight," said Sarah.

"Yes, do you want me to drop you off?" asked Emma.

"No, I want to walk Poppy before, the flight is so long for her."

"Okay, it's great that she is so easy with flights."

"Yeah, I got lucky."

They got up and hugged.

"Bye, honey, send me photos, okay?" said Emma.

"I will, bisous," replied Sarah.

Once again, Sarah and Poppy enjoyed the trees, flowers, and cute little streets on their walk back home.

Sarah ordered an Uber to go to the airport. She made sure she had hers and Poppy's traveling papers. They waited at the entrance for the Uber with two bags. She got a notification on her phone that the Uber was outside.

"Okay, baby, let's go," said Sarah to Poppy.

Poppy eagerly wiggled her tail, and they headed for the car.

The Uber driver rolled down his window.

"For Sarah?" said the man.

"Yes, thank you," replied Sarah.

They get into the Uber, Poppy sat on Sarah's lap. The radio played an old rock song. The Uber driver was an older man and a bit shy. Sarah looked out the window as they drove. She thought about the night at the gallery and the emotions she experienced when her thoughts were interrupted.

"We have arrived," said the driver.

"Thank you," replied Sarah, as she got up.

She put Poppy on the leash and got her suitcase from the trunk before heading to security. Sarah never checked-in her bags; she just took small roll-ons to avoid the hassle of waiting for her belongings at the other end.

They stood in line at security; Poppy was in her traveling bag; she had done this many times and knew the drill. When it was their turn, Sarah removed Poppy from her bag and put her on the leash. They walked through the security checkpoint. Sarah put Poppy back in her traveling bag. They went to their gate and sat down on a bench. Sarah opened Poppy's bag. Poppy stuck her little head out.

"We are going to see Papa," Sarah smiled at Poppy.

Sarah's flight started boarding passengers. She got on the plane and went to their seat to settle in, while more people boarded.

Half an hour later, everyone was seated, and the plane got ready to take-off. Poppy fell asleep in her traveling bag at Sarah's feet. Sarah took out a good book that Emma recommended. She started reading; it was an interesting book about an orphan from Austria. Sarah tried to sleep a bit to not be too jet-lagged upon arrival. She slept for an hour and then woke up.

She got a coffee from the attendant and started reading again. While reading, she suddenly saw a painter painting. It seemed like a flash, but it looked so real. She could see a man with brown hair, green eyes, medium built, forties, painting. He was in a loft. Sarah saw the light come through the windows, wooden beams on the ceiling, red paint on the brush, the canvas, and a Golden Retriever sleeping on the floor next to the painter.

Eli Johnson was in New York City, in his loft painting avidly. He looked entirely immersed in what he was doing. The sun came in through the windows while he painted on a canvas next to his Golden Retriever.

Sarah didn't understand how she could possibly see what this painter was painting. The painting looked a lot like the paintings from the gallery; she recognized the style. She was completely bewildered. She went back to reading and finally fell asleep again.

The plane landed.

Forty-two ∞ Paris

Sarah got off the plane, out of the airport, and into a taxi to her father's house. She looked up Eli Johnson's name on her phone and found a photo of him that looked exactly like the man she visualized on the plane. She thought about everything that happened since she went to the exhibition. She arrived at her father's house.

"Hi, Papa!" said Sarah.

"Hi, honey," replied her father, Simon.

They hugged and Poppy was happy to see Simon as well.

"I am almost done preparing dinner. Are you hungry?"

"Yes, I'll just go take a quick shower, and then I'm ready."

Sarah went upstairs to her room, put her bag down, and took a shower; Poppy followed along as usual.

Twenty minutes later, Sarah was back downstairs.

"Can you set the table, honey?" asked Simon.

"Yes, of course," Sarah replied.

"Dinner will be ready in five minutes."

"Great, what are we having?"

Sarah was always excited about delicious French food.

"I made a raclette," said Simon, knowing it was one of her favorite dishes.

"Thank you, Papa," Sarah smiled.

They sat down to have dinner and chatted for a few hours. They talked about philosophy and life as they often did; they loved spending time together.

"I'm getting tired," said Sarah, feeling the jet-lag kick in.

"Yes, I am surprised you are still up."

"Good night, Papa," said Sarah as she kissed him.

"Good night, honey."

The next day they spent the day together walking the streets of Paris, talking. Debating subjects they believed they had answers to.

They stopped at a little French Bistrot, called l'Ecurie, which they often went to; it was one of their favorite restaurants. They served the best steak with pepper sauce. They finished their late lunch.

"I'm going to see Anne, I will be home late," said Sarah.

"Okay, honey, have fun, I'll take Poppy on a long walk," replied her father.

"Thank you, Papa, bisous."

"Bisous."

Simon was a retired concert pianist but since his wife's death, he stayed home all day waiting for time to pass; he had lost all life enthusiasm. They didn't speak much about Martine, Sarah's mother; it was too painful.

When Sarah was in Paris, she usually went to her typical little boutiques to buy things she couldn't find in the US; she was too broke to go shopping this time. She went to a cute restaurant called the Café de l'Industrie to meet with Anne, her best friend.

She arrived at the restaurant and saw Anne sitting at a table. Anne was beautiful; she had gorgeous brown hair and big green eyes. She looked very French with her little purse and the typical Parisian mannerisms.

"Anne!" exclaimed Sarah.

They hugged and kissed each other on each cheek, Parisian style. Anne and Sarah grew up together in Paris, they had been friends forever. They were excited to see each other and talked as if they hadn't seen each other for years. Sarah tried to go to Paris once a year, but they always had so much to catch up on.

Anne was a ballerina and told Sarah the big news; she just booked the lead dancer in The Nutcracker. It was a big show at a reputable ballet company in London; this had been Anne's dream since she was a little girl.

They celebrated the event, finished their dinner, and decided to go to Place de la Bastille to have tea. They sat down at their table and got comfortable.

"I have a bizarre story to tell you," Sarah started.

"What is it?" asked Anne.

"I don't really know how to describe it because it's so particular."

"What happened?"

"I went to an art exhibition with Emma the other day, and I saw these paintings that were incredible, I had never seen anything so beautiful-"

"That's not weird."

"No, that's not weird at all, no, what's weird is that since I went to this exhibition and touched one of these paintings, I feel like I can see what the painter sees; I know it sounds totally crazy, but I was on the plane, and I am telling you I saw him painting in his loft. I could see the colors, the canvas, I even saw that he has a dog!"

"I don't get what you mean? You see what he paints?" asked Anne.

"No, well, yes, I mean, I feel like I can see what he sees or what he does without actually being where he is. I saw him painting in his loft while I was on the plane coming here. I don't know how to explain it, but that's what happened."

"Wow, that sounds pretty intense. I've heard of stories where people would wake up one morning and speak an entire language fluently overnight, I don't think I've ever heard of anything like this, but I think it's pretty awesome. Do you think he can see what you see?"

"I have no idea, I am not too sure what to think."

"I wouldn't overthink about it, just go with what you feel, and if you saw him painting, then that's cool. I think we all have so much to learn about life. I wouldn't worry too much," reassured Anne.

"Yes, I guess you're right."

The two friends chatted away until two in the morning. Anne told Sarah about this Colombian guy, Juan, she just met in her ballet company and how happy she was for new love. Sarah went on about her travels and her worries about her father. The night finally came to an end.

"I have to go to bed, I have a big day tomorrow," said Anne.

"Yes, it's really late, will I see you before I leave?" asked Sarah.

"Yes, I'm going to London tomorrow, but I'll be back in three days. We should have dinner before you leave."

"Sounds great, break a leg! I love you!" Sarah kissed Anne, goodbye.

"I love you too!"

The next day Sarah spent with her father. They went for walks in the streets of Paris. Sarah loved Paris, the sounds, the atypical people, the cafés, the art in the streets, and the buildings. For her, it was a beautiful city. She was accustomed to living in Los Angeles, but Paris was her home. They went to a cute bookstore called Shakespeare and Company. Sarah grew up in that neighborhood and always went to that bookstore with her parents when she was younger. They enjoyed themselves, walking and sitting for a coffee in the afternoon.

They went back home and watched a movie before going to sleep early. Sarah was taking the train to Normandy the next day to see her grandmother that resided there.

The next morning, after a good night's sleep, Sarah woke up to the smell of a toasted baguette and coffee. They had breakfast together on the balcony; the birds sang; it was a beautiful morning. Her father was happy when Sarah came to see him because he was alone all year. They finished having breakfast and then got ready to leave. Simon took her to the train station.

"I'll see you in a couple of days, Papa."

"Have a good time, sweetheart, bisous."

Forty-three ∞ Normandy

Sarah and Poppy got on the TGV to Normandy; it was a lovely train ride. They sat in the café area on the TGV when Sarah heard Americans speaking. She looked, listened, and smiled. It was a couple from Texas, it was their first time in France, they were very excited to travel to Europe. They seemed very much in love; Sarah believed they were on their honeymoon.

Sarah enjoyed her train ride, having coffee, looking out the window, not thinking about anything. Suddenly she was struck with a vision. She saw Eli in a meeting in an office in New York; he was surrounded by three people, all sitting in armchairs. They looked like businessmen. Eli stood and walked to the window; he looked outside; Sarah could see the people he was looking at and the New York traffic. She felt what he was feeling; he was very professional, business-oriented, focused. She was amazed by what she saw and felt; it was like she was him at that very moment. She wasn't frightened; she found it spectacular and intriguing. She continued to look out the window and wondered why she could see what he saw and feel what he felt.

A few hours later, Sarah arrived at her train stop. She got off the train and saw her grandmother. Sarah hadn't seen her grandmother in years. Her grandmother was a fascinating character, brilliant, fluent in several languages, a quick thinker, but a pain in the ass. Her grandmother loved Normandy, its countryside, the ocean, and the fantastic food that one could find there. Lilianne, her grandmother, was very tall, had beautiful piercing blue eyes and very blonde hair.

As soon as Sarah stepped off the train, her grandmother kissed her and pulled her by the arm.

"Let's go to the market. Oh good! You brought your dog," said Lilianne.

"Yes, I take her when I can," replied Sarah.

"Good, let's go to the market before all the good fish is gone."

"Okay, grandmother," said Sarah, not surprised at all.

Her grandmother had been going to this same open market for over 40 years. They went to the market and got all kinds of tasty food; fruits, vegetables, fresh fish from that morning's fishing, the best oysters one could find in France, and the most amazing butter and bread.

After a few hours spent at the market, they drove to the farm near her grandmother's house to get eggs from the chickens.

Life at her grandmother's house was an adventure, a great experience. It was always so relaxing to be there; eight hours of sleep at Lilianne's was equivalent to fifteen hours of sleep anywhere else.

They spent two days talking, laughing, eating, and going for long walks on the beach with Poppy. They talked about the family tree, good books, Sarah's trips, and history. Every time Sarah went to her grandmother's house, it was like going to the best spa on the planet.

The two days flew by very quickly. Sarah's grandmother was back at the train station, dropping her off on her way back to Paris. Lilianne handed Sarah a huge basket full of food.

"Take this, bring it to your father, he will be so happy to have real food," implying that Normandy was the only place one could get good food.

Sarah had experienced this many times and knew that there was no point in refusing; it would offend her. Sarah's grandmother had been spoiled by the ways of Normandy. She had pride in making sure that her grandchildren ate well and left Normandy with everything they could bring. Sarah carried an additional basket full of food, Poppy, and her roll-on bag, but Sarah knew it made her grandmother happy and thought her father would enjoy the food.

"Thank you," said Sarah.

They kissed each other goodbye. Lilianne watched Sarah and Poppy get onto the train and leave.

Sarah looked out the window; she was full of energy yet calm and rested. She read on the entire trip back to Paris. She thought once again about the strange events she had experienced with Eli; she couldn't get him out of her mind.

Forty-four ∞ Martine

Sarah got to Paris a few hours later. Her father picked her up at the train station.

"Oh, I see that you have extra luggage," said Simon smiling.

"Yes, she said you would enjoy," replied Sarah.

"I know; she is very sweet."

They went home, had some of grandmother's food, and started watching a classic movie.

"What a great movie," said Sarah.

"Yes, it was good. I am going to sleep, I am tired," said Simon.

"Yes, me too. Remember the boxes I left here before I moved to Los Angeles?" asked Sarah.

"Yes."

"Where did you put them?"

"They are in the attic."

"Okay, I wanted to go through some stuff."

"Sure, you want to go there now or tomorrow?"

"No, tomorrow, it's a bit too late."

"Okay, good night, honey."

"Good night, Papa."

The next morning Sarah woke up to birds singing and the sun shining through her window. Poppy was next to her, cuddled up closely. Sarah heard a noise coming from downstairs; her father must be up already. Sarah and Poppy went to the kitchen and found her father preparing breakfast.

"Good morning, honey," said Simon.

"Good morning, Papa," replied Sarah.

"Did you sleep well?"

"Yes, very well."

"If you want, after breakfast, we can go into the attic to get your stuff?"

"That would be great."

Sarah's father opened the hatch to the attic and got in. Poppy stood at the bottom of the ladder while Sarah climbed up and went into the attic; she saw boxes and spider webs all over.

"I put all your boxes here."

Sarah went over to the right corner of the attic and opened the first box; it was full of winter clothes. She opened another and found old books.

"What are you looking for?" asked her father.

"I am looking for a box with photos; I put all my first pictures in one place," said Sarah.

He turned around and saw old boxes in the other corner. He was silent for a moment, Sarah felt it.

"What is it, Papa?" asked Sarah.

"Those are all your mother's things," said her father.

"Oh... Should we take a look at them together?"

Her father hesitated for a moment.

"I haven't touched anything since she left us," said Simon.

"Yes, I haven't been up here since."

She went to the other side of the attic, where her mother's belongings were. They both sat next to each other on the floor. Sarah opened the first box and took out a huge stack of photos; it was photos of Martine's childhood, their wedding, and of Sarah as a child. They looked at the pictures together; her father got nostalgic.

"Should we put them away?" asked Sarah.

"No, it's fine, I haven't seen these in such a long time is all."

"She was so beautiful."

"Yes, she was."

They continued to go through boxes when Sarah found a small wooden case with her mother's diary and two letters in it. One of the letters was addressed to her father, and the other was addressed to Sarah. They were in disbelief; they had not seen these before. Sarah handed him his letter and kept hers.

"They must have been packed away with all her belongings," said Simon.

"Are you going to open it now?" asked Sarah.

"No, I'm going downstairs to prepare some lunch."

"Okay, Papa."

Her father left the attic. Sarah knew that he wanted to be alone for a moment. She read a few pages of her mother's diary; she read how her mother described the love she had for her father. How they met and how much she loved him the first moment she saw him. She put her mother's diary back and closed the box. She sat in the attic and looked at her mother's letter but didn't open it.

She got up and went to the boxes on the other side of the attic. She opened a carton and saw letters and files. She opened another one and saw all the photos she took years ago. She went through the box and found the photo she took in India; the picture she looked up in the middle of the night. She looked at it for a moment and set it on the floor. She closed the boxes and put them back.

She left the attic, closing the hatch on her way down, Poppy was there, shaking her tail.

"Good girl, Poppy."

She went downstairs to check on her father. He was quietly preparing lunch. She saw his letter on the table; he hadn't opened it.

"Can I help you, Papa?" asked Sarah.

"You can set the table if you like, lunch is almost ready," said her father.

She set-up the table. Her father brought food to the dining room a few minutes later; they sat down and started eating.

"It's delicious," said Sarah.

"Thank you."

They ate. Her father was silent; he occasionally looked at his letter on the table in the living room.

"Do you want to go for a walk afterwards, Papa?"

"No, I might go and take a nap, but you should go for a walk," said Simon.

She kissed him on the cheek before she left with Poppy.

Sarah walked through the streets of Paris. They departed from rue Maître-Albert, in the Latin Quarter near Notre-Dame de Paris, passing by the Shakespeare and Company bookstore. Then they went up to the Parc de Luxembourg to admire the statues and the gardens. Poppy ran in the park before they went to the Pantheon.

An hour later, they walked back home.

Meanwhile, her father had been pacing back and forth in front of his wife's letter. He didn't dare open it. He walked in front of it and then went to the kitchen to bake a cake. Half an hour later, he put the cake in the oven. He went back to the living room and observed his letter again. He stood in front of it for a while. He went back to the kitchen and took out a watering can. He filled it up and watered the flowers on the balconies of the apartment. He went back to the kitchen and put the watering can away. He came back to the living room and stared at the letter before returning to the kitchen.

Sarah walked into the apartment. She smelled the chocolate cake; it smelled heavenly. She saw her father in the kitchen, taking the cake out of the oven.

"Ah, you're back," said her father.

"Yes, it smells yummy!" replied Sarah.

"I made a chocolate cake. How was your walk?"

"Great, we went to the Parc de Luxembourg and then to the Pantheon, it's so beautiful. What have you been up to? Did you take a nap?"

"No, I didn't, I made a cake and watered the flowers, nothing special. Anne called, she said she wouldn't make it back in time, they asked her to stay in London, she seemed very happy though, I think the rehearsal went very well, she will call back in half an hour."

"Oh, okay, that's so good that it went well. Can you imagine that it has been her dream since she was a little girl?"

"Yes, I am very happy for her," said her father.

"So what do you want to do for the rest of the day?" asked Sarah.

"I want to take a small nap, and then I thought we could get a hot chocolate at Les Deux Magots?" said her father.

"Yes, that sounds great, I'll get my luggage ready while you rest."

Sarah went to her room and packed her belongings; she was flying back to Los Angeles the next morning.

She sat on her bed and looked at her mother's unopened letter; she hesitated to read it but decided not to, before putting it away. She looked at the picture she took in India and thought about Eli.

The phone rang. Sarah picked up; it was Anne.

"Hi! How are you?" said Sarah.

"I'm doing great! Rehearsals are going so well! I am so excited!! But I won't make it home tonight," replied Anne.

"I am so happy for you! I remember when we would speak about this moment when we were nine years old! Such a long time ago, you did it!"

"Yes, I still can't believe it!" said Anne proudly.

"I'll be back in Paris in a year; by then, you'll be a huge dancer! I am so proud of you!"

"Thank you, I have to get back to rehearsal, I'm sorry. I love you," said Anne.

"I love you too, have so much fun!"

They hung up the phone; Sarah felt how excited her friend was.

She finished packing her bag and looked out the window. Sarah's parents bought this loft before she was born. It was a beautiful old fashioned duplex right in front of Notre-Dame. She could see the top of Notre-Dame when she looked out the window from her room. Sarah looked at her ceiling; some stars lit up in the dark that her mother glued when she was a little girl. Sarah remembered what her mother used to always say. *These stars are so you always continue to dream, my love.* Sarah missed her mother; they were very close.

She heard her father get up; she was about to close the windows but stopped to watch the sun glitter through the glass. She looked at the rooftops of Paris; she used to climb out as a teenager and sat on the roof.

Her parents never found out about it. She took amazing pictures of Paris's roofs, the people in the street, and people in their apartments. She would people-watch all the time, imagining what they were talking about, where they would go, and how they had met.

"Honey, I'm ready," said her father.

Her thoughts were interrupted; she closed the windows and came out of her room.

"Should we go?" asked her father.

"Yes, it's such a beautiful day," replied Sarah.

They left their apartment with Poppy, enjoying the walk to Les Deux Magots in silence. Her father was very pensive. The streets were full of people sitting on the benches, drawing, painting, and reading books while Poppy was chasing the pigeons. They arrived at Les Deux Magots, sat down, and ordered a hot chocolate.

"Can you imagine that Ernest Hemingway would just sit here all day and write?" said Sarah.

"Yes, those were amazing times, your mother and I would come here together and imagine all these writers together talking about their views of the world and what they wanted to do to change it," said her father.

"I didn't know you came here with Mama?"

"Yes, this was our café when we first met, she would always have a hot chocolate, and every time she would get a mustache as she drank it."

Sarah smiled and looked at her father, who was lost in his memories.

"And every time I would kiss her and I would get chocolate on my lips, she knew this and did it on purpose every time we came."

"You are so cute, Papa."

"She was the love of my life, I feel lost without her."

"Yes... I know... If you knew where she was, maybe it would be easier for you?"

"What do you mean?"

"I mean that when someone dies, their body dies, but they still exist as a spirit, right?" said Sarah.

"Oh, I think so, when she died, I felt someone in the apartment a lot, it's been such a long time now, I don't know what to think anymore."

"Did Mama ever tell you what she thought would happen after?"

"Not really... She often spoke about this little village called Soller in Spain, that's where I told her I loved her for the first time."

"How romantic," said Sarah.

He was lost in his thoughts once more; Sarah would have loved to see her father happy again. He broke the silence.

"Should we go to Shakespeare and Company?" asked her father.

They walked through the streets of Paris, enjoying every bit of it. They entered the bookstore; they used to come here as a family when Sarah was young. Her father went upstairs, Sarah followed him and they sat in an armchair near the stairs under the slanted roof.

"We used to sit here every time we came," said her father.

"Yes," replied Sarah.

"She would read us stories, do you remember?"

"Yes, I remember."

Sarah took a book on the shelf near them and started to read a passage. Her father listened to her, smiled, and had teary eyes; he enjoyed the moment immensely.

"Should we buy it and go home?" said Sarah.

"Yes, thank you, honey," replied her father.

Sarah was not sure why he thanked her, but she saw that her father looked slightly better. They bought the book and went back home.

"If you want to rest, I was planning on making dinner," said Sarah.

"How about we cook together?" said her father, smiling.

They had fun making ratatouille and an entrecote. They had a delicious dinner and ate the chocolate cake he made earlier.

"I am exhausted, we should go to sleep early if we need to be at the airport at eight in the morning," said her father.

"Yes, good night, Papa, thank you for this wonderful day," said Sarah.

He took his daughter in his arms.

"Good night, honey," said her father.

Sarah went upstairs.

Her father looked at his wife's letter; he got closer to it; picked it up and put it back down. He stood in front of it for a moment and then decided to go to his room.

Sarah fell asleep next to Poppy.

Her father was in bed, tossing and turning; he couldn't fall asleep. He got out of bed in his pajamas and went downstairs. He looked at the letter again and picked it up. He sat in an armchair in the living room and opened it; he read.

My love,

Thirty-six years together was the highlight of my life. Each day taking care of each other and understanding each other. All these moments spent together are priceless. I will miss you terribly. I don't know what is to come, but I know that I will take you with me. All our moments together. The day Sarah was born, when your face lit up. The first time you told me you loved me in Soller. I knew at that instant that we would always be together, to help each other and love each other. I feel honored that you chose me to be your wife. I want you to remember us when we were happy, living life together, not in the last few months when I was sick. You must continue to live, to create, smile, and laugh; this will permit me to go on. We have a beautiful daughter that will need your help and advice. Maybe you can take her to Soller to show her this beautiful town you brought me to? I think about our times in Soller often. The peaceful walks, the breeze, the times spent on the beach talking into the night. Who knows, if life after death exists, I might meet you there one day? I will always love you; thank you for this beautiful life you gave me.

Love,
Martine

He cried for hours, rereading the letter over and over again. He thought about all the moments they spent together. He thought about the time they spent in Soller. He remembered the evening they decided to spend their life together; they were lying on the beach next to the fire watching the stars whispering to each other, imagining their future together. He remembered thinking at that time that he would never love her less than he loved her then. He loved her more and more from that day on. That was the real beginning of their life together. He remembered all these moments, in their detail, that he had forgotten. He thought about what she wrote. That they would probably see each other again. He started to smile, and gradually his smile became a laugh. He laughed and laughed and laughed. He felt at peace for the first time in years. He got up, took the letter with him, and went to bed.

"Good night, my love," he whispered.

He fell asleep instantly.

The next morning he woke up feeling great. He went downstairs. Sarah hummed a tune while she prepared breakfast. Poppy was next to her waiting for Sarah to drop food. Her father joined her.

"Hi, Papa," said Sarah.

"Hi, darling," replied her father.

She looked at him; he looked like he was twenty years younger.

"You look great!" said Sarah.

"I feel alive again! I found peace with myself, honey."

He smiled and hugged her tightly; she looked at her father and felt like he had come back to her; the jolly man she always knew. Sarah was delighted to see him like this once again.

They went to the airport in her father's old, well-kept car. They sang to George Brassens in the vehicle. Family tradition.

They arrived at the airport—Sarah put Poppy in her traveling bag.

"Bisous Papa, thank you, I love you," said Sarah.

"It was so nice to have you, I love you," replied her father.

She went into the airport and through the usual security routine with Poppy and got onto their flight.

Sarah thought about her parents and her trip to France. She thought about her mother's letter; she was not ready to read it. The flight went by quickly. Sarah read her book, took a few naps, and wondered about Eli.

They arrived in Los Angeles. Sarah was happy to be back home but wouldn't have much time to relax because she was headed to Ethiopia in two days.

Forty-five ∞ Ethiopia

The next morning Poppy and Sarah woke up at 6am. Sarah had a coffee in the backyard, enjoying the sunrise while Poppy chased a squirrel; the squirrel got away, as usual.

They went on a long morning walk, up to Los Feliz Boulevard, up the hill on Winona Boulevard, and then back down through Hobart Boulevard.

Once home again, Sarah prepared her bag for her departure the next day. She had never been to Ethiopia and was excited to go somewhere new. She went through her cameras and picked out her Leica camera and a few lenses that she really liked.

Her phone rang; it was Emma.

"Hi, honey, how are you?" asked Emma.

"I'm good, getting everything ready for my trip to Ethiopia; how about you?" said Sarah.

"I'm doing really well, I'll tell you everything tonight. Are we still on for dinner?"

"Yes, should we meet there at 6pm? I don't want to go to sleep too late as I have an early flight."

"Perfect! I'll see you tonight."

"Bisous."

Sarah finished getting her stuff ready. She packed a small bag for Poppy and put it in her roll-on suitcase.

Sarah called Jake from the office.

"Hi, Jake," said Sarah.

"Hi, Sarah. What's up?" asked Jake.

"I just had a question about my guide, Yonas," said Sarah.

"Yes?"

"It doesn't say on the document where he will meet me?"

"I'll tell my assistant. She'll email it to you."

"Thanks."

"Bye," said Jake as he hung up.

Sarah double checked everything, her camera bag, Poppy's documents, her passport, and visa. She was all set. She took a quick shower and then got dressed before heading out to meet Emma.

They walked to the Figaro Bistrot on Vermont Avenue. Sarah and Poppy got there first; they sat outside, the sun was still shining. Sarah ordered a Kir Cassis, a typical Parisian drink.

Emma arrived fifteen minutes later.

"Hi, honey! It's so nice to see you! I have so much to tell you!" said Emma excitedly.

"Hi!"

"Hi, Poppy," said Emma as she pet her.

Emma sat in front of Sarah, the waiter arrived.

"Hi! What can I get you?" asked the waiter.

"Hi, I'll have the same as my friend," said Emma pointing to the glass of Kir Cassis.

"Yes, are you ready to order?" asked the waiter.

"I am, are you ready to order, honey?" asked Emma.

"Sure, I'll have the Salade de Chevre Chaud," replied Sarah.

"And I'll have the Croque Monsieur," said Emma.

"Okay," replied the waiter.

"Thank you."

"So, how was your trip, how is your father?" asked Emma.

"Why don't you tell me about you? You seem so excited."

"Okay! Liam asked me to move in with him! What do you think? Is it too fast?" asked Emma.

"Oh my god, that's incredible! I think that you should do what you think; time has never been a thing for me, I think that you simply know; I've seen people move in together within a week of meeting each other, and it worked. Look at my parents. They met, and my father asked my mom to get married eight days later; they got married a month later. They had a good life together, I mean until she passed away, of course," said Sarah.

"Yes, I'm sorry... But it's true, it's not about time spent together; it's about how we get along. I have never been this happy in my life, and Liam is so sweet, understands me, helps me, and we make a good team. We are moving in together, oh my god, I am so excited!" said Emma.

"I am so happy for you! It's so exciting! When are you moving in with him?"

"I don't know, probably this weekend, he wanted me to move in last night!"

"I'm sure it's all going to be perfect!"

"Yes, I'm so excited! So, how was France? How is your dad holding up?"

"Actually quite a bit happened in France; first of all, my father is doing much better. He's finally smiling again. We got some stuff out of the attic, and we found a letter from my mother. I can't believe we never knew about them."

"Oh my god."

"Yeah, I think he is ready to move on. We went to Shakespeare and Company, you know the little bookstore we would go to with my parents? And then we went to their café, and he told me about their time together, it was adorable."

"Oh, wow, I am so happy to hear he is better."

"Yeah, I mean, he looks like a different man, you wouldn't recognize him," said Sarah.

"That's so great!" replied Emma.

"And then something else happened," said Sarah, avoiding to talk about her feelings about her mother.

"What?" asked Emma.

The waiter brought their order.

"Voila," said the waiter.

"Thank you."

"I was on the train on my way to see my grandmother, and I saw Eli Johnson," said Sarah.

"What do you mean?"

"I mean, I didn't actually see him, I saw what he was doing without being with him. I saw that he was in New York in some office, very business-like, and I saw him painting. It was so... it was so, I don't know, it's so weird like if I could see what he was seeing, I honestly don't know how to explain it," said Sarah.

"Oh wow, that sounds incredible, sometimes we can't explain things, but they exist, you know?"

"I am sure I'll figure it out eventually. It's just kind of strange," replied Sarah.

"Yeah, I get it," said Emma.

"Oh, and totally changing subjects, Anne booked the lead ballerina dancer for The Nutcracker in a great ballet company in London!" said Sarah.

"Oh my god, that's a huge deal!"

"I know! She is so excited!"

"I am so happy for her, my god, she has worked so hard."

"Yes, I know, so amazing!"

The waiter interrupted them.

"Would you like anything else?" said the waiter.

"I'm fine, thank you," replied Sarah.

"Me too, the check, please," said Emma.

Emma payed, and they got up.

"Thank you, honey," said Sarah.

"Of course," replied Emma, knowing how broke Sarah was.

"Where's your car?" asked Sarah.

"I gave it to the valet, do you want me to drop you off?" said Emma.

"No, thanks, we will walk so that Poppy gets her walk before we go to sleep."

"Okay, see you in a week and have a great trip!"

"Bye, honey, have fun moving in! Bisous."

They parted ways.

Poppy and Sarah walked home, there was a little breeze, but it was still warm.

They got home and went straight to bed.

Sarah laid in bed next to Poppy; she was about to fall asleep when she saw Eli again. He was in a hotel room in Singapore. She could see what he saw, he was looking out the window, he was in a skyscraper. She saw the people walking in the streets from his point of view. She thought to herself that he must be there for an art exhibition. She found it fascinating and fell asleep shortly after.

Sarah and Poppy were at the airport once again; she was in travel mode. People were hustling, the usual airport scenario. They get onto the plane, Poppy was in her little bag sleeping while Sarah worked on her laptop.

Sarah was preparing for her mission in Ethiopia. Her mission was to take photos of several villages, focusing on the living conditions and children's treatment.

The first flight was not too bad; it went by quickly. The second flight seemed longer; Sarah couldn't wait to land.

They finally got to the airport in Ethiopia. Yonas, her guide, was there waiting for them.

"Hi, I am Sarah."

"Hi Miss Sarah, my name is Yonas, I will be your guide while you are here."

Poppy smelled Yonas and liked him; he pet her to say hello.

"Thank you," said Sarah.

Yonas seemed like a nice guy.

"We have to drive for six hours to get to Awassa," said Yonas.

"Okay," replied Sarah.

"You tell me if you are too tired and we stop, okay?" said Yonas in his best English.

"Thank you, I will just walk my dog for a moment before we go, okay?"

"Yes, of course, over there it is good, I will stay here," said Yonas.

"Okay."

She walked Poppy for five minutes and then met up with Yonas again before getting into the car. It was an old car, but it was clean. They started driving on rough, bumpy roads. Yonas put on traditional music from Ethiopia.

"This is Rahel Getu," said Yonas.

"I really like it."

Sarah enjoyed the ride; she looked out the window as they drove through a lot of small towns.

"This is Lake Koka," said Yonas, as they drove near it.

"It's beautiful," said Sarah.

There were people fishing, and others washed clothes in the lake.

"The people come here to get fish to eat," said Yonas.

"Oh."

Sarah was amazed by the number of people that smiled when they drove by them.

They continued the drive, the roads were quite bumpy, but the view was beautiful with wild animals every once in a while.

"We have almost arrived," said Yonas.

"Thank you."

"This is Abijatta-Shalla Park," said Yonas.

"It's wonderful," replied Sarah.

Half an hour later, they got to Awassa; they arrived at the Lewi Resort.

"We have arrived," said Yonas.

"Thank you."

She was delighted to arrive after almost two days of travel. They entered the hotel; Yonas spoke with the receptionist in Amharic.

"Hello, Madam," said the receptionist to Sarah.

"Hi," replied Sarah.

"He will show us your room," said Yonas, who followed the receptionist.

They all went to a room; it was pretty; Sarah could see the lake from her window. She saw monkeys outside in the garden of the resort.

"You need something, you call here," said the receptionist pointing to the phone.

"This is key," said the receptionist handing it to Sarah.

"Thank you," replied Sarah.

The receptionist left.

"This is okay?" said Yonas.

"Yes."

"I will go now, you can rest; I come back tomorrow at 7am, we go to the orphanages in the different villages, yes?" said Yonas.

"Okay, thank you," replied Sarah.

Yonas left.

Sarah was delighted to be able to take a shower and rest. She unpacked and went into the shower while Poppy sat on the mat in the bathroom before they took a nap.

Sarah woke up an hour later and prepared everything she would need for the next day.

They went downstairs together and sat in the outside dining area. Sarah ordered a traditional salad with meat for herself and some shredded beef for Poppy. There were a few monkeys in the garden that stayed away. The waiter came with the food. Sarah and Poppy ate; a monkey got closer to Poppy to try to get some of her food. Poppy growled slightly, and the monkey retreated. The monkeys in the garden were used to humans and not aggressive at all. Sarah finished her food and stood up. Poppy kept looking at the two monkeys that were not too far, eyeing her food's remains. As Sarah and Poppy left, the monkeys went onto the table and finished the left-over food.

They went back to their room; Sarah put her camera equipment in her backpack to be ready for the next day before hopping into bed.

She started reading when she saw Eli doing an art exhibition in Los Angeles. These visions were still surprising to her, but she was beginning to get used to it. She continued to read and then finally fell asleep.

The next morning Sarah was rested and felt very energetic. She had breakfast and was waiting for Yonas in the lobby. He arrived at 7 o'clock sharp.

"Hi Miss Sarah," said Yonas.

"Hi Yonas."

"Did you rest well?" asked Yonas.

"Yes, thank you, I feel better," replied Sarah.

"Okay, so we will go to the first one, we will arrive in about twenty minutes," said Yonas.

"Thank you."

Sarah and Poppy got into the car; they drove for about half an hour through some smaller roads until they got to the first orphanage.

When Yonas, Sarah, and Poppy stepped out of the car, children came running to them. The children touched Sarah and Poppy. Some children jumped, others sang, while some simply stared at them.

The Administrator, Neela, greeted Sarah, and Yonas. They accompanied this kind looking lady inside and visited the orphanage, followed by the children. The living conditions were better than Sarah expected.

Sarah took photos of the orphanage as well as the children.

An hour later, they sat on the floor together and had some food. A little girl stood in the corner of the room and didn't come to eat with them; Sarah went to see her.

"Hi, my name is Sarah, what is your name?" asked Sarah.

She didn't say a word; Neela came to join them.

"She never speaks, her name is Fana," said Neela.

"Oh, what do you mean, she never speaks?" asked Sarah.

"She hasn't said a word since her arrival, she was brought to us a year ago by a lady that found her in a field," replied Neela.

"How old is she?"

"We think she is about three years old."

"She is beautiful," said Sarah.

"Yes."

Neela went back to have lunch with the other children.

Sarah looked at Fana and smiled. Fana stared at Sarah but didn't do anything or smile back. Sarah imitated Fana; when Fana scratched her head, Sarah scratched her own head. Fana then wiped her mouth, and then Sarah wiped her own mouth. Fana saw this and smiled. Sarah then smiled. Fana put her arm up in the air, and Sarah imitated her again. They played this imitation game for about twenty minutes.

Neela looked at Sarah and Fana and could not believe what she saw; she had never seen Fana smile or engage in any activity before.

Now, Sarah touched her head with both hands and waited to see what Fana would do. Fana did the same thing. Sarah then touched her own arm, and Fana touched her own arm in return. Sarah touched her own nose, and then Fana touched her own nose. They played this for quite a while until Fana started giggling. It was the cutest sound Sarah had ever heard, an adorable high pitched giggle.

Neela came over to see them.

"I have never seen Fana laugh before, how did you do it?" asked Neela.

"I am communicating with her," replied Sarah.

"You are very good with children."

"Thank you."

Sarah got up and started taking more photos.

Fana followed her everywhere she went, not saying a word but merely observing Sarah. Poppy followed Sarah as well. Neela and Yonas watched from afar.

"Fana has been here for over a year and has never even smiled at another child. She really likes Sarah," said Neela.

"Yes, Miss Sarah is a kind woman," replied Yonas.

Sarah spent the whole day taking photos, talking to the children, and playing with them.

Fana did not leave her side; they smiled at each throughout the day and Sarah continued to imitate Fana who did so as well.

The day came to an end; Sarah, Yonas, and Poppy were about to leave. Sarah said goodbye to all the children, some of them jumped into her arms.

Sarah crouched in front of Fana.

"Bye, beautiful," said Sarah.

Fana tagged onto Sarah's shirt to prevent Sarah from leaving; Neela came and took Fana to let Sarah go. Fana looked upset; she watched Sarah leave, sulking. Sarah turned around to get a last look at Fana who was angry.

They got into the car, they were on their drive back to the hotel. Sarah thought about Fana during the entire trip. They definitely had a strong connection. But Sarah didn't know what to do. It was the first time a child seemed so upset to see her leave.

They got to the hotel.

"Here you are, Miss Sarah," said Yonas.

"Thank you, at what time will you come tomorrow?" asked Sarah.

"I will come at 7 o'clock again; we go to a smaller orphanage tomorrow, it's a bit further away," replied Yonas.

"Okay, see you tomorrow," said Sarah as Yonas left.

Sarah and Poppy went into their room, she took a shower unable to think about anything but Fana. That giggle was priceless. She then thought about how upset Fana was when she left.

Sarah and Poppy went downstairs to have some dinner before going to bed. There were very few people in the garden area. Sarah ate rather quickly and went back to her room with Poppy.

She laid on her bed and started researching on her computer what she would have to do to adopt Fana; it seemed pretty complicated.

"I can't adopt her, my life is not organized to have a child, right? She wouldn't be happy with me. What do you think, Poppy?" said Sarah, not expecting an answer from her dog.

She laid in bed and saw Eli doing an art exhibition, but this time he was in New York.

Shortly after, she fell asleep; Poppy cuddled up next to her.

They woke up the next morning, ready for day two; Sarah had not slept too well.

She had breakfast and was waiting for Yonas to pick her up in front of the hotel. Yonas arrived, he was in a great mood. They got into the car and drove off.

"Today we take a bumpy road to go to the other orphanage, it's a very small orphanage," said Yonas.

"Okay," replied Sarah.

They started driving, Sarah was very pensive; Yonas saw this. There was traditional Ethiopian music playing on the radio.

"Are you all right, Miss Sarah?" asked Yonas.

"Yes, I'm okay, thank you," replied Sarah.

She didn't feel like talking; she was trying to understand what was going on herself. She had been to many countries and had seen many children, but it had never upset her like this before.

After a bumpy drive through a small forest, they got to the orphanage. They got out of the car, children came running towards them. There were about ten children; it was a very small orphanage composed of a few huts. An old lady came out, she strolled and looked exhausted. She greeted them; she only spoke to Yonas because she didn't speak any English.

"Hi," said Sarah.

The old lady smiled slightly.

The children touched Poppy who was thrilled to have all the attention. Sarah and Yonas toured the orphanage, following the mistress. The children followed behind. Some of the children touched Sarah's camera.

The living conditions were not as good as the ones in the orphanage they saw yesterday; it was dirtier. The mattresses on the floor look used and old. It smelled like urine in one of the huts.

"Yonas, can you ask her where they get water from?" asked Sarah.

Yonas asked the mistress. She pointed to an area outside, which looked like an old well. The mistress took them to the well, Sarah looked inside it; the water was opaque and yellowish.

The mistress offered them coffee; they all sat in a circle in a hut with a small piece of wood for a table.

"Yonas, can you ask her what they are missing the most?"

Yonas asked the mistress.

"She said that the other lady that was working here left; it has been harder since. Small orphanages are usually the last ones to get help," said Yonas.

"Can you ask her where the other lady went?"

"She said that the other lady was called to help in another orphanage," said Yonas.

"Okay, I will see what we can do to help," replied Sarah, preoccupied with the situation.

Some of the children played with Poppy.

"Can you ask the mistress if I can take photos?" said Sarah.

Yonas asked the mistress, who nodded. Sarah took photos of the living conditions and the children.

The day went by quickly; before they left, they gave the mistress all the water, food, and supplies they had. They said goodbye to the mistress and the children; the children pet Poppy before she got in the car.

They were on their drive back to the hotel, Sarah was silent. Every time she traveled, she knew that she needed to do more, help more.

About half an hour into the drive, Sarah saw Eli, once again, doing an art exhibition; it looked like he was in Amsterdam.

Yonas looked at Sarah in the rearview mirror.

"Everything is okay, Miss Sarah?" asked Yonas.

"Yes, I guess... Do you think you could take me to the orphanage to see Fana tomorrow morning before we go to the airport?" asked Sarah.

"Yes, of course, I take you where you want to go."

"Thank you, would it be okay if you came at 7 o'clock tomorrow?"

"Yes, of course," replied Yonas.

"Thank you."

She looked out the window as they drove; she thought about Fana, she thought about the orphanage they just saw and how terrible the living conditions were.

Shortly after they got to the hotel.

"Thank you, Yonas, I'll see you tomorrow," said Sarah.

"Yes," replied Yonas, smiling as he drove off.

Sarah and Poppy got to their room. Sarah gave food to Poppy and then went to take a shower. She was very quiet, pensive. She got dressed and went over all the photos she took.

They went downstairs to have dinner an hour later. There were several monkeys nearby.

"Good girl, Poppy," said Sarah.

Poppy did not move.

The waiter arrived.

"Hi, what would you like?" asked the waiter.

"Hi, can I please have the Wat with chicken?" replied Sarah.

"Yes, and would you like something to drink?"

"Yes, just some water please."

"Okay," replied the waiter and left.

Sarah looked at Poppy and pet her.

"You are such a good girl," said Sarah.

Poppy wiggled her tail, delighted by the attention Sarah gave her.

The waiter came back with bottled water.

"Thank you," said Sarah.

"You're welcome," replied the waiter.

A few minutes later, he came back with the Wat.

"Thank you."

"Yes, enjoy."

She ate and gave some of her food to Poppy; the monkeys didn't approach them. She finished her dinner and they went back to the room.

Sarah laid in bed and watched the movie *Casablanca*. She had seen this movie many times but loved it as much each time.

She finished watching the film and was about to fall asleep when she saw Eli on a private plane. She saw him look out of the window. It looked beautiful; there were heavenly clouds and a sunset. She could see the horizon; it was breathless.

Being able to see what Eli saw was becoming more familiar to her; she was used to these moments. She decided to not overthink about why she could see what he saw as she didn't understand.

She fell asleep, she felt calmer than she had all day.

The next morning she woke up, packed her bags, had breakfast, and checked-out of the hotel.

Yonas came to pick her up at 7 o'clock.

"Good morning, Miss Sarah," said Yonas.

"Hi Yonas, did you rest well?" asked Sarah.

"Yes, and you?" replied Yonas.

"Yes, thank you."

They got along well; he was straightforward and charming. He put on some traditional music, Sarah smiled.

The drive was nice and slightly bumpy; Sarah recognized the road they took two days before.

She thought about Fana, she wondered if Fana would recognize her.

They got to the orphanage. The children heard the car approaching and ran towards it; Sarah looked out the window but didn't see Fana. Once they got out of the car, Fana came running from behind the other children. She ran into Sarah's arms; Sarah looked at Fana with teary eyes.

"You remember me?" said Sarah, smiling.

Fana didn't say anything but smiled.

"You came back?" said Neela to Sarah, pleased to see them.

"Yes, just for a little bit, I am going back to America in a few hours," replied Sarah.

"Oh," said Neela, a bit disappointed that they were leaving so soon.

"I wanted to come and say goodbye," said Sarah.

"You want some coffee?"

"Yes, I would love some."

The children played with Poppy and asked Sarah to take photos of them, which she did.

Several children played a jumping game with marks on the ground, they looked happy.

Fana followed Sarah everywhere she went. She tagged on Sarah's t-shirt to get her attention; Sarah looked at her, and Fana started putting her hands on her head. She wanted to play. Sarah laughed and put her hands on her head. Fana then put her hand on her cheek. Sarah did the same. Fana jumped and touched her feet. Sarah did the same once again. They played for quite a while; Fana loved this game.

"Now *you* do the same as me, okay?" said Sarah.

Fana observed Sarah and imitated her each time Sarah did something, they had a great time.

A few hours went by, Sarah had to leave or would miss her flight.

"Thank you very much, I hope to see you again," said Sarah to Neela.

"Thank you, you are always welcome here."

Sarah said goodbye to the children; some of them hugged her, and others waved at her.

Fana didn't look happy and opened the car door, trying to get in.

"I am sorry, you cannot come with me, you understand? I can't, can I please have a hug?" said Sarah.

Fana crossed her arms, sulking.

"I am sorry, I can't," said Sarah.

Neela came to take Fana away, who started to cry. This was breaking Sarah's heart. Sarah took Fana in her arms, calming her down before putting her back on the ground and then got in the car.

"No," said Fana quietly.

Everyone was surprised, Fana had never said a word. Sarah started to have teary eyes and Neela held Fana's hand. Sarah rolled down the window and looked at Fana one last time.

"I am sorry," whispered Sarah.

Fana stared at Sarah intensely as Yonas drove away.

The ride to the airport was very silent; Sarah was getting over her emotions. She kept thinking about Fana and how she said *no*.

"I don't know what to do," said Sarah.

"Sorry?" asked Yonas.

"I mean, I can't adopt her, can I?"

"I can find out for you if you want, Miss Sarah?" offered Yonas.

"Yes, okay, please find out."

She felt better already; maybe she could adopt Fana, why not? Sarah started to smile again and looked out the window until they got to the airport.

"Thank you for everything, Yonas, you have been amazing."

"It was my pleasure," replied Yonas.

He thought well of Sarah, and she could feel it.

She went into the airport and once again through the usual airport routine with Poppy. They got onto the plane, the plane was relatively empty.

Sarah went through all the photos of Ethiopia. She looked at the pictures she took of Fana. She was so beautiful, she thought about that giggle, it reminded her of the cute girl in Monsters Inc.

While going through her photos, she saw Eli again. He was in a beautiful art exhibition in London. It was a much bigger space than the other exhibits she saw him in. The walls were very white with all his paintings on them. There was a vast crystal sculpture in the middle of the room. She saw the people he was looking at. She heard him talk; he was describing one of his paintings. She felt his happiness, he was calm, he seemed satisfied with his art exhibition. He was content with himself but in a humble way. She was amazed by what she felt and saw. She smiled to herself and wondered if he could see what she saw.

She closed her eyes and fell asleep.

A few hours later, she was awakened by the flight attendant serving dinner. She ate and gave some food to Poppy. Poppy was quietly under Sarah's feet in her little bag. She finished eating and had tea before watching a movie.

She saw Eli again; this time he was brushing his teeth. She saw him from his point of view. He was brushing his teeth while watching himself in the mirror of a hotel bathroom. The sink was made of beige marble, the walls were white, the mirror was round, and there was a white towel to his left. She saw all the details of what he saw. She was intrigued by what was happening.

She continued watching her movie and fell asleep again.

They got to their layover in Istanbul.

They had a few hours before their next flight took off to Los Angeles.

They stopped at a café, Sarah got some coffee and then went to a newsstand to get water before boarding the plane. She saw an art magazine with a photo of Eli Johnson on the front page. She opened the page to his article and saw that he had been in Los Angeles, New York, and Amsterdam; she couldn't believe it. It amazed her that what she saw during her trip had happened, but mainly it reassured her because she sometimes wondered if she was not losing her mind. She bought the magazine with her bottle of Evian water and walked to the gate with Poppy.

They got onto the plane. Sarah took out the magazine and read the whole article. She still couldn't believe that she really saw where he was; she was very excited about it but at the same time really wondered how it was possible.

She watched a funny movie and then went to sleep again for a few hours. She woke up and went to the bathroom with Poppy. Poppy peed on a little pad that

Sarah threw away afterwards. She walked through the plane for a minute before going back to her seat.

She took out her book and started reading. Half an hour later, the flight attendant brought her some food. Sarah was not really hungry but ate some anyways, she gave most of it to Poppy. Sarah read for a few more hours and then went to sleep again. She was woken up by the smell of coffee. They were about to land; Sarah was excited about being back home. Half an hour later, the plane landed, they got out of the airport and took an Uber home.

Sarah was always delighted to be home. She unpacked, took a shower, and put on some comfortable clothes. She opened her mail and saw that she had another letter from her landlord; she didn't open it, she knew what it said. They went for a long hike at Griffith Park, the sun was shining, there was a slight breeze. The leaves on the trees were abundant, the flowers were blooming, it was gorgeous. After an hour of walking, they got to the top of a hill in Griffith Park; there were few people, they did this same hike once a week. They could see the observatory to their right, on an adjacent hill.

Sarah sat on the grass on the top of the hill and took out some water for Poppy. Poppy drank and then laid next to Sarah. They sat for a while, observing the horizon. Sarah thought about Fana; she would be happy here. The sun started to go down. They got up and left before it became pitch black.

They got home forty-five minutes later. Sarah was fatigued by the walk, but she loved feeling tired from physical activity.

She made some dinner and watched a movie on the couch. She wanted to go to sleep early as she had to go to the office in the morning. She went to bed with Poppy next to her as usual. Sarah started reading her book and fell asleep an hour later.

She woke up in the middle of the night and felt Eli again. She saw Eli, herself, and a little newborn baby in a room. It looked like they were together and just had an infant. She was confused. It was the first time she saw them together instead of seeing him or what he was doing. She felt a connection with Eli that she had never felt with anyone before. She sensed everything he felt and still wondered why. Did he see her or think about her? Was he imagining having a child with her? She fell asleep half an hour later, still thinking about what she just saw.

The next morning she woke up, got ready, and went to the office, parking in her usual spot.

"Hi, Sarah!" said Carlos.

"Hi Carlos, how are you?"

"Good, good, how was your trip?"

"It was good, interesting."

"Going to see Jake, huh?"

"Yes," said Sarah as she walked to the elevator.

They got to the 5th floor; Sarah waved to colleagues in the office as she walked by their cubicles. She got in front of Jake's office and knocked.

"Come in," said Jake.

Sarah opened the door.

"Hi, Sarah, did you get some good pictures?"

"I hope. I'll drop everything at the lab, I'll come by tomorrow so we can go over them," said Sarah.

"Okay."

"When is the next press?" asked Sarah.

"Friday."

"Okay, I'll see you tomorrow then," said Sarah.

"Yes, bye."

"Bye," said Sarah as she left his office.

They went to the other side of the 5th floor in front of a door that said *Laboratory* on it, she entered.

"Hi Sean, how are you?" said Sarah.

"Oh, hey Sarah, how's it going? How was the trip?" asked Sean.

"Great, it was good."

"Hey, I saw your picture in the last issue, beautiful," said Sean.

"Thanks," replied Sarah, blushing slightly.

"What you got for me today?" asked Sean.

"Here, can I have them by tomorrow? I am meeting with Jake, in the morning."

"Anything for you, Sunshine," replied Sean.

"Thank you, Sean."

"Sure, how's the little puppy holding up? Still taking her everywhere you go?" asked Sean.

"Yes."

Sean pet Poppy; she really liked him.

"Okay, I'll see you tomorrow," said Sarah.

"Yup, bye," replied Sean.

They took the elevator to go to the parking lot. Carlos was sitting in his little booth.

"I'll see you tomorrow, Carlos, say hi to the family from me," said Sarah.

"I will; see you tomorrow."

Sarah and Poppy drove back home before going on their usual walk around the neighborhood. They walked for half an hour and then went home. Sarah started putting everything away; she put her lenses on her shelf and then put in a laundry load.

She started cleaning her house while listening to music. Music, in general, always made her feel free. She cleaned and danced at the same time; she was happy. She started dancing in her living room, making beautiful motions with her hands.

Eli was in his loft in New York, painting a woman dancing. The movement of his brush aligned with Sarah's dancing movements. They seemed to connect completely. He was in the same loft Sarah saw previously; the walls were white, there were beautiful wooden beams on the ceiling, and huge windows letting the light in. There were paintings everywhere, hanging on the walls and piled up against the walls. There were paintings of Egypt and the countryside. There was a woman in all the paintings; all was clear but the woman's face. He was painting Sarah dance in her living room; he was very swift while creating his art piece. Sarah finished cleaning her house. Eli finished his painting of her dancing and observed his work of art for a while. He added a touch of red on the bookshelf of her living room. Sarah put her camera bag on her red bookshelf.

She went to take a shower and got ready for her dinner with Emma.

"I'll see you in a few hours, okay? Good girl, Poppy," said Sarah as she gave her a bone.

They met at the Stinking Rose in Beverly Hills.

"Hi, honey," said Emma.

"Hi! It's so nice to see you," replied Sarah.

They hugged. Emma looked beautiful; she had the glow of a woman that was in love. They were seated by the waiter.

"Can I get you something to drink?" asked the waiter.

"Yes, I'll have a glass of Burgundy," replied Emma.

"Me too," said Sarah.

"Okay, I'll be back in a minute to take your order," said the waiter.

"Thank you."

"So, how was your trip?" asked Emma.

"It was great, I have so much to tell you. Should we decide what we want and then I tell you everything?" said Sarah.

"Yes," replied Emma.

They looked at the menu.

"Should we have the Garlic Soaking like last time? Oh, and the Baked Brie, remember it was so good?"

"Yes, and maybe a pizza? I'm starving," said Sarah.

"Yes, pepperoni?"

"Perfect."

"So, how was your trip?" asked Emma.

"It was interesting."

"What happened?"

"I met someone."

"What?!"

"No, not like that, I met this little girl, her name is Fana, I think I want to adopt her," said Sarah.

"Oh my god, wow, that's big news!"

The waiter came back with their drinks and took their order.

"So you were saying, you want to adopt a girl, I mean that's huge!" said Emma.

"Yes, I know, but if you saw her, she is... she is, I don't know, I never had a connection like that with any other orphan I met, and she talked to me," said Sarah.

"What do you mean, she talked to you?"

"Well, she was brought to the orphanage a year ago and never talked to anyone. Then I came, we got along really well, and she said *no* to me when I was leaving."

"Oh, how sweet, how old is she?"

"The Administrator told me that they think she is about three years old."

"Wow, I mean that's great news!"

"I know, I can't leave her there. If you saw how upset she was when I left, it was heartbreaking."

"I trust you entirely. If you decide to adopt her, I am sure it is the right thing to do."

"Yes, I am still trying to figure all this out; it all just happened," said Sarah.

"Did you file the paperwork when you were there?" asked Emma.

"No, I haven't done anything yet, I am still thinking about it."

"I think it's a great idea!" said Emma, smiling.

"I have to help her," replied Sarah.

"Yeah, I was speaking to Liam yesterday. He asked me to help him with a film against slavery; when he went to India, he saw crazy stuff and wrote a script about a little kidnapped girl," said Emma.

"Oh, I had no idea he was interested in that; I really want to get to know him better," said Sarah.

"Yes, he's amazing, I love him more each day," said Emma.

"How is it living together?"

"It's completely natural as if we have lived together forever, we already have our habits. It's really nice, I am happy."

"That's really great!" said Sarah.

The waiter came with the food. The girls started to eat.

"God, this Brie is so good," said Sarah.

"Yes, it's amazing," replied Emma.

"And then more stuff happened with Eli."

"What happened?"

"I keep seeing him in different places, I don't know what to think."

"Like what do you see?"

"I see him doing exhibitions, and I see him in other places. The craziest thing is; I saw him doing exhibitions in LA, New York, and Amsterdam. Then I saw that he had *actually* done exhibitions in those cities in a magazine, so I can really see what he does," said Sarah, waiting for her friend's reply.

"I don't know what to say, I think it's incredible, I've never heard anything like that before, but I think it's pretty cool," replied Emma.

"But what should I do?" asked Sarah.

"I don't know, things will probably sort out by themselves," replied Emma.

"Yeah, I guess you are right."

"We should definitely go to his exhibition next time he comes to LA, you might meet him," said Emma.

"Yeah, I've been trying to not think about it too much, but I can't help myself."

"Yeah, I get it."

They finished having dinner.

"Are you free on Friday? I wanted to invite you over for dinner at our place," said Emma.

"Absolutely!"

They paid and left the restaurant.

Sarah went home, opened for Poppy, and went in the backyard. Victoria was outside having a drink on her own as she scrolled through her phone.

"Hi, honey!" said Victoria.

"Hey! How are you?"

"I'm great! How about you? How did it go?"

"It went well, I guess..."

"What happened?"

"I met this little girl, she's so cute, I am thinking about adopting her."

"Oh, wow! That's a big deal, but you are broke; are you sure that's a good idea?"

"I know, I've been thinking about that, anyhow, I don't know we'll see," replied Sarah.

"Yeah, but it's nice of you."

"Yeah... I've been feeling a bit confused lately," said Sarah.

"Talk to me, honey, what's going on? You don't seem like your usual self."

"I don't know, it's this weird thing. Do you... do you think you are a spirit, Victoria?"

"I mean, yeah, of course."

"Well... I went to a gallery with Emma a while ago, and since, I've been able to see the painter, I see what he is painting even though I am not with him."

"What are you talking about?"

"I know, it's strange, I can see where he is even though I am not with him."

"Dude, you are hallucinating?! I think Jake is stressing you out so much that you see things that don't exist; I am worried about you."

"Forget it," Sarah said, offended.

"Honey, don't be upset, you are telling me that you can see someone when you are not with him. It sounds crazy, I am just worried about you, is all."

"Yeah, I guess you are right, it's crazy."

"You should get some rest and work less."

"I can't, I can barely get by, I am taking all the jobs Jake gives me."

"I told you, come and work with me."

"I don't know, I love my job."

"Yeah, but sometimes you don't have a choice, you know?"

"Yeah, you are right."

"Look, maybe things will get better, and Jake will give you a raise."

"I hope so."

"I have to go, I am meeting with a client early tomorrow, I might make another sale!"

"That's great! Good night."

"Good night, honey, let me know if you need anything, okay?" said Victoria as she started walking away.

"Yes, thanks, I really appreciate your offer, I know you want me to be happy."

"Sure."

Sarah went inside with Poppy and got ready for bed. She thought about what Victoria said about Eli and adopting; she wondered if she was losing her mind.

The next morning Sarah woke up and got ready to go to the office. She took Poppy on a short walk, and they went to the office together. Sarah went to see Sean directly.

"Hi Sean," said Sarah, as she entered the lab.

"Oh, hi, Sunshine," replied Sean.

Sean looked down at Poppy.

"Hello, little one," said Sean while petting Poppy.

"And here you are, they are fantastic, there is a photo of a little girl sitting in a hut alone, which is spectacular," said Sean to Sarah.

"Thank you, I hope Jake will like it as much as you," replied Sarah.

"I am sure he will."

"Thanks, I have to go, he is waiting for me," said Sarah.

"See you soon."

"See you," said Sarah as she left with Poppy.

She knocked on Jake's door.

"Come in," said Jake.

Sarah entered.

"Hi, Jake," said Sarah.

"Hi Sarah, so, what do you have?"

Sarah sat down and took out all the photos from a big brown envelope; Jake went through them.

"This one is good; we will definitely use it."

"Thanks," said Sarah.

It was a photo of the smaller orphanage with all the children sitting outside it. Jake continued to go through her pictures, he saw an image of Fana in the orphanage and looked at it for a while.

"This one is not bad," said Jake.

"She is adorable," replied Sarah.

"I'll suggest it for the front cover."

"Really?!" said Sarah excitedly.

"Don't get too excited."

"Does that mean you'll give me a raise?" asked Sarah.

"Sarah, you have to stop asking me for a raise, I have tons of people that want your job, okay?"

"I love my job, I just thought..."

"Well, don't think... I can't pay you more, get it?"

"Yeah."

She felt crushed but didn't show it. Jake continued to go through the photos and picked a few.

"Okay, well, that's all," said Jake.

"Okay."

"I'll see you for your next mission," said Jake.

"Yes, any idea when that will be?" asked Sarah.

"No, my assistant will let you know."

"Okay."

"Bye, Sarah."

"Bye."

She went to the parking lot, she felt depressed.

Poppy saw that Sarah was unhappy and stayed close to her. Sarah drove to a store in West Hollywood called Sockerbit to buy some salty licorice.

Eli was at an art show in New York, he was being interviewed by a journalist.

"Mr. Johnson, these paintings are spectacular," said the journalist.

"Thank you," replied Eli.

"People have asked you this question many times to no avail, will you let us know who this mystery woman is?" asked the journalist.

"No, not today," replied Eli.

"As you can imagine, we are all very eager to know."

"Yes," said Eli, ending the interview.

Everyone left the exhibition. Eli was alone in the gallery, looking at his paintings. He stood in front of the painting *Thebes, the City of Love,* and stared at it for a while. Tears came scrolling down his face while he observed the girl in the picture.

"Who are you?" whispered Eli.

He stayed in the gallery for a while, looking around. There were so many paintings of this woman with no face.

Sarah got home and sat in the backyard, eating her licorice, while Poppy chewed a bone. She broke down in tears; Victoria saw her from her balcony and came down.

"Are you okay, honey?"

Sarah tried to hide her tears.

"What's happening?" asked Victoria.

"Everything is fucked up; I am two months behind on rent, Jake won't give me a raise, and my love life is nonexistent!" Sarah exploded.

"I'm sorry, I didn't know it was this bad. Did you ask Emma, I am sure she'd help you?"

"She just moved in with her boyfriend, I don't want to bother her."

"Yeah, I get it, I would help you, but I can't, I haven't received my bonuses yet."

"It's okay, I am just having a bad day."

"Okay, are you sure you don't want to come and work for me?"

"Let me think about it, I don't really have a choice; I was just hoping that after all this hard work I'd be fine, you know?"

"Yeah, I get it. Life is tough."

"Yeah, and now I'm eating all this candy, I am going to get fat!" Sarah started to laugh through her tears.

"Everything is going to be okay, you'll see."

"Yeah, thanks, Victoria."

"I have to go, but think about it, okay?"

"Yes, thanks," said Sarah trying to smile.

Victoria left, Sarah stayed in the backyard eating licorice, trying to get over her emotions and decided to call her father.

"Hi, Papa, how are you?" asked Sarah.

"I am doing great! I started playing the piano again!"

"I am so happy for you, Papa."

"So, how was your trip?" asked Simon.

"It was good, I met a little girl in an orphan that I really like, the trip was very eye awakening," said Sarah.

"Was it different from the other trips?"

"Yes, this little girl, I am considering adopting her," replied Sarah.

"Wow, that's incredible, Mama would be really proud of you!"

"Yes, I've been thinking about how I can help more lately," said Sarah.

"That's great, honey."

"How about you? What have you been up to?" asked Sarah.

"I've been taking nice walks around Paris, and playing Pétanque with Antoine almost every day."

"That's great," said Sarah.

"Yes, things have been good, I am doing better each day, I feel like I have been given a second chance at life."

"I am so happy for you, this is such good news."

"Yes, is everything fine with you? You sound quiet," asked her father.

"Everything is fine, don't worry!" said Sarah, forcing enthusiasm in her voice.

"I am so proud of you, honey."

"Okay, I have to go," said Sarah, starting to break into tears again and not wanting her father to hear it.

"Okay, speak soon, I love you," said Simon.

"I love you, Papa," replied Sarah.

She hung up the phone and sat silently for a while; she felt very lonely. She considered the job offer from Victoria. Maybe she could do it for a time until she was afloat again and then get back to her art.

They went inside, had some lunch, and then Sarah got her laptop. She started looking into what she would need to do to adopt Fana.

The day went by rather quickly.

They had dinner and went to sleep early.

The next morning they woke up, had breakfast, and then went for a hike to Griffith Park. They went to their usual hilltop. It was beautiful; they could see the entirety of Los Angeles.

Sarah took out a thin blanket, some water, and a book. She started reading while Poppy walked around on her own.

Sarah took out the early lunch and whistled a tune Poppy had been trained to respond to. Thirty seconds later, she appeared and they had lunch together.

It was a beautiful day, not too warm, just perfect with a little breeze. Sarah continued to read, Poppy laid on the blanket next to Sarah.

She saw Eli again; he was in a house next to a beach; she saw the light beige curtains moving from the wind blowing through the opened window. He was sitting on a couch reading, he was wearing dark blue jeans and a black t-shirt, his bare feet were on the coffee table. He looked towards the moving curtains, looked outside, and saw the beach and sand.

Sarah could feel what he felt, his thoughts, his emotions. It was very intense. Sarah was falling in love with a man she had never met. Every time she saw what he saw or felt what he felt, she questioned why she was able to, and started to think she was crazy.

She continued to read for an hour and then packed everything up. They walked back home. Sarah took a shower and went through all the photos she had taken on her missions; she was not satisfied with them. She received a text message from Emma with the address for their dinner the next evening. Sarah was excited about spending the evening with Emma and Liam, she felt too depressed and was looking forward to seeing Emma and wanted to get to know Liam better.

She went to Trader Joe's to get her usual groceries.

"I'll be back soon, good girl Poppy," said Sarah, giving her a bone.

She came back home and prepared dinner.

They watched Serendipity; Sarah had seen this movie many times but never tired of it.

Sarah took Poppy to the backyard for a minute, and then they went to bed.

The next morning Sarah woke up to an email from Yonas. Yonas found all the information that Sarah needed to be able to adopt Fana. She was excited for a second but then immediately doubted herself, she thought about what Victoria said. She hesitated for a while before filling out the paperwork and did so knowing that it would not get approved anyways.

Sarah and Poppy had lunch in the backyard. The fountain's soothing sound reminded her of her grandmother's garden in Normandy.

After lunch, Sarah went through all her pictures and organized them in chronological order. She was bored.

"Should we go for a walk, Poppy?" said Sarah.

Poppy started wiggling her tail.

They went for a nice walk in the neighborhood and came back home.

Sarah took a nap before going to Liam and Emma's house for dinner. When she was depressed she slept a lot more and she still felt a bit jet-lagged. She fell asleep right away.

Fifteen minutes later, she was partially awakened by a strong emotion of despair. She saw and felt Eli.

In New York, she saw him enter a tall building, she saw him in a conference room talking to a beautiful woman wearing a trench coat. The woman didn't seem particularly kind. They were discussing an important matter. There were other people in the conference room with them. A moment later, Sarah saw this lady leave the building. Sarah saw Eli go to the rooftop. He paced back and forth on the rooftop, thinking. He looked towards the streets of New York; he was very upset.

Sarah was now on the rooftop as well. She looked towards Eli, he saw her, there was a very definite connection.

They talked for what seemed to be hours, he told her about his whole life. Where he was from, his childhood, his relationship with his parents, his family.

How he started painting. He told Sarah about his ex-wife, who was giving him a hard time. She told him all about her life. They talked about everything they loved, the music they listened to. At the end of the night, he looked at Sarah and realized that he was utterly in love with her. Everything between them was so simple, communication was effortless. Being together seemed so natural.

"You are the woman with no face," whispered Eli.

"Yes," whispered Sarah.

He looked at her, got closer, and kissed her; it was a passionate kiss; they became one.

Sarah woke up and looked around, confused. It felt like she spent the whole night with him. It felt so real. Her feelings for him were so present, she remembered everything he said. She remembered the sounds, the movements, the lights on the rooftop, how he was dressed, what he said, how he looked at her, how he touched her, and their kiss. Everything. She didn't know what to think. It was so real.

She went into the shower and wondered if she was not completely losing her mind. Poppy sat on the mat in front of the shower door as usual. Sarah took a long shower. She thought about Eli; she didn't know how to explain it, and it was really starting to bother her. Sarah got out of the shower, got dressed, and then drove to Emma's house.

She rang the doorbell and was greeted by Emma.

"Hi honey, I am so happy to see you, hi Poppy," said Emma.

"Hi, honey," replied Sarah.

"You doing good?" asked Emma.

"I'm fine," replied Sarah in a quiet voice.

Liam came to join them into the garden.

"Hi Sarah," said Liam.

"Hi Liam, it's really nice to see you again," said Sarah.

"Please come in, Emma will show you around; I am almost finished cooking dinner," said Liam.

"You are cooking? A man of many talents," said Sarah, smiling.

"And this must be Poppy, Emma told me a lot about you," said Liam to Poppy while he pet her.

"Come, let me show you our house," said Emma proudly.

She was very excited. Emma showed Sarah the house; they had two bedrooms, a pool, and a beautiful garden; Poppy followed them around.

"Dinner is ready in a minute," said Liam from the kitchen.

"We are coming, honey," replied Emma to Liam.

"We will have dinner in the garden, the weather is perfect," said Emma to Sarah.

They went to the kitchen and helped Liam bring out the food to the garden table. There were beautiful lights set-up, lots of trees, and a small fountain; it was very cozy.

"So, Emma tells me you are thinking about adopting, that's incredible!" said Liam.

"Yeah, I mean... I don't know if my application will get approved," replied Sarah.

"What do you mean?" asked Emma.

"I don't know, we'll see, these things can take time," said Sarah.

"Oh, okay," replied Emma.

"I think it's brave; if more people helped, we'd all be better off," said Liam.

"Yes," replied Sarah.

"I thought we could all do an art exhibit together?" said Liam.

"I love your idea, honey," said Emma, proud of her boyfriend.

"It sounds nice," replied Sarah quietly.

"Emma could exhibit her paintings and stories, you could exhibit your photography, and I could exhibit my short films?" suggested Liam.

"I don't know that people would come to see my photos," said Sarah.

"What are you talking about? Your pictures are amazing!" replied Emma.

"I don't know," said Sarah.

"And some of the proceeds could go to children in Africa," said Liam.

"Yes, great idea!" said Emma.

"It sounds nice," said Sarah quietly.

Emma looked at Liam and kissed him. They had a great time together, eating and talking about remaking the world.

"It's time for dessert," said Liam.

"You made a dessert?" asked Sarah.

"No, Emma did, she made her amazing Tiramisu," replied Liam, proudly.

Liam went inside to get the dessert.

"He is charming," said Sarah.

"Yes, I feel very fortunate. Is everything all right, honey?" said Emma worried about her friend.

"I'm okay, just had a tough few days."

"Are you sure? Do you need anything?"

"I'm fine, don't worry."

There was a silence, Sarah broke it.

"I wanted to talk to you about Eli, a lot of things happened," said Sarah.

"What happened?" asked Emma.

"Liam might think I'm crazy if I talk about this in front of him," said Sarah.

"No, not at all, you'd be surprised," replied Emma.

"Really?" asked Sarah.

"He's very spiritual, you know," said Emma.

Liam arrived with Tiramisu. He could sense that the girls were having a private conversation.

"You ladies talking about me?" said Liam, smiling.

Emma served the Tiramisu.

"No, actually, Sarah was telling me about someone she has never met that she can sense," said Emma to Liam.

"Oh, how so?" asked Liam.

"This is going to sound very weird, if someone would have told me what I am about to tell you, I am not sure I would have believed them," said Sarah.

"Now I really want to know," said Liam.

Sarah smiled timidly. She explained everything to them, everything that had happened since the beginning. The times she saw him, she could feel him, the magazine she saw at the airport. The dream that seemed so real a few hours ago.

"Wow, I mean, this is incredible, I love your story," said Liam.

"I think people would think I'm nuts," replied Sarah.

"Do you realize, you can actually feel someone you have never met, I mean, I think it's fucking amazing!" said Liam.

"I don't know what to do?" asked Sarah.

"I think you should meet him for sure," replied Liam.

"That's what I said," said Emma.

"Yeah, but I mean, what would I say, Hi Eli, I *feel like I know you*? It's too weird, he'd think I'm crazy," said Sarah.

"You don't know; maybe if the two of you met, he would recognize you as well?" said Liam.

"Yeah, but what if he doesn't?" replied Sarah.

"Well, at least you would have tried, right?" said Liam.

"Yeah," said Sarah.

"Next time he does an exhibition in Los Angeles, we should all go together," said Liam excitedly.

"Sure," replied Sarah.

"I can't wait," said Emma.

"This Tiramisu is amazing," said Sarah changing the subject.

"Thanks, it's my grandmother's recipe," said Emma.

"So good," said Liam.

They finished their dessert.

"Thank you so much, I had such a great time," said Sarah.

"You are welcome anytime," said Liam.

"I'll see you tomorrow for lunch, and then we go to the beach, right?" asked Emma.

"Yes, do you want to meet in front of the Farmers Market or inside?" asked Sarah.

"I thought I'd come to pick you up so we can drive together?" said Emma.

"Okay, perfect," replied Sarah.

"I'll come at 11am, is that good?" asked Emma.

"That's great, bisous, see you tomorrow," replied Sarah.

Sarah and Poppy left. Sarah listened to music in the car, a song came on the radio. She knew that Eli loved this song; she didn't know how she knew but simply did.

Eli was in his loft, painting a rooftop. The painting was very colorful; there were beautiful colored lanterns, a little table in the middle of the roof, and two people sitting at a table. You could see the lights and buildings of New York in the background. Eli was absorbed; he was painting and painting, perfecting his piece of art.

Eli's manager walked into the loft. He got closer to Eli and stared at the painting.

"Wow, this is a masterpiece," said Kelvin.

"It came to me in a dream. Yesterday after I saw Crystal with the lawyers, I went to the rooftop to get some air, and I had this incredible dream," said Eli.

"This painting is amazing," said Kelvin, absorbed by its beauty.

"Thank you, I think it might be my favorite," replied Eli.

Sarah went to sleep, Poppy laid next to her.

The next morning when Sarah woke up, she felt rested. She had her coffee in the backyard with Poppy and checked her emails; she received another email from the landlord as well as a late notice from a credit card. She took a shower and got ready before Emma arrived.

"Hi, honey," said Sarah.

"Hi, did you sleep well?" asked Emma.

"Yes, I feel like I'm finally over the jet-lag," replied Sarah.

"Cool, are you ready to go?"

"Yes," said Sarah.

She closed up her flat, and they all got into Emma's car. Music played on the radio.

"So what did you think about Liam?" asked Emma.

"He's great, I really like him, and he seems like a genuinely good guy," said Sarah.

"Yes, he thought you were great too, he loves your story with Eli, he kept asking me questions after you left," said Emma.

"Oh, I thought I sounded crazy," said Sarah.

"Honey, what are you talking about? This is so romantic, we really want to know how it will end," said Emma.

"Yeah," replied Sarah.

A popular song from the '80s started to play on the radio.

"You see, I know that Eli likes this song, but I don't know how I know," said Sarah.

"You know because he told you, that's how you know," replied Emma, smiling at her friend.

"Yeah, I guess you are right, it's either that or I'm losing my mind completely," said Sarah, laughing.

"Don't say that," said Emma.

Sarah started to feel better; Emma always believed in her and wanted her to be happy, Sarah felt it. They arrived at the Farmers Market and went to their usual pizza place.

"God, these pizzas are so good," said Sarah.

"I've been thinking about this pizza since I woke up!" said Emma laughing.

Sarah gave a few pieces of pepperoni to Poppy.

"You're the best mistress ever, you take her everywhere you go, and you feed her human food," said Emma.

"I know, I love her," replied Sarah mocking herself.

"You are lucky, Poppy," said Emma.

They finished their pizza and drove to the beach.

"So when do you start?" asked Sarah.

"We start rehearsals in two days; I still can't believe they picked my pilot," said Emma.

"I know, it's fantastic, I'm sure your show will be amazing," said Sarah.

"I'm a little nervous."

"It's going to be great! We can rehearse on the beach if you want?"

"If you don't mind, I'd love that," replied Emma.

"I love rehearsing with you; it's always so much fun."

They listened and sang to music on the radio for the rest of the drive and then arrived at the beach.

Poppy was off the leash, running around chasing after the seagulls.

They set up a little blanket on the sand and sat down. They started rehearsing. Emma made Sarah laugh by doing all these funny different voices and accents. They rehearsed for two hours.

"I feel pretty good about it," said Emma.

"Awesome."

Sarah's phone rang; it was Jake.

"Hi, Jake," said Sarah.

"Hi Sarah, listen, David can't go to India, can you go instead of him?" said Jake.

"Yeah, of course, when would I need to go?" asked Sarah.

"Tomorrow," replied Jake.

"Oh, tomorrow?" said Sarah.

"Yes."

"I'll do it."

"Good, come by the office in the morning, my assistant will give you all the info about the mission," said Jake.

"Okay, see you tomorrow," replied Sarah.

"Bye," said Jake.

She hung up the phone.

"Who was that?" asked Emma.

"Jake wants me to go on a mission to India... tomorrow," said Sarah.

"Oh, wow, so soon?" asked Emma.

"Yeah, David can't go, and I can't refuse any work right now," replied Sarah.

"Okay," said Emma.

"Should we go for a swim?" asked Sarah.

"Yes, it's so hot," replied Emma.

Poppy followed them, her little muzzle sticking out of the water. They had a nice swim.

It was the end of the afternoon.

"Are you okay if we go home? I have to prepare everything for my trip," said Sarah.

"Of course," replied Emma.

Poppy played in the sand. They got dressed and headed back to the car.

"Poppy, come here," said Sarah.

Poppy came running; Sarah cleaned all the sand off Poppy. They got into the car, and Emma drove them back home.

"Thank you, honey, it was such a great day! Say hi to Liam for me," said Sarah.

"Bye honey, yes I will, see you in a week, have a great trip!" said Emma.

"Thank you, let's have dinner at my house when I'm back," said Sarah.

"Absolutely!" replied Emma.

They hugged, and Sarah and Poppy went to their apartment. Before they had time to enter, Victoria yelled from her balcony.

"Sarah!"

"Oh, hi, Victoria, how are you?"

"I'm good, I haven't seen you since, you better?"

"Yeah, thanks! Sorry, I was a mess the other day."

"No worries! Should we hang out tomorrow?"

"No, I am going to India on a mission, but I'll see you in a week!"

"Oh, okay... Have a good trip!"

"Thanks!"

Sarah took a shower; she was exhausted from the day spent in the sun. She prepared a light dinner, her bag for the trip, and went to sleep early.

Sarah laid in her bed, thought about Fana, and wondered why anyone would let her adopt a child. She closed her eyes and fell asleep.

Sarah and Eli were making love; it was very intense. They made love to each other as if they had been together for years. They were so connected that they seemed to be one. They spent the night talking, laughing, and making love. She woke up in the middle of the night and looked next to her; Eli was not there.

Forty-seven ∞ India

The next morning, Sarah got up early and went to the office to see Jake's assistant for her mission.

She loved going to India; she had been there many times. The photo which Eli looked at in the middle of the night was a picture Sarah took on her first trip to India.

She got to the office with Poppy.

"Hi Carlos, how are you doing?" asked Sarah.

"Hi Sarah, hi Poppy, things are great! Where are you going this time?" asked Carlos.

"I am going to India," replied Sarah.

"I'd love to go there one day," said Carlos.

"Yes, it's beautiful, but the poverty is tough to see," replied Sarah.

"Yes, I'm sure," said Carlos.

Sarah and Poppy went to Jake's assistant's office; she was not there. They went to Jake's office, and she knocked.

"Come in," said Jake.

Sarah entered.

"Hi Sarah," said Jake.

"Hi, Jake, your assistant is not at her desk, do you have the documents?" asked Sarah.

"Yeah, she had to leave, here is everything; James will pick you up at the airport," said Jake.

"Oh great, James is fantastic," replied Sarah.

"Yeah. There's a bit more to this mission, we want you to inspect the orphanage carefully, we have reasons to believe that children are being sold illegally," said Jake.

"Oh... okay," replied Sarah worried.

"It's fine. James is aware of the mission; you can ask him anything," said Jake.

"Okay, thanks," replied Sarah.

"Bye," said Jake.

"Bye."

It was the first time that Sarah went on a mission like this.

She went home and sat in the living room. She opened the brown envelope, there were photos of the orphanage, missing children and one man. The man was named Akhil, he created the orphanage. Amnesty International believed that he smuggled children from his orphanage and sold them to wealthy men for sexual slavery. The orphanage was in a small town near a jungle an hour away from New Delhi. She read all the info about the mission.

Sarah and Poppy went on a walk. Sarah thought about her mission, she was a bit stressed out.

They went back home and took an Uber to the airport. They got stuck in traffic; Sarah knew she was going to miss her flight and called Jake.

"Hello?" said Sarah.

"What's up?" replied Jake.

"I am stuck in traffic, I'm going to miss my flight."

"What the fuck Sarah?!"

"There's an accident on the highway, I'm sorry."

"You are so irresponsible! I can't believe I trusted you with this mission!"

"I'm sorry."

"I'll tell Angela to do the changes, she'll send you the new flight ticket," he hung up.

Sarah was very annoyed at herself.

An hour later, they arrived at the airport. Sarah and Poppy went through the airport's typical hustle and boarded the plane. Poppy was in her little bag under Sarah's feet as usual.

She studied more about her mission, and this man named Akhil; he came from a wealthy family from New Delhi. He had several orphanages in India. Sarah finished going over all the documents and then watched a film before taking a nap.

The flight went by quickly. They got to their first lay-over, waited for about an hour, and then got onto the second plane. The second flight was shorter.

Sarah read and slept for a bit. They landed in New Delhi and found James at the arrivals.

"Sarah!" said James.

"Hi James, it's so nice to see you again, it's been a while," replied Sarah.

"Yes, it has been too long," said James.

Sarah and James had known each other for years.

"Let me help you with your bag," said James.

"Thank you."

"Hi Poppy," said James.

Poppy wiggled her tail while James pet her.

"Did you have a nice trip?" asked James.

"Yes, it went by rather quickly."

"Good, we have an hour drive to get to the hotel," said James.

"Okay."

They started driving, the weather was hot and humid.

"How are things?" asked James.

"Good, I've been doing a few missions," replied Sarah.

"I saw your photo in the last issue; I love it."

"Thank you."

"So, have you met your husband yet?"

"No, not yet. How are the children?" asked Sarah.

"Very good, very good, Gunbir is learning how to write."

"They grow so fast," said Sarah.

"Yes."

They continued on the drive until they got to a small hotel. They all got out of the car; James took Sarah's bag, and they entered the hotel. A man was behind a reception desk.

"Yes," said the receptionist.

"We have a reservation for two rooms," said James.

"Under what name?" asked the man.

"James."

"Ah, yes, here you go, you go straight down the hall and take a left," said the receptionist as he handed them two keys.

"Thank you," said James.

Sarah, James, and Poppy went down the corridor.

"Get some rest, we can get some dinner later?" said James.

"Yes, that sounds great. Should we meet at 7pm?" asked Sarah.

"Yes."

She went into her room, it was small but clean. The walls were pink with a big green painting on the wall above the bed. Sarah took a shower and then took a nap.

Two hours later, she woke up feeling rested. She got ready and went to James's room and knocked on his door.

"Yes?" said James.

"It's Sarah, I'm ready, I'll wait for you at the reception."

"Ok, I'll be there in a minute."

James met Sarah at the reception two minutes later.

They walked to a little restaurant, not too far away; Poppy walked next to Sarah, off the leash.

They sat down and the waiter came.

"Hello, what would you like?" asked the waiter.

James nodded for Sarah to order first.

"I'll have the chicken curry with some rice, please," said Sarah.

"And I'll have your special," said James.

"Okay, would you like something to drink?" asked the waiter.

"I'll have a green tea, please," said Sarah.

"Me too," said James.

"Okay," replied the waiter.

He left and came back a minute later with the tea.

"Thank you," said Sarah.

The waiter nodded and left.

"So tell me about this Akhil guy," said Sarah.

"I don't know much more than what is in the report. He is from New Delhi, his family is very wealthy, and he has orphanages everywhere in India," said James.

"Okay, and why do we think that he is illegally selling children?"

"About a month ago, a 9-year-old girl almost died in a hospital. She had been escorted by boat to a very wealthy man in Africa, had been abused for 2 years, and came from Akhil's orphanage. It's not the first time we hear this about Akhil."

"Okay."

They had dinner and spoke about the mission before they went back to the hotel.

"We should leave at 8am," said James.

"Okay, I'll see you tomorrow."

"See you tomorrow."

They went to their respective rooms. Sarah went to bed but had a hard time falling asleep.

The next morning she woke up and got ready to go to the orphanage. James was at the reception, waiting for her; Sarah arrived with Poppy.

"Good morning Sarah," said James.

"Morning," replied Sarah.

"Are you ready to go?"

"Yes."

They drove for an hour on a decent road and then got to a narrow, bumpy dirt road and drove through a jungle.

"I didn't realize the orphanage was really in the jungle?" said Sarah.

"Yes, it's pretty secluded," replied James.

A few minutes later, they arrived at the orphanage and parked. Fakhil came out of the orphanage, there were some children next to him. Sarah, James, and Poppy got out of the car.

"Hello, welcome!" said Fakhil.

"Hi," said James.

"Hi, my name is Sarah," said Sarah, as she shook hands with Fakhil.

"Nice to meet you both, please come in," said Fakhil in perfect English.

Fakhil was charming and very elegant.

They followed him into the orphanage. It was spotless and in a better condition than what Sarah was used to seeing.

The children pet Poppy; they seemed happy to play with a dog. When they entered the dining room, the children were quietly seated. Sarah was surprised to see orphans this calm; she was used to seeing noisy children running around everywhere.

A mistress arrived, she was gorgeous.

"This is Saira, she manages the orphanage," said Fakhil.

"Nice to meet you," said Saira.

"Nice to meet you, too," replied Sarah.

"Hi," said James.

"If you have any questions, you can ask Saira," said Fakhil.

"Thank you," replied Sarah.

"Saira will show you around," said Fakhil.

Sarah and James followed Saira. She took them around the orphanage, they went to very tidy rooms.

"The orphanage is very clean, I have never seen anything like this before," said Sarah.

"Yes, we try to do our best for the children to live in good conditions," replied Saira.

Sarah looked around; she was impressed. They continued their visit of the orphanage, Sarah took photos as they went.

They came back to the dining room; Fakhil was speaking to a child in Hindi.

"Have you been to the kitchen yet?" said Fakhil to Saira.

"No, we are on our way there now," replied Saira.

"Would you like some coffee?" asked Fakhil.

"Yes, I would love some," replied Sarah.

They sat down in the kitchen; Poppy sat on the floor next to Sarah. A teenage girl poured them some coffee; Sarah smiled at her, she smiled back.

"This is the nicest orphanage I have ever seen," said Sarah to Fakhil.

"Thank you, we take pride in having the best orphanages in the country," said Fakhil, smiling.

They spent a moment in the kitchen chit-chatting.

"I must leave, but feel free to take all the photos you want; if you need anything, Saira will help you," said Fakhil.

"Thank you," replied Sarah.

"It was a pleasure," said Fakhil before he left.

"How long have you been working here?" asked Sarah to Saira.

"I grew up here, I am an orphan myself, Fakhil helped me a lot and then offered me a job here," replied Saira.

"That's very nice of him," said Sarah.

"Yes, he is like a father to me," replied Saira.

They went outside.

Sarah spent some time with the children and took pictures of them; some of the children played with Poppy.

"We should get going before it gets too dark?" said James to Sarah.

"Yes," replied Sarah.

They said goodbye to the children.

"Thank you very much," said Sarah to Saira.

"Of course, thank you for your visit," replied Saira.

They got back into the car and left; Sarah was silent.

"What are you thinking?" asked James.

"I don't know, everything looks perfect, but I have a weird feeling," replied Sarah.

"I have the exact same feeling," said James.

"We went everywhere, I don't think there is anything suspicious, I don't really see what more we can do," said Sarah.

"We could go back there when they are not expecting us?" said James.

"Yes, good idea, let's go back tomorrow," said Sarah.

When they got back to the hotel it was fully dark outside.

"Let's meet at 8am," said James.

"Yes, good night, see you tomorrow," replied Sarah.

"Good night," said James.

They both went to their rooms; Sarah was followed by Poppy.

Eli was in his loft in New York painting. He was painting a girl in a jungle. The image looked very much like the jungle Sarah went through to get to the orphanage.

Sarah fell asleep rapidly. She woke up in the middle of the night, not feeling too well. She went to the bathroom and vomited. She felt very hot. She went back to sleep an hour later, feeling extremely dizzy.

The next morning James was waiting for Sarah at the reception. He waited for fifteen minutes and then went to her room and knocked on the door; there was no answer.

"Sarah?" called James.

Still no answer. He heard Poppy whining and knocked a few times.

"Sarah, are you there?"

There was still no answer, but Poppy was now barking. James was worried, he went to the reception.

"Have you seen the lady from room 103?" asked James.

"No, sir, I haven't seen anyone this morning," said the receptionist.

"Can you open room 103? I need to see if everything is okay," said James.

"Yes," replied the receptionist.

They went to Sarah's room, and the receptionist opened the door. Sarah was in bed; she looked very pale with dark circles under her eyes.

"Oh my god, Sarah," said James.

Poppy was on the bed next to Sarah, whining. James touched Sarah's forehead, she was burning hot.

"Call a doctor!" said James to the receptionist.

The man left the room in a hurry.

"A doctor is coming," said James to Sarah.

Sarah was delusional; she was mumbling something that James didn't understand. James took a wet cloth and put it on her forehead.

The man from the reception came back a few minutes later.

"The doctor is coming," he said.

"Thank you," replied James to the receptionist.

The receptionist left.

"Sarah, can you hear me?"

Sarah mumbled again. James didn't know what to do; he continued to wipe her forehead with the moist cloth.

The doctor arrived half an hour later. He took her temperature and looked at James; the doctor seemed worried.

"What is it?" asked James.

"She has a high fever," said the doctor.

He gave Sarah medication.

"I hope the fever will come down with this, I believe she got food poisoning," said the doctor.

"Will she be all right?" asked James.

"I hope so, give her some every four hours, and she should be fine," replied the doctor.

"Thank you," said James.

"If she is not better by tonight, call me," insisted the doctor.

"Okay."

The doctor left leaving James in a worried state. He sat next to Sarah, who mumbled and tossed in bed.

A few hours went by; Sarah didn't look any better. James sat next to her and spoke to her, hoping this would help.

"Sarah, please, you have to wake up," said James.

Sarah mumbled something that sounded like a name. James didn't understand what she was saying. He paced back and forth and then went back to the reception.

"Please call the doctor again," said James.

"Yes," replied the receptionist.

James went back to Sarah's room, Poppy was whining.

"What about Poppy?" said James to Sarah.

The doctor arrived an hour later and took her temperature and pulse.

"So?" asked James.

"It's not very good," replied the doctor.

"What should I do?" asked James.

"There is nothing more that can be done; it depends on her," said the doctor.

James was devastated when the doctor left.

Poppy pushed Sarah with her head, she was trying to wake her up. Sarah's breathing was very slow.

"Please, Sarah, come back," insisted James.

James sat on a chair next to Sarah and fell asleep.

Two hours later, Sarah opened her eyes. Poppy started barking joyfully; Sarah turned her head and pet her softly, James woke up.

"Thank God," said James.

"James," said Sarah.

"You scared us," said James.

"Sorry," replied Sarah, with a weak smile.

James brought Sarah some warm soup, she drank it seated on her bed. She looked better; her cheeks had some color in them. Poppy wiggled her tail and pushed Sarah with her head.

"Hi Poppy," said Sarah as she pet her.

"How do you feel?"

"Better, thank you," replied Sarah.

"Good, good, maybe you should eat some more?" said James, still worried.

"I think I need to sleep; I will feel better when I wake up. Did you take Poppy outside?" asked Sarah.

"This morning," replied James.

"Would you mind taking her out for a minute?" said Sarah.

"Yes, of course," replied James.

He took Poppy out for a short walk and came back a few minutes later.

"Get some sleep, I will check up on you in a few hours," said James.

"Thank you."

She quickly fell asleep, Poppy cuddled up next to her.

James came back a few hours later; Sarah was sound asleep. He touched her forehead; she no longer had a temperature and looked much better. He went back to sleep in his room.

Sarah woke up in the middle of the night; she was wide awake. She took a stroll with Poppy outside; they walked and got to a small garden bench. Sarah sat down and watched the moon. She took out her mother's letter from her jacket and read it silently. She read it several times and cried and smiled.

"Everything is going to be okay, Poppy," said Sarah determined.

The next morning when James woke up, he went straight to see Sarah. When he entered her room, she was awake, had showered, and was dressed, ready to go.

"You scared me, Sarah," said James as he hugged her.

"What would life be without a bit of an adventure? So are you ready to go? I've been waiting for you!" said Sarah, teasing him.

"What? *You* are waiting for *me*? No, I am waiting for you, but seriously, you actually want to go?" asked James.

"Yes, I am fine, let's go back to the orphanage," replied Sarah.

"Okay, I'll meet you in fifteen minutes at the reception," said James.

They met at the reception and drove to the orphanage.

Eli was once again in his loft painting; he was painting a girl in bed in a hotel room. The walls in his image were pink, and there was a big green painting above the girl's bed. The painting looked exactly like Sarah's hotel room; the girl's face in it was blurry.

James and Sarah got to the orphanage. Saira came out of the orphanage and looked perplexed. There were no children outside. Sarah and James got out of the car, Saira smiled.

"Have you forgotten something?" asked Saira.

"Hi Saira, no, we wanted to come by one more time before I head back home," replied Sarah.

"Oh, of course, please come in," said Saira.

Sarah and James felt like they had interrupted something.

"Would you like some coffee?" asked Saira.

"No, thank you, we just had some," replied Sarah.

They entered the dining room and said hi to the children that were seated. The children were happy to see Poppy again and played with her; they made some noise while playing with Poppy; Saira looked annoyed.

"Go outside to play with the dog," said Saira in a stern voice.

She smiled at Sarah, wondering if Sarah noticed her tone of voice; Sarah smiled back at her.

They stayed for a couple of hours, Sarah took some photos. They were outside the orphanage getting ready to leave.

Poppy was outside playing with the children when she ran into the jungle.

"Poppy!" said Sarah.

Poppy didn't come back. Sarah was surprised that Poppy didn't return; it was not in her habits.

"What is she doing?" said Sarah.

Saira looked a bit worried.

"Poppy!" yelled Sarah.

Still no sign of Poppy, Sarah started to worry.

"James, can you help me?" asked Sarah.

Sarah headed into the jungle where Poppy ran.

"Poppy! Poppy!" yelled Sarah.

They walked for a minute and heard Poppy barking.

"Poppy! Come here!" said Sarah.

Poppy still didn't come. James and Sarah continued to walk towards the barking and finally saw her.

"Poppy, what are you doing? Come here!" said Sarah.

Poppy didn't move. Sarah was confused; Poppy never disobeyed her. Sarah and James walked towards Poppy, who continued to bark. They got to Poppy and saw a metal gated cell that went underground; they saw children behind metal bars.

"Call the police right away!" shouted Sarah to James.

James called the police. Sarah tried to open the cell but couldn't. They tried to force the gate, but it didn't even move slightly.

"What should we do?" asked Sarah.

"I think we should wait for the police, I don't think it's safe to go back to the orphanage," replied James.

A few minutes later, the police arrived; sirens could be heard. Saira left the orphanage in a hurry from behind and ran into the jungle. Sarah and James walked towards the police cars next to the orphanage.

Several policemen came running out of their cars, Sarah and James explained everything to them and showed them what they had found.

An officer talked to one of the orphans; he asked where Saira was, the child pointed towards the jungle.

Three officers managed to open the cell, eighteen children came out of the hole; they were dirty and look drugged. Most children were younger than the age of ten, they all wore white cotton dresses.

Sarah took photos.

The entire area was locked down by the police; ambulances arrived.

A few hours went by, Sarah and James gave all the information they had to the police, who thanked them for their help and explained that they had an eye on this orphanage for years.

Sarah and James left the orphanage and drove back to the hotel.

"You are such a good girl, Poppy!" said Sarah.

"She is a hero," said James.

"Yes," said Sarah as she kissed Poppy.

They got to the hotel. Sarah took a shower before meeting up with James to have dinner. She was exhausted from all the events of the last few days.

"What a day," said Sarah as they sat down to have dinner in the hotel.

"Yes, we saved children's lives today," said James, proudly.

"Yes, we did," replied Sarah.

She looked at Poppy, lovingly. They ordered Tandoori chicken and plain chicken for Poppy.

"I still can't believe it, I wonder if they found Fakhil?" said Sarah.

"I am sure they will find him," replied James.

"Yes."

They had a pleasant dinner going over the events of the day before going back to their mutual rooms.

"Good night Sarah, good job!" said James.

"Good night James, we were a great team today! I'll see you in the morning," replied Sarah.

Sarah went to bed and fell asleep immediately.

The next morning Sarah woke up very early, packed her bags, and met James at the reception at 7am.

"Good morning Sarah," said James.

"Hi James," said Sarah.

"Are you ready to go home?" asked James.

"Yes, I am," replied Sarah.

They drove to the airport; it was a pleasant drive. James talked about the events from yesterday and imagined being a superhero saving children all over the world. They enjoyed this moment together and got to the airport.

"I hope I will see you soon, Sarah," said James.

"It's always a pleasure working with you, James, thank you for everything, I'll see you soon," said Sarah as she hugged him.

"Have a good flight," said James.

"Thank you," replied Sarah.

Once again, Sarah went through the usual airport scenario with Poppy and got onto their first plane. Sarah looked at all the photos she took and thought about all the recent events. The flight was smooth; Poppy slept throughout most of it.

They got to their layover and had a snack in a burger joint at the airport; Sarah gave Poppy some hamburger meat.

They boarded their second flight, the plane was relatively empty. Sarah watched two movies and took a nap.

They finally got to Los Angeles. Sarah was delighted to be back; they took an Uber and got home.

Sarah took a shower; Poppy waited for her on the bath mat. She dressed up comfortably, and they went on a long walk in their neighborhood.

Sarah was exhausted from the jet-lag. After their walk, they got home, had a light dinner, and went to sleep.

She woke up at three in the morning and could feel Eli more than usual; she felt like he was waiting for her. She saw that he was in a coffee shop in London, sitting by himself. She fell asleep again a few minutes later.

Forty-eight ∞ London

Eli sat in a coffee shop in London, wearing a thick trench coat and a scarf. It was cold; there was condensation on the windows in the coffee shop. He rubbed his hands together and blew hot air on them.

Sarah arrived in the coffee shop, wearing a red dress and a coat. He saw her, waved, and smiled. She got closer to him and kissed him. She sat in front of him; they looked like a couple meeting up in their usual coffee shop. They gazed at each other, talked, laughed, and kissed.

Once again, they spoke about everything; she told him about India. He told her about his latest paintings. They spent hours together talking about their lives and their dreams. They talked about their future, about getting married and having children. They enjoyed themselves immensely; they were in love.

Sarah woke up the next morning, looked next to her; Eli was not there, but this didn't bother her because she knew she spent time with him, and they had a great time. Once again, it was so real.

She got out of bed and had a coffee in the backyard, the sun was shining, birds were singing, it was a beautiful morning. Sarah put on some hiking clothes, and Poppy and Sarah went on their usual hike at the top of the hill in Griffith Park. They got to the top, Sarah put down a small blanket and took out some water and snacks. Sarah thought about her life, about the mission in India, about Fana, and about Eli.

Poppy ran around and came back every few minutes to check up on Sarah.

Forty-nine ∞ Hope

Sarah and Poppy went back down the hill and walked back home, taking their time. Sarah hopped into the shower and got dressed before calling Emma.

"Hi, honey, how are you?" asked Sarah.

"I'm doing great!" replied Emma.

"Great, are we still on for dinner at my house tonight?" said Sarah.

"Yes, we'll come at about 7pm, is that good for you?" replied Emma.

"Yes, that's perfect, I'll see you tonight, bisous."

"See you tonight, I can't wait, bisous," replied Emma.

They hung up the phone.

Sarah took her camera bag and went to the office with Poppy; they got to the parking lot and headed to the fifth floor. Sarah knocked on Jake's door.

"Come in," said Jake.

Sarah opened the door.

"Sarah," said Jake, still reading a document.

"Hi, Jake," said Sarah.

"I'm still upset you missed your flight; you know it cost me, but I am willing to forgive you because the mission went well, they arrested Fakhil," said Jake.

Sarah looked at Jake in disbelief.

"Jake, you know what... I quit!" said Sarah.

Jake was flabbergasted and speechless. Sarah stormed out, proud of herself.

She drove home with Poppy as she listened to loud music in her car. She couldn't believe she quit; it felt so good, but at the same time, she thought about her rent.

Sarah went to Trader Joe's to get everything she needed for dinner; she would make a raclette. She finished all her groceries and came back home, greeted by Poppy as usual.

Sarah put everything away and prepared a few things for dinner.

While cooking the potatoes, she saw Eli on a plane looking out the window.

She put a laundry to go and cleaned her house.

She went through her emails. She received an email from the adoption agency indicating that her application had been taken into account, but there was a waiting list, she couldn't believe it, she might be able to adopt Fana!

She read an article on the internet about Eli. He was to do an exhibition in Los Angeles in a month. Her heart stopped. She couldn't believe she might meet him. She was excited and stressed out at the same time. She thought about all the different possible scenarios of meeting him. She decided to take her mind off Eli and went to the living room.

She thought about the art exhibit Liam talked about and went through the different photos of her missions. She had tons and tons of pictures; she put everything on the floor in various stacks and went through them. She piled everything up to continue the next day.

Emma and Liam were arriving soon. She finished preparing dinner–the doorbell rang, and Poppy started wiggling her tail. She knew they had come and was excited to see them.

"Hi, honey!" said Emma, with a big smile on her face.

"Hi, honey, it's so nice to see you," replied Sarah as she hugged her friend.

"Hi Liam," said Sarah.

"Hi Sarah, thank you for having us over," said Liam.

"Of course, come in," replied Sarah.

Liam handed Sarah a bottle of wine.

"Thank you," said Sarah.

"Of course," replied Liam.

Poppy welcomed Emma and Liam effusively as they entered the house.

Emma stood in front of Sarah, staring at her with her hand in the air. Sarah saw an engagement ring on her finger.

"Oh my god!! Congratulations!!" said Sarah.

"Thank you, I am so happy!" said Emma as she jumped in Sarah's arms.

"It's incredible!! Tell me everything!" said Sarah.

"So, Liam took me to the film set where we first met, he set up a table in the middle with candles, beautiful lights, and our song played in the background," said Emma.

"Wow," said Sarah.

"So I sat down, he poured me my favorite wine and in the middle of the meal he asked me to get married!" said Emma.

"Oh, you are so romantic, Liam," said Sarah.

"I love you," said Emma as she kissed Liam.

"I love you," replied Liam.

Sarah was really happy for them; they were so perfect for each other.

"Are you guys hungry?" asked Sarah.

"Yes!" replied Liam.

They sat down at the table and Liam poured them some wine.

"So how was your trip?" asked Emma.

"It was incredible but a bit scary, so much happened," said Sarah.

"What happened?" asked Liam.

"I arrived and went to an orphanage to take photos. My mission was different this time because the orphanage owner was being investigated. We had reasons to believe that he was selling children to the black market," said Sarah.

"Oh my god, I can't believe you didn't tell me," said Emma.

"I didn't want to worry you before I left," replied Sarah.

"Okay," said Emma.

"Anyhow, so I got there. The first day, nothing seemed weird, except that things were immaculate, almost too clean compared to what I had seen before, so I took photos, met with the owner and the children, and then left," said Sarah.

"Yes," said Liam.

"And the next day I got extremely sick, I had the highest fever I ever had. James, the guide that we work with in India, actually thought I wasn't going to make it," said Sarah.

"Oh my god," said Emma.

"And while I was delusional, I kept thinking about the orphanage. Anyhow, James had suggested that we go back to the orphanage when the owner was not expecting us," said Sarah.

"Yes," they said, eager to hear the end of the story.

"So the next day when I woke up, I was feeling much better, and we went to the orphanage. When we got there, Saira, the lady that manages the orphanage in the owner's absence, was weird; something was different; it felt like we were not welcome; so we went through the orphanage again, but we didn't see anything unusual," said Sarah.

"Yes," said Emma.

"So, we were about to leave when Poppy went running into the jungle," said Sarah.

"The jungle?" asked Liam.

"Yes, the orphanage was in the middle of a jungle," replied Sarah.

"Oh," said Liam.

"Anyhow, so we went looking for Poppy, I kept calling her, and she wouldn't come back, you know, it was bizarre," said Sarah.

"Yes," said Emma.

"So, we finally went to where she was, and she found an underground cell with lots of children that had been locked up," said Sarah.

"Oh my god!" said Liam and Emma.

"So we called the police and helped the children out, and they found the owner, and he got arrested," said Sarah.

"Holy shit, I can't believe it!" said Liam.

"Poppy, you are such a good girl," said Emma kissing her.

"Yeah, it was pretty crazy, anyhow, everything ended up for the better," said Sarah.

"Wow, that is great, honey!" said Emma.

"Yeah, and in other news, I quit my job."

"Oh my god! What happened?" asked Emma.

"Honestly, I couldn't take it anymore; Jake doesn't appreciate me or what I do. I've been thinking about the exhibit, I'd love to be part of it!" said Sarah.

"Wow! A new start!" said Emma.

"Awesome, we need to get rolling!" said Liam.

They ate raclette.

"This raclette is amazing," said Liam.

"Thanks, it's one of my favorite meals," replied Sarah.

"Yeah, remember when we drove for an hour to go to that little French restaurant to eat a raclette?" said Emma.

"Yeah, that was such a fun drive," replied Sarah.

"Yeah," said Emma.

"Anything new with Eli?" asked Liam.

"Yes, I feel like we had a full-blown conversation in a coffee shop in London, I know, it sounds so wild," said Sarah.

"I love it, it's so exciting!" replied Liam.

"Anyhow, I just saw that he is doing an exhibition here in a month," said Sarah.

"Oh my god, we have to go," said Emma.

"Yeah, I'm stressed out," replied Sarah.

"Can you imagine if you see him, and he recognizes you instantly?" said Liam.

"It would be amazing, so romantic," said Emma.

"I don't know, maybe I'm the only one that feels anything," said Sarah.

"I think if you can feel him so well, he must also feel something, I think it's fascinating," said Emma.

"Can you imagine meeting someone from a past life? I'm so excited for you," said Liam.

"Okay, guys... We'll see," said Sarah, smiling at their enthusiasm.

They finished having dinner. Liam took a call and went into the backyard; Sarah and Emma were alone.

"You look better, honey," said Emma.

"Thanks. I had a bit of a wakeup call; when I was in India, I read my mother's letter."

"Oh, wow. And?"

"She just reminded me of who I am," said Sarah, smiling.

"That's so great!" said Emma, relieved to see her friend doing much better.

Liam came back into the apartment; Emma got up, they were getting ready to leave.

"Thank you for dinner, it was delicious," said Liam.

"You're welcome," replied Sarah.

"Thank you, honey, bisous," said Emma.

"Thanks for being such a good friend," said Sarah as she hugged Emma tightly.

"Bye," said Liam.

"Bye guys," said Sarah.

They left, Sarah cleaned up a bit and then went to bed. She laid in bed and thought about Eli. She wondered if this could all be true. What if two people could meet over and over again in different lives? How would they be when they saw each other? How could they recognize each other? Tons of questions came rushing, which she didn't have an answer for.

Sarah finally fell asleep with Poppy cuddled next to her.

The next morning Sarah woke up feeling excited. She went to the backyard and had coffee in the warm sun. The colors were beautiful, flowers were blooming everywhere. The sun reflected in the water in the fountain. She spent time in the backyard observing the beauty of life while Poppy tried to play with a squirrel in a tree. Victoria interrupted Sarah's peace.

"Hey! How are you?" asked Victoria.

"Hi Victoria, I'm great! How about you?"

"I'm fine; I am surprised you never got back to me about the job?"

"Oh, yeah, I wanted to think about it. I decided to do an exhibit with Emma and Liam to show and sell my photos," replied Sarah.

"Oh."

"And I quit my job, so I have time to work on it."

"What? But how are you going to pay the rent?"

"I'm going to sell my art."

"I doubt you're going to sell photos right away."

"I will."

"It sounds reckless to me."

There was a long awkward silence.

"Listen, Victoria, I am tired of your constant comments about how hard it is and how I won't make it. I am an artist, and I'm not going to stop creating. Thank you for the offer, but I will persist and succeed."

"Sure, whatever Sarah, don't come to me when you are completely broke."

"I won't."

Victoria stormed up the stairs.

Sarah took a shower and then went on a walk with Poppy in the neighborhood.

They came back home, and she continued to go through her photos, putting those aside that she wanted to show at the exhibition.

Her phone rang; it was Jake.

"Hi, Jake," said Sarah.

"Sarah, what was all that about yesterday? Have you lost your mind?" said Jake.

"No, Jake, you don't appreciate me or my art, so I'll take it elsewhere."

"You're not going to get a better job anywhere else, you know?"

"I will," said Sarah, confident.

"Fine, I'll give you a fucking raise."

"No, thank you, I'm fine."

"Are you turning me down? Are you crazy?!"

"I'm just fine, thank you, I wish you well, bye," said Sarah, as she hung up.

"Bitch!" yelled Jake, before Sarah could hear it.

At sunset, Sarah went to the Hollywood Overlook on Mulholland Drive with Poppy. Sarah and Poppy got out of the car and sat on the mountain, looking at the incredible view. She thought about Fana, she would manage to adopt her. Sarah took out her mother's letter and read it once more.

My beautiful Sarah,

I have loved you since the moment you were born. When you were barely three years old, you would help me in the house, always wanting to set the table and participate like an adult.

You are an incredible artist, don't let anyone tell you otherwise. Artists create the future. I believe in you, I always have, and I always will.

You are a fighter; some people might come along and try to crush you but remember, people can only hurt you if you let them.

I love you, Sarah, you are the best person I have ever met. I am always here with you, loving you, kissing you, and congratulating you.

I love you always,
Mama

Sarah had tears in her eyes; they stayed there for an hour, observing the horizon and then drove back home.

Sarah ordered a pizza from Lucifer's Pizza and watched Serendipity again; she knew most of the dialogue of the film.

She took Poppy out to the backyard; Victoria was on her balcony but didn't talk to her. The moon was visible; it was beautiful. She stayed in the backyard, observing it as she thought about her mother and what she wrote in her letter. She was in a hopeful mood, lost in her thoughts.

"Let's go to sleep Poppy," said Sarah.

They went inside and to bed.

The next morning Sarah received an email from the adoption agency. They were concerned about Sarah's financial stability; she thought about this but knew she would find a solution.

She had lunch and then went through all her pictures; she decided to show forty different photos.

A week went by, Liam, Emma, and Sarah were getting everything ready for their exhibit. Liam found a gallery that was excited to show their art.

Fifty ∞ Art

It was the big night; their art was on the walls and small tables in the gallery. Sarah's photographs were on the wall to the room's right while Emma's paintings were to the left. In the center of the room were small tables with Emma's poems and stories. At the entrance, there was a projector with a screening of Liam's short films.

There was a champagne reception; the place was filled with people and the press. Next to the champagne reception, there was a podium with a man standing behind it. Near this, there was a sign that read: *Help the Children of Africa.* Emma and Liam looked at each other with pride, Sarah was next to them, smiling.

The auctioneer stood up straight in front of the podium and began.

"The first piece is a painting from Emma Davis, titled, *The Lost City*," said the auctioneer.

People raised their paddle numbers and started to bid. The first painting went to a bigger woman in the back. The auction continued.

"The tenth piece is a photograph from Sarah Lavigne, titled, *The Girl with Sad Eyes*," said the auctioneer.

It was a photo of a young girl in a white cotton dress from India; people raised their paddle numbers and bid. The photograph went to an older lady in the front. The auction went on for a few hours until every piece of art was sold.

"The artists would like to say a word," said the auctioneer.

Emma, Liam, and Sarah were behind the auctioneer and stepped next to him.

"We would like to thank you all from the bottom of our hearts, our association will help children in Africa, this means the world to us. Thank you for all your support," said Liam.

The people at the auction applauded. They went to the champagne reception and had a glass of champagne.

The press did interviews, and the public asked various questions about the exhibition until everyone left.

They were now in the gallery on their own; they looked at the now empty walls.

"We are a good team," said Sarah.

"Yes, we are," they replied.

Fifty-one ∞ Fana

Sarah got home and hugged Poppy; she felt free. She had made more money in one evening than with her three last missions.

They went to sleep, Poppy cuddled next to Sarah.

The next morning when Sarah woke up, she had tons of emails offering her work.

"We did it, Poppy!!" said Sarah, excitedly.

Poppy saw how joyful Sarah was and jumped on her while wiggling her tail. Sarah called Emma.

"Did you see the articles?! I am so happy!" said Sarah.

"I know; I have received so many emails, it's crazy! Two galleries asked Liam to do an exhibition, this is amazing!"

"Yes! Thank you, thank you for believing in me, it means the world to me," said Sarah.

"Of course; I love you!"

"I love you!" Sarah hung up.

A few weeks went by, they were flooded with offers and worked harder than ever to prepare the next exhibitions.

One morning, Sarah received an email from the adoption agency. Her application had been approved; she could come and adopt Fana!

Sarah and Poppy landed in Ethiopia. Yonas drove them from Awassa to the orphanage; Sarah was slightly stressed out.

"Everything is going to be all right, Miss Sarah," said Yonas.

"Yes, I am just eager to see her," replied Sarah.

They arrived at the orphanage, Neela, the administrator, came out.

"Hello, Miss Sarah, it's very nice to see you," she said.

"Hello, Neela, it's very nice to see you again!" replied Sarah.

Neela hugged Sarah tightly.

"Where is Fana?" asked Sarah.

"She will be here in an hour; she is with the doctor. The adoption agency wants to be sure she has a final medical exam before we sign the papers," replied Neela.

"Oh, okay," said Sarah, disappointed to not see Fana right away.

"Are you hungry?" asked Neela.

"No, thank you," replied Sarah.

"You can wait here or go for a walk while you wait," said Neela.

"Okay, maybe I will go for a small walk," said Sarah.

"Don't you worry, Miss Sarah, Fana will be here soon," said Neela.

Sarah was reassured.

"Thank you, Neela," said Sarah.

Sarah went on a walk with Poppy and wondered how it would be to see Fana again.

They walked to a charming river, the sun shined and reflected on the water; there was a vast field next to the river. Poppy jumped in the water, Sarah looked at her and smiled. She wondered if Fana came to this river to play. They stayed there for half an hour before heading back to the orphanage; Sarah got emotional.

They arrived, and Sarah saw Neela come out, followed by Fana; Fana saw Sarah and ran into her arms.

"It's true, you came back!" said Fana.

"Yes, I came back," said Sarah, amazed by how much she was speaking.

Sarah cried with joy and hugged her tightly.

"Should we go inside to sign the papers?" asked Neela.

"Yes," replied Sarah.

They all went into the orphanage; Sarah signed all the papers with Neela while Poppy and Fana played together.

"Thank you, Miss Sarah, I know Fana will be happy with you," said Neela.

"Yes, I will take good care of her," replied Sarah.

Neela hugged Sarah again.

"Thank you for all your help," said Sarah.

"Of course, thank you," replied Neela.

"Fana?" said Neela.

"Yes," replied Fana.

"We will miss you here," said Neela.

"I will miss you too," replied Fana.

Fana hugged Neela and then got into the car while the children waved goodbye to her from the orphanage. She waved back, smiling.

They drove away. Fana and Sarah stared at each other; Fana giggled. The same priceless laugh Sarah heard once before. Yonas looked at them and smiled.

Fifty-two ∞ Exhibition

They got back to Los Angeles and settled in. Fana adapted quickly. She spent her days with Sarah on her photoshoots and played with Poppy. Sarah was making more money than she ever had.

Sarah and Fana found a cute duplex house in Los Feliz and moved; there was a beautiful room for Fana and a quaint garden, which Fana and Poppy spent most of their time in.

Fana loved Emma and Liam; they became her godparents. She spent a lot of time with them and regularly had sleepovers at their house.

Sarah was going through her photos in their new living room, while Fana and Poppy played together in the garden.

Her phone rang; it was Emma.

"Hi, honey," said Emma.

"Hi, how are you?" said Sarah.

"I'm doing great! You remember about tonight, right?" asked Emma.

"Yes, of course, I do. I have butterflies in my belly!" said Sarah.

"I am so excited, we'll pick you both up at 6pm, okay?" said Emma.

"Okay, I'll see you soon," replied Sarah.

"Bye," said Emma.

They hung up the phone; Sarah was nervous, Eli's exhibition was tonight. What if he didn't come? What if he did come?

She got ready, dressed Fana, and waited for Emma and Liam. She was pacing in the living room, talking to Fana.

"What do you think, Fana, do I look okay?" asked Sarah.

"You look beautiful, Mama," giggled Fana.

Sarah was wearing a lovely dress and had red lipstick on; Poppy wiggled her tail and went towards them.

A few minutes later, Emma called Sarah.

"We are outside," said Emma.

"Okay, we're coming," replied Sarah.

"We are coming back, good girl Poppy," said Sarah.

Fana gave Poppy her usual bone.

"Hi, honey," said Sarah.

"Hi, this is so exciting! I love your dress, Fana!" said Emma.

"Hi!" said Fana, excited.

"Hello ladies," said Liam.

They got into the car, Sarah was nervous.

"It's going to be great," said Emma seeing that she was apprehensive.

"Yes, I'm sure it will," said Sarah as she held Fana's hand.

Emma drove off.

"Are you both well?" asked Sarah.

"Yes, very good, we have been so busy, we might go away for a week to get some rest!" replied Emma.

"Nice, where are you thinking about going?"

"Liam wants to go to Utah, to Bryce Canyon," replied Emma.

"It's beautiful there, I went once a long time ago," said Sarah.

"I want to go," said Fana.

"We will, honey," replied Sarah.

Sarah sat back and looked out the window.

"We are almost there," said Emma.

"I am so excited!" said Liam.

"Oh my god, I'm so stressed out," said Sarah.

"Why are you so stressed out?" asked Fana.

"Um... I'm not sure, honey."

"Everything is going to be fine, Mama," replied Fana.

The three adults looked at each other; Fana was too cute.

They arrived in front of Blum & Poe and parked. Sarah and Fana got out of the car; Sarah looked towards the exhibition. A few people were standing outside, she could see that there were a lot of people inside.

"It's going to be great," said Emma.

"Yes, we will for sure see his beautiful paintings," replied Sarah, smiling.

They entered the exhibition. Emma and Liam started looking around; searching for Eli.

As soon as Sarah walked in, she saw a jungle painting in India; she looked at its colors and beauty. It looked exactly like the jungle she was in.

"We are going to look around and see if we can find him," said Emma.

"I want to come with you!" said Fana.

"Okay," replied Emma, taking her by the hand.

Sarah barely nodded, lost into Eli's world of art. She stared at his paintings in awe. She saw one of a sick woman in bed in India. The walls in the painting were pink, and there was a green painting above the bed, precisely like in India's hotel room. She couldn't believe it. She thought this must mean that he could feel her as well. She continued to look at his art and saw one of the rooftop in New York. She halted and reached towards the painting about to touch it.

Eli entered the gallery. He stopped abruptly when he saw Sarah observing the painting of the rooftop in New York. Sarah sensed that someone was watching her from behind and turned around. Eli looked at her intensely; he was a few feet away from her. They locked eyes for what seemed like hours. He got closer to her, keeping eye contact.

"Rooftop in New York."

"Coffee in London."

They were both very emotional. They got closer and closer to each other; he put his hands on her face and kissed her passionately. Time stopped. The movements were very gentle and soft. They were in a different world as if they were spinning, going into a dream. The kiss lasted a while. It was the most incredible kiss she could have imagined. They stopped kissing, stared at one another for a while; they finally found each other.

Emma, Liam, and Fana saw everything from the other side of the gallery; Emma smiled and had tears in her eyes; Liam took Fana in his arms.

"Mama found her love," whispered Fana.

"Yes, she did," they replied, emotionally.

Sarah saw that her friends and Fana smiled at her and smiled back, teary-eyed.

Eli looked at Sarah and, without saying a word, took her by the hand, as if he was taking her somewhere.

Sarah looked at Emma, who motioned with her hand to go; Fana would stay with them.

They left the gallery and walked in the streets of Los Angeles for a few hours, talking and laughing.

"I love how ugly LA is," said Eli.

"Yes," replied Sarah, understanding precisely what he meant.

They reiterated everything they felt throughout all this time and couldn't believe how magical it was. Sarah told him about Fana and about India, but he already knew.

They walked to Sarah's house. Poppy was at the door, eagerly waiting for them to enter; when they did, Poppy smelled Eli and liked him instantly.

"Hi Poppy," said Eli.

Poppy wagged her tail.

"I heard a lot about you," said Eli.

They sat and talked in Sarah's living room. She showed him all of her photos, he loved them and was moved by them. He felt like he had already seen them, but they became more tangible to him.

He started kissing her, took her by the hand and brought her to her bedroom, and laid her down gently on the bed. He undressed her; she undressed him. They made passionate love. They were completely and utterly connected. Time stopped completely, they were simply together, they became one. When they were together, it was as if they had never left each other in the past; it simply was.

The next morning when Sarah woke up, Eli was staring at her lovingly. It seemed like a déjà vu to her.

"Good morning, I thought we were in France for some reason," said Sarah.

"Maybe we were," replied Eli, smiling.

"Yes, I guess anything is possible."

"Yes."

He kissed her, and they made love again.

An hour later, they got out of bed and went downstairs. Sarah was at the bottom of the stairs, next to the kitchen.

"I'm making breakfast. Eggs and bacon?" asked Sarah.

Eli was standing at the top of the stairs looking at Sarah wearing his t-shirt.

"Eggs and bacon it is," said Eli as he went down the stairs admiring how sexy she was.

Sarah started taking out eggs and bacon; she poured some orange juice and made some coffee.

"Coffee, monsieur?" said Sarah.

"Yes, madame," replied Eli, smiling at her.

She prepared breakfast as he stood in the kitchen, admiring her every move.

Sarah was cutting a baguette in half when Eli went completely pale.

"What is it?" asked Sarah, worried.

"Stop!" yelled Eli frantically.

"Stop what?"

"You're scaring me with the knife."

"I'm just cutting bread."

"Please stop, it's freaking me out."

"It's okay," said Sarah, reassuring him.

"Please just stop."

Sarah put the knife down and hugged Eli.

"I'm sorry, I don't know what's happening, it's scaring me."

"It's okay, everything is fine."

"We are together," said Eli with teary eyes, touching her face to be sure she is there.

"Yes."

Sarah finished preparing breakfast, and they enjoyed it with Poppy in the sunny garden. There was a slight breeze and the sound of birds singing.

"Emma and Liam want to have dinner with us tonight, and of course, Fana will be there as well," said Sarah.

"I can't wait to meet Fana! That sounds great, I'd love to meet them," said Eli.

"Yes, I'm sure you'll love her. I was thinking about going to this restaurant called République; the food is amazing," said Sarah.

"I'll go anywhere you want as long as we are together," replied Eli.

Sarah smiled.

"I won't lose you this time," said Sarah, looking at Eli from the corner of her eye.

"You mean, I won't lose *you* this time... I love you for eternity, remember?" said Eli.

Emotion flooded Sarah; she cried as she remembered.

"Yes... yes... I do remember... I love you for eternity," whispered Sarah.

Eli took Sarah in his arms.

"We are together again, everything is going to be fine," said Eli.

"Do you think we had children?" asked Sarah.

"Yes, I think we did, and we will have more children together in this lifetime and then in the next lifetime and the next one," replied Eli.

"Yes," whispered Sarah.

She was pensive.

"But how will we find each other again?" said Sarah.

"I think we should decide on a location and meet there lifetime after lifetime," said Eli.

"Where?" asked Sarah.

They looked at each other for a while and smiled.

"Okay," replied Sarah, implying they had agreed on a place they both remembered.

They spent the day talking, going on walks with Poppy, and making love again and again.

It was the end of the afternoon; Eli was on the phone with someone in the kitchen while Sarah was in the living room, cleaning up; Eli hung up the phone and looked at Sarah.

"I was thinking of taking you and Fana on a trip for a couple of weeks?" said Eli.

"Couple of weeks? What did you have in mind?" asked Sarah.

"It's a surprise," said Eli looking at her eagerly.

Sarah smiled.

"Can you give me a clue?"

"It's not on this continent."

"Oh, wow, so it's far then?"

"Kind of," replied Eli.

"But that's not really a real clue," said Sarah laughing.

"That's all I am going to say for now. So, is that a yes?" asked Eli.

"Yes, it sounds great, I've been working so much, a getaway sounds perfect!" said Sarah in a cute voice as she kissed him.

"Can we leave tomorrow?" asked Eli.

"Tomorrow?" said Sarah.

"Yes..."

"It sounds totally crazy, but, I guess... yes!" said Sarah.

"Done!" replied Eli as he kissed her.

"We need to get ready; we have to leave in 20 minutes," said Sarah.

"Okay," replied Eli.

They got ready quickly.

"Bye Poppy, we are coming back, good girl," said Sarah as she gave her a bone.

"Are they meeting us directly at the restaurant?" asked Eli.

"Yes," replied Sarah.

They got into the car and drove to République restaurant. They listened to music in the car. Eli started singing the lyrics of a song, Sarah laughed.

"You are very cute when you sing," said Sarah, teasing him.

"Are you spying on me?" said Eli, playfully.

"Yes, I am," Sarah laughed.

They get to République Restaurant; Emma, Liam, and Fana had not arrived yet.

They entered the restaurant and were seated by a waiter.

"Hi, would you like something to drink?" asked the waiter.

"Yes, can we please have a bottle of your Bourgogne Pinot Noir 2015?" asked Eli.

"Yes," said the waiter and left.

"That's one of my favorite wines," said Sarah.

"I thought you might like it," replied Eli, smiling.

"So, are you going to tell me where we are going?" asked Sarah.

"No, it's a surprise," said Eli, smiling.

"It's so hard... Tell me..."

"I am not going to tell you."

The waiter came back with a bottle of wine.

"Would you like to taste?" said the waiter to Eli.

"I'm sure it's fine," Eli replied.

He poured a glass for Sarah and then a glass for Eli and left the bottle on the table. Emma, Liam, and Fana arrived as the waiter left.

"Hi, Fana! I missed you!" said Sarah as she took her in her arms.

"Honey, I want you to meet Eli," said Sarah to Fana.

Fana looked at Eli for a few seconds; she smiled but didn't say anything. Eli smiled at her and started imitating her; she giggled.

"It's very nice to meet you!" said Eli to Fana.

Fana ran into his arms and hugged him. Everyone looked in awe. Sarah introduced Eli to everyone.

They sat down; there was silence for a second.

"So?! Tell us everything; we want to know," said Emma.

Sarah and Eli laughed. Fana kept staring at Eli from the corner of her eye.

"I don't know what to say, we found each other, we could both feel each other, it's kind of like magic, I guess," said Sarah.

"Oh my god, it's amazing," said Liam.

Emma had teary eyes.

"I am so happy for you both," said Emma.

"Thank you," they said together.

The waiter came back.

"Hi, would you like something to drink?" said the waiter to Emma and Liam.

"We ordered some Pinot Noir if you like red wine?" said Eli.

"Yes, that's great," replied Emma.

The waiter poured wine for Emma and Liam.

"Fana, what would you like to drink?" asked Sarah.

"Apple juice, please," replied Fana.

"I'll be right back with your apple juice," said the waiter.

"Do you need a minute to order?" asked the waiter.

"Yes, please," replied Sarah.

The waiter came back a minute later with Fana's apple juice and then left. Sarah raised her glass.

"To new beginnings!" said Sarah.

"To new beginnings," replied everyone.

Everyone looked at the menu; the waiter came back and took their order.

"Honey, Eli wants to take us on vacation, is that okay with you?" asked Sarah.

"Yes! Is Poppy coming as well?" Fana asked as she smiled.

"Yes, she is. And Eli has a dog as well, so you'll be able to play with both of them," said Sarah.

"How fun!" replied Fana.

"That's great; where are you guys going?" asked Emma.

Sarah looked at Eli, who smiled.

"He won't tell me," said Sarah.

"I love it," said Emma as she laughed.

"Come on, give me one hint," said Sarah.

"No, it's a surprise," replied Eli.

"You are both so cute," said Liam.

"When are you leaving?" asked Emma.

"We are leaving tomorrow," replied Eli.

"Oh, wow!" said Emma and Liam.

"When did you have time to organize this?" asked Sarah.

"Magic!" said Eli, laughing.

"You are so cute," said Sarah, as she kissed him.

"Now, I am very curious," aid Emma.

"I'm sure Sarah will call you when we arrive," said Eli, smiling.

They finished their dinner; the party of five got along really well.

Eli got up to go to the bathroom.

"I'll be right back," said Eli.

He touched Sarah's shoulders and hair as he walked behind her.

"He is fantastic!" said Emma.

"I know, I can't believe it, I keep wondering if I am not in a dream," said Sarah.

"So tell us, what happened?" asked Emma.

"We want all the details," said Liam.

"We just knew each other already; when I told him about India, he already knew. It was like you said; he could feel everything I was feeling. I can't explain it. It is honestly just magical. I feel like I have known him forever. We are so natural together. I have never experienced anything like this before."

"Wow, it's great," said Liam.

"Are you going to get married?" asked Fana.

"I hope so..." replied Sarah.

"I told you not to worry," said Emma, smiling.

"I know, you were both right, it's so unbelievable."

"It's so romantic," said Liam.

They were very happy for Sarah. Eli came back.

"Should we go?" asked Emma.

"We have an early start tomorrow," said Liam.

"Yes, let's get the bill," said Sarah.

"I took care of it," said Eli.

"Oh, thank you," said Emma and Liam.

Sarah looked at Eli and kissed him.

"Thank you," said Sarah.

She knew that he was elegant enough to go and pay when he said he was going to the bathroom. They left the restaurant and said goodbye before parting ways.

"And you call me when you know where you are, okay? Bye, honey," said Emma to Sarah.

"Yes, I will, bye!" said Sarah.

Emma took Fana in her arms.

"You are going to have so much fun! Call me every day, okay?" said Emma to Fana.

"Yes, I will," replied Fana.

"I am going to miss you, Munchkin," said Liam to Fana.

"Me too," replied Fana.

Fana, Eli and Sarah got into the car and drove off.

"So?" said Sarah discreetly.

"I think your friends are great," said Eli.

Sarah smiled.

"So, where are we going tomorrow?" asked Sarah.

"Yes, where are we going?" asked Fana, joining the game.

"It's a surprise, I am not going to tell either of you..." said Eli.

"I bet I can guess, are we going to France?" asked Sarah.

"No," said Eli.

"India?" said Sarah.

"No," said Eli.

"Are we going to the beach?" asked Fana.

"No..." replied Eli.

"Okay fine, I'll stop," said Sarah, laughing.

Fana giggled.

"You'll both know soon enough; we need to leave the house at 7 in the morning," said Eli.

"Okay," said Sarah and Fana.

They got home; Poppy was thrilled to see them. They went to the garden for a moment with her. Fana played with Poppy while Sarah and Eli kissed in the moonlight. They had a nice moment before going back into the house.

"I will pack a bag. Do you have everything you need for the trip?" said Sarah.

"My assistant will bring me my bag in the morning," replied Eli.

"Okay," said Sarah.

She packed her bag with all of Fana's clothes and took what she needed for Poppy, along with her favorite camera.

They put Fana to sleep.

"Can you read me a story?" asked Fana.

"Yes, which one do you want?" replied Sarah.

"The one with the rabbit."

"Okay."

Sarah read for twenty minutes, Fana was almost asleep.

"Good night, honey," said Sarah as she kissed her.

"Good night, Mama," replied Fana before closing her eyes.

Sarah and Eli went to bed and made love before going to sleep. Poppy slept next to Sarah; Eli didn't mind it at all.

Fifty-three ∞ Vals

The next morning they woke up, had breakfast, got ready, and left. Eli drove Sarah's car to Bob Hope airport, Fana was in the back next to Poppy playing.

"So we are leaving from Bob Hope, that could be a clue," said Sarah looking at Fana and then at Eli.

Eli laughed. He entered from behind the airport and parked the car in a private parking spot. Sarah had never been on this side of the airport before. They got out of the car, Eli took Sarah's bag and Sarah carried Fana.

"Where is your assistant?" asked Sarah.

"She's coming," replied Eli.

A beautiful Golden Retriever came running to Eli.

"Fluffy!" said Eli petting his dog.

Poppy and Fluffy got to know each other, Fana looked at them.

They walked for a few seconds and arrived in front of a private plane; his assistant was standing there.

"Good morning Mr. Johnson, I see Fluffy found you," said Edith.

"Good morning Edith, Yes, he did. I would like you to meet Sarah and Fana," said Eli.

"Hi Sarah, hi Fana, it's a pleasure to meet you both," replied Edith.

"Hi Edith, nice to meet you, too," said Sarah.

"Hello," said Fana.

"I put your bag in the plane," said Edith.

"Thank you," replied Eli.

"Shall we?" said Eli to Fana and Sarah.

"Yes," said Sarah, smiling.

"I will see you in a couple of weeks, Edith, we will keep in touch."

"Yes, Mr. Johnson, enjoy your trip," said Edith.

"Thank you," they replied.

Eli let Fana and Sarah on the plane first; followed by Poppy and Fluffy. The aircraft was empty; it was a private jet that had ten seats in it.

A professional-looking lady arrived.

"Hello Mr. Johnson, would you like something to eat or drink?" said Martha.

"Good morning Martha, yes, if we could have a hot chocolate for Fana and some coffee and breakfast, that would be great," said Eli.

"Yes, right away," replied Martha.

"This is Sarah and Fana," said Eli.

"Good morning Sarah, hello, Fana, pleased to meet you both; I will be right back," said Martha.

"Thank you," said Sarah to Martha.

"Thank you," said Fana politely.

Sarah looked at Fana proudly; she was well mannered and kind.

"Private plane, are you trying to impress me?" asked Sarah.

"No, I mean, a little bit maybe," said Eli, laughing.

"Thank you, this is really great, so where are we going?" asked Sarah.

"It's a surprise, you will know in about ten hours," said Eli.

"Okay," replied Sarah, looking at Eli and trying to read his mind.

Fana drew in her coloring book for a few hours and then fell asleep.

"She is so cute," said Eli.

"Yes, she likes you already," said Sarah.

The flight went by quickly; it was a pleasant trip. Poppy and Fluffy slept most of it, while Sarah and Eli talked about their future.

"We will be landing in twenty minutes, Mr. Johnson," said the Captain in the flight's loudspeaker.

Sarah was excited; she looked out the window and saw mountains and snow everywhere.

"Do you like to ski?' asked Eli to Sarah.

"I love skiing! This is so beautiful," replied Sarah.

Eli saw how excited she was; it made him really happy.

"We are about to land in Vals Switzerland," said Eli.

"It's gorgeous, I have never been to Switzerland," said Sarah, kissing him.

"I think you might love it here; this is one of Switzerland's nicer places; I bought a cottage here a while ago," said Eli.

Sarah looked out the window.

"Wow, you must come here often, then?" asked Sarah.

"Every time I want peace, I come here," replied Eli.

"These mountains look amazing," said Sarah.

Eli smiled and looked at her for a while. She looked like a little child that just opened a gift; he could feel her excitement. Fana was still asleep; Sarah gently touched her arm to wake her. She opened her eyes and looked out the window.

"There is snow!" said Fana, very excited.

"Yes! We are in Switzerland, it's a country with lots of mountains," said Sarah.

"It's beautiful," said Fana, still looking out the window.

The plane landed at a small private airport. A car was waiting for them outside–Eli handed Sarah and Fana a ski jacket.

"Thought you might both need this," said Eli, smiling.

Sarah took the jacket and put it on.

"It's perfect, thank you," said Sarah.

She helped Fana put on her jacket.

"Are you both ready?" asked Eli.

"Yes," said Sarah as she zipped Fana's jacket.

They got off the plane; Sarah felt the frosty air go into her lungs. Everything around them was white with snow; it was breathtaking. Fana, Poppy, and Fluffy jumped in the snow and played.

"I never took them to the snow," said Sarah.

"I think they both like it," replied Eli.

"Yes," said Sarah.

They got into the car.

"Hello, Mr. Johnson," said the driver.

"Hi Martin, how have you been?" asked Eli.

"Very good, thank you, Sir," replied Martin.

"I would like you to meet Sarah and Fana," said Eli.

"Very nice to meet you, ladies," said Martin.

"It's nice to meet you, Martin," said Sarah as Fana smiled.

Martin was an elegant English gentleman.

They drove for about twenty minutes and got to a gated private property. Martin entered a code, and the portal opened. They drove through a long path that took them to a massive cottage. Sarah looked around; she felt like she was in a fairy tale. Fana looked out the window.

"Wow!" said Fana.

They arrived in front of the house.

A man came out to greet them and took their bags.

"Good evening, Sir," said Gabriel.

"Good evening Gabriel, thank you," said Eli.

"Hello, Miss," said Gabriel.

"Hello, my name is Sarah, and this is Fana," said Sarah.

"It's a pleasure to meet you both," said Gabriel.

Eli took Sarah by the hand and walked her into the house. Fana walked in just behind them, playing with Poppy and Fluffy.

Sarah looked around; the house was beautiful. There were apparent wood beams on the ceiling and white marble on the floor. A grand piano to the left side of the living room, a chimney in the center, and a huge Chesterfield couch; to the living room's right, there was an old wooden spiral staircase. The first floor was open, like an interior balcony. There was a large chandelier held by thick boat ropes in the middle of the room. Sarah could see a library on the entire back wall on the first-floor balcony with a sliding ladder.

"It's gorgeous," said Sarah.

"I am happy you like it, do you like it here, Fana?" asked Eli.

"Yes," she replied in amazement.

Eli took them around the house and then to the back to a hot spring. There were mountains as far as the eye could see; it was spectacular.

"God, this is amazing," said Sarah.

He kissed her passionately.

"You are real, aren't you?" asked Sarah.

"As real as you," replied Eli.

Fana, Poppy, and Fluffy played in the snow right next to the hot spring.

"Should we get a snack?" asked Eli.

"Sure, are you hungry, Fana?" asked Sarah.

"Yes, a little," replied Fana.

Eli took Sarah by the hand and went to the dining room. He pushed a wall in the dining room, which moved and brought them into the kitchen.

"It's a magic wall," said Fana.

"Yes," replied Eli smiling at her.

The dogs rushed through and went into the kitchen.

"I love this moving wall, I had it imported from a French barn in Auxerre," said Eli.

They walked into the kitchen, it looked like a kitchen from a French farm. There were terracotta tiles on the floor. The back wall was filled with old bronze pans.

Eli opened the fridge, took out some cheese and some saucisson and some apple juice, and opened a bottle of red wine. They sat in the kitchen on an old bench against a wall and enjoyed their snack together; Fana discreetly gave the dogs cheese; Sarah and Eli pretended like they didn't see it. Fana got tired.

"Do you want to go to sleep, honey?" asked Sarah.

"Yes," said Fana, half falling asleep.

"I'll put her to bed, I'll be right back," said Sarah.

"Do you want me to come with you?" asked Eli.

"No, it's okay, thank you," replied Sarah.

"We can go to the hot spring after if you want?" said Eli.

"Sounds perfect," said Sarah, smiling.

Sarah put Fana to bed, already fully asleep in her arms, before coming back to the kitchen. Eli took the bottle of wine and they went to the hot spring. He undressed himself and then undressed Sarah.

"Come, it's freezing out here," said Eli.

They went into the hot spring, it was incredibly warm. Poppy and Fluffy walked around and occasionally jumped into the snow.

The love birds had some wine and talked while in the hot spring and then made love; it was intense.

Back in the bedroom, fire from the chimney warmed up the entire room. Sarah and Eli fell asleep, spooning each other while Poppy and Fluffy slept at the tip of the bed.

The next morning Eli woke up before Sarah. He watched her sleep. She woke up to his gaze, and they made love to each other.

"Good morning, honey," said Sarah to Fana as she entered her room.

"Hi, Mama," said Fana.

They went to the kitchen and had breakfast, the dogs followed them.

"Do you want to go skiing today?" asked Eli.

"Yes!" replied Fana.

"I would love to," said Sarah.

"Great!" said Eli.

"Can I go outside and play with the dogs?" asked Fana.

"Of course, honey," replied Sarah.

Fana went outside while Eli and Sarah stayed in the kitchen; they were inseparable. They both seemed to have habits from the past with one another. When Sarah poured some coffee for Eli, she knew he liked cream in his coffee and added cream without asking him. Everything was effortless. They knew each other and understood each other without having to speak much.

They all got ready to go skiing. Eli took Sarah and Fana to a beautiful skiing spot. Eli taught Fana how to ski, she enjoyed it very much.

Gabriel, Poppy, and Fluffy waited for them in a coffee shop at the mountain's bottom.

The three skied together, having a lot of fun. Eli and Fana got along like a sock and a shoe. When they got to the bottom of the mountain, they decided to stop at the coffee shop to get a hot chocolate. The dogs wiggled their tail as they saw them arrive.

"With all the snowfall from last night, the snow must be perfect," said Gabriel.

"Yes, it is. Do you want to go while we stay here?" asked Eli.

"No, thank you, Sir, that's all right," said Gabriel very elegantly.

"Okay," replied Eli.

They had hot chocolate, and Eli made a chocolate mustache to make Fana smile. An hour later, they headed back to the slopes. Fana stayed with Gabriel as she wanted to play with the dogs. They spent some time skiing before all heading back to the house.

The evening went by quickly, watching Mary Poppins with Fana in front of the chimney in the living room.

Two weeks went by. Fana spent a lot of time outside in the snow playing with the dogs. Sarah and Eli enjoyed their time together skiing, bathing in the hot spring, and loving each other.

Two days before they left, Eli went to find Fana outside. She was trying to play hide and seek with the dogs.

"Fana?" called Eli.

Fana came out from behind a tree.

"Hi, honey! Are you having fun?" asked Eli.

"Yes, I am playing hide and seek, but they don't always find me," replied Fana, giggling.

"Yes," he laughed.

Fana looked at Eli lovingly.

"I wanted to ask you something?"

"Yes?" replied Fana.

"I want to ask Mama to marry me," said Eli.

"Oooh..." replied Fana.

"Is that all right with you?"

"Of course, Mama loves you," said Fana.

"Would you like to help me prepare a surprise for her?"

"Yes!!"

"Thank you, honey," said Eli.

They left together and went to a private office to prepare everything.

That evening during dinner, Fana looked at Sarah and giggled.

"What is it, honey?" asked Sarah.

"Nothing, Mama," said Fana, having a difficult time holding back.

Eli and Fana looked at each other as accomplices; he put his finger in front of his mouth, Sarah saw this.

"What's going on?" asked Sarah.

"Nothing," replied Eli.

"It's a surprise, Mama," said Fana.

"Yes, it's a surprise," confirmed Eli.

"Another surprise?" said Sarah, smiling at them both.

"Yes," they said in unison.

The next day, they all made a snowman together and then bathed in the hot springs.

"I love it here," said Fana.

"Me too," replied Sarah, smiling.

The evening before departing, Eli took Sarah's hand and brought her to his private office. Sarah had never been there before.

It was an entirely oval room with art everywhere; it was vast; she could see the sky through the glass ceiling. There were paintings on all the walls, a bookshelf created inside the wall with thousands of books on it, and an old vinyl player.

Sarah was amazed by what she saw, she felt like she was in the room of a magician.

There was an area with flowers, a small round greenhouse with hybrid blue and pink roses in it. Eli opened the greenhouse and handed her one of the roses.

"It's so beautiful," said Sarah.

"I named it *Sarah*," said Eli.

He looked at his roses and whispered something to them.

"You talk to your roses?" asked Sarah, smiling.

"Yes, I believe they can hear me," replied Eli.

"Yes, I believe they do," confirmed Sarah feeling like she already saw this before.

They kissed, surrounded by art and love. It was magical. He took Sarah to the other side of the room.

An easel covered up with a white sheet stood in a corner. Eli removed the covering and revealed a beautiful painting of Sarah, she looked timeless in the portrait.

She stared at his painting for a while; emotion came rushing through her body, tears started coming down her cheeks.

"It's so beautiful," said Sarah.

"The woman finally has a face," said Eli, smiling.

They kissed passionately while Artur Rubinstein's Chopin Waltz Op 69 No.2 in B Minor played.

They started to dance, they were in their own world together, as if they were creating a beautiful dream together. They felt like they were floating in the air. Memories came pouring; their life together in Egypt; their life in France; their children. They felt like they were drifting out of their bodies.

The vinyl stopped playing and they came back to a more present reality.

"I am so sorry, I didn't know in Egypt," said Sarah.

"I know, my love," replied Eli.

"In France, was her name Margot?" whispered Sarah.

"Yes, and John," said Eli, tears running down his cheeks.

They held each other tightly for what seemed to be an eternity.

"Sarah?" whispered Eli calmly.

"Yes?" said Sarah.

He took out a beautiful, old fashioned ring and went down on one knee.

"Will you marry me?" asked Eli.

Sarah smiled, her eyes were teary.

"Yes, I will marry you a million times," replied Sarah.

He put on the engagement ring; it fit perfectly, and they kissed passionately.

"I love you for eternity."

"I love you for eternity."

They looked at each other for a moment, and Eli took her in his arms and kissed her.

"One more lifetime together," said Sarah.

"Yes, and many more," replied Eli.

"Yes."

Fana came barging in the room and stared at them enquiringly.

"Did she say yes?"

"Yes, of course, I said yes!" said Sarah.

Fana ran into their arms and the three hugged.

Fifty-four ∞ Eternity

It was the 29th of January 2019. Eli and Sarah sat on a blanket on their hilltop at Saint-Dié-des-Vosges. Eli had a wicker basket with some cheese, wine, and saucisson; they enjoyed a moment together.

"I still can't believe you found our hilltop," said Sarah.

"How could I forget?" said Eli.

Poppy and Fluffy ran around and played together.

They enjoyed their picnic and time together when they heard the all too familiar bell tolling. They looked at each for a moment and laughed before getting up and walking to the farm, followed by their dogs.

As they got to the farm, they saw lights hanging from the trees and tables outside. An older man, Paul, was at the door waiting for them.

"Did you have a good walk?" asked Paul in a thick French accent.

"Yes, thank you," replied Sarah.

"Dinner is ready," said Paul.

"Thank you," said Eli.

They entered the kitchen to find Catherine, Paul's wife, setting up the kitchen table. Fana was in the kitchen with Catherine observing her every move.

"Are you hungry?" asked Catherine, also in a thick French accent.

"Yes," replied Sarah.

"Good, I like it when there are many people on the farm; it is plein de vie," said Catherine, smiling.

"Thank you," replied Eli.

"Are you having fun, honey?" asked Sarah to Fana.

"Yes, Catherine showed me how to bake bread," replied Fana.

Sarah looked at the bread oven; it seemed all too familiar as well. They all sat down and started to eat.

"How long have you lived on this farm?" asked Eli.

"My father moved here after the war, I have lived here since," said Paul.

"Oh," replied Eli.

"Who lived here before you?" asked Sarah, eager to know what people said about the farm.

"It's a sad story, my father told me that the family that was here before left during the occupation, you know, the Germans?" said Paul.

"Yes," said Sarah with teary eyes.

"You are too young to know, but those were tough times," said Paul.

"Yes," said Sarah, actually understanding what Paul was talking about.

"Was your father a friend of the family?" asked Eli.

"My father knew the family; they helped the villagers with food during the occupation. It was a very generous family, the farm was abandoned after the war," replied Paul.

"Oh," said Eli.

"They were a good family, bénisse leur âmes," said Paul.

"Yes, god bless them," replied Sarah and Eli.

"We were surprised when you asked to have your wedding here; not many people come to the village," said Paul.

"We love it here," replied Sarah.

"If it *makes you happy* like we say in France," said Catherine, smiling in excitement.

"Catherine has been very excited; she likes the festivities," said Paul.

"Yes, thank you very much," said Sarah.

"It's a blessing to have our wedding here," said Eli as he touched Sarah's hand.

They finished having dinner.

"I thought I could read a story tonight in the living room," said Sarah.

"Yes! I will make some chamomile tea," said Catherine.

"That would be perfect," said Sarah, smiling.

They all took place in the living room; Paul made a fire; it was very cozy. Sarah looked at Fana and Eli lovingly and began to read.

They all had a wonderful evening and then went to bed.

Sarah and Eli made love; they sensed all the moments of love they experienced on the farm in their past life; they felt incandescent happiness.

The next morning when they woke up, they heard noise coming from below. They went downstairs and saw Fana in the kitchen with Catherine tasting the cake doughs and laughing; Fana was amused.

"Good morning, honey," said Sarah as she hugged her.

"Hi, Mama," said Fana.

"Did you sleep well?" asked Catherine.

"Yes, very well, thank you," replied Sarah.

"It's tranquil here, it's the air from the countryside, good for sleep," said Catherine.

"Yes," said Eli.

They had coffee in the kitchen, while they heard people outside, setting the tables, and finishing all the wedding preparations.

"Would you like to go for a walk, love?" asked Eli to Sarah.

"Yes, I would love that, do you want to come with us, Fana?" asked Sarah.

"No, I want to stay here with Catherine," said Fana putting her finger in cake dough.

"Okay, honey," said Sarah, amused.

"This little one, she loves the cakes," said Catherine, as she touched Fana's head.

"Yes," replied Sarah, smiling.

She kissed Fana, and they left to go on a walk around the farm; they saw the well that was lit with beautiful lights and stood in front of it.

"I think something happened here," said Sarah.

"It's very possible," replied Eli.

They continued on their walk and arrived in front of the greenhouse; Eli walked in front of it and opened the door, which squeaked; the greenhouse looked abandoned. They entered the conservatory and felt a strong emotion of love; Eli turned to face Sarah.

"I feel like I am home," said Eli.

"Me too," replied Sarah.

They stared at each other for a moment and kissed passionately. He took her by the hand and walked further into the greenhouse; he looked at the wildflowers that had survived and whispered to them. Sarah observed him; she felt like this was another déjà vu; her love for him intensified.

"I think I used to spend a lot of time here," said Eli.

"Yes, I think so," replied Sarah.

"We have so much more to create together," said Eli.

"Yes," replied Sarah.

"I love you for eternity, remember?" said Eli.

"Yes, I remember, I love you for eternity," replied Sarah.

"Eli?"

"Yes?"

"I am with child."

Eli had teary eyes and held Sarah tightly and kissed her. It seemed as if the love they built in the past added to the love they were creating presently; it was a timeless moment.

"Are you ready to write another chapter?" asked Eli.

"Yes, I am," replied Sarah, smiling.

They went back to the farm to get ready for their wedding.

Anne, Juan, Emma, and Liam, as well as Eli's parents, had arrived. Sarah's father had come and was getting ready to officiate their wedding.

Everyone was rushing around the house.

Emma and Anne helped Sarah with her hair and make-up. Catherine came into the room while Sarah got ready.

"You have what you need?" asked Catherine.

"Thank you, I was wondering if you had a needle?" asked Sarah.

Catherine didn't understand what a needle was.

"You know, to sew?" said Sarah, motioning with her hand.

"Ah, une aiguille, yes, I have one," said Catherine.

Sarah followed Catherine into another room to get a needle; when Sarah entered the room, she felt like she had been in it many times before; she looked around silently.

Catherine opened an old dresser and took out a sewing kit; Sarah stared inside the drawer and saw Eli's old pocket watch; tears started coming down her cheeks.

"Non, why you cry?" said Catherine.

"Oh, no, it's okay, everything is okay," said Sarah.

"You will sew, and it will be okay."

"Yes, yes, of course. It's the watch, can I buy it from you?" asked Sarah.

"This old watch, you like it?" said Catherine.

"Yes, I want to give it to Eli for his wedding gift. He loves watches."

"You can have it, you don't need to buy it," said Catherine, handing Sarah the pocket watch.

"Thank you, thank you so much," said Sarah hugging Catherine.

She looked at the watch closely and turned it around to see Eli's name engraved in the back of it. She had a flashback of the birthday Eli received it and smiled profusely. Catherine was amazed at how happy Sarah was about an old pocket watch.

"Is okay?" said Catherine.

"Yes, thank you," replied Sarah.

She went back to the other room and finished getting dressed. She looked stunning in a white, old fashioned wedding dress. The wedding ceremony was about to begin. Fana wore a beautiful light pink dress; she was the flower girl and the ring bearer and was very proud of it. Poppy and Fluffy both had a ribbon with flowers on it. Everyone was seated, waiting for Sarah to arrive.

The wedding ceremony took place on the hilltop, where Eli asked Sarah to marry him in their previous life. Sarah walked down the aisle while Eli stared at her as she approached. Sarah's father handed Sarah to Eli and then took place to officiate the wedding.

The ceremony began; Emma and Liam looked at each other; they were part of the bridal party. Anne cried of joy while Juan looked at her with admiration, also part of the bridal party. Sarah and Eli were in their own world; they saw only each other at this very moment. Sarah's father took out their vows and handed them to Sarah and Eli.

"I, Eli, pledge to thee," said Eli.

"I, Sarah, pledge to thee," said Sarah.

They continued saying their vows.

"To love you for eternity, to always remember you, to help you when you are down, to encourage you when you need it, to honor you at all times, to trust you always, to persist for us, to have courage at all times, to never go to sleep on an upset, to ensure your growing love for the world and its people, to remember you lifetime after lifetime, to meet you life after life to continue our journey, I pledge to thee one million years," said Eli and Sarah.

Fana gave Sarah Eli's ring; Sarah put it on his finger; Fana then gave Eli Sarah's ring. He put it on her finger.

"I pronounce thee, husband and wife, you may now kiss the bride," said Sarah's father.

They kissed and stared at each other.

"I love you for eternity."

"I love you for eternity."

Everyone congratulated them, and they went to the farm to celebrate with dinner and cake. Cindy Lauper's *Time after Time* song started to play. Eli took Sarah's hand, and they danced their first dance. They had eyes only for each other; experiencing happiness they thought was possible only in movies. The song came to an end, and everyone else started to dance; the party went on for hours. Fana danced with Eli and Liam many times; she was having the best night of her life.

Sarah and Eli sat at their table alone.

"I have a gift for you," said Sarah.

She handed him a little wrapped present; he looked at Sarah inquiringly. He undid the wrapping and saw a small box; he opened it to find his old pocket watch. Tears rolled down his cheeks; he looked at it and turned it around to see his name engraved on the back of it.

"How?" asked Eli.

"I found it in Catherine's dresser, she said you could have it," replied Sarah.

"Thank you," said Eli kissing her passionately.

Anne and Juan came and sat next to them.

"It's such a beautiful wedding, congratulations!" said Juan.

"Thank you," replied Sarah and Eli.

"You look so happy," said Anne, hugging Sarah.

"I am," said Sarah.

Sarah took off her ring and showed Anne the engraved infinity symbol inside it; the letters S and E were in each symbol's oval.

"It's breathtaking," said Anne.

"I love him so much," said Sarah.

"Yes, you look radiant," said Anne.

"How is it going with you two?" asked Sarah.

"It's going very well, I believe he is the one for me," said Anne, with a giant smile.

"I am so happy for you, you both look so cute," said Sarah.

They looked at each other for a moment, remembering their childhood and dreams.

"Who would have thought we'd be this content?"

"I know. Life is beautiful. Should we dance?" asked Anne.

"Yes," replied Sarah as she stood up and took Eli by the hand.

They all went dancing until the wedding came to an end.

It was fifty years later. Sarah and Eli laid in bed in their house in Vals, cuddled up. Their room was filled with paintings and photographs. On their nightstand, there were pictures of Fana and their other children.

They turned to each other and kissed before cuddling up body to body like a couple of kitchen spoons.

"I will see you next lifetime," said Sarah.

"I will see you next lifetime, my love."

They closed their eyes and departed bodiless from their room into the sky. They floated through their house, above the house, and looked at Vals from the sky.

Printed in Great Britain
by Amazon

81483133R00332